BETRAYAL AT FALADOR

T.S. CHURCH

TITAN BOOKS

RUNESCAPE: BETRAYAL AT FALADOR
ISBN: 9781848567221

Published by Titan Books
A division of Titan Publishing Group Ltd
144 Southwark St
London
SE1 0UP

First edition October 2010
10 9 8 7 6 5 4 3 2 1

Visit our website: www.titanbooks.com

Did you enjoy this book? We love to hear from our readers. Please email us at readerfeedback@titanmail.com or write to us at Reader Feedback at the above address.

To receive advance information, news, competitions, and exclusive Titan offers online, please register as a member by clicking the "sign up" button on our website: www.titanbooks.com

A CIP catalogue record for this title is available from the British Library.

Printed and bound in the United States.

BETRAYAL AT FALADOR

To my grandparents, parents, and the Giraffe, and to my nephews, who I hope will take as much enjoyment from the book as they do from the game. And also to the talented staff at Jagex who have devoted so much of their time to this project.

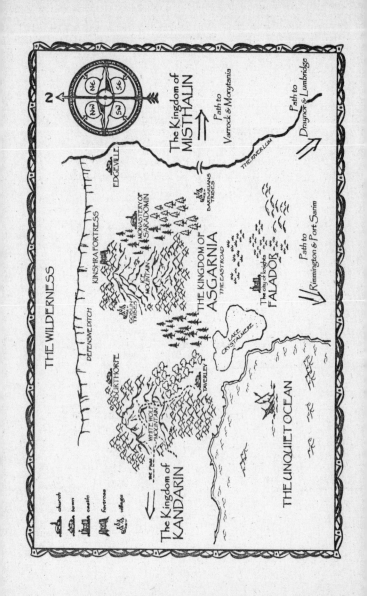

ONE

"Get some light over here! We need some light!"

Master-at-arms Nicholas Sharpe shouted loudly into the wind in order to be heard by his fellow knights on the bridge. A fair young man ran forward, shielding his blazing torch from the anger of the winter storm.

"Thank you, Squire Theodore. Now, let us see what damage has been done."

Half a dozen men stood around as firelight flickered over the fallen masonry. It was a life-sized statue of a knight which had come crashing down from the castle heights an hour after midnight, when the storm had been at its most ferocious. The crash had been loud enough to raise the alarm.

"That's more than a thousand pounds of solid stone," Sharpe said, peering up into the darkness from whence it had plummeted. "Must've been a wicked gust to move it.

"We can't leave it here," he added. "Get hold of it. On three we'll lift."

There was some jostling as the knights moved closer, every man packing himself as close to the statue as possible.

"One... two... *three*!" Sharpe counted out, and on his last call the small group of men lifted the marble statue with a collective groan of effort. "Carry him to the courtyard. We can't leave one of our own out here in the cold!"

The men staggered under their burden, moving slowly from the exposed bridge toward the open gates, Squire Theodore lighting the way.

The statue will be safe there until the morning, the master-at-arms mused, *as long as the damage wasn't serious enough to break it into a thousand pieces as they moved it.*

And as long as nothing more comes down on our heads, he added silently. It wasn't safe in the streets of Falador that night; several people had already been killed by falling debris, and the quicker their party was back inside the castle, the better.

But the pessimistic thought turned to prophecy. A sharp crack, a sudden cry, and the statue dropped again to the paving, scattering the men who had lifted it. Only two had retained their grips on the polished marble, and now they held the right leg between them, detached from the rest of the figure.

"Get the torch back here!" Sharpe hollered, his temper rising. He swiftly noted the anxious faces gazing toward the courtyard. "Where's the torch?" he called. "Where has Theodore got to?"

A sudden gust of wind, biting cold in its journey south from Ice Mountain, swept across the bridge. The squire emerged from the gatehouse, bringing the torch with him and carrying a heavy bundle under his arm. As soon as he reached the shivering party, there was a crack from above and a cry of warning rang out.

"Watch your heads!"

Each man instinctively looked up, crouching low in readiness. Spinning from the rooftops, a tile crashed onto the bridge and exploded on the stonework scant yards away, sending sharp chips of slate into the turbulent moat below.

"Come on; we must not stay out here any longer," Sharpe said decisively. For all the statue meant, it wasn't worth the lives of the young men who stood close to him. "Theodore, don't run off again. We need the light to see what we're doing."

He noted the look of disappointment on the young man's face. Theodore was an excellent squire; the master-at-arms couldn't recall any better. Yet he took himself too seriously, making him an easy target for any of his peers who envied his dedication, or even despised him for it.

"I have blankets, sir," Theodore said. "We can carry the statue on that. It will allow more of us to help lift it and prevent any more accidents like the last one…" His voice trailed off as a couple of the knights regarded him coolly.

But Sharpe nodded.

"It's a good idea, Theodore. Pull the blankets under the statue when we lift it—on three again!" And as soon as the men around him had obeyed, the master-at-arms began the count.

"One…

"Two…

"*Three!*" Each man issued a grunt as they hefted their burden.

A sudden flash erupted from the polished marble above the entrance to the courtyard, and once again the stone knight fell, the impact knocking several of the knights off their feet. One stumbled against Theodore, so that he was forced to loosen his grip on the spluttering torch and the light vanished as it splashed into a puddle.

Immediately, concerned voices called out in the darkness.

"What was that?"

"Are we under attack?"

"There's been no thunder—it must be magic!"

Sharpe bellowed from the side of the bridge.

"Get me a light!"

Theodore crouched and seized the torch, only to find that it was soaked from the puddle. He was on his feet in a second, running toward the gatehouse where the night watch kept lights burning.

He was careful to avoid the dazed knights who risked tripping him in the dark.

"Help me!"

A voice called out nearby. It was faint and unusual, and Theodore dismissed it, knowing he could not help anyone until he had light. As he entered the gatehouse, the voice groaned again, closer now.

When Theodore emerged holding the burning torch, he nearly dropped it in surprise. For lying not far away was a young girl, shivering from the cold. Looking closer, he could see that she was in shock from the savage injuries that covered her body. In one hand she held a strange flower, and in the other a golden ring, broken in two, that appeared to be smouldering in her open palm. It boasted a crystal clear gem, and an acrid scent hung heavy on the night air.

Her eyes, wide and dark, looked into his. He had never seen anything so...

"Help me... please."

The girl blinked once and opened her eyes. Then with a sigh she closed them again, and her head lolled back.

Sir Amik Varze's mood reflected the weather outside.

Freezing winds howled down from the mountain and The Wilderness that lay beyond, and his order had been busy dealing with food shortages and a desperate population. Though the night was black as pitch, on a clear day, from his room in the tower of marble overlooking the city of Falador, Sir Amik could see Ice Mountain in the distant north, a foreboding sharp pinnacle which could look deceptively beautiful on those evenings when the sun reflected off the frozen summit.

Beautiful, but deadly, he thought as the gale blew open a shutter. It struck the wall with a raucous clatter.

From his younger days as an ambitious squire and all

through his long career, Sir Amik had travelled more than most throughout the lands of Gielinor, east to the borders of the dark realm of Morytania where even the dead could not find rest, and south to the vast wastes of the Kharidian Desert which no man had ever crossed.

Yet of all his achievements, he was most proud of his role in manoeuvring the Knights of Falador as a serious political force within the realm of Asgarnia. He had ruled in old King Vallance's place, making and enforcing the laws that kept the nation safe. For two years the king had been bedridden, and Sir Amik had made certain that the knights had filled the vacuum before instability could threaten.

Not everybody had been happy about that, however. The Imperial Guard—under the direct rule of Crown Prince Anlaf—had questioned Sir Amik's intentions, and were aware that his knights controlled the nation's treasury. The prince had governed the town of Burthorpe in northwest Asgarnia for many years, placed there by his father to amass experience and prepare him for his inevitable succession to the throne. Under Anlaf's management, the Imperial Guard kept the nation safe from the trolls in the northern mountains, and rarely interfered in Asgarnia's wider affairs.

Yet the rumours swirled. Some predicted that a power struggle would plunge the nation into civil war, but Sir Amik would not let it come to that. As long as he lived, honour and truth would conquer the petty politics of such self-interested men.

It was the will of Saradomin.

Amik was old now, though. Not so old, however, as to be confined to the almshouses in the city, which the knights maintained to shelter those who had survived to reach the age of retirement, spending their days in the parks and lecturing the younger generation about the virtues of truth and honour.

No, not yet, he thought as he stood up to close the offending shutter. He was still capable of putting in as many hours as were required to guarantee the security of Asgarnia and the blessings of Saradomin.

Rather than closing the shutter, however, he pulled it back, taking a moment to glance down to the courtyard. Even over the wind, which sung its shrill song amongst the rooftops, he could hear raised voices. He saw several torches flickering in the darkness and shadowy men running in animated confusion. Before he could call out, however, footsteps sounded on the steep stairwell outside the door to his private study, and a moment later it shook under the anxious hammering of a man's clenched fist.

"Sir Amik? Are you awake?" a familiar voice said. The man's tone betrayed his excitement.

The knight sighed, knowing that he was going to be forced to postpone his sleep.

"What is it, Bhuler?" he called out, closing the shutter and turning to cross the room. "What catastrophe has you running up these stairs at this hour?" He unlocked the door, and there stood his personal valet.

"It's a woman, sir!"

Sir Amik raised an eyebrow. "At your age, Bhuler?"

"No, sir." The man looked to the floor, disarmed by his master's quick humour. "Outside, in the courtyard. She just appeared on the bridge—it has to be magic. But she's badly injured—Sharpe doesn't think she'll pull through."

Sir Amik's expression hardened.

"Where is she now?" he asked. His curiosity was piqued. The knights had many enemies, and in order to counter any hostile entry, the castle was guarded by more than walls alone. It was supposed to be impossible to teleport anywhere within the perimeter of the moat.

"She's been taken to the matron in the east wing, sir."

They exited the room, and the valet led the way down the spiral stairs and across the courtyard.

The entire castle had been roused by the news, and Sir Amik couldn't imagine a swifter call to action. Lights shone from the dormitories of the peons—those boys who worked to attain the rank of squire and who carried out the menial labours. Above the howling of the wind, he heard a squire muttering of an elven princess, sent to warn the knights of impending disaster.

Already the rumours have started, he thought. *Even ones as foolish as that.* He smiled thinly, for the elven race had vanished from the world long ago—if they had ever existed at all. Yet this was a point the young squire ignored entirely.

Then his smile disappeared. Some things he would not allow.

"Turn out those lights!" he roared. Hastily the young peons extinguished their lamps and ceased their speculations, aware that tomorrow would bring a punishment drill. Sir Amik's attitude toward discipline was well-known: it was at the heart of their order.

Arriving at the matron's quarters, he found master-at-arms Sharpe and the young Squire Theodore there, as well. But it was no elven princess under the matron's anxious care, rather a very human young girl. Her blonde hair was matted with dried earth and sharp thorns were entangled in the long strands. Her skin was deathly pale. She looked like some feral animal.

"What do you think, matron?" he asked.

"She is badly injured, Sir Amik." The heavy-set woman's eyes flicked to the patient. "Prayer is her best hope now."

"Then I may help. The will of Saradomin is not known to me, but his wisdom has never failed to aid me before." The elderly matron nodded. Her considerable skills were of no use to a girl with such savage injuries.

"Clear the room," Sir Amik ordered briskly. The matron complied, taking the others with her. When he was alone, he

knelt at the bedside to pray, clearing his mind. His head bowed
in reverence and his hands rested on the girl's cold forehead.

"My Lord Saradomin, I have served you without question
since I was old enough to govern the path of my life, and I do
not claim to know your will. I pray now for the sake of this
unknown girl. I pray that you will give her the strength to live."

He felt the power within him, stemming from his heart and
cascading along his outstretched arms and into the still body.
His eyes snapped open with surprise. Never before had he felt
so much energy. He struggled to keep his hands steady and his
mind clear, lest the conduit that he had become be broken.

After a minute the charge ceased, and Sir Amik called to the
matron.

"Saradomin be praised!" he claimed as he stood. "She will
live."

At his words, the girl stirred as if gripped by a fitful
nightmare. She *would* live.

As he left the room carrying the mysterious girl's belongings,
Theodore glanced back at her.

He didn't want to leave her side, and Sir Amik's order to clear
the room had made him unusually angry, though he knew better
than to voice his feelings. Instead he decided to keep himself
busy, accompanying Sharpe toward the armoury to catalogue
the girl's property.

"I saw the way you looked at her, Theodore," the master-at-
arms said as they ascended a polished stairwell. "You know that
as a Knight of Falador there can be no chance for romance. A
lonely but honourable life in the service of Saradomin is our
reward—not for us a hearth and a home."

"I know that, sir," Theodore replied, his face warming. "But
as the only person she has spoken to, I felt it might be best if I
was there when she wakes."

Sharpe looked sympathetically at the squire.

"You should prepare yourself, Theodore," he said calmly. "She might not wake up." He didn't slow as they entered the armoury. The squire stopped for a moment, shocked at the fatalistic thoughts of his tutor.

"She will wake up, she will!" he declared.

Bending down and opening a wooden box, Sharpe didn't even look up at the young man's brief tirade. After a moment Theodore followed him.

It only took them a few minutes to catalogue the girl's property. Her leather armour was cut deeply in a dozen places, to the degree that it would offer her no protection should she wear it again, and her clothes were so torn that they would have to be replaced. The nurses had found no weapons save her sword, which the knights had retrieved from the ground at her side. Her scabbard was empty and bent, as if she had fallen on it, and her quiver—slashed viciously from one side to the other—contained no arrows.

The items that she had held in her hands were the most interesting, however. The white flower offered a clue as to where she had come from, and the ring that had broken into two pieces could help to identify her. Theodore could recognise neither of them. He knew nothing of botany, and herblore wasn't among the skills he had studied.

Such was the case with Sharpe, as well. Both men stared at the flower for several minutes before admitting their total ignorance of where it might have grown. The only thing they could determine was that neither of them had ever seen one like it before. But there were people who were well-practised in the identification of such things, chief amongst them the druids.

"I can take the flower to Taverley, sir," Theodore offered. "It is two days' ride. The druids will know where it grows, and it should be clear to them, for how many other flowers bloom in winter?"

Sharpe nodded.

"I shall put your idea to Sir Amik tomorrow," he said thoughtfully. "But it is not the flower that I am so interested in Theodore—not yet. It is the ring in her hand."

The older man's eyes glazed over as if he were searching for some memory of an event long past, the ring held closely before him, its small diamond faded to a milky white since Theodore first retrieved it.

"Do you recognise it, sir?" Theodore asked eventually.

Sharpe shook his head.

"No. No, I do not. I thought it was something that it was not, something it could not be. But I shall be certain in the morning, when I discuss this with older heads than yours."

"What did you think it might be, sir?"

Sharpe peered at him for a moment.

"It was a foolish idea, Theodore, and it is time you went off to bed. It will be light in a few hours, and if I know Sir Amik he is going to want a reliable squire to drill some sense into the peons for their boisterous behaviour. They had no business being up at such an hour."

Theodore bowed his head and left, yet he felt entirely unsatisfied at their findings. He returned to his chamber to try and snatch a few hours' sleep, which he knew he would find evasive. All his thoughts were on the girl.

Sharpe did not sleep either. He sat silently in the armoury, alone under a burning torch, his eyes fixed on the broken ring.

Could it be? Is it possible? His mind ached with questions, none of which he could answer.

Finally, as the cold grey light of a winter dawn began to appear in the eastern sky, he stood, his bones cold and weary from his long vigil. He stretched briefly and then took the ring in his hand, carefully, reverently. With a furtive glance around him, he left the armoury.

TWO

It was the dream again.

She felt the fear and cold that always came with it. It started with the screams of the villagers and the shouts of the black-armoured attackers.

She had escaped the men. It was always that way. She always escaped, just as she had done all those years before. Yet she knew what was to come.

She ran for the cover of the trees, but as soon as she touched the frozen bark the cry went out. She had been seen.

Her father's bag was heavy enough to slow the eight-year-old down, but she gritted her teeth and ignored the thin whips of the branches that tore at her face and hands as she ran, leaving red welts across her exposed skin.

She could hear the baying of the starving dogs the men had brought with them. The animals had her scent and her running figure caught their attention. She heard their growls and the jeers of the men who watched the spectacle, certain of the outcome.

And yet she knew she would escape and live. She knew it even as the first animal—running far ahead of the others—drew back to leap at her. For she had been taught how to protect herself.

Instinctively she ducked as the dog jumped, its eyes flashing in the winter sun, its red tongue anticipating the taste of young flesh. But its anticipation would be denied.

With a speed and skill that was unheard of in one so young, she slashed at its jaw with a knife from her belt. The dog howled. Then, startled at finding an enemy capable of fighting back, the beast fled—content to return to the warm corpses that lay unclaimed in the burning village.

But that was only one animal from several, and she knew already what she would be forced to do to escape the others. She knew of an island that stood in the heart of a frozen pool, not far away. In the summer evenings she had enjoyed the peace of the forest there, comfortable in the knowledge that her father, a woodcutter, was never far away.

With the baying of the other dogs close behind, she reached the pond and stepped onto the ice, making for a fallen tree that had toppled years before and lay like a bridge across the frozen pool. Clambering atop it, she was halfway across when the first dog leapt onto the fallen trunk, its starving eyes fixed feverishly upon her.

Her young heart was consumed with an anger that she had never imagined possible, a hate for the men who had destroyed her life and burned down everything she had loved.

For the first time in her life, she *wanted* to kill.

The dog advanced along the trunk, cautious at the sight of the girl's savagery, wary of the angry tears that came into her eyes as she suddenly realised that all she loved was dead.

The girl kicked downward and shook the trunk as hard as she could. Then she shifted slightly and stamped her feet onto the frozen surface of the pond. At once it began to crack.

The end of the trunk shuddered.

The starving dog dug its claws into the decaying bark, trying to steady itself, aware that something was wrong.

The other dogs arrived and bunched, displaying the pack instinct, then crept to the edge of the pool. But they were unwilling to commit their full weight to the ice.

With a sudden loud crunch, the ice shattered. Losing her balance, the girl fell into the freezing water. She clung to the trunk to keep herself from drowning, yelling in shock, unconcerned whether her cries were heard. The trunk twisted, taking the dog under the water, trapping it beneath the icy cover and condemning it to a frigid end.

Then the trunk twisted again, rising as it turned, carrying her up and lifting her clear of the biting cold water.

For a brief minute she lay on the bark, shivering uncontrollably, indifferent to the dogs that stood a dozen yards from her, separated only by the dark eddies of the water. They didn't matter, she thought to herself, nothing did. Her family was gone, her home destroyed.

Let them take me, she thought. *Let them do with me what they will.* For the cold was too strong for her to fight, too seductive in offering its escape from the weariness that was replacing her rage. Ignoring the hungry growling of the starving dogs nearby, she lay her head gently on the bark to rest.

Despite the many hundreds of times that she had relived the episode in her dreams, whether or not she had found sleep she could never tell. If she had, she knew it could not have been for more than a moment.

It was the voices that stirred her—harsh words of men drunk on plunder and violence, rejoicing in their wickedness. The dogs stared at her in hungry desperation, their appetite dimmed as they became aware of the men and their metallic boots stamping over the frozen ground.

She had to hide, for if she failed to do so she would die—the final victim of the men who had destroyed her village. But it was hard for her to move farther along the trunk toward the snow-covered island. She had gone only a yard when her strength failed.

As her thoughts began to dim, she recalled the stories her father had told her, of centuries gone, when the gods fought for the destiny of the world and their terrible powers reshaped the continents and destroyed civilisations. There was one amongst them, her father had told her, who would give aid to those in need.

"Saradomin…" she whispered. The word felt awkward on her lips, as if she only half-believed the tales her father had told her on those winter nights in their cramped log cabin at the edge of The Wilderness.

"Saradomin… hide me." The word gave her strength now— the strength necessary to clamber across the trunk and onto the small island. Her energy spent, she half-fell and hid behind a crimson bush of thorns.

She could not move, certain she was going to die on the island she had made her own in happier times.

"Well, Sulla! It looks like she got away!"

The man's voice was hard, and he spat the words as if he meant to insult his companion.

"You think so? With no shelter? If the dogs didn't get her then the cold will—or did you not hear the cry as we approached? Now round up these animals and muzzle them. We don't want their yelps attracting any attention on our way back to camp."

The other man swore under his breath as he turned to leave. In a breathless moment the girl knew she had to see this man, this "Sulla," who had taken everything from her in a single afternoon. Carefully she raised her head, her numb hands parting the branches of the thorn bush.

The man Sulla, the commander of the attackers, had his face hidden by a black helm. As the wind picked up and tugged at his bearskin cloak, she noted that his entire armour was black, as if he were a being of soulless metal.

Then, even in her sleep, the girl shuddered involuntarily.

For she knew what would come next.

Sulla removed his helm in the dream, exactly as he had done in life nearly ten years before, and it was his face that made her bury her head into the snow to stop herself crying out. His entire face was a single hideous scar, as if a heated mask had been forced onto it, burning flesh and leaving the skin blistered. From the pale left eye that stared blindly without a pupil to the cracked fissures of skin around his mouth, the man called Sulla and his hideous visage was something the young girl promised herself she would never forget.

"Sulla," she whispered as the men left, dragging their dogs with them, encouraging them with vicious kicks and the lash of the whip. "You killed me—and I will never forget you."

And finally, when she was alone in the freezing forest under the clear pale sky, she closed her eyes, expecting never again to open them.

THREE

A clear dawn painted the white walls of Falador a noble gold, the sunlight from the east warming the stone and making the inhabitants forget about the weeks of gusting winds and damaged homes.

For Sir Amik, the morning brought questions that needed answering. He had been awake since the first rays of light had caressed the highest tower of the castle, hours before any lawful citizens had begun to stir from their beds, going over what little he knew about the mysterious girl. He estimated her age at seventeen, but there was little else he could tell.

Of one thing he was absolutely certain, however—the girl was important. The powerful response to his prayer at her bedside was evidence of that.

"Gods move in mysterious ways," he said to his valet, Bhuler, when the servant entered the room to stir the fire.

"When they choose to move at all, my lord—which is either too rare for some…" Bhuler jabbed at the logs with the poker, "… or too frequently for others."

Sir Amik didn't answer. He knew what Bhuler meant. His valet had himself once been a capable knight, many years before, and still his body was strong, a hangover from the many years of hard training. But Bhuler had been unlucky. During his first year as a knight, a joust between the two men had ended in disaster. Sir Amik had unhorsed him, and a bad landing had resulted in a leg injury that had forced Bhuler to retire from active duty. For although fit and strong, Bhuler had never since been able to run any great distance, and all knights who travelled abroad in the world needed the use of two good legs.

Since then he had spent his years managing the castle and ensuring that the knights had the home they deserved, often training with the squires and peons, for he was still a strong and skilled warrior.

On some occasions, Sir Amik secretly wondered if Bhuler harboured any anger against him for rising to the head of their order—a role to which Bhuler himself might once have aspired.

Perhaps, he thought sometimes, *our roles could have been reversed. I could have been the servant, and Bhuler the master.* More often he was certain that the man didn't blame him for the ruination of his career, for that was not a knight's way. Yet he knew it had caused his valet a crisis of faith.

For how could Saradomin let such a thing happen to a man filled with nothing but faith and love for his god?

"Are these false gods we worship?" Bhuler had once cried in a brief moment of anguish. "Does Saradomin even exist?"

And then a senior knight had stood up, so quickly as to upset his chair. His gaze had locked the distraught valet into a sobbing retreat, and the words he spoke with passion made everything seem so simple and true.

"Saradomin exists," he had said with conviction. "Yours was an unfortunate fate, no doubt the doing of Zamorak. He exists as well, and some say his will is as great as our Lord's."

The senior knight had bowed respectfully toward the four-pointed star that was the symbol of Saradomin, a symbol that the knights displayed proudly on their pennants and arms.

Slowly Bhuler had followed his example, uttering the words of Saradomin with a hesitant yet renewed confidence.

"Strength through wisdom."

Never again had he shown such doubt. Accepting that he could not be an active knight, Bhuler had organised the running of the castle, elevating it to a higher standard than ever before. If he could not fight Saradomin's battles in the world at large, he would ensure that his brother knights would be equipped to do so.

And to Sir Amik, Bhuler's quick mind had proved an invaluable asset. It allowed him to concentrate his efforts on the knights' political affairs, knowing that the domestic matters of the castle were left in good hands.

It was therefore no surprise to any of the most senior knights that Bhuler should be present at the private counsel they convened to discuss their strange visitor.

Sir Amik recounted the tale of the young girl's arrival to the dozen men who sat before him. All had already heard some version of it—each slightly different, for the story had been told and retold a dozen times—and like all stories it had grown in the telling. Once he finished he sat down, gesturing to the master-at-arms to reveal what he could about the girl's belongings.

"I shall start with the sword."

He held it up for the men to see. It was a weapon of fine workmanship, and Sir Amik noted the look of admiration in the eyes of the onlookers. He especially enjoyed the look Sir Vyvin gave it, for his sword had been smelted years before by the Imcando dwarfs, before their defeat at the hands of raiding barbarians, and so precious had it become that Sir Vyvin only used it on ceremonial occasions.

"It is neither steel nor iron. I believe it is adamant." A murmur of respect ran through the men. Adamant was one of the strongest and rarest of all metals, and beyond the craft of any smith in Falador.

"I would draw your attention to the symbol on the blade, which is replicated on the scabbard." Sharpe pointed to the engraving. All were familiar with the four-pointed star of Saradomin, yet this was different, imperfect, as if it had been carved into the metal by someone replicating it from memory.

The sword was handed around the circle of men, each weighing it in his hand, their faces expressing their pleasure at the quality of the blade.

"How could she have come by such a weapon?" Sir Vyvin asked.

"We have two clues that might help us answer that," Sharpe said. "The white flower she clutched in her hand might give us an indication of her location before she teleported onto the bridge. I propose to send Squire Theodore to Taverley and the druids. They have the knowledge needed to identify the plant— knowledge none in Falador would likely possess." He surveyed the uncertain looks of the men. "But if the case be otherwise, then here is the flower. If any of you can identify it and tell us where it grows, it would save Theodore the journey."

The master-at-arms passed a silver tray around the company, the white flower resting at its centre.

"Do we not have books in the library that can help us?" Sir Vyvin asked as he too gave a resigned shake of the head and passed the tray back to the start, thus completing the circle.

"We do not," Sharpe replied. "I have spent the night checking for both the flower and this ring that the girl possessed. It, too, might tell us who she is." The broken ring began its round on a second tray, and each knight carefully scrutinised it.

"Do you think it a family heirloom, perhaps?" a voice said from the entrance, and each man looked to the newcomer. He was older than Sir Amik by nearly ten years, and his clear grey eyes shone with a penetrating intelligence. Nature had favoured his mind over his body, however, for he walked stiffly in his armour, as if he had worn it for so long that taking it off was beyond him. The knights stood as he entered the room, two of the nearest rushing to help him to his chair.

He glared at both of them, and they stopped before they could reach him.

"I am not that old," he said gruffly. "The almshouse may be where I hang my cloak, but I am not yet a permanent fixture."

He read their thoughts with a glance, Sir Amik thought, and the idea amused him. *For he has spent his life reading men and divining their intentions, and he was very good at his job.* Then he spoke aloud:

"Come in, Sir Tiffy. I am glad you came. You have been apprised of the situation?" he asked.

Sir Tiffy moved slowly toward his chair, sitting himself down with dignified care. He ran a hand through his white beard.

"The peon who fetched me was eager to tell me everything, doing his best to be indiscreet. You should tell the youngsters to keep their tongues from wagging, Sir Amik. Loose talk costs lives!"

Several of the knights glanced at one another. Sir Tiffy ran the knights' intelligence network, mostly from the quiet confines of the park close to the pond, where he could happily feed the ducks that lived in its reeds. He had developed an eccentric reputation amongst the citizens of Falador, and enjoyed a degree of fame as a harmless old man who was enjoying his retirement. Yet the reputation was a ruse, a shield to put his enemies off guard and to gain the confidence of others. Inside the castle, with his peers, he removed his mask, ever eager to bring his burning intellect to the problem at hand.

The three items were brought before him: the sword, the flower and finally the broken ring.

"Neither the sword nor the flower mean anything to me," he said, considering each in turn. "But the ring! I have seen one like it before... though not recently. Indeed, not for a long time."

"Do you remember where that was, Sir Tiffy?" Sharpe asked, an unusual intensity in his gaze.

"I do not immediately recall—but give me time." He looked up at the master-at-arms, a slight glimmer in his eyes. "Please, tell me your suspicions."

The company of men turned in anticipation to Sharpe, who swallowed before he began.

"I was hoping one of you might confirm my suspicions," he said slowly. "I spent the night in the library, after Squire Theodore and I catalogued the items. I found nothing conclusive, but I strongly suspect that this is a Ring of Life."

His eyes passed briefly over the men assembled. No one spoke, so he continued.

"It must have been what brought her here. It is broken now—most likely it was broken the minute she arrived. Is that not in keeping with the Rings of Life? That they offer a last chance to teleport a dying individual to a place of safety?"

"But are these Rings of Life powerful enough to breach the barrier?" Sir Vyvin spoke quietly. "This in itself was thought to be impossible."

Before Sharpe could reply, Sir Tiffy spoke.

"If it was a normal ring, then that might be so, but I see what Sharpe is getting at." His face was drawn as he spoke. "If this is one of the few Rings of Life that was issued to our very own agents, many years ago, then it would possess the ability to pierce the barrier, would it not?"

Suddenly someone laughed.

"What is so funny, Sir Ferentse?" Sir Amik demanded.

The knight rose.

"Those rings were given out decades ago," he said scornfully.

"The man who crafted them has been dead for ten years. Only a few were unaccounted for, and surely you cannot expect one of those to have fallen into the hands of a simple girl, and after all this time?"

"Stranger things have happened, Kuam. It is a possibility." Sir Amik scolded the man lightly.

"It raises an important question." Sir Tiffy looked intently at the ring again. "It could be, Sir Amik, that the girl you are harbouring upstairs, unguarded and unrestrained, is a murderer."

A murmur arose. The Rings of Life were near-legendary artefacts the knights had created with the help of a sorcerer sympathetic to their goals. They had been issued to those who undertook the most dangerous missions, men who would spend years living amongst the enemy and learning their intentions. From nearly fifty Rings of Life issued over a decade-long period, only eight were yet unaccounted for.

"Speculation, Sir Tiffy," Sir Amik stated, remembering the results of his bedside prayers. "We need facts, and I shall send Squire Theodore to Taverley to find out about the white flower."

The meeting ended and the men rose from their chairs. All save Sir Tiffy, who politely refused the offers of assistance.

He's certain that he's right, Sir Amik realised. A Ring of Life had been used to teleport the wearer out of danger and away from certain death. But the question remained.

Just how did this girl come to possess such a precious object?

FOUR

The cold air of winter stung Theodore's face.

He travelled northwest, driving his mare hard in his eagerness to reach Taverley. He had been on the road since morning and had stopped only once, to bow his head in respect to the graven statue of Saradomin that stood several miles to the north of Falador, its hand pointing to the city as a guide for travellers.

He had not been alone, for several others were preparing a fire on which to cook some game. They sat a respectful distance from the squire, eyeing him with distrust, as if expecting him to accuse them of poaching. The Knights of Falador were known not only for their honour and their dedication to truth but also for their zealousness. Many perceived them as self-proclaimed lawmen, and a few even called them a militant judiciary, too eager to ensure that the law was upheld to the letter.

After a long silence, an elderly man spoke.

"Have you heard the news from the south?" he asked nervously of one of his fellows, who warmed his hands before the fire.

"Aye," the younger man replied. "I was there a week ago when we found her. Not far from Old Farm on the Draynor Road. It was a young woman. She'd been dragged from the road shortly after darkness." There was bitterness in his voice.

"So it's true then? Did you see her?"

"What was left of her. There's something south of Falador that lives amongst the woods and hills, something wicked that preys upon the local people." As he spoke the hood slipped back from his face and his eyes settled on Theodore, who listened quietly.

He had heard of nothing amiss in the south, and yet as a simple squire there was no reason why he should have. It was the knights themselves who would attend to such business, or the Imperial Guard.

"What will you do about it, knight?" the man called over to him in anger. "Two people seized and devoured in the last month!" He stood and walked over, striding aggressively, confident that some code would prevent Theodore from retaliating against an unarmed traveller.

"Or do you go elsewhere in the service of your God?" the man continued. "Attending to matters of greater urgency. Are we peasants not important enough to warrant your attention?"

"That is not true," Theodore replied calmly. "I knew nothing of this monster that plagues you, but when I have finished my journey I shall see that action is taken. You have my word."

The man stopped and turned his head aside, unable to meet Theodore's clear gaze. When he spoke again, some of the anger had left his voice.

"You knights have to do something," he said, returning to the fire to join his companions. He faced the squire again, looking him straight in the eye.

"There have been strange men in purple robes—hunters they call themselves—stirring up anger, telling the people there is a monster in their midst. The men in robes have even started questioning folk about it. They will lynch some poor fool if they can, and it will be the wrong man."

Theodore knew of the men in purple robes. They were

an organisation from neighbouring Misthalin, a group of individuals who preached human superiority and were intent on driving out non-human populations, stirring up anger and violence in the villages. Their most common target was the goblins that wandered Asgarnia.

He had encountered goblins on several occasions, and felt a certain sympathy for the creatures. As a tribe they posed no threat to the human cities. They were incapable of organising any standing army and as individuals they were to be found wandering the roads where they were akin to beggars. He had fought only one goblin, the year before, when he was sixteen. It had been stealing from a farmer, and he had killed it with a deft thrust through its neck. But he had taken no pride in the act. He had even lost sleep over it, for goblins were not worthy enemies.

After allowing his mare an hour's rest, Theodore continued north. The men's hostility had ceased after they vented their anger at the slayings, and they seemed satisfied with his promise to investigate.

Night fell, and yielded a full moon. He planned to sleep by the roadside, and when the winter darkness deepened so that there wasn't enough moonlight for him to continue, he led the mare off to the west. He found a hollow, sheltered from the wind by a briar. It was well back from the road, invisible to other travellers. There was no way in which any man-sized foe could approach him other than entering the hollow the same way he had.

He tethered his mare, ensuring that she was comfortable. She was a horse of the knights, a companion to Theodore from when she was very young, and since her days as a foal she had become accustomed to the long days of riding and the hard nights of unsheltered sleep. Without complaint she dipped her head, her eyes carefully fixed on her master.

Then he stretched out beneath the shelter of the briar, drew his sword and laid it by his side, ready for immediate use. Wrapped in his cloak, he was soon asleep.

The night was still. The northern winds that had rent the land had finally exhausted themselves, and the darkness was ideal for the hunt.

He had gone many miles out of his way, fearful of the large city of men with its white walls and armed guards, and it had cost him a week before he had picked up the scent of his quarry. He had feared that it had been lost, that he would have to continue onward until chance favoured him. But he had come upon the scent close to the road, and it was strong enough for him to follow.

And he had decided to celebrate.

He watched some gypsies at the roadside, the lights of their caravan luminescent in the blackness. The land of his youth had had gypsies, as well, hardier folk than these travellers, accustomed to the land they were living in and its unforgiving way of life. Those people knew their place, but here the people were soft, well-nourished, peace-loving, and unsuspecting.

He knew he shouldn't attempt it. But the risk that such an adventure suggested, here in these fatted lands, served to spur on his appetite.

A plump child wandered to the edge of the darkness, and he drooled. He heard the sharp cry of a young woman's voice, calling to her son, and recalled the week before when he had dragged another woman from the roadside, excited by her fear.

I am spoiling myself, he thought, his red eyes glowing under the still trees.

It was still dark when the sound awoke Theodore, a noise that instantly set him on edge, his hand grasping his sword instinctively.

Something was moving nearby, something big was forcing its way through the briar circle that sheltered him. He breathed out slowly, silently, waiting for the intruder to come closer. Yet with each second his fear grew.

I am a squire of Falador, Theodore told himself. *Fear is paralysis. Fear is a greater enemy than any mortal foe.*

He moved swiftly, his cumbersome armour giving him away as he stood, his sword drawn back in readiness. As he summoned his breath to give a yell of challenge, the briar parted and an animal's wizened head appeared through the thicket. The moment it saw him, the creature's dark eyes widened in fear.

"A badger!" he breathed as the intruder scurried off, loping swiftly into the darkness. He glanced at his mare, noting that she hadn't moved—indeed, she seemed barely awake—and he was reminded of an old maxim of the knights. *Evil to he who thinks evil.* It was the talk of the travellers that had set him on edge, putting thoughts of vicious beasts in his mind. Meanwhile his mare displayed the wisdom of all animal kind, dreaming in an untroubled sleep, oblivious to the fears of humanity.

Fear, Theodore told himself, as he lay back down on the earth still warmed from his sleep. *Fear is the greatest enemy.*

He had ridden for two hours before he came across the caravan, just beyond the tenth mile marker that indicated the distance to Taverley. He had left before daybreak, catching only an hour's added sleep after his rude awakening, unable to relax enough to get any more.

He noted the soldiers first, standing away from the brightly coloured wagon, its red tint gleaming in the morning sunlight. As he rode closer he noted the blanched faces of the men and their suspicious glances as they looked toward him.

"What has happened here?" Theodore asked. These were Imperial Guards, men who viewed the knights as a rival military force in Asgarnia. He ignored their hostile gazes as his eyes swept over them hastily, and then moved onto the caravan. That was when he realised that the red tint hadn't been the gay colours of a gypsy's pride, but rather a spray of blood.

The guards noted his sudden comprehension, and one of the older men spoke.

"A savage attack on a gypsy peddler and his family. There is a body inside, mauled by a beast, and the body of a woman lies in the woods. Their child's clothing has been found…" The guard removed his helm as he spoke, as if he needed a diversion to gather himself before continuing. "… bloodied. There is no sign of its body."

Theodore entered the wagon, and felt his gorge rise. He had seen death before—from accidents in the lists to the violence he had encountered while accompanying a knight in his role of squire—but he had never seen such carnage. The beast had forced itself in through the slim wooden door at the back of the wagon, and even the killings had not satisfied its rage, for the wooden walls and cupboards had been ripped and household objects overturned as if the very idea of a home had been offensive to it.

"We think the woman ran into the woods with the child…" A younger man began to speak, but his commander interrupted him.

"What are your intentions here, squire?" he demanded. "Will you join us in the hunt and slow us down, or will you go on your way?"

"My interest here is the same as your own—to see that justice is done. However, I am needed urgently in Taverley, and will gladly take any message to the authorities there.

"I will not put politics above justice," he added firmly.

"Nor will I," the man responded. "You can take a message to Taverley. That would be a useful service to us, for we need men who know the local lands if we are to start a hunt."

The guard moved to one side and wrote briefly on a parchment, which he then rolled and handed to Theodore, telling him who to give it to.

As the squire pulled on his reins, ready to depart, a sudden thought occurred to him.

"Is this related to the events in the south?" he called, making the guard turn.

"What events?"

"Another murder, a week or so ago. I met some travellers on the road yesterday who told me of a woman who had been slain. From his description it seems as if it might be the same creature."

The guard bowed his head, his face darkened by the news.

"Thank you, squire—that is useful news, indeed. I am glad you chose to share it, despite the differences of our politics."

Theodore returned the bow, knowing that he had done the right thing.

FIVE

The blue banners with the symbol of Saradomin embroidered upon their centre fluttered in the cleansing breeze over Falador. It was less bitter and violent than the wind that had buffeted the land in previous weeks.

The matron mopped the girl's feverish brow. Despite Sir Amik's assurance that she would live, the woman's optimism had begun to wane. Unless she woke soon, the girl would be too weak to survive.

"What is your name, child?" she asked softly. The matron had tended the sick since she was young, and she was sure that even in such a comatose state the patient would respond to her soft tones. She had spent a good deal of her time that morning singing the old nursery rhymes she had crooned to infants in her days as a midwife, hoping that the words might be familiar to the strange girl and stimulate a recovery.

But the song died on her lips when the girl suddenly turned her head. It was the first time she had moved since the knight's prayer. Was she ready to wake?

Her eyelids remained closed, her breathing unchanged, and the matron's heart sank. She gathered the damp rag she had used to wipe her patient's brow and moved to leave the ward.

She had just reached the door when a hard voice called out, uttering words that she did not understand, words unknown in the common tongue of men.

The patient had spoken.

Yet still she lay motionless, asleep, her breathing barely heightened from the exertion. The matron peered at her, unsure about what to do.

The girl suddenly moved again, tossing her head to one side.

That launched the woman into motion. Gathering her long skirt in her hands, she abandoned the rag on the flagstones and ran as fast as she could, down the wide staircase and across the courtyard, the winter morning cold on her face.

Theodore stood near the window overlooking the small fountains and gardens for which Taverley was famous. It was a very different place from Falador—far more peaceful, in harmony with nature. The houses reflected two styles, either thatched, wooden structures or moss-covered stone buildings that seemed to grow out of the earth itself.

He enjoyed the serenity of the town, for it did not have cobbled streets like Falador but fine earth tracks on which a horse could walk almost silently. The peace was exactly what the squire needed after the shocking scenes at the caravan.

Casting his attention outward, he surveyed the country around Taverley, looking first to the northwest, to White Wolf Mountain. He had heard tales of the huge wolves from which the mountain derived its name. Few were brave enough or foolish enough to attempt a journey over the narrow passes and into the sun-filled land of Kandarin beyond, and in winter it was said that the mountain was impassable.

To the south, a great calm lake extended as far as he could see. He remembered the tales he was told as a child, of dragons that prowled its depths, away from the prying eyes of men. As a squire, Theodore had been taught of the special equipment needed to successfully combat a dragon, and of the abilities these creatures possessed. More often they were seen on land, but they were rarely sighted in civilised regions, rather making their lairs deep underground and far north in the most distant Wilderness.

A soft voice interrupted his reverie.

"I cannot help you, Theodore," it said. He turned to see an old man in a plain white robe, his chin boasting an even whiter beard.

"Then you have no idea where it grows?" Theodore could not hide his disappointment. He had been so sure the druids would know.

"I have consulted our specimens, but there are none that match," Sanfew replied, handing the flower back to Theodore. "I still have some of our coven going through them, however," he continued, speaking slowly and quietly as if he were afraid his very words might be an intrusion against nature. "If you would be happy to wait, I suggest that you explore Taverley. The calm here would do you good."

As soon as Theodore had arrived he had relayed the message of the Imperial Guards and informed the druids of the monster's attack on the gypsy caravan. A dozen militiamen had headed south to aid in the hunt, while the druids had offered him soothing tea to calm his nerves.

Yet still he felt a lingering panic.

"I could do with a brief rest," he admitted gratefully to Sanfew.

"Then please, avail yourself of the opportunity," the druid said. "Meanwhile, I have sent for Kaqemeex. He's the most knowledgeable of our coven, although he spends much of his time in the ancient stone circles to the north. He will be here by afternoon, however, and with luck he may be able to answer all your questions."

The manner in which Sanfew spoke drew the squire's curiosity.

"All of my questions?" he echoed. "I have only one."

"I thought you might have more. About the beast that stalks the countryside?"

Theodore hadn't considered the possibility that the druids might be able to ascertain the nature of the savage creature that had committed the brutal murders. Yet the druids knew more about the world and its magical ways than they let on. It was said that they could conjure animals, compelling them to do their bidding in guarded rituals.

"Do you know anything that might help in its capture, Sanfew?" Theodore's voice was urgent. *What do they know about the monster?*

"You must ask Kaqemeex," the druid replied calmly. "He hears things, from the birds and the beasts."

Theodore nodded, content to wait, for he didn't wish to appear rude. The druids were well known for doing things at their own pace, regardless of the pressures of the wider world. Instead, he decided that he would use the time to attend to his horse, to explore Taverley, and then to get some rest.

He had found his mare a warm stable as soon as he had arrived, and was pleased to see that a young groom had provided food and water. He found her asleep, tucked amid the warm hay that was a rare luxury in winter, her saddlebags and reins hanging nearby.

Then Theodore had only himself to look after, so he spent half an hour strolling amongst the fountains and the flower beds. He wondered whether he had time to pass through the fence to the south, to gaze upon the still waters of the partly-frozen lake.

"Squire Theodore! What are you doing here?"

Theodore recognised the youthful voice at once, and turned to see a familiar face and a shock of red hair. They belonged to a young man in a long blue robe that marked him as an apprentice to the Wizards' Tower. The robe was too big, however, and seemed prone to being caught underfoot while the sleeves hung too far over the man's hands.

"Castimir!"

The young apprentice bowed to the squire, but there was a look in his eye that took Theodore back to a childhood friendship that predated his own decision to dedicate his life to the knights.

Straightening, the wizard showed an eager smile.

"The druids have not ceased talking of your arrival," he said. Then his face darkened. "Nor of the caravan."

"That is not my concern, at least not yet," Theodore replied, his own mood sombre for a moment. "The Imperial Guard are handling it. I will help when I am able, and when…"

"… when your duties are done." Castimir finished Theodore's sentence for him. "You see, young squire, I know you too well."

"Your wits may be sharp, but how would your magic fare against the true steel of a knight?" Theodore drew his blade, the sharp sound of steel on steel reflected in the eager gleam of his eyes. He stood as if to attack the defenceless blue figure before him.

And then he laughed, lowering his weapon. It seemed as if it had been a long time since he had laughed so genuinely.

"I have moved beyond such childhood games, Theodore," Castimir replied earnestly. "We no longer compete on the same level." He opened his hand to reveal a dozen pebble-like stones resting in his open palm, with mysterious markings engraved upon them. The wizard smiled daringly at Theodore. "Do you think you could deliver a blow before I could stop you? Or do you lack the courage to try?"

Theodore's eyes narrowed as he regarded his childhood friend coolly, but after a few seconds his icy demeanour evaporated and a large grin spread across his face.

"And what spell would you have used, Castimir? A fire strike?" The squire laughed again as he sheathed his sword. Yet the wizard remained serious.

"My abilities have grown considerably in the months since we last met in Falador. With these runes in my hand, I could snare you to the spot and bind your limbs." He gestured dramatically. "You'd be defenceless! As for fire strike, that would be child's play. It is one of the very first spells we wizards learn."

"Truly, I remember when you first cast that one, Castimir. It was a day after the talent scout had identified your magical potential and gave you a few runes to practise with. You tried to kill that rat, and ended up setting fire to Rommik's crafting store! No wonder he disliked you, even *before* you destroyed his entire inventory!"

It was Castimir's turn to laugh.

"My uncle had tried to apprentice me as a crafter under Rommik's guidance. What a mistake that was. I attempted to mould a ring and ended up breaking everything. He scowled at me for years afterwards!"

"Well, I hope you make a better wizard than crafter, Castimir. Your luck can only take you so far!"

Despite his words, it had always seemed to Theodore that Castimir had been the brighter of the two of them, and to have risen so quickly in the ranks of the wizards in the legendary tower only served to prove his point. It was a great accomplishment.

His face must have reflected his thoughts, for his friend spoke up.

"Let's get something to eat, Theo," he said, calling the squire by his childhood nickname, "and I'll answer all your questions as we dine."

The table was laden generously with food.

Theodore had heard tales of how the druids would only eat meat if it was specially prepared. The animal had to have been killed in a fashion that was respectful of its nature. Now several meat dishes sat between the two friends. Brightly coloured fruits, some of which he had never seen before, were piled in wooden bowls, their red and orange skins stirring the squire's appetite.

"That one is chicken." Castimir pointed with his fork to the dish that sizzled in front of them, his manners abandoned in the company of his friend. He seemed entirely intent on enjoying himself.

Theodore helped himself to the delicacy, careful to avoid filling his plate excessively. He noted Castimir's wilful abandon, however, and a moment's fleeting jealousy flashed through his mind when he considered his old friend's new station in life.

Castimir was destined for great things, and even the shock of bright red hair that once had been such a cause of merriment now seemed to distinguish him from other men. It had darkened as he had aged but still stood out. And its owner moved with a confident assurance that he had lacked only a year before—especially in the company of Theodore, against whom he had always been physically weaker.

"I am nearing the end of my year's travels." Castimir said, recounting his wanderings. "I crossed over the mountain a few weeks after leaving you in Falador. The snows were not so bad, and I went with a party of travellers. If I had crossed alone, however, I doubt very much I would have survived. The wolves up there are huge, and always ravenous."

He paused to poke his knife in the direction of White Wolf Mountain, using the moment to swallow a tender morsel.

"And Kandarin! When you get over the summit, round the highest pass, you see a land drenched in golden sunlight, and the ocean as vast as you can imagine." He paused, and his eyes peered at something far away. "It is the most beautiful thing I have ever seen, Theo, amid the freezing snows and the howls of the white wolves!"

Theodore said nothing, though his envy grew unbidden. He had heard stories of Kandarin that lay beyond the mountain. Many knights had travelled there, and he had listened to their accounts with eagerness, dreaming of one day walking there himself.

"It has strange beasts as well. My mule died shortly after we descended the mountain. A wolf injured him near the end of our journey, and the poor creature did not survive. Thus, I was forced to purchase a replacement from a fur trader who had journeyed south all the way from Rellekka, the city of the Fremennik peoples who live on the northern edge of the world."

Castimir looked at Theodore with an amused glint in his eyes, hastily swallowing another piece of chicken.

"It is a yak, Theodore!" he said, his enthusiasm youthful again. "A yak! He's a stubborn creature, but he is a perfect substitute for my poor mule, and he is better suited to carrying my belongings with a purpose-built leather harness. I shall introduce you to him. I think he is far more useful when travelling in cold climates than a mule—he's sure-footed and his shaggy hair is warm, if ever you need to shelter from the cold." Then he looked wistfully at the rapidly diminishing food, as if debating what to eat next.

Theodore found himself turning sullen, yearning for the adventures his friend had already experienced. Before he could speak, the young wizard continued.

"I honestly think I might be the first person to bring a yak into Asgarnia. I thought I could sell him as a curiosity to one of these natural philosophers, but then they would probably cut him up to see how he works, and I couldn't accept that!"

Then Castimir paused, studying his companion's expression.

He bit greedily into a rose-tinted apple an ' changed the subject.

"So how are things in Falador?" he inquired. "You look well—but then you never looked amiss!" His grin failed to turn Theodore's humour.

"I have been with the knights since I was nine, Castimir," the squire replied. "I have seen my parents only once in that time, when I graduated to the position of a squire after the long years as a peon. I still have another two years before I become a knight."

Castimir gave him an encouraging look.

"It will pass quickly, Theo," he said, certainty in his voice. "Of course, you must have doubts. What knight would you be if you did not?"

"A true one, Castimir! One who would not question my life's direction."

But the young wizard was undeterred.

"You don't doubt your choices, Theo, you doubt your own ability," he said. "Your parents weren't rich, and many squires come from exclusive backgrounds. To them, having a spare mount or lance is something they take for granted. That is why you feel left out—you cannot afford the same entertainments as the other squires when they head into Falador for a night off."

"I do not take nights off, Castimir."

"And the others do?" A pained look appeared on his face, and Theodore stared down at the table.

"Sometimes," he replied. "Not often."

"Your hard work will be rewarded, Theo—I can promise that. Stick at it long enough and keep in the game, and you will be there at the end, ready to reap the rewards."

At that, they allowed the subject to drop, and both friends refilled their plates, Castimir unafraid of excess, and Theodore refusing to let the food go to waste.

SIX

"I want you to meet someone, Theo."

The young squire's mood had lifted since their meal. After they had refilled their plates, Castimir had gone over memories of their childhood, many of which Theodore had forgotten. They had brought the smile back to his face, and as they left the room he had gripped his old friend's hand, in gratitude for making him remember what he had forgotten in the pursuit of duty.

Castimir spoke as they made their way toward the wizard's lodging.

"This man has been in Taverley for several weeks, after returning from Catherby. He is eccentric—and possibly mad, I haven't decided yet—but he is certainly worth meeting. I call him the alchemist because he has all sorts of strange theories about the world."

"Nothing too blasphemous, I hope?" Theodore said smiling, seeing if Castimir would rise to the bait—for he had always been more open-minded than the squire.

"Well, he's not a worshipper of Saradomin, Theo. I do not think he worships any of the gods as we know them. He believes them all to be one being, that each element of the traditional gods—such as order and wisdom from Saradomin, and chaos and death for Zamorak—are parts of a single entity. He believes that such differences are akin to different fingers on the same hand."

"But surely he favours one aspect over the others? The wisdom of Saradomin, the balance of Guthix, or the chaos of Zamorak? How can you believe in all three when they run so contrary to one another?"

"That is what I said," Castimir agreed. "And he remarked that the differences I had mentioned, just as you have done, are created by mortals to serve their own political ends."

Theodore's expression hardened.

"If he speaks too loudly, then, he will be declared a heretic," he muttered.

"Maybe," the wizard agreed. "But what kind of world would it be if it were true? Would your ideals change? Would you still pursue the followers of Zamorak with your sword in hand on your white charger?"

"You sound as if you almost believe him, Castimir."

"I do not, Theo. The old gods aren't so weak as to be knocked off their pedestals by the words of old men. But we wizards must be open to new ideas."

They stopped outside a white-walled house with a thatched roof. Castimir entered without knocking.

The bitter smell was the first thing Theodore noted as he ducked his head under the low lintel. A large table stood in the centre of the room, behind which stood an old white-haired man. His thick-rimmed glasses glistened in the afternoon sunlight, which struggled to make its way through the fug in the room. Theodore's hand instinctively covered his mouth as the smell began to choke him, and the man looked up.

"Ah! Leave the door open, Castimir," he said. "Your friend is unfamiliar with *chemistry*!" The alchemist beamed with pride at the word, and said it with an exaggerated flair. "Chemistry!" he hollered. "Surely there can be no more noble an art."

He spread his arms wide, gesturing to the strange implements that lay scattered throughout the laboratory. Theodore noted test tubes suspended over the open fire or arranged upon the table, contentedly boiling away the suspicious liquids they contained, in some cases until there was nothing left.

"I had understood you to be interested in science, Ebenezer," Castimir reminded him gently, and the old man's eyes gleamed at the mention of the word. "What is this newfound enthusiasm you have embraced?"

"Science, yes, that's right my young friend," the man replied. "It's one and the same. My chemistry is a study of science, Castimir—one of the many facets of knowledge that may reveal the workings of the universe." A suspicious furrow wrinkled his brow, and he peered at Theodore. "But Castimir is a wizard, and wizards already think they know all there is to know." He scowled darkly at the young man.

"Sir, Castimir told me that you don't believe in the gods," Theodore said cautiously. "Is this true?" He had met men like this before, men who preyed upon the discontent of the masses, preaching impossible solutions to the hardships of life. *Liars, heretics, and con men*, he thought.

But the alchemist didn't respond as he expected. He shook his head.

"That's not entirely true, squire." The man gazed darkly once more at Castimir, pushing his glasses back up to the bridge of his nose. "The evidence supports their existence, despite the fact that the prayers of the faithful still seem to go mostly unanswered. Yet in my travels I have seen miraculous demonstrations of faith, attributable to any member of the pantheon of gods who are currently worshipped."

"Currently worshipped?" Theodore countered. "It is not for mortal-kind to pick and choose the gods."

The notion was absurd to the aspiring knight, whose ideology was built around serving justice in Saradomin's name.

"Isn't it?" the alchemist parried. "I have seen terrible things done in the name of religion, by people who were good in all other respects. Isn't the pantheon like a noble house, wherein each member is fighting for dominance?"

Theodore felt the blood rush to his face.

"It is not for men to pass on their own folly to the gods—they are above that!"

"A god above jealousy?" The old man seemed amused by the idea. "And yet legends tell of the God Wars, when the continents were devastated by their quest for dominance over one another." But then he turned away, adding, "Perhaps you are right though. Who can know the will of higher beings?"

Theodore cursed himself inwardly. Was his faith in Saradomin so weak that it could be upset by a remark from an eccentric traveller? The Knights of Falador believed that Saradomin was the most powerful god, and their education was not accepting of all other religions. Some faiths could be tolerated, certainly, but those such as the followers of chaos, of Zamorak, were to be opposed wherever they were found.

He breathed deeply to calm himself before speaking again.

"I am sorry, alchemist, if my words seemed harsh. You have seen much more of the world than I, but surely you must acknowledge that Saradomin's way is best? If all followed it, there would be no war, no dishonesty. Would we not have a perfect world?"

The alchemist raised his head.

"People boast too many differences for us to have a perfect world. What is perfect for you might not be perfection for anyone else." He saw Theodore open his mouth to respond, and held up his hand to prevent him. "As for only worshipping Saradomin, that would make the world a boring place, wouldn't it?

"But if the pantheon were incorporated as one god, that god

would possess aspects of your Saradomin to reflect justice and order, and Zamorak to reflect the need for chaos. After all, even chaos exists in the natural order of things. The fox takes a rabbit where it can, following its nature—its attack chaotic, unplanned, the strong against the weak. That is how the natural world goes," he said firmly.

"And what aspect of order does the natural world possess?" Theodore asked, his tone sarcastic. "Any at all?"

"Order is in nature every bit as much as chaos," the old man replied, seemingly unperturbed. "If the fox eats too many rabbits there will be no more and it will starve. Thus there will then be fewer foxes the next year to hunt the fewer rabbits. In time, however, the rabbits will breed and once their numbers are back up then they will be able to sustain a greater population of foxes. There is order there, and chaos as well, but at a level that is hard for us to see. The natural world is something that is still largely hidden from us."

Before the argument could continue, a door slammed, and a youth with dark hair and astonishingly black eyes appeared behind Ebenezer. He stood uneasily, looking at Theodore with what the squire could only think of as fear, hiding himself partly behind the alchemist as a shy child might hide behind its mother.

He looked about a year younger than Theodore, an adolescent slightly taller than the squire. His teeth were very white, and his dark hair was thickly matted and unkempt, growing long to his shoulders. When he moved he did so with the natural grace of an animal, his thin body sinewy and tough. He noted Theodore's gaze on him and stepped back farther still behind the old man, his white teeth showing in a feral snarl of distrust that startled the squire.

There was something about the lad that made him feel distinctly unsafe, as if he were in the company of a wild creature.

At the sound of the low growl, Ebenezer turned to reassure the lad, his hand resting on the youth's shoulder in a gesture of reconciliation.

"You must excuse Gar'rth, young squire," he began as the newcomer calmed. "He has had a hard life, and does not speak the common tongue. Plus he is hostile to armed men, even if they be of your righteous order."

"He has nothing to fear from me, sir—unless he has broken the laws of the land." As he spoke, Theodore was surprised to see Castimir glance knowingly at Ebenezer.

The old man shook his head.

"I found him on the road a few weeks ago," the alchemist explained, "starving outside the walls of Taverley, a stranger to human kindness. Is a man guilty if he steals to prevent himself from starving?"

Theodore did not answer. In his mind theft was a crime, and crime—no matter what the cause—was inexcusable. His expression darkened, and Castimir moved closer to him, speaking quickly.

"You must excuse Ebenezer, Theodore," he said. "He found the man that Gar'rth stole from and made full reparation. The farmer was entirely satisfied."

"But has Gar'rth been punished?" the squire responded. "Simple reparations are not enough. He must be made to understand that what he did was unacceptable." His hand had instinctively travelled to the hilt of his sword, caressing it unconsciously.

Before Castimir could reply, the alchemist spoke, anger colouring his voice.

"Did I not explain? He does not speak our language!" he said, his eyes flashing. "How can he be made to understand?" Ebenezer's eyes darted between him and Castimir, and with a clear effort he calmed himself. "But I am teaching him. We are learning, aren't we, Gar'rth?" He smiled at the youth as a teacher might smile to encourage a pupil.

After a moment of struggling, a broken phrase passed between Gar'rth's lips.

"Thank you…"

"That is one of the few phrases he has mastered," whispered Castimir. "The lad is a strange one, Theo, savage and astoundingly strong. To any other save Ebenezer, he is decidedly hostile. Even toward me." He grinned broadly as he finished speaking, and Theodore decided again that there was little in life his friend took seriously. As always he found it inexplicable, yet it caused him to appreciate the friendship all the more.

Ebenezer returned to his chemistry. Carefully he took a glass vial from the tabletop. It contained a clear, still liquid. With exaggerated care he mixed the calm fluid with a cup of water.

Immediately, the compound began to froth, spitting droplets onto the tabletop and beyond.

"Oil of Vitriol! Who would have thought that adding cool water could cause such a reaction?" He laughed manically.

Castimir's curiosity was sparked by the experiment, and he moved closer, reaching out.

"Water did this? I would not have thought it possible…"

"Do not touch it!" the alchemist shouted. "The reaction heats the liquid, and it's still quite hot," the old man added. "It would have burned you."

"Heat without flame?" Theodore muttered to his friend. "Surely that is magic."

"I told you he was worth meeting, Theo," the young wizard responded, as a knock at the door drew their attention.

A druid stood in the entrance, the sunlight illuminating his white robes, his green cloak shining as if it were made of living plants. He had an old face that spoke of many days and nights spent outdoors and in the company of nature. His grey eyes possessed wisdom that could not be learned save by an honest journey into old age.

He focused his gaze on Gar'rth, and the youth hung his head to avoid the attention of the new arrival. When the druid spoke, his voice was deep.

"How is Gar'rth today, Ebenezer?"

"He is well, Kaqemeex," the alchemist replied. Upon hearing the name, Theodore straightened with curiosity. "The affliction seems to have quieted since your intervention. We are all thankful for that."

The old druid noticed Theodore's interest, and nodded to him.

"You are the young squire from Falador, who wishes to know about a particular white flower," he said. "The birds have told me of your coming."

Theodore bowed his head in respect to the old man. He opened his mouth to answer the druid's query when a high-pitched chirping sounded from nearby. A blackbird perched upon the lintel, her black eyes flicking warily from one person to the next, taking in the entire group with a flurry of motion.

"I know already, my small feathered friend," Kaqemeex said gently, and her chirping ceased. "Go and take your fill in the cool waters of the fountains." The small bird fluttered away, leaving Theodore to stare at the druid with undisguised scepticism.

"The birds are the most useful spies of all," the elder man said as if giving a lecture. He seemed not the least bit daunted by the squire's overt disbelief. "There are very few of us who can still converse with wild creatures, and of those I am possibly the most adept at doing so." He smiled sorrowfully, as if his memory dwelt on better times.

Yet Theodore remained unconvinced.

Surely he cannot expect me to believe…

"What did she tell you?" Castimir asked in all earnestness.

"What I have known for some weeks now. There is an evil abroad in Asgarnia, that has entered the lands recently. A creature that seeks something, or someone." He bowed his face and a cloud hid the sun, deepening the shadows.

The killer, Theodore realized with a start, and he spoke up, all thoughts of blackbirds driven from his mind.

"Sanfew told me to ask you about the monster," he said quickly, eager to learn anything that might help him in the quest for justice. "He told me you might have some useful information?"

"I do not know what the beast is, if that is what you ask," Kaqemeex answered. "I know only that it pursues something. It heads north, hiding by day and moving toward its goal each night. I suspect that what it is searching for is here, in Taverley. The birds seldom sight it, for it is a canny creature."

His eyes moved swiftly to each of them in turn, much as the bird's had done. Castimir looked uncertainly away, and Theodore held his grey stare without moving. He turned his attention to Ebenezer, who cast a knowing look in return. Finally they came to rest on Gar'rth.

"How are his lessons, Ebenezer?" Kaqemeex asked, turning back to the alchemist.

"Slow," Ebenezer replied ruefully. "Gar'rth is not a linguist, I fear. Teaching him the common tongue will take time. Castimir has helped, however."

The druid nodded in Castimir's direction and then he turned his eyes back on Theodore.

"I understand you have a query about a white plant, as well," he said.

At that, Theodore reached into his pack and drew the specimen out reverently.

Kaqemeex stared at the flower in Theodore's upturned palm. He did not touch it at first, and after a minute he bent low to smell what fragrance remained with the flower. As far as the squire could tell, there was none.

"Do you recognise it, sir?" Theodore asked with ill-disguised anticipation.

"Yes, it is a White Pearl, so called because of the fruit it produces," the druid replied, and at his words a shiver passed through the squire. "They are found up on White Wolf Mountain." He nodded his head northward to where the range of icy peaks marched into the distance as far as the eye could see. "They do not grow exclusively on that mountain range. Ice Mountain also harbours its own population of White Pearl."

At last, a clue!

Theodore's excitement caused him to smile broadly. He extended his hand in gratitude to the old man.

"May the blessing of Saradomin be upon you! This is excellent news indeed." He turned to his friend. "I will return to Falador at first light tomorrow."

SEVEN

It was night. The faces of the men were eerily lit by the burning brands they held in the crowded dell.

Before them stood twelve men clad in purple robes, addressing the audience and engaging them with swift hand movements and carefully chosen words.

"What kind of men are we, citizens of Asgarnia, who would let monsters roam the countryside?" one said. "How many more of our womenfolk must we see seized by the roadside and devoured? How many of our children? The attack on the caravan is not the first of its kind, and even now a conspiracy amongst the Imperial Guard and the knights exists to deny it— to prevent us knowing the truth!"

The speaker paused for breath, clenching his fist as he raised his hand and then pointed to the onlookers theatrically.

"Do you know what that truth is, fellow citizens?" The faces looked expectant under the light of the burning torches. "Do you?" the speaker cried loudly, he bunched his hand in a tight fist and punched the air, challenging the crowd.

"No! Tell us!" someone shouted from the back, and immediately his call was backed by others in the crowd. The speaker in the purple robe let them continue for a moment before calmly raising his arms in a gesture that bespoke of reconciliation and peace.

The crowd fell silent, everyone captivated by these strange men who had come amongst them, preaching humanity's superiority over all other creatures.

The speaker resumed.

"The truth is that they *can't* protect you! They cannot protect any of you! Not the elitist Imperial Guard, too concerned with protecting the crown prince in Burthorpe. Not the knights, too caught up in their righteous ways to care about the needs of the so-called common people!

"And both..." He pointed at the crowd once more, emphasising his point, "...and both caught up in their own militant rivalry!" He spat the words in disgust, and a few voices shouted out excitedly from the crowd, agreeing with him.

"They do not want us out here, hunting for the monster ourselves! They feed on our insecurity, on the belief that simple men like us cannot protect our homes—making us believe we need them! Look around you! Look at your neighbour! Can he not protect himself? Would he not *die* to save his family?" He spread his arms wide before him in a suddenly sweeping gesture, and the audience of men, glaring now at one another, nodded their heads and shouted in agreement.

"They rule only by our consent. They govern us only by our own leave. They exist only because we allow them to!" The speaker's finger once more extended toward the night sky, and he paused for a moment to let them consider the enormity of his words. If the authorities had heard him speak in such a manner in one of the cities, he would be arrested for sedition. He knew that well. But here in the open country, and with Falador a day's ride south, standing amongst farmers and travellers and men to whom the monster was a very real thing, he was free to do as he wished.

"But in truth, we are to blame," he continued. "Look again at your neighbour—if he can protect himself, then why does he rely on the goodwill of others? If he can fight, why then is he so eager to extol the virtues of the knights and depend upon them for safety? Why, if a common man has faith in the strength of his own arm, are we so eager to let the strutting knights and officers of the exclusive Imperial Guard collect their taxes and rob us of our livelihood, just to pay for the silver buttons on their ceremonial coats?

"Remember, they rule only because we let them. They rule only because we fear to take our destinies into our own hands!"

A pungent smell made the speaker smile inwardly. His fellow believers had done well, passing the strong brew amongst the onlookers, feeding their frenzied minds with the potent alcohol. Such was their animation that he doubted the crowd would be willing to disperse without some activity to vent their rage.

It is so easy, he thought to himself before continuing, *to take advantage of their innate fear.*

"They say a monster is loose!" he cried. "A creature that devours its victims! They say they do not know what it is, and they secretly encourage us to let our own imaginations build their monster into something mythical.

"Werewolves!" He punched the air viciously. "Vampires! Ghouls!" With each word another savage punch, and with each blow a roaring tempest of voices shouting encouragement.

"But what has it attacked so far? A single woman barely out of girlhood! A lone gypsy caravan, isolated from any help, with just a grandfather and young mother to protect a defenceless child! Look at your neighbour, my friends, and ask yourselves why we should be afraid. Search amongst you for any who would not fight to protect their families from a beast that kills the old and the weak. This is no werewolf. This is no vampire or ghoul. But it is not human either. What human would do such a thing?"

The faces of the men showed doubt under the torchlight.

"It is something masquerading as a monster—something designed to instil fear into our souls," he said, his voice filled with certainty. "What else could it be?"

The men shook their heads.

"Goblins can be found in these parts—we all know of the settlement north of here. Could it be a goblin?" he asked, facing the foremost onlookers directly, one after the other.

"Goblins aren't smart enough." The voice was thick with the rural accent.

"But what else can it be?" This second voice was familiar to the speaker, for he had told the man exactly what to say.

The result was exactly as he had hoped.

"There's a dwarf that lives hereabouts. Just off the road to Taverley, a few miles north of here. He lives on his own, as a hermit."

Doubtful expressions drew the speaker's attention. Some of the crowd still needed convincing.

"A hermit?" the speaker yelled suddenly. "Does he show a hatred of people?"

"He don't like them getting too close!" the rural voice shouted out, and several nodded in agreement. The dwarf was a well-known hermit who had lived in the lands of Asgarnia for two dozen untroubled years, but as the farms of men had grown closer, he had become an angry neighbour.

He's perfect, the speaker mused.

"Dwarfs are known for their cunning," he said in a thoughtful manner. "They are the masters of metal, hoarding their treasures, unwilling to share even the basest trinket. What lengths would he go to in order to protect his privacy? How well do we know him? We cannot trust a creature like that!" His fiery eyes observed new jugs of alcohol being passed amongst the crowd, and to his delight he noted several men swaying uncertainly.

"How can we trust a thing that hoards its wealth?" he

continued. "Dwarfs are known for their love of shiny metals. They share the magpie's lust to decorate their homes with what is precious to humankind. Gold! Silver! Rubies! Where a dwarf makes his home, you will find such things."

The speaker had lit the fire of envy in the eyes of the onlookers, and as they drank he could see the effects of his appeal to their greed. Each of them pictured what secret wealth the lone dwarf might possess in his isolated log cabin.

"I say we go and see the dwarf," the rural voice called from the rear of the crowd. "Ask him about the murders!" A dozen voices rose in agreement.

"It will know something, my friends! The caravan was only a few miles from its lair when it was attacked." The speaker had changed his approach. The dwarf had been demoted to an "it", his home rechristened a lair.

He smiled as the angry voices echoed amidst the dell. A lair was so much easier to burn than someone's home.

The clear night glittered with so many stars that Theodore thought they must be beyond count.

He had sat up late with Castimir, talking extensively of their childhood together in Rimmington, a town that lay several days' travel from Falador. The two had shared laughter, reliving the halcyon days of their youth, their faces lit under the strong moonlight that softly touched the thatched rooftops and white walls of Taverley. The fountains glistened in the gloom, their faint music of cascading water an eerie enchantment.

Now Theodore looked once more at the stars, a great loneliness in his heart, a sudden feeling of smallness as he observed the heavens above him.

"Is it true, Castimir?" he asked. "What they say about the stars?"-

The young wizard looked at him for a long minute, aware

that their conversation was nearing its end and that it would soon be time for them to part. It had taken considerable effort to break through Theodore's reserve, a protection the squire built around himself to keep others at a distance.

You didn't have that before you joined the knights, Castimir thought with sadness. *If you have changed like that, how must you think I've changed?*

"What do they say about the stars, Theo?"

"That if you travel far enough, they change." Theodore stared wistfully skyward.

"I cannot say, for I have never travelled so far. The stars in Catherby are the same as they are here—fixed in the heavens by the gods to guide seamen and reveal the secrets of the world to astrologers."

A sudden cough sounded from nearby, and Theodore's hand instinctively found the hilt of his sword. A moment later Ebenezer emerged from behind a fountain, his hand holding a clay pipe as he walked tentatively toward them.

"Did I hear you correctly, saying that you believed the stars to be fixed forever in the heavens, just to be used by astrologers?" He eyed Castimir with a sparkle in his eyes.

"That's what we were brought up to believe," the young man replied. "I know you well enough, however, to know that you do not agree." The wizard looked at Theodore warily, knowing that he would not approve of Ebenezer listening in the darkness.

And still the squire kept his hand resting on the hilt of his sword.

"I have a number of different theories about them," the old man replied. "Though I have yet to decide which one best suits the facts as I know them. But nothing is forever—not people, not places, not worlds and not stars. Everything is subject to change."

"Must you question everything, alchemist?" Theodore

asked, unwilling to be drawn into another argument in his final moments with Castimir.

"Absolutely!" the old man replied proudly. "If you do not ask, you do not learn—a favourite maxim of many mothers, that too few children bother to practise. It is a philosophy of mine that everything must be questioned. To leave the natural world in the hands of the gods is to give even them too much credit."

With that, Ebenezer lit his clay pipe and stood close to the two young men, pointing out the constellations to both squire and wizard. As they observed the heavens on that cold, cloudless night, a shooting star sped across the horizon and vanished behind the glistening peaks of White Wolf Mountain to the northwest.

Not a hundred yards away, Gar'rth lay in a pool of cold sweat.

Curled beneath some blankets they had laid down in the hall, he had watched as Ebenezer, finished with his chemicals, decided to stroll out for his evening smoke. The alchemist had paused at the door before opening it, looking down at Gar'rth's shadowy outline.

"Are you all right, Gar'rth?" he asked the motionless youth. Although he did not understand any of the words save his name, Gar'rth was familiar with the manner in which they were spoken. Soft words, comforting words, the words of someone who cared. It had been long years since Gar'rth had heard any words like that.

"Thank you," he had responded. The only words that Gar'rth had so far been able to learn, he said them with a sincerity that would make the most practised dissembler feel envious.

Gar'rth had struggled to keep himself from shaking as Ebenezer spoke to him, but when the old man shut the door he stopped trying to fight it. He lay in utter silence, his body shivering so much that even the glowing embers of the fire offered him no comfort.

Shortly afterward he began to sweat, a cold sweat that erupted from his pores and drenched the bedclothes. He was familiar with his ailment, and despite the potions that the druid had brewed for him, he knew he could not expect his condition to improve. He doubted that he would *ever* be rid of it.

Lying there, he recalled the taunts that his blood-brothers had heaped on him those many months ago, before he had escaped.

You can't change what you are, Gar'rth. You're one of us. You can't change the way you're born!

He had escaped, crossing rivers and borders, living off charity where he could before accepting the fact that he had to steal to survive. The one thing he never did was to harm an innocent person—that was a rule he would not break. He could never do that, for if he did then he knew he would be lost.

After the sweating came the spasms, which wracked his body as if there were something inside that hungered to be released. As he tasted his own blood in his mouth, he sniffed the mixture of crushed herbs that Ebenezer had prepared for him. Usually they soothed him, but now they affected him little.

It was the most violent attack his ailment had ever made against him, and he knew it would be worse the next time.

Crying was rare where he came from. It showed weakness, and a youth of Gar'rth's age crying would have incurred a harsh punishment. But he was far away from that place. Covering himself entirely with the sweat-drenched blanket that was now cold against his skin, he wept, his black eyes pools of anguish.

EIGHT

The furnace bathed the room in a red glow of warmth, enough to heat the entire log cabin in winter, when the ground was frozen and the trees had shivered off their leaves.

But something had awakened him.

Living in isolation had given him a sense for trouble, and he could feel in his old bones that something was amiss. Something was coming—something dangerous.

The old dwarf's hand shot out and grasped the heavy battle-axe that he never let out of his sight. The weapon was a comfort in his hands, yet as he stood he became aware of a sensation that he had rarely felt before. Cold fear knotted his stomach.

There was something outside the cabin, something truly terrible, something that exerted a fearsome presence through the stout wooden doors that he knew would not offer him any protection should the source of his fear decide to enter.

His mouth was dry and the words he had been preparing to shout died on his lips. Never in all his many decades of life had he felt such a presence.

Something sniffed at the door and the hardy dwarf stood back, whispering a half-remembered prayer to his most favoured deity, Guthix.

Let it come, he thought. *It'll find me ready to defend my home.*

He did not feel the cold when he was hunting, and the only danger the snows presented was the possibility of leaving tracks for hunters to follow.

Only chance had put the gypsy caravan in his way. His mother had told him, years ago, that it was wrong to waste an opportunity. Ever since he had feasted on the family, he had watched warily as armed men searched the frozen woods and questioned travellers on the road.

His treats were becoming more of a risk.

This made the bloodlust stronger.

So strong had it become that the thought of taking an unprotected maiden or errant child no longer excited him. His dark thoughts had turned their attention to the isolated farmhouses and log cabins that populated the forested land between Falador and Taverley. How the residents would fear when he devoured a family in their own home!

The log cabin that he had decided upon was a squat building more isolated than any other. For two nights he had watched it from his vantage point on a steep rise. Tonight he had ventured closer.

But when he sniffed the door frame the scent was different. The occupant was not human, he realized, and he was unfamiliar with the smell.

No matter, he thought. *Variety is what makes life interesting.*

He jumped away from the cabin, gathering his strength in readiness to throw himself into the oakwood door.

The dwarf had fought worse than goblins in the dark caverns of his race's mines, but something here was very wrong.

He heard the creature sniff the ground outside, just a few yards from him, and he heard it back slowly away from the door, most likely readying itself for an assault.

It's intelligent, he thought to himself as the cold fear once more wound his stomach in a knot. *It knows I am alone.*

I have lived a hundred years, he told himself firmly, *and if I am to die this night, then it shall be in the way in which I have lived my life—with my axe in my hands, facing my foe.*

He took a deep breath and summoned his courage. Then he stepped toward the door to open it.

He stopped at the last second, his head turning in the night air. He could hear people—many people—stomping over the frozen earth and shouting.

Too many, he thought, *and likely armed.*

Through the trees he could see at least a dozen burning brands held aloft, and as the wind changed direction he caught their scent. They were human men given the false confidence that came with alcohol.

He wondered for a second whether he could take them, whether he could defeat all of them. But then he remembered what he had come into Asgarnia to do, and with a bitter glance back at the oak door, he fled across the clear ground and into the darkness.

Spoil yourself with children and maidens, he thought, *but not groups of men.*

The door clattered open and a wave of warm air flooded out from the cabin. The dwarf stood silhouetted by the red glow of the fireplace. His eyes swiftly adjusted themselves to the dim light under the trees where the moonlight could not penetrate. He caught sight of a cloaked figure vanishing silently into the darkness, running close to the ground.

"Who's there?" he shouted in the common tongue, trying unsuccessfully to rid all trace of fear from his voice. He gazed intently in the direction the figure had gone, his eyes attuned to see in the darkness, but so thick were the trees that he could make nothing out.

Still he could feel it. Out there, nearby, something was watching him.

Then he heard a shout, and as he walked a few yards from his cabin and onto the icy ground, out in the blackness, he saw a large body of men coming from the direction of the road.

The group was being deliberately noisy, as if the sound of their own drunken shouting was enough to protect them from whatever lurked in the darkness. For an instant the dwarf was relieved, pleased by the sudden approach of the men.

Perhaps they would let me join the hunt for the creature.

But then he noted the hostile looks and the gestures of anger that they made toward him. He recognised some of their faces, farmers from the surrounding country, lumberjacks and hunters he had lived amongst for years.

And he remembered why he kept to himself, more often than not.

As they strode up into the clearing in front of the cabin, he saw the looks of hatred on their faces. He was an experienced fighter, but he knew this many men would easily overwhelm him, unless he could get inside the cabin and into the escape tunnel that he had dug as a hidden exit, years before. It led out into the woods, a hundred yards or so to the east.

But he knew that running would be an admission of guilt in their eyes. *Let them say what they will,* he thought, shifting the weight of his axe more comfortably. *Let me hear what my crime is.*

A tall man strode forward, his purple robes unfamiliar to the dwarf. He raised his hands as the crowd shouted. Some began to throw stones at the cabin, while a few of the bolder youths walked closer, eyeing him intently.

Never before had he seen a mob, and it began to terrify him. Not the terror he had felt earlier, but a fear that was no less real, and he was lost for words.

More of the group turned their attention away from his home and toward the dwarf himself. One of them shouted and pointed accusingly in his direction.

"There is the creature!" the man in the purple robes declared. "It must know about the murders. Let us force it to confess!"

Before he could react, the men surged forward, the smell of drink rife amongst them. His axe was impotent—he couldn't risk killing any of them, for then he would surely be lost.

This must be a misunderstanding, he thought. *A mistake.*

"What are you talking about?" he shouted above the din. But they paid him no heed. His arms were seized, his axe taken from him, and he was lifted bodily off the ground, his protests ignored. Vicious hands tore at him and clenched fists clubbed him in drunken rage as a dozen men forced their way into his cabin.

He could hear the crashes of his handmade furniture being overturned and broken, and he knew then what they were looking for.

"Gold!"

A cry louder than the rest silenced them all.

He knew the find would spur them to greater efforts. Kicking feebly against his captors, the dwarf could hear men ripping up the wooden panels of the floor, using his own axe to destroy his home.

He had watched the men approach the cabin. He had heard enough of their words and seen enough of the looks on their faces to know that they had only unintentionally rescued the dwarf from becoming his next victim. He looked on with an amused growl, watching the events unfold with anticipation.

The thought that an innocent creature would pay for his crimes amused him. He lowered himself to the earth underneath a small group of fir trees, whose low-lying foliage concealed him against the whiteness of the snow.

His red tongue slowly made its way around his white teeth, hunger making him salivate. The clearing was beset by the scent of fear from the dwarf, from the mob, and even from the men in purple robes.

He had encountered such men before—men who preached human superiority and lied to achieve their ends. He examined the speaker, a man who was gesturing and talking with righteous animation, and in the darkness his red eyes glinted sadistically.

He was no longer interested in the dwarf.

The fire started accidentally.

One of the men, careless from intoxication, dropped his burning brand on the stack of dry straw that the dwarf used to bed his goats during the winter. As the flames roared the looters cried out in alarm and rushed outside, the last of them barely escaping as the roof collapsed behind him.

Some men clapped and hallooed, their voices slurred and their eyes burning with aggression. Others looked suddenly downcast, as if the fire marked the end of a fever.

Quickly the mob began to disperse. Some dropped their plunder in the clearing, ashamed of their behaviour—though it could not be undone. The thought of the monster still loose in the land made them remember their loved ones, defenceless at home, not far away.

With growing alarm the mob vanished.

Lying in the snow, forgotten, the dwarf's face was curiously expressionless as he watched the burning pyre that had once been his home. He shed no tears and he uttered no curses at those who had done this deed.

The leader of the mob, his pockets now heavy with coins and

jewels, knelt by the dwarf while his fellow purple-robed men stood close by.

"You should see this as a warning," he sneered. "Some of the men might regret what they've done tonight, but they will convince themselves they did the right thing—they always do. Yours is not the first home I've burned to the ground!"

He stood and brushed the snow from his robes, careful to check that none of the coins had fallen from his swollen pockets.

"Heed this warning and return to your people. Asgarnia is a human realm!" He kicked the dwarf in the ribs. "Your goats are ours now. We'll eat them, as you have no more use for them."

The dwarf watched as the twelve robed men departed, until they became shadows in the darkness, dragging his goats behind them. Standing, he looked back at his burning home, wondering what to do. Should he return to the mountains, or go to Falador to demand justice?

Neither option appealed to him. If he returned to the mountains, the men in purple would have won. If he went to Falador, then he would be humiliated. The monster had stirred up this fear, and it was the monster that would have to pay.

He brushed off the snow, giving a final look at the tiny figures of purple-robed men as they disappeared in the darkness. His foot tripped on something heavy in the snow. Leaning down he found his axe, which had been dropped when the mob had fled the fire. Carefully he picked it up, weighing it in his hands gratefully.

It's funny, he thought to himself, *but I could have sworn there were only twelve purple-robed men. Not thirteen.*

NINE

The men lay close to the fire, their blankets covering their heads to keep the cold away.

Only the speaker sat upright, his mind pondering the value of the stolen goods. He smiled, wondering whether there were any other dwarfs nearby living in isolation, a convenient target for the stirred hatred of men.

He shivered and moved closer to the fire, contemplating if he should try to sleep once more. He cast a jealous eye to his fellows, each perfectly still, corpse-like, hidden beneath their thick blankets.

He was about to stand when a movement caught his eye. It was the guard, his purple robes hanging loosely about him. The speaker watched him move toward the glow of the fire. The guard sat down opposite, his head bowed, his face hidden in shadow.

"It was a good day," the speaker said. "A few more like that and we will be rich men."

The guard laughed, sounding satisfied with everything the night had offered. Then he swivelled his head, peering into the shadows around them, expectantly. Watching him, the speaker continued.

"Wake your replacement and get some sleep," he ordered.

"The monster may take lone women and children, but there are twelve of us and we are all well armed."

The guard nodded, and yawned.

"This killer is perfect for us to rally people to our cause," the speaker added. "With the fear so rife we can make the whole of this land monster-free!" He checked himself as his voice rose, a habit from his speeches.

Swiftly he cast an eye over the silent men. Despite his words, not one of them had stirred. That was odd. He knew two or three of them were light sleepers. Then it occurred to him that even the overweight Thwait was not snoring. That was unusual.

He stood up and kicked the obese figure under the blanket, pushing back the cloth that covered him. As he did so he gave a cry and staggered back, his gold coins forgotten. Thwait lay still, unmoving, the blood already dry on his exposed throat, that had been torn open in his sleep.

"Wake! Wake!" the speaker yelled, fumbling for his dagger, pulling back the blanket of the man nearest him. He recoiled instantly when he saw another torn throat, the lifeless eyes staring up at him.

The guard had not moved. As the speaker turned in his direction, he raised his head. Burning red eyes stared hungrily from the shadow beneath the cowl.

"They cannot hear you, speaker." He spoke harshly, like a feral animal holding back his instinct to enjoy the moment. "None of them can."

"Where is the guard?" the speaker stuttered, knowing that no weapon he possessed could possibly be of any defence against the creature that had done this.

"I tore open his throat like all the rest, and left him where he fell."

The speaker felt the tears blurring his eyes. It wasn't supposed to be like this.

He was supposed to be the hunter!

"No!" he said as he wept. "Please, take the money, take the jewels. Take *everything*. You don't need me for anything!"

"You are right. I don't need you," the dark figure said. "But I am a monster, aren't I?"

The cowl fell away from the face. The speaker shouted for mercy as the burning eyes narrowed and the long tongue shot forward to taste his hot tears.

He let the man scream, relishing each second.

Let the cries awake the countryside, he thought. *Let the people of this land know that I can take whom I wish, unopposed.*

It lasted for nearly two minutes. Then the scream ended abruptly, the sudden silence sending the birds flying from their nests, their cries a witness to the atrocity under the first of the dawn light.

A minute later, several goats left the clearing and headed north.

Theodore had not slept. So much had happened in the three days since the girl had arrived—the appearance of the monster, the return of Castimir, his introduction to Ebenezer and to Gar'rth.

He wondered if this was what life was like for a knight all the time. Indeed, he hoped so, for he had loved every minute of his small adventure.

Except for the gypsy caravan. His thoughts darkened at the memory of such gruesome sights. Then again, he remembered, a knight's life had to be like that. Such evil would remind him of his duty, to ensure that it would never be repeated.

He left Taverley before daybreak, intending to get as far south as he could before halting. Ebenezer had sent Gar'rth to prepare the mare, but she had shied away from him. Even Castimir's yak, indifferent to much that was going on around him, pushed himself to the farthest end of his enclosure in an effort to be away from the feral youth.

Only when Theodore had soothed the mare would she let Gar'rth fit her saddle. It took careful instructions issued by example for Gar'rth to see how it was done. Theodore wondered what kind of life Gar'rth must have lived to have never saddled a horse before.

As he left the stable the youth bowed his head.

"Thank you, Gar'rth," Theodore said. He was startled to see the surprise that his words had provoked. Was the young man really such a stranger to kindness and common decency?

Castimir was standing in the courtyard, and Theodore embraced him. The young wizard's red hair was dishevelled from his sleep, his eyes half-shut as he said goodbye to his childhood friend there under the dawn sky. Even Ebenezer bid him a fond farewell, and Theodore, not wanting to leave with any ill words between them, took the alchemist's hand.

Then he hoisted himself into the saddle, and headed off along the road to Falador.

He had gone no more than five miles when he pulled on the reins to halt the mare. Her breath was visible in the cold morning air, and she shied a bit, as if aware of the sudden change in her master's mood.

Theodore stood in his stirrups, looking to the east.

A black pall of smoke was rising from the dense woods not far from the road, and he could see the black shapes of carrion eaters flocking to the south. He knew well what the black wings meant.

Slaughter.

He had no choice but to investigate. Dismounting, he led the mare off the road and into the drifts that carpeted the forest floor. The going was slow and Theodore had to keep the sun before him to ensure that he was travelling in the right direction, for the tall trees obscured his view of the smoke.

After several minutes of stumbling through the soft snow that crunched underfoot, he came upon a track. Here he could see that the snow had been churned up by a large but disorganised body of men that had passed over it very recently. They had not taken the time to hide their numbers, and to Theodore's eyes it looked as though they had deliberately tried to make themselves known to the forest. He wondered if they were the hunters led by the Imperial Guards that he had encountered. Perhaps the smoke was from a pyre they had used to burn the body of the monster?

Then a cold shiver ran through him. *Perhaps they had burned the bodies of more victims?*

The smell of smoke grew stronger and the faint breeze could no longer hide its presence. Ensuring that his sword was loose in his scabbard, Theodore followed the trail to the edge of a clearing.

The smoke came from the smouldering remains of a cabin on the edge of the tree line. The road from Taverley to Falador had often harboured highwayman and bandits, he knew, although he had never heard of them attacking the farms that lay scattered and isolated across the countryside.

Warily he drew his sword, his free hand covering the mare's mouth to indicate that silence was required.

It was the angry voice he heard first. A great shout issued from the ruin, followed by a loud crash as several timbers were knocked aside.

Still Theodore waited, his sword in his hand, craning his head to see. He could make out a small figure, his face blackened from the wreckage, using an axe to dig through the hot embers. Sheathing his sword loudly so that the dwarf would hear, he walked confidently into the clearing, leading his horse by the reins.

"Can I be of any assistance to you, master dwarf?" His voice was loud in the stillness of the forest. Theodore had met several dwarfs before, in Falador, and knew that good manners would be needed to get a civil response—or any response at all.

The dwarf started back at the sound of Theodore's voice, his axe raised. He peered intently at the squire, who kept a respectful distance between them, his hands empty and open.

The dwarf's lips pursed but he said nothing.

Then, approaching a small collection of belongings that he had rescued from the ruins, he swung his axe with perfect precision onto the padlock of a stout metal box. The metal shattered with a spark. Somewhere nearby birds cried out in protest at the sudden noise, and flew raucously into the sky.

"I keep my most precious items in here!" the dwarf spat, lifting the lid with the blade of his axe. Inside, Theodore could see the heads of bottles glinting in the early morning sun. The dwarf reached in and picked out the nearest one, leaning on his axe for support as he unscrewed the lid. He took a swig.

"Hid it well, too," he said. "The mob never came near it!"

Theodore walked closer, a faint smile on his face.

"What happened here?" he asked, looking curiously around the clearing. "There are tracks of a large body of men coming and going down the path to the road. Did they do this?"

"Aye!" the dwarf said, taking a second swig, and Theodore was close enough now to smell the alcohol. "Called me a monster! Thought I'd killed the gypsy and the child. A mob of farming men and hunters—some of whom have known me for years! They were led by men in purple robes."

At the mention of the robed men, Theodore thought back, to the words of the man at the campfire, near the statue of Saradomin.

They will lynch some poor fool if they can, and it will be the wrong man.

"Then you must come with me to Falador," he said

emphatically, "to lodge a complaint with the authorities. The criminals must be brought to justice."

The dwarf looked on impassively, until he seemed to have made up his mind.

"Criminals! It is the monster that needs tracking," he said, and a strange look passed over his face. "It makes everyone afraid—and fear makes men do bad things."

"True words, master dwarf," the squire said. "But you have not answered my original question—can I be of any assistance to you?"

The dwarf took another swig from his bottle and looked sternly at the squire. No doubt he needed help, for digging through the ruins with an axe was tiring work. Two pairs of hands would make the work far easier and quicker, and Theodore was certain the dwarf wouldn't want to be standing in the clearing after dark, not with a fiend on the rampage.

"I accept your help, Knight of Falador," he said finally. "I have a rope here, and your horse can help drag the timbers aside. I need to get two more boxes such as this one." He patted the upright lid with his hand, and the bottles jingled in the rack.

Theodore stared back suspiciously.

"You want to spend time digging up beer and wine?" He shook his head. "I will aid you, master dwarf, if you sincerely need my help. I can take you to Falador if you wish, but I will *not* help you waste our time digging for liquor."

"Very well then," the dwarf said, kneeling down. He lifted the rack of bottles from the box, and Theodore perceived that there was a hidden space beneath. From it the dwarf pulled out a solid bar of polished metal that glowed mysteriously with a green tint. He used both hands to hold it, turning it for the squire to see as if he were trying to sell it to him.

"What is it?" Theodore asked.

The dwarf raised his eyes to the morning light, grimacing in frustration.

"It is adamant!" he said. "One of the finest ores that can be mined. It takes years of practice to craft it into a weapon, and that is something that is no doubt beyond the skill of any human smith! I have another two boxes down there, each with four bars in.

"Now, will you help?"

TEN

Sulla spat.

He had been dreaming again, the same dream that he did not understand. It was the girl, the same girl of whom he had dreamed before.

He ran his large hand over his scarred face. It was damp with cold sweat. His mind was suddenly fearful that he might be developing one of the many dreadful illnesses that afflicted those folk who chose to live in The Wilderness. He went to the open window to look down into the darkness of the castle's yard. Daylight was still some minutes away, for the castle stood on the lower slopes of Ice Mountain and the yard was shaded by the foreboding walls of black stone.

Suddenly the dream was pushed from his mind. A small group of chained prisoners drew his attention.

"Recruits" was his term for describing the unfortunate people—and creatures—his men enslaved in their raiding parties. Amongst the thirty or so captured this time were several goblins, stumbling clumsily in their shackles. Sulla frowned. Goblins were not very useful as slaves. In truth the only useful task they could accomplish was to mine ores from the endless miles of tunnels that honeycombed the mountain on which the fortress stood.

"Check they all have good teeth, guard!" he roared out of the window to the men below. "If they have good teeth, they can eat. If they can eat, then they have the strength to work!"

Turning, he moved back into the room.

He thought uneasily about the dream again. He had had the same dream for the third night in a row now. And he knew he needed advice. He would consult with the sybil, the old hag of a woman who lived in the depths of the castle near the dungeons, close enough that she could hear the screams of those unfortunates whom the Kinshra wished to interrogate.

He pulled a bearskin cloak about him and unlocked the stout wooden door that led to the stairwell beyond, seizing a torch to light his way. The castle moaned with the cold drafts that ran down off the mountain peaks to the west. Some of the younger men believed that the castle was haunted by the souls of their victims, but in all his years Sulla had never seen anything that resembled a ghost. He had decided long ago that such superstition was only a weakness, and had chosen not to believe in anything that was said to be as relentlessly vicious as he could be.

Those men who knew him believed he was probably right. He knew well the rumors, and they served his purpose.

Some said that Sulla had made a pact with Zamorak, back in his youth, and to uphold his end of the bargain he needed to commit an evil act every single day. No one knew what Zamorak had offered in exchange for this worship.

Others whispered that he had sealed the bargain to gain control of the Kinshra, and that he was destined to lead them to conquer all the lands of Asgarnia. But no one knew for certain.

What they *did* all know was that Sulla was hated by his superiors—hated by them because they feared him—and factions were emerging amongst the Kinshra as they anticipated a struggle for supremacy.

As he descended, Sulla could hear the piteous cries and moans of those creatures under interrogation in the bowels of the fortress. He pursed his lips as the smell of despair reached him, pausing outside a wooden door that seemed to have twisted itself in response to the evil inside.

"Come in, my brave soldier!" a voice hissed. Before he could raise his hand to open the door it swung inward of its own accord, creaking as if it were imitating the sounds of the dying inhabitants of the dungeons.

Sulla blinked, his one good eye not used to the artificial haze which bubbled up from the huge black cauldron that sat upon a fire. He could make out the sybil behind the cauldron, her yellow teeth catching the light of his torch as her lips peeled back in a malicious smile. Sulla hated her, partly because he needed her, but also because he didn't understand her ways or powers.

"I have had the dream again," he said. "About the girl."

"Do men ever dream of anything different?" she replied, mocking him. Instinctively his powerful fists clenched.

If she were anyone else I would kill her, he thought.

"It is definitely her," he said. "Yet I saw her as the bolt pierced her, only days ago. She pulled it out and fell down the cliff face. She *must* be dead!"

The sybil looked at him with her bloodshot eyes, regarding him coolly.

Without a word she hobbled to a bench and began picking through the iron pots and knives that lay scattered about. Then, having set aside a pan and a knife, she hobbled toward a set of dark drawers that stood nearby. Her head bent low to examine the plants and dead animals that lay heaped atop it.

Sulla lost patience.

"Did you not hear what I said?" he demanded. "Why do I dream of her again after killing her? I dreamed of her before I even saw her, and I continue to do so now! What does it mean?

Is she dangerous to me still? Answer me!"

The hag turned from the drawer and peered at him intently. Sulla felt suddenly very weak under her vicious gaze.

"She is dangerous to you, Sulla," she replied. "And you have only yourself to blame for that! An obsession—that is what she is. Who can this girl be who killed your men? Who fought like an animal? Who is she who knows your name when she has never even met you?

"You fear her Sulla, for her hate burns hotter than yours!'

He considered her words... and laughed. It was a sound he rarely made, and whenever he did, it sounded as if he were out of practice.

"Fear her?" he responded. "A dead girl? She ambushed my men and killed them with her hunter's tricks, but she is no warrior. My men wounded her and I killed her myself with my crossbow. I do not fear her, witch!" He spat the words, his anger giving him the power to believe them.

"Let us see, Sulla," the hag said quietly. "Do you have something that belonged to her? Any trinket? A piece of hair? Of torn clothing?"

Sulla knew her ways and he had come prepared. He handed the hag a dagger that the girl had hurled at his head. The witch took it reverently, eyeing it closely, and then she wrapped it in several leaves that she had taken from the drawer. She placed it in the iron pan, then picked up a dead creature, which Sulla dared not examine too closely, using her knife to expose its entrails. Swiftly she stirred them, the knife scraping the bottom of the iron pan, making an excruciating noise.

Sulla held his breath.

The sybil leaned over her foul concoction and looked at it very closely, her beady bloodshot eyes examining it in fine detail. For several minutes she remained silent.

Sulla shifted his weight from one foot to the other impatiently.

Finally he could stand it no more.

"What does the augur say, witch?" he demanded.

"Only that which the gods wish us to know, Sulla!" she snapped suddenly, clearly angry that her meditation had been interrupted. Sulla thought for a second that he saw a fearful look upon her face.

"Well?" he asked, a conciliatory tone in his question.

"She lives and her spirit grows. She is still in danger, but with each passing moment she gains strength. Something is protecting her, though. Something is hiding her from my sight. But it cannot protect us from her, Sulla. Her hate and her anger are enough to burn. She has been chosen as a pawn of the gods, in the latest of their long games!"

"Is she where I left her? Where she fell from the cliff top?"

"I cannot tell you that, Sulla," she said. The hag was clearly exhausted from reading the augur.

"Then I will send men out there to scour the area. If she is alive they will bring her back to me. I shall enjoy dowsing the fires of her hatred with my own hands!" He clenched his fists once again in savage delight as he recalled the girl's blonde hair and pale skin.

ELEVEN

The mare struggled to obey Theodore's uncompromising commands. Her breath was heavy and labored, and her eyes shone feverishly.

The dwarf who sat in front of the squire looked nervously up at him.

"She cannot keep the pace! You're killing her!"

"I will not stop," Theodore responded. "You saw what I saw! It is close." He had never known true fear before—he knew that now. In his training he had been taught to master his emotions, and he had been good at it, too. But that was behind secure walls and in the company of others.

Out here the fear was pure, undiluted.

And he was afraid.

It had taken them an hour to retrieve the dwarf's boxes, and they had placed all the adamant bars into a single iron box that they roped to the mare's back.

Then they had made their way back to the road, where they had once more seen the crows flocking to the south.

"It's the monster!" the dwarf said with grim certainty. "It's struck again!"

They had ridden down the road without haste, Theodore

conscious that the mare might need all her speed later on. But with every yard their nervousness grew.

Soon they found the hollow occupied by the bodies of the men in purple. It was daylight by then, and the mutilated corpses lay where the monster had slaughtered them in their sleep. On all bodies the carrion eaters had left their grim mark.

As they dismounted and examined the scene, the squire had felt sick, his body numbed and his face paled.

"We should leave here," the dwarf whispered urgently.

"Whatever did this is gone, do you not think?" Theodore asked hopefully.

"No, squire, I do not think so," his companion replied. "This thing is clever. These men were killed in their sleep."

The mare whinnied, suddenly and fearfully. Theodore glanced about quickly, his hand instantly on his sword hilt. There was a change in the wind, and the birds had fallen silent.

"We should leave here now, squire!"

But Theodore was still uncertain.

"Look, squire!" the dwarf growled, reaching down into the earth. He held his clenched fist to Theodore and opened his hand. Lying in his palm were several golden coins. "These are the men who incited the others to burn my house! They took my gold and jewels, all of which are no doubt lying scattered about." He eyed the nearby trees nervously. "You know the reputation of my race, squire—how we covet gold and precious metals. I am willing to leave all of it behind if it means we leave now. There is something unnatural here. Can't you feel it on the wind?"

Theodore had indeed felt something. The world had gone quiet, as if nature was holding her breath as she stalked up behind them. He cast his eyes skyward to see if the carrion eaters were still circling. They were, but higher than they had been before, as if they waited for a powerful predator to take its fill first.

He strode hastily over to the mare, who had become increasingly skittish.

"Come on! It is close!" the dwarf said. Theodore mounted and hauled the dwarf up in front of him. The horse needed no urging to leave, and she found her own way back to the road at a smart trot, keeping her feet well despite the hidden roots that lay under the deep snowdrifts.

And when they were on the road, she had felt secure enough to pick up her pace, putting as much distance as she could between them and that blood-stained hollow.

"We do not stop until Falador!" Theodore cried to the dwarf as they looked anxiously at the nearby trees, both unable to shake off that horrible feeling—the sensation of being *stalked*.

"What if we meet any travellers? We must warn them!" the dwarf replied.

We will deal with that when we come to it, Theodore told himself. He whispered a quiet prayer to Saradomin to ensure that the road ahead would be empty, and that there would be nothing to slow them down.

He caught the scent on the morning wind, brought to him by the northern breeze. The smell excited him. It was more poignant than it had been in a long time, sweeter and more recent.

He had woken from his half-sleep salivating, the wet jewels of his hunger dampening the robe that he wore to conceal himself. As he raised his head to the early light, his bed still shaded amongst the warm pine needles that carpeted the forest floor, he noted that the birds had fallen silent. He cursed them. They were too quick for him to catch. The best he could do was to make them afraid, but their silence would alert others.

The scent grew as he left his bed, chasing it through the forest toward the west, toward the road a mile away. Once, he lost it as the wind changed and he stood absolutely still, distending his feral nostrils and breathing in deeply. Within seconds he picked it up again, continuing his journey at a lope.

He heard them before he saw them, and he recognised the scent of the dwarf. He could hear them talking in the hollow where he had stood only hours before, the sweet smell of human blood still dominant over all others.

It only made him salivate more, his long red tongue lolling from his mouth, curling itself in anticipation. He had gorged himself on the body of the guard he had slain, but it was not a meal he had enjoyed. Adult men were too sinewy for his taste. Maidens and fat children were more his appetite.

He watched as they mounted the horse, observing as the fair-haired man cast his eyes woefully about the carnage, looking sorry to leave the dead untended. It was on him that the scent was strongest, and yet his quarry was not present.

For months he had trailed the scent of his prey and only now—as he had indulged himself to dangerous levels that would surely attract the attention of armed hunters—had he come so near his goal.

Patience, he told himself as the mare left the clearing. *You will find him. He is near.*

His red eyes glinted in the morning light. Knowledge was what he needed now. Who was this young squire who carried the scent of his prey? He would follow them wherever they were headed and keep hidden.

TWELVE

It always snowed in the dream and in her bed the girl shivered, her mind far away.

Outside the window the day was dawning, the low sun not yet high enough to warm the white towers. There was not even enough of a breeze to make the proud flags stir and they hung limply, as if they were no more than sodden rags put out to dry by one of the city's washerwomen.

The girl's brow wrinkled and she breathed sharply. Somewhere in her mind she told herself that she need not be afraid, that she had experienced the dream hundreds of times before. But it would not be enough, she knew.

She opened her eyes as small flecks of snow chilled her bare skin, her face raw in the winter afternoon. It was already dark, and the bright stars that shone through the wispy clouds were the first sights that made her realise she was still alive.

She sat up, knowing instinctively that she would have to move if she was to survive. Her father's pack was still tied to her back, its heavy weight causing her to struggle as she crouched low, peering intently from her hidden vantage point.

For several minutes she watched the still scene, her senses

alert for any sign that some of the men might have remained.

The world was absolutely silent.

She crept quietly to the trunk that now lay partially submerged, the ice once more covering the black water, hiding any indication of her struggle with the savage dogs.

Tentatively she tested the ice with her foot, her weight pressed against the trunk. She hardly dared to breathe but the ice seemed thick enough to support her weight. She took a single step. Then, emboldened, she took another.

With a *crack* the ice broke, plunging her into the freezing water. The shock of the terrible cold made her cry out.

Overwhelmed with utter isolation and despair, she pulled herself out onto the frosted shore. For long moments she could do nothing but hold herself and weep, cursing the unfairness of the world and the men who had taken everything from her— and most of all her parents, who had so suddenly left her alone.

Anger replaced despair, and then she ran. She ran west, toward the mountain that loomed ominously above her, blocking out the clouds with its high summit and treacherous crags. All her life she had gazed at it, wondering what lay beyond.

But now she knew only that she had to keep running.

After several hours the forest grew less dense and the trees sparser. With each step the snow swallowed her to her knees and tested the very limits of her strength. Only then did the fatigue quench her burning rage. Only then did she fall.

It was the howls that forced her to her feet again. She was so tired that she imagined that the fleeting glimpses of the wolves might be an illusion. But they were not. They were real. Their yellow eyes glowed at her from the growing shadows on the white landscape, their predatory growls gathering in intensity as more of the pack added their voices to their terrible chorus.

Let them come, she thought to herself. *I have done everything*

I possibly can, and the world has gone against me. She loosened her grip on the dagger that hung from her leather belt.

She took deep breaths, forcing the fear from her mind, intent on making peace with the world in her last few minutes.

Darkness gathered, and close behind her she could hear the soft tread of padded feet digging into the snow, a low growl emanating from a lupine throat.

She was ready to die, to submit herself to Saradomin.

And then she caught sight of stars that twinkled in the dark haze. It was the constellation of Saradomin himself, made up of four brilliant stars that stood out in the heavens. Her father had made certain she would recognise it.

The growl sounded again, closer this time, but now she knew what she had to do. Her hand tightened on the hilt of her dagger.

The wolf leapt and she turned, crouching low and swinging inward with the blade. She felt it bite deep into the creature's flesh, her hands turning warm from the hot liquid that spilled out from the mortal wound.

The wolf rolled onto its back as it tried in vain to reach the deadly injury in its throat. The howling had ceased and the bright eyes that had looked at her hungrily withdrew into the night, suddenly aware of the savagery in this eight-year-old girl.

She watched as the wolf gave a final yelp and died, and she knew that she needed warmth to survive. She lay atop the animal's body, gripping its fur tightly in her bloodied, clenched fists. The sweet scent from the wound sickened her as she embraced the warm corpse.

The matron noted a slight smile on the face of the girl as she slept. It was the first sign of any happiness that she had seen, and she prayed it heralded a recovery.

"Run and inform Sir Amik, Elise!" she barked. "I think she might be waking."

The warmth of the wolf made her sleep. She was exhausted and hungry, but she knew she was safe.

"Wolf Cub" was what they called her when they found her some hours later—"Kara-Meir" in their language. A dozen hardy dwarfs led by the master forger Phyllis had set off from the mountain to investigate the flames from the village. They were dour folk who rarely mixed with the humans who lived in the shadow of the mountain, but they knew how hard life on the edge of The Wilderness could be.

She had woken to see them standing over her, their ashen faces wrinkled in concern. They had talked for an hour amongst themselves, speaking in a language she could not understand, forcing her to drink a hot liquid that made her cough and splutter but which restored feeling to her chilled limbs. The dwarfs had ventured as far as they dared, unwilling in their small band to confront the likes of Sulla and his Kinshra, for it was a rescue mission, not one of war.

Master Phyllis lifted her up onto his own back, her bare arms clasped about his neck, taking comfort in knowing that they had not failed—not entirely—that they had rescued at least one innocent from the ravages of the wild.

Outside, in the courtyard, the sound of hooves clattering over stone could be heard, followed by the white mare's neigh of celebration now that she was home and safe.

In the ward, Kara-Meir's eyes opened as the smell of clean linen and a warm fire blazing in a hearth reminded her of something she thought she had forgotten. It was the smell of happiness and people, bringing back memories of her family in their cabin and of her happy youth, before the time of Sulla.

She knew then, as she had known all those years ago when

Master Phyllis had taken her from the mountainside and adopted
her as his own, that she was safe.

THIRTEEN

The man was dying. He wiped his lips and saw with wide-eyed shock that the back of his hand was coated in blood.

"When?" he stuttered. "Who has done this to me?"

He sank to his knees, an invisible force draining him of his strength. Somewhere a door slammed.

"It will not be long now, my lord," a woman's voice murmured behind him. It was his mistress, a slave girl he had taken years before and for whom he had developed a true fondness.

"I am not ready…" he murmured through blood-stained lips, his hand outstretched in a plea for mercy he knew would not be granted.

"You were ready a long time ago!" a harsh voice snapped, rejoicing in the sight of a dying man. It was Sulla. He had orchestrated this man's murder as only Sulla knew how—totally without pity, using a loved one as the instrument of death, corrupting someone who had been trusted.

The dying lord of the Kinshra noted Sulla gesture toward his mistress. She looked despairingly into the scarred man's face, his grimace the closest thing to a smile that he could manage. His blank white eye shone with an inner delight. He was revelling at the spectacle.

"Do it!" he told the woman. "Kill him!"

"Is the poison not enough for you?" She bowed her head in fear, looking with genuine sympathy to her dying master. "He will be dead shortly as it is!" Her voice broke into a wail at the thought of what Sulla had made her do.

"Not soon enough!" Sulla growled. "And poison is too easy for him. I want him to know that I now possess everything he treasured in life!"

"Do as he says!" the dying man cried out. "Kill me, but only if it frees you after this day!"

Sulla nodded.

The woman stepped forward, a pillow grasped tightly in her hands, her knuckles white from the grip. With a cry she forced it over his face, holding it as tightly as she could, ignoring his muffled words. Her weeping grew louder in contrast to her lover's efforts, which began to weaken and finally ceased altogether.

Her weeping was the only sound in the room.

Sulla regarded the woman coolly. He removed the curved knife from his belt and tossed it onto the floor beside her.

"I am offering you your freedom," he hissed in anticipation. "Take it!"

She looked at him, her eyes uncomprehending.

"You die today, or I will keep you alive for months. I don't need to tell you what that will mean for you. You are a murderess."

Slowly it dawned on her what he meant, what he had planned from the very outset of his coup. She took the dagger gingerly in both hands and turned it slowly, fearfully, upon herself.

Sulla watched as she threw herself forward, thinking for a second that she would turn on him. But she fell next to her dead master, and Sulla's eye shone as he watched her body contort itself in the agony of the wound, but she did not scream.

That was brave of her, he thought, nearly as brave as the girl who had ambushed him some days before, and whom he had shot from his horse. She hadn't cried out as she had fallen from the cliff's edge, although he remembered with a slight shudder that his men had not found any trace of her body.

Surely the wolves had taken her.

With a snarl he banished such thoughts. The girl would not spoil his triumph!

Sulla knelt next to the dead Kinshra lord. The signet ring sparkled on his limp hand, tempting him to take it.

"How long have I coveted you!" Sulla said, breaking the finger in order to force the ring from its former owner. Without any delay, he slipped it onto the finger of his right hand. Now he was the lord of the Kinshra.

After a moment more, alone with the two bodies, he called the guard.

"Take them outside for the beasts," he instructed, "or give them to the starving miners, if necessary!"

The winter had been harder than they had expected, and their slaves would starve for lack of food. This year they needed slaves, for Sulla had grand ambitions, and the miners were worked to death, pulling as much coal from the mountain as they could. *Coal*, Sulla thought to himself, as he shouted to his men and called a council of senior Kinshra, *coal to fuel my war machine*.

My war machine! he suddenly thought. He was now the lord of the Kinshra, and he would make certain the world knew it.

FOURTEEN

Theodore had made his report to Sir Amik and master-at-arms Sharpe, answering their questions as accurately as he could and with absolute truth. Even when he admitted to the fear he had experienced he spoke clearly, never seeking an excuse, unafraid to admit to it.

Sharpe knew that other squires might have chosen to disguise their fear, and Theodore's open honesty drew appreciative nods from both men.

The dwarf was called in after the squire had given his version of events.

Respectfully removing his helm, he began.

"My name is Doric. For many years I have lived away from my kin, in the company of the men south of the mountain. I have known several knights throughout my life. I have trust enough in your order to know that I have nothing to fear by telling the whole truth, in the hope that my tale will help somehow in bringing this monster to a swift end!"

Doric's telling of their adventure supported Theodore's version in every way, and the dwarf didn't hesitate even when revealing the existence of his adamant bars. When he finished speaking, a quiet settled over the four of them.

"So you know the metal well, Doric?" Sharpe asked, breaking the silence.

"Aye!" the dwarf said. "I know it as well as any father can know a son."

The men glanced furtively at one another, and Doric followed their looks.

Sir Amik noted his sudden unease and sought to calm him.

"Your coming here at this time is surely fated, my aged friend," he said. "I would have your opinion on a matter of which we are unsure. A weapon has come into our hands in the most exceptional circumstances—a sword we believe to be made of adamant. Would you be willing to examine it, to confirm or deny our suspicions?"

Doric nodded without hesitation.

And following an order from Sharpe, Theodore left the room at once.

As the young man walked swiftly across the courtyard he could feel the excitement in the air. He felt eyes focus upon him from high windows and shaded arches. He could feel the jealousy of the younger knights, who envied the fact that fate had dropped the girl into his life, and his subsequent adventure to and from Taverley. It wasn't that the town was far from Falador—many of the squires and all of the knights had been farther afield— but the existence of the monster had given his short journey an adventurous tone that few of theirs could equal.

He saw the longing looks of the young peons, and in them he noted a different light—an aspiration, an increased willingness to be more like him. But he noted too the jealous looks of his fellow squires. To them, he had always been seen as the hardest worker, and recent events would most likely turn their envy into anger.

He knew his life would be more difficult from that moment on.

The excitement that permeated the castle was enhanced

by the fact that the mysterious girl had awoken, lending a breathless fever to all who crossed his path. One old knight, whom Theodore held in high regard as the ideal of restraint and humility, glanced at him with open curiosity.

"She's awake, is she?" he asked the squire.

"Yes, sir—so I've heard."

The old knight pulled on his moustache in excited thought.

"What can it herald?" he mused aloud. "There is a meaning to this mystery, Theodore, I know there is!"

The squire bowed in acknowledgment of the knight's experienced words before continuing.

The excitement had also seized Theodore. He tried to resist it, but couldn't. As he retrieved the sword from the armoury, wrapping it in a dark cloth under the watchful gaze of the duty guard, he decided to take a different route back to the interview, one which would take him directly past the ward.

He stepped rapidly as he descended the steep spiral staircase that wound itself inside the tower. His footsteps were louder than he would have liked, as if the stone were intent on betraying his presence. As he turned a corner he caught sight of two peons he knew by name, keeping a secret vigil outside the doorway in case any person left it open long enough for them to catch a sight of the mysterious girl who lay within.

"Be on your way Bryant! I expect better of my peons!"

The peon farthest away fled immediately, but the boy Bryant stood his ground.

"I am sorry Squire Theodore. We meant no harm."

Theodore nodded. Bryant was one of his twelve charges, and it was his duty to coach them in the best traditions of the knights, looking after their physical and spiritual needs. He had tried hard with Bryant—more so than with any other peon—for the boy was neither dexterous nor strong, and often he would lag behind the others in their exercises. But he was popular nonetheless, for his great strengths were history and lore, much as Castimir's had been when they were children together.

He was imaginative, clever, and quick-witted.

Still, Theodore often doubted if it would be enough. Knights had to be fighters first and thinkers second.

"Everybody is talking about her, Squire Theodore," the peon stammered. Theodore knew Bryant was right. The thought of the girl and her identity was irresistible to him, as well.

Am I any different? I too have made my way to the ward when there was no need for me to do so.

Theodore drew a long breath and put his hand on Bryant's shoulder.

"I can't fault you for your curiosity Bryant. I would be a hypocrite if I did so. But skulking in shadows and passageways is not a habit I wish to see continued. Have you said your midday prayers?"

The peon nodded.

"Then I have a task for you. Go to the stables and ensure that my mare is being adequately looked after. And make sure she has enough hay. It's scarce enough in this winter and I suspect that Marius's peons have been taking more than their share for his animals."

"Yes, Squire Theodore." The boy ran from him quickly, no doubt glad of so slight a reprimand.

Finally, when he was alone, he put his hand gently against the the door to the ward.

It wasn't locked, and swung open with ease.

She was there, in her bed. The sunlight was broken into bright shards by the high windows and it played upon her sheets, lighting her face.

For a long moment he watched her, not daring to move. Then her dark eyes opened and she stared at him in silence, her gaze unmoving.

"How do you feel?" he asked, the words feeling awkward in his suddenly dry mouth. He knew she could speak the common tongue, since she had done so upon her arrival. As far as he knew, however, no one had been able to convince her to talk since.

"It's you." She spoke slowly, as if she hadn't done so in a long time, yet there was an excited tone in her voice that made Theodore step forward instinctively.

"I was on the bridge the night we found you," he acknowledged. "I carried you here." The blood pounded in Theodore's head. He couldn't think straight.

"I remember," she said. "I was dying." She blinked slowly and shivered slightly. Her blonde hair fell across her face and she raised a bandaged hand to wipe it back so that she might see Theodore more clearly.

He was about to speak when the matron's song reached his ears, echoing down the ward toward him. She was singing one of the many nursery tunes that she claimed had finally revived her patient. The squire tried to leave before he was discovered.

But the girl would not let him. Her dark eyes would not release him, and he stood rooted to the spot, as though she had worked some unknown enchantment on him that surpassed the most powerful magic that even Castimir could summon.

"Theodore?" The matron's voice was sharp and accusing. "Leave here at once, young man! The patient is not fit to be disturbed."

That broke the spell. The squire bowed immediately and backed away, still unable to turn from the girl's dark gaze.

"Thank you, Theodore," she said as he retreated, and he thrilled at the sound of her voice speaking his name. Then her head fell to the soft pillow, her eyes closed again, and she seemed instantly asleep.

As he passed through the door the matron followed him and clicked it firmly shut behind them, careful not to awaken her charge. Then she turned and fixed her eyes on the squire.

"What have you done, Theodore?" she asked angrily.

"Nothing!" he protested. "She woke when I opened the door—that is all!" Theodore felt guilty. He had done nothing wrong save go into the ward, yet he felt as if he were lying. He could feel the hot flush on his face and could not meet the matron's stern gaze.

"She's never spoken before," the matron said. "This is the third time she's been awake, and no one has been able to convince her to say a word." The woman's face was red with anger. "I shall inform Sir Amik of this shortly, after I have tended to my patient. Who knows what damage you may have done."

She re-entered the room, slipping through the gap so that he could not see past the door. As soon as she had shut it, he heard a firm *click* that told him it had been locked.

Theodore strode across the courtyard, his head bent low toward the ground—so much so that he did not notice the shadow that barred his way until he was within an inch of colliding with its owner.

He looked up, startled, and immediately knew that he was in trouble.

It was Marius, standing a full head taller and with his arms crossed.

There was a long-standing rivalry between the two squires. Marius was expected to rise to the height of his profession, yet Theodore—with his monkish adherence to duty—had advanced more quickly and had been entrusted with the trip to Taverley.

"Well, Theodore," he said, "it seems you've attracted a lot of attention. Rescuing damsels and stalking monsters... You've become quite the hero!" His tone was openly mocking.

Several other squires stood behind Marius, and they shared amused glances. The large youth was more popular than the rest. His family was wealthy and he was more confident than

Theodore, who drew more comfort from his duties than from
the often raucous pastimes the other squires enjoyed.

"Get out of my way, Marius," Theodore said softly, his face
darkening. "I am on duty for Sir Amik himself—if that means
anything to you."

The insult was obvious. Marius was not as hard-working as
Theodore—none of these squires were—and he and his followers
would often break the less important laws of the knights, either
in pursuit of their own pleasure or due to their own laziness.

Marius's mocking expression turned hard.

"You cannot hide your cowardice behind the mask of duty!"
he declared.

Theodore's eyes flashed at the implication. As the blood
rushed to his head, he forced himself to remain calm.

"I will not fight you here, Marius," he replied loud enough for
all in the group to hear. "Not today. But you have insulted me,
and I demand justice—as is my right. The choice of weapon will
be yours to decide."

A gasp went out. Most such arguments were settled in an
instant by a fist and a scuffle, with supporters cheering their
champion on. The result usually was no more than a bloodied
nose. But Theodore's words were far more serious.

Trials of this sort were solved by skill in combat and it was
believed that Saradomin himself judged the outcome, thereby
ensuring that the victor was in the right. Men had been killed in
the course of such challenges.

Theodore didn't hesitate. The shocked silence gave him the
advantage. He brushed by Marius with a strong look of resolve
etched on his youthful face.

Sir Amik took the sword gently in his hands and laid it reverently
on the table. With a quick look at Doric he pulled back the
dark cloth.

The dwarf leaned closer, his eyes intent on the mysterious metal.

"It is adamant! I have no doubt of that," he said after only a few seconds. His short finger traced its way across the surface of the blade, which was without a single mark.

"No human made this weapon," he continued. He grasped the handle of the sword and turned it over, holding it up to study it closely. "It is of dwarf-make, as I think you have guessed." His eyes fixed on the symbol of the four-pointed star. "Yet Saradomin is not the primary god of the dwarfs." He raised his head, and his grey eyes looked into Sir Amik's. "Our god is Guthix, so this sword was made by a dwarf for a human. It is too long for any of my folk to wield."

"What you say confirms our suspicions. We think the girl came from Ice Mountain," Sir Amik said. "She appeared in circumstances that are unknown to us."

The dwarf nodded, his attention still on the sword.

But Theodore knew something was amiss. He saw the uncertain look that passed between Sir Amik and Sharpe. Then the two men thanked Doric for his help, and instructed Theodore to find lodgings for him in Falador, for the dwarf had decided to remain in the city and pursue his claim for compensation via the magistrates. Such thoughts accounted for the dwarf's silence as he and Theodore walked under the high white walls and across the bridge into the city.

But the squire was quiet for a different reason. He was certain Sir Amik and Sharpe knew more than they had let on.

FIFTEEN

He entered the city at dusk, his true nature concealed from the guards who cast a wary eye over those passing through the gates.

Rumours of the monster had driven many people to the city. Farmers and hunters had sent their loved ones south for the protection of Falador's high white walls and crowded streets.

He hated the crowds. There were too many people and the smell of human fear taunted him, for he knew he could not act upon it.

With the cloak pulled tightly about him he kept to the shadowy alleyways. A child's cry from the window above forced him to master his hunger. The mother's soothing voice angered him still further.

Just two more, he thought to himself, *and then I will go after the knight who knows my quarry.*

He felt his heart quicken at the thought of the hunt and he salivated at the thought of the kill. His long fingers curled into fists.

There will be no more killing! a sinister voice whispered in his mind.

At once he stopped, admitting to himself that he was afraid. Since beginning his chase he had never been afraid, not in these human lands.

The alley across the street darkened. It seemed to him as if it had become a gateway to a different place, a land in perpetual shadow. Several people passed it by, unaware of its existence, seeing nothing unusual in the passage that had been there for many years.

No human could see the gateway.

He sensed a great power reaching out to him. He had only been in the presence of such power once before, months ago when he had been chosen to travel across the holy barrier to the human realm.

There will be no more killing! the voice repeated in his head, louder now and in the darkness a shadow moved. He could sense the terrible strength of its stare and instinctively he placed his long hands over his head in a reverence born out of fear.

"Only two more, my lord," he said pleadingly, keeping his voice low so that none would hear. "These lands are so well stocked!"

No more! came the reply. *You have work to do in Asgarnia. You have to bring him home.*

The shadow seemed to be drawing closer, but it stopped at the very edge of the darkness, its features hidden.

You have spent long months here already—too long. Remember who I am! Know what I can do. Killing endangers your mission.

"Then I shall hunt no more," he replied. "All my energies will be devoted to my task."

See that it is so. Even from so far away, I can still reach out to you. Even here, you are not immune to my will!

The shadow raised its hand and pointed directly at the robed figure. Immediately he felt very afraid. He knew it was pointless to run, however, for no speed could outrun the powers that this shadow possessed, perfected throughout the many centuries it had ruled its dark domain.

He cringed, awaiting the pain that did not come. So he straightened, and spoke.

"I swear to you it shall be done. I shall bring him home!"

The shadow lowered its hand and receded. The fear lessened, but did not abate altogether. Soft voices drifted down from the window, the mother soothing her young child in the cold winter night.

He couldn't remember anyone ever speaking to him in such a way. His childhood was a thing not of memory but of fabrication, for so much time had passed that he had forgotten it.

Such is the life of a monster, he thought—more than a century of living, and now forbidden to hunt by his dark master. He knelt in the narrow alley, his eyes staring at the castle that housed the Knights of Falador and towered over the centre of the city.

That was where his quest would take him. For a young squire there knew where his quarry was to be found.

SIXTEEN

The darkness was kept at bay by a sole flickering torch that cast a furtive light on the meeting. The three men talked in hushed tones.

"It must be the case, Sir Amik," Nicholas Sharpe said anxiously.

"Yet it changes nothing," Sir Tiffy Cashien cautioned, his voice calm. "What we need to know is how she came to possess the ring. Until we ascertain that, we will not know whether she is a friend or foe."

Sir Amik nodded.

"You are right, Sir Tiffy. We must be cautious. Though she possesses one of the remaining rings, it does not mean she is necessarily a friend."

"But the matron hasn't been able to get a word from her, and we shall never learn her origin if she refuses to speak." The master-at-arms was suddenly loud, his frustration getting the better of him. "We are at an impasse."

"That is no longer the case," Sir Amik said. "I spoke to the matron this evening. The girl *will* talk—not to her, but to Squire Theodore."

Sir Tiffy propped his chin in his hand, intrigued.

"It would appear that young Theodore has been seized by

fate in this matter," he said, his age-wrinkled hand stroking his white-bearded chin.

Sir Amik nodded.

"And who are we to deny the will of Saradomin?" he said.

An hour after their secret discussion, Sir Amik sat alone in his high chamber, considering all that had been said.

The Ring of Life that had spent its magic in teleporting the girl to the bridge matched all the descriptions contained in their secret texts. Even Sir Tiffy, who was old enough to remember the days when their agents had been issued with such powerful objects, was certain of its nature.

There were eight men who had been issued with such rings and as yet remained unaccounted for. All were dedicated knights who after years of service had decided to accept the dangerous task of living close to their enemies, gaining knowledge of their ways and agendas.

Two had been sent west, into the neighbouring realm of Kandarin: one to live amongst the hardy Fremennik peoples in the north, and the other amongst the vicious Khazard race of men, who were known for their war-like ways.

Three had been sent into The Wilderness, that great expanse of land that was untamed and unmapped, where the only certainty was a brutally short life lived in total lawlessness. A sixth man had headed into Morytania to live amongst the monsters that dwelt there. A seventh had gone south to the tribes of Al-Kharid, before venturing as far as he could into the Kharidian Desert to see what lay beyond.

But it was the last man who intrigued the knight most, for he had headed to Ice Mountain to live in exile, dangerously close to the Kinshra. Sir Amik was certain that this was the man who had passed the ring onto the girl, though whether willingly or not was something beyond his knowledge.

He was equally certain that the girl had nearly been killed on Ice Mountain, but whether she was one of the Kinshra herself or an enemy of theirs was a question he knew would keep him awake at night.

Theodore lay sleepless in his bed, his head supported on his hands as he stared at the high ceiling in the cold dormitory.

The twelve peons who slept in the same room as him were forbidden to talk after the tenth bell sounded from the sentry tower, its dolorous tone echoing across the courtyard.

He could not get the girl out of his thoughts. He was certain a special bond existed between them, and he felt a strange pride that he had been the only one to whom she had spoken. As he rolled onto his side his heart softened, yet he grew grim.

For it was forbidden for a knight to entertain such feelings. A life spent in devotion to Saradomin could not be shared by another love on earth.

A peon coughed somewhere in the room. All the others were silent, exhausted after a ten-mile run. It was one of Theodore's duties to ensure that his peons were well disciplined and fit for their tasks, and under his firm guidance these twelve boys held him in high esteem. They made no secret of their fear—that if Theodore ever had to accompany a knight on his travels then another would take over their training. Marius never wasted the opportunity, regaling them of how he would treat them if ever they came under his management. He taunted them, and persuaded his own peons to undermine Theodore's influence at every possible turn.

Firm, but fair. Theodore knew that was what they said of him. This reputation had garnered him unrivalled respect amongst the peons, he was certain, but it served to make his enemies hate him even more.

There was another reason Theodore couldn't sleep. He was

certain Sir Amik had lied to him and Doric about the girl's
origins. Yet all in his order were taught from the very start that
lying only demeaned oneself, that a true knight's conscience
must be clear. Saradomin prized peace as one of the chief
virtues, and by lying a knight could not be at peace with himself.

He rolled onto his back once more, in an effort to find sleep.
Yet even as he did so, he knew it would not come any time soon.

SEVENTEEN

Doric, too, found sleep elusive. He had been unable to find any lodging in the city, due to the many extra people who had come to seek sanctuary for fear of the monster.

That afternoon, Theodore had walked with him from one inn to another, beginning with the famed tavern The Rising Sun, yet none of them had a room to spare.

Neither did any of the lesser-known establishments. Theodore had even dragged him to the almshouses of the knights, situated near the park at the northern wall of the city. But they had already offered what spare accommodation they possessed to the more vulnerable of the country folk seeking refuge.

Finally they returned to the castle and found Doric a bed in a vacant peon dormitory. The usual inhabitants were away on an exercise south of Falador, learning how to forage amongst the natural elements. Thus Doric was left to his own devices, and he welcomed the time on his own. He felt awkward in crowds, and Falador boasted many of those, with its bustling peoples and offensive smells.

The only thing he didn't like about his temporary bed was the fact that he knew it to be in a room that was high above the ground. He would never admit it, but he hated heights such as these.

His suspicion of human engineering and the thin stone walls that they insisted on constructing made him nervous. As a young dwarf he remembered when the ground had shaken beneath him, causing a cave-in, and he had never discovered what it was that had caused the earth to move in such a frenzy.

To be underground amongst the foundations of the earth was one thing, but to build towers of stone that touched the sky could only be folly. If the earth ever decided to shake again, then the white towers would come crashing down.

With such thoughts making sleep impossible, he decided to get some air in the courtyard. He pulled on his soft doublet and boots, but decided not to don his armour. He rarely went anywhere without wearing it, yet he forced himself to remember that he was in a castle in one of the biggest cities that men had ever built.

Patting himself down with a satisfied sigh, Doric opened the door and stepped warily down the spiral staircase beyond.

He crossed the moat soundlessly, concealed in the shadow of its high banks. Despite his many years he had never learned to swim, and while he had a very real fear of water, he possessed a far greater fear of his dark master.

He used a log to support himself as he forced his way across the still water, moving slowly enough to appear natural and to ensure that he did not make a splash.

No one challenged him as he swiftly ran to the base of the wall, soaked through, his hunter's instinct alert to anything that might give him away.

He could smell the men on the wall above, his glowing red eyes enabling him to see them in the darkness. He was not there to kill, however—he was searching for the young squire who knew the location of his quarry.

He would need to wait until he was dry before continuing.

When the moment arrived, long claws found purchase in the white stone which would have defeated any human.

But he was no human.

With a grunt he began to climb, his shape obscured by a tower that stood scant inches to his left. His wide nose took in the night air cautiously. The men on the wall and at the bridge were not alarmed, for the scent of their sweat was no more than was usual on a human being. Swiftly he ascended, always keeping at least two points of his body gripping the white stone.

It would not take him long now; the parapet was near.

"Halt! Who goes there?"

The sharp scrape of steel sounded as the guard drew his sword.

Doric sighed.

"It's me! Doric—the dwarf who arrived with Squire Theodore today," he growled. It was the third time he had been challenged, and now—here on the northern wall, as he gathered the courage to walk upon the parapet—the man's words raised his ire.

"I beg your pardon, my friend," the man said with a nod of his head. "Vigilance is imperative, you know." The sword scraped as it was returned to the man's scabbard. "You may proceed—but I should warn you of the guard at the other end."

Doric thanked him and stepped warily onto the walkway. The stone gave him comfort, and with each step he gained confidence until he was striding as if he had forgotten his fear of heights.

Squire Theodore!

He felt elation as he hung from the wall only yards away. He could smell the dwarf—the very one he had stalked in the forest—and his animal senses enabled him to discern every word.

And now his prey had a name.

He waited for the footsteps to cease. As soon as he heard the next sentry's challenge and the dwarf's gruff reply, he reached for the parapet.

But try as he might, he couldn't grasp it. His hand could not touch the lip of the nearest merlon. Even though he put as much strength into it as he dared, he was prevented from touching it by only the slightest distance.

He had felt this power before. He was not a creature of this land and coming into it had been exceptionally difficult for one of his kind. The sacred river that separated his homeland from the realms of men could be crossed only by the vilest desecration and the most powerful will. Only the power of his master had enabled him to do so. But he could not turn to his master here, many miles from his home. He would have to find another way to reach Squire Theodore.

He looked to the moat below. He hadn't planned on climbing so high only to be forced to climb down again. He wasn't even sure he could. But if he leapt from the wall his presence would be betrayed, and he might drown.

No, he would have to climb back to the ground.

As he lowered his leg he knew his efforts had not been in vain. He knew the squire by name now. He would lure him out into the city and away from the castle's holy protection on some pretext, and then take his time in the interrogation.

He would have to kill again, and soon.

EIGHTEEN

"You look concerned, Castimir. Tell me, what is on your mind?" Ebenezer gently disturbed the young wizard's reverie, and he looked up.

"Soon I shall return to the Wizards' Tower to complete my training," Castimir replied. "For my year's journey is nearly at an end." His voice trailed off as his hand unconsciously squeezed one of the many pouches on his belt. Those pouches held the most precious things a wizard could possess, the alchemist knew. For they contained the rune stones he needed to control his magic. Without them, he could no more accomplish magic than the meanest charlatan.

Ebenezer didn't speak, leaving it to the young man to reveal his concerns in his own time. Gar'rth entered the room and stood nearby, awaiting the first instructions of the new day. The old man drew a large book from the shelf and ignored the scowl Gar'rth adopted when he saw that it was a book on human language.

"It was the mages' discovery of the rune stones that enabled human civilisation to thrive," Castimir mused aloud. "Using them we were able to dominate the lands of Gielinor at the end of the Fourth Age."

Ebenezer glanced sympathetically at the young man. He knew, of course, the history that was preached by the wise, but he didn't necessarily believe it himself. He knew the mages saw themselves as the saviours of humanity, whose actions had enabled mankind to dominate the world so much that the Fifth Age was often called "The Age of Humans."

And yet Ebenezer could recall times from his youth when the blue-robed wizards had been a more common sight. It seemed to him that they had lessened their wanderings, as if they were growing afraid to send members of their order abroad.

In fact, Castimir was the only wizard he had seen in months.

"Are you having doubts about the path you have chosen, Castimir?" Ebenezer sat down next to Gar'rth and took a long sip of his coffee, savouring in the taste.

The first of the season's trading caravans had made its way across White Wolf Mountain, arriving the day before and bringing with it exotic fruit and coffee beans that had found their way from the southern islands to Catherby. Being the first to cross the mountain, they had expected an excellent profit, but they had been disappointed. Fear of the monster had deterred many Falador traders from making the usually safe journey to Taverley.

Recognising that fewer buyers meant better prices, Ebenezer had decided to purchase several sacks of coffee beans. He had tasted coffee before, but not for a long time.

The alchemist sipped from his cup while he waited for the blue-robed youth to reply. The wizard was obscured from view by the steam that rose from the hot liquid and fogged his glasses. With a sigh he finished his drink, set the empty cup down, and wiped his spectacles on a small cloth that he kept for that purpose.

As he did, Castimir finally spoke again.

<hr />

"Not about the path, Ebenezer," Castimir said. "I have no doubt that I am best suited to be a wizard. Could you imagine me as a farmer, or a miner, or a blacksmith?" He shook his head. "I grew up with books, learning about places far off, entertaining the other children with legends. My most eager student then was Theodore." He smiled at the fond remembrance. "No, Ebenezer, my worry stems from something else, which could have severe implications for us all, over time."

But he fell silent again, reluctant to explain further, for to do so—even to a trusted friend like Ebenezer—was strictly against the rules of his order.

And how could Castimir ever admit the truth, and tell Ebenezer that the rune stones were actually running out? Existing supplies could not be replenished, and the wizards were thus restricting the number of mages allowed to use them. Castimir had been granted permission because of his unusual aptitude for magic. His masters were certain he could be a great asset to the Wizards' Tower, and an invaluable force for protecting the human realms from their enemies.

Only the royal households of each nation knew of the dwindling supply of runes, for it was a secret that could unleash panic amongst the citizens who believed that the wizards would always be there to protect them. Castimir feared that his would be the last generation of wizards. So limited were the runes that even to use them for practice was a rare privilege, reserved for only the most skilled mages.

Each time Castimir conjured a spell, he felt guilty watching the pebble-like objects dissolve in his hands as they were consumed to summon his magic.

"I am sorry, Ebenezer," he said. "Pay no heed to my mutterings." Castimir thought of a lie that would divert his friend's attention, and he was summoning the courage to speak, when a knock on the door distracted them both.

It was Kaqemeex. His face was grave.

"Ebenezer, would you be kind enough to walk with me? I have some thoughts on your proposal."

The druid looked kindly at Gar'rth, who bowed his head in respect.

The alchemist stood up.

"I would be happy to," he said, following the druid out of the room, leaving the two youths alone.

NINETEEN

"Theodore will be here shortly," the matron whispered to Bhuler. The valet was sitting at the girl's bedside, a bowl of thick, warm broth in one hand, a wooden spoon in the other.

"You must eat," he pleaded with the girl, who stared at him darkly. She still hadn't spoken to anyone other than Theodore, despite the matron's comforting words and his own attentions.

With visible reluctance, the girl took the spoon and proceeded to eat. She managed only two mouthfuls before she handed the spoon back to him and shook her head.

"But it's delicious," Bhuler insisted, tasting some in an effort to convince her. His smile vanished as he struggled to swallow the foul-tasting broth, and his eyes watered as he tried hard to ignore the taste.

The girl managed a stiff smile, as if she hadn't smiled for a very long time and was unused to it.

And her expression did not go unnoticed by the canny valet. He decided not to try to force her into conversation, fearing that her good mood might vanish if she thought he was taking advantage of it.

Instead he decided to gain her goodwill by forcing a smile from her once more.

"It's really not that bad, my dear," he whispered, lowering his head to speak to her privately, while the matron turned her back to dispose of the bandages that she had removed from the girl's hand. He risked another mouthful and exaggerated the natural grimace that the taste inspired. His suddenly grotesque appearance had the desired effect, for the girl smiled once more, looking at him as if she thought him a fool.

Saradomin knows what they put in this, Bhuler thought as he prepared himself for a third mouthful, wondering how he could survive such punishment. He stopped the spoon just before his open mouth.

"No, I cannot lie to you," he confessed. "It *is* awful!"

He put the broth down by his side and stuck the spoon in its dark surface. It stood upright without support from the bowl, as a dead log might stand in a thick swamp. To Bhuler it looked horrible, and it tasted even worse than it looked.

So the valet reached inside the folds of his white robe, and withdrew a red apple. He saw the girl's eyes light up.

"Why don't I leave you this, then?" he said as her eager hands reached for it. "But don't let the matron see!" He looked back at the broth with a sorrowful expression. "She has interesting ideas about food."

He patted her arm gently as he stood, and was shocked when he found her unwilling to let him go. Gently he brushed her hair back from her pale face.

"I have to leave now, my dear. I have my duties to attend.

I must ensure the castle's seamstress and tanners are finishing off your new clothes as per my instructions." He gave her a conspiratorial wink. "I have commanded they be fashioned in a similar way to your previous dress, even replacing your stubbed leather brigandine. They should be ready for you tomorrow. But do not fear, I will not be gone for long."

With a smile on her face, she watched him go, her head resting on the pillow. Bhuler reminded her of the last person who had called himself father to her, the old dwarf who had picked her out of the snow all those years before.

"Kara-Meir" was what the dwarfs had called her, and while she knew she had possessed a human name before that time, she could not remember it. Nevertheless, her traumatised mind was reliving her youth again, when she had been in the company of humans. Slowly she was recalling her life in the village.

The tune that the matron had repeatedly sung was familiar to her. She envisioned the long summer evenings when her father, the woodcutter, would return to their house singing a similar verse.

She recalled the evening that her father had returned to the cabin with an injured bear cub. She had nursed it back to health before he had decided to return it to the wild the following year. It shocked her that she could ever have forgotten something like that. It was as if a door had been opened in her mind, through which she could witness those peaceful days of village life.

Suddenly she needed to talk to someone about her experiences, to tell another human being about her childhood and to confide in someone as she had never done before.

The door to the ward opened and Theodore strode in quietly. She turned to look at him.

"Theodore!" she said, and a look of surprise swept over his face. Nearby the matron gasped.

The young squire sat by her side, looking unsure of what to say. But Kara-Meir needed no spur to the conversation, for she wanted to tell him of her life in the shadow of the mountain.

For an hour she talked ceaselessly.

Sir Amik's face was impassive as Theodore told him the girl's story.

He began with her name, Kara-Meir, which was the only name she said she could remember. Her father had been a village woodcutter, often staying away from the community for days at a time. One of her first memories was being taken from the village to a monastery some days' walk from her home. There, her father had asked for Saradomin's blessing upon her, and the monks had given it.

The young girl had received special attention, for children were very rare visitors to the monastery, and the monks had been enchanted with her innocent smile and wide, enquiring eyes.

Under her father's loving tutelage she had learned how to stalk and forage, how to live in the wild, how to shoot a bow and how to wield a sword. Her upbringing had been that of a hunter rather than a maiden.

It was toward the end of her story that Sir Amik grew more interested.

Her father had stayed away from the village for several weeks, and one evening he had returned badly injured. He had been in a battle. A few weeks after that, as the winter snows had fallen thick upon the earth and isolated the village, a man had come with others at his side, and her happy life had ended.

She had not mentioned the man by name, for her focus was on the happy time before he had entered her life.

Moved by her tragic story, Theodore had not wished to press her for details.

"You must find out more," Sir Amik told him. "It seems as if her father's actions might have brought the men to the village. I believe them to be the Kinshra."

"Am I to give this priority over my other duties, Sir Amik?" Theodore asked.

"You are, Theodore," Sir Amik ordered, not taking his eyes off the young man. "But I know your reputation. I know you will not neglect your duties." With that, he dismissed the squire.

Sir Amik watched Theodore go, his brow furrowed in thought. He was indeed an excellent squire, but he wondered if the youth had enough aggression to succeed as a knight. Training against others was not a mark of ability—fighting for your life against your enemies was what counted.

All of the squires had yet to prove themselves in this manner.

TWENTY

Theodore returned to the ward to continue his discussions with Kara-Meir. The sky was grey and overcast with low clouds which threatened rain, and the blue flags of the kingdom shook energetically in the breeze.

"Tell me about the knights, Theodore," Kara said as soon as he sat down by her side. A swift glance told the squire that the matron was nearby, her vigilance unrelenting.

"We are an old order, Kara," he said. "We were formed at the end of the Fourth Age, before the founding of Asgarnia as a nation under King Raddallin more than a hundred and fifty years ago. We were charged with protecting Falador, and gained new prominence during the war with the dark wizards, followers of Zamorak, who were once welcome in the order of mages.

"It was their betrayal and subsequent burning of the Wizards' Tower that gave our cause impetus and righteousness, for all men had until that time lived as one, their actions not governed by their religion. But then the world lost its most powerful mages, and since that time our cause has been at odds with the followers of Zamorak, especially the Kinshra."

"And have you yourself ever fought any of these 'followers'?" she asked eagerly, her eyes flashing.

"No." Theodore dipped his head slightly. "Not yet. I am still a squire, training to be a full knight."

"What about the men who attacked my village? Surely they are followers of the god of chaos?"

"I think it very likely that they, too, are the Kinshra. The people of Falador refer to them as the 'black knights'. They are our most hated enemy, yet they still wield some political power in Asgarnia, albeit a shadow of their former influence.

"Their founders were once men of wealth and power, fighting alongside the knights under King Raddallin at the founding of Asgarnia, until our differing religious views—heightened by the sacking of the Wizards' Tower—forced them to leave the city. Yet with King Raddallin's help, and in repayment for their services in uniting the nation, they built a castle on the eastern slopes of Ice Mountain, promising to guard the kingdom from the dangers that populate The Wilderness.

"Many families of influence in Falador today have members amongst the Kinshra nobility, though there is never any contact between them. When they left, the Kinshra vowed to return, to make Falador their own one day. For generations they have been attempting to do that, by strength as well as by subtlety."

Theodore smiled ruefully.

"There are even rumours that the crown prince and his Imperial Guard are content to leave the Kinshra be, as long as they do not threaten the people of our nation. Some have said that the Kinshra have a special envoy in Burthorpe, seeking to turn the crown prince and his guard against us, and to pervert our rivalry into open hostility."

"And do you believe these rumours?"

"I do not know," he admitted. "But I do not believe even the decadent prince would permit it."

Kara lay back on her pillow, her eyes burning in quiet anger.

"I wish they were all dead," she said simply. She caught

Theodore's look and turned her head away. "The Kinshra do not deserve to live. I am going to kill them."

"What happened to you on the mountain, Kara—before you came here?" In his mind he already knew. The White Pearl he had found in her hand revealed her location, and her attitude toward the Kinshra confirmed it.

"I would rather not talk about it," she said flatly.

"You went after them, didn't you?" he pressed. "You fought some of the Kinshra?'

She turned her head away from him and pulled the blanket over her as if she planned to sleep.

"I am tired, Theodore," she said. "Please leave me alone."

For a moment he did not know what to say, but Sir Amik's words came back to him, reminding him that uncovering the knowledge this girl possessed was his most important task.

"You did go after them, Kara," he said. "And you lost."

The girl turned to glare at him with a feverish light in her dark eyes, and it pained him to think that he had hurt her so.

"Yes, I went after them—and I didn't lose. Even if I avenged myself on just a single member of their order, then it was a triumph worth dying for.

"And I will go back there, Theodore." she continued. "When I am strong again I shall take my sword and find the man they call Sulla and his Kinshra and I will not stop hunting them. You cannot stop me!"

The force of her words, and the hatred they bespoke, shocked him. As a squire, losing control of his emotions was unacceptable. But now he had a name. Sulla. He had never heard it before, but he would carry it to Sir Amik.

He rose and spoke gently.

"I am going to go now, Kara. I will come back soon, when you have rested. I am sorry to have upset you."

His tone calmed her and she looked at him, seeming

embarrassed. He turned and began to walk to the door.

"Theodore," she called. "Please, wait. Can you promise me something?"

"What is it?"

"I want you to teach me how to fight, Theodore. When I am strong again," she said, her voice determined. "I want you to teach me how to be a knight."

He looked at her in astonishment. She was a young woman, barely out of girlhood, and the only thing she wished to do with her life was to fight. To kill. No woman Theodore had ever encountered had been of such a mind.

He did not know what to say, and so he laughed.

Her face fell and he saw tears appear in her eyes. Suddenly he felt very ashamed.

"Kara, please forgive me," he said. "There has never been any woman in the order. It is not permitted, of that I am certain. What you ask for is simply impossible."

She turned away, and did not look at him again. Finding himself lost for words, he left her under the watchful gaze of the matron who had heard everything.

TWENTY-ONE

It had been two days since he had scaled the wall of the castle, and a plan had developed in his mind.

He had yet to put it into action. Instead, he was going over every detail of what he would have to do, and the resources he would need.

The main problem was his lack of privacy. He had no base in the city, and for the third night running he would have to sleep in one of the narrow alleys. That was no problem for him—he had been sleeping rough in the country for the majority of nights during his hunt—but he needed seclusion to subdue the squire and conduct his interrogation.

An irate voice attracted his attention and he found himself looking at a short, crooked-backed woman who was raising her voice in anger at a market trader.

"My husband's been dead for three years!" she said loudly. "How am I to afford food for my grandchildren and fuel to keep my home warm?"

Her pleas were greeted by muted laughs, and several people shook their heads.

"It's the crazy woman!" someone said quietly to a friend.

His hard eyes, hidden from view by the cowl he always

wore in populated places, focused on the madwoman. He saw an opportunity.

"Is she really crazy?" he asked the market trader. He could sense the man's fear rise.

"She's been m-m-mad for years," the trader stammered. "She wanders the streets, b-begging and cursing. The children think she's a witch."

A few people overheard the words, laughed, and someone called over in agreement. Thus buoyed, he pressed for more information.

"And does she truly have a home and grandchildren?" He managed to make his voice sound suitably curious, hiding the feral rasp that sometimes asserted itself.

"A home, yes, but no children." The trader peered at him with nervous curiosity, then glanced away to avoid being discovered. "It's a lie she tells in order to get money from gullible strangers. The guards will move her along in a moment."

And a moment later they did, ushering her out of the market and commanding her not to beg. She did not notice the tall figure in the robe follow her from the crowd and down the narrow streets.

He moved without sound, catching up with her swiftly. Finally, just as she was fumbling with a key outside a door in a poor part of the city where the rooftops touched each other above the alleyway, he reached forward, his large hand resting on her shoulder.

She gave a small cry, and tried to twist away from him.

"Do not be alarmed," he said. "I am new to this city. I have come in from the country. I have nowhere to rest. I have money—a great deal of it." He smiled as he watched her fearful expression turn to curious greed. "I seek lodging, only for a few nights—nothing more." He spoke softly and his voice purred with temptation. "I would be out in the daytime. I'm a busy man."

"How much have you got?" she asked, her voice sharp and rude.

He reached into his robe and withdrew a bright red gem that caught the afternoon light as he held it up to her face. His smile grew as her eyes fixed themselves upon it.

"I think that will be enough," he said, letting her grab the gem that he had taken from the purple-robed men some days before.

"But you won't be getting food," the woman snapped, and for one of the few times in his life he grinned in genuine humour.

"No, dear lady, I will not be asking you for food," he agreed. "I am entirely self-sufficient."

With a curt nod she opened the door and ushered her lodger in, no doubt wondering about this strange man from the country who seemingly conjured riches from the pockets of his robe. Likely she wondered what other surprises he might provide.

Without doubt, she would find out in due time.

TWENTY-TWO

She stepped carefully, balancing her weight before taking a second step.

It was the first time she had stood since coming into the castle, and she was doing so in secret. It was after midnight and she was alone in the ward, save for a snoring nurse who slept every time she was on duty.

Kara took a third step forward, keeping her hands outstretched, ready to catch herself if she should fall. She stumbled once, her hands seizing the bed frame as she caught herself. Silently she stood once more, her breathing sharp. The nurse's snoring was the only other sound in the room.

Cautiously, as if she were a burglar, Kara put one foot in front of the other. Her legs held, and within a minute she stood at the entrance to the ward. She turned to make her way back to her bed, feeling suddenly strong again. Her legs obeyed her now.

But she would not stop there. Furiously she recalled Theodore's words.

There has never been any woman in the order. It is not permitted.

Upon reaching her bed she turned and, moving more quickly now, returned to the door again and then back to the bed. She ran back and forth from one point to the other, back and forth, minding her stance to run silently—for when she had to be, Kara was as silent as the stealthiest cat.

After a moment she stopped. Though winded, she was satisfied that her legs had strength enough for what she needed to do. It was her arms that now needed testing.

She lowered herself to the floor and did fifty brisk push-ups. Her stomach muscles cramped together from the strain of keeping her body straight, and before long her arms shook from the effort. She bit her lip to quiet herself as her arms finally gave way. Breathing heavily, she climbed back into her bed, her muscles warm and her skin breaking out in a sweat.

Though frustrated, she was happy. In the darkness of the ward, with the nurse mumbling nearby, she smiled. Despite her injuries, her body had not lost too much of its strength, and she knew that within a few days she would be sufficiently recovered to do what she needed.

For she was going to escape.

"Do you think you can walk?" Theodore asked Kara gently. "Perhaps you should try and get some fresh air." He was anxious to make peace with her after their previous harsh parting, and in hopes of doing so he intended to show her the castle.

Kara remained as silent as she had been since he entered the ward. Now, without a word, she pushed back the sheet and lowered her legs to the stone. With an angry glance in his direction she stood for a second, and then—as her legs began to shake violently—she collapsed into his arms.

When she looked up at him, it was still with anger in her expression.

"Does that amuse you, Theodore? Do you want to laugh at me again—the girl who wanted to be a knight and who hasn't the strength even to walk?"

Not knowing what to say, he lifted her up and returned her to the bed as gently as he knew how. Finally he replied.

"I do not want to laugh at you, Kara. Surely you know that."

When she didn't respond, he felt an irritation of his own welling up. To prevent himself from speaking hastily he disappeared into the depths of the ward, returning a minute later with a wooden chair that ran on squealing wheels.

"If you cannot walk, you can still get some fresh air. Can you climb in or do you wish me to help you?" He allowed no malice in his words.

Kara stared at him, as if looking for an excuse to refuse.

Theodore remained patiently silent.

"I can do it," she snapped suddenly, and quicker than Theodore had expected she lowered herself off the bed and into the chair, pulling the bed sheet after her and wrapping it about herself. "I do not want to be cold," she said, before he could ask.

Without another word he wheeled her out, guiding her gently down the wide stone staircase one step at a time.

Kara's bad mood waned as Theodore showed her the fortress. Her eyes widened in wonder at the grand towers and marble edifices. But more amazing to her still was the city that lay beyond the moat. Having climbed the spiral stairway to the battlement, leaning on Theodore's shoulder to maintain the illusion of her weakness, she gazed from the ramparts.

It was like nothing she had ever seen before.

"Take all the time you need," he said, watching her intently as her dark eyes absorbed everything.

"There are so many people," she said quietly. "I didn't know." For the first time since climbing the high wall, she turned to look him in the eye. "I remember my father telling me stories of Falador. He must have been here, but he never told me why, and he never told me how many people there were. Thank you,

Theodore, for showing me the city. I am sorry for being angry with you earlier."

Theodore nodded. "Thank you, Kara," he said. "I was rude to you before and I am sorry for it."

He held her hand tightly, and suddenly a cold wind rolled down from the north. She shivered involuntarily the cold air turning her skin to ice under the white garments worn by patients of the ward. She stepped closer to him, to shield herself from the wind, resting her head upon his shoulder. The squire said nothing and made no effort to move away. After a moment Kara lifted her head and gazed at the mountain.

"That is Ice Mountain," Theodore told her.

"How far is it?" she asked. "How many days' travel?"

"It would take three days to get to the foothills, but the mountain itself is beyond our authority, for a colony of dwarves lives there, and we respect their territory."

At the mention of the dwarf race, Kara's eyes shone. She had not told Theodore of her discovery and adoption by Master Phyllis, the dwarf who had taught her so much. Back then, it had taken her weeks to regain the confidence to speak any words. Once she had, however, her foster father had educated her, speaking to her in both the common tongue and his own language. Kara was fluent in both.

She thought back to her final months in the underground city. She had lived there for eight years, rarely seeing the surface world, and by her estimation she was seventeen years old. Master Phyllis had been unwilling to keep her amongst his people any longer. One night she had discovered him at work in his forge, and it was then that he had presented her with a long sword crafted from adamant.

"It is yours, Kara," he revealed. "It will cut through the toughest armour of any surface dweller, and through the hides of most beasts."

Thinking about her sword, she turned her gaze from the mountain and looked up into the squire's honest face.

"Can I have my sword, Theodore?" she asked suddenly. "It's very important that I have it—it was made by someone very dear to me."

He cast a wary look in her direction.

"Does fighting mean so much to you, Kara?" he asked. "You are safe here, in the most fortified city in the world. You do not *need* to fight any more."

Kara turned her gaze from the mountain and looked down into the courtyard below. There were several peons and squires practising with their wooden training swords, trying out different combinations and fighting amongst themselves. They were uncommonly loud in their competition, and occasionally one or more of them glanced up in her direction, as if showing off for her.

One of them, however—slightly older and wearing training armour—did not shout out, and he seemed to pointedly ignore Kara's presence on the ramparts, taking a greater interest in the peons' practice.

"Who is that?" Kara asked, watching him command.

"Marius," Theodore replied, and his voice sounded tight. "He's a squire, like me."

"Is he your friend?"

"No." Theodore looked away. Kara noted his pained look.

"Theodore, you are upset." Her hand rested on his arm.

"Marius is my rival." He looked at her intently. "Rivals in all things, it seems."

A cold wind blew again from the north and Kara shivered. Theodore pulled her sheet around her and carefully escorted her down to the waiting chair.

In the courtyard, one of Theodore's own peons, Bryant, was

fighting against one of Marius's, their wooden blades clacking as they sparred. Kara had decided against sitting back in the chair and she walked with uncertainty, leaning on Theodore's arm.

"Come on, Bryant!" Marius shouted.

Theodore's eyes narrowed in anger.

Bryant yelled as his opponent's blade smashed his knuckles and caused his fingers to bleed. He dropped the practice sword in shock. Several peons laughed in triumph, while others gathered around him to protect him from any further attacks—something Marius was quick to seize upon.

"So, Theodore's peons rush to aid their fallen comrade," he taunted. "Why do we not make a mock battle of it then? You five shall defend the fallen Bryant against my six. What say you, Theodore?" he added, turning to face the newcomers. "Are your peons up to facing mine?"

"I would favour any of mine against yours, Marius," Theodore replied. "I teach my charges to be honourable men in the highest traditions of our order."

"Yet you don't teach them how to win," Marius snarled. "There will come a time when they will have to fight for their lives. Where then will their honour get them?"

"I have faith in Saradomin's way, Marius," Theodore countered. "I believe in his teachings." Making certain Kara was leaning securely against the wall, he approached the small crowd.

"As do I, Theodore," Marius replied. "But we cannot anticipate his will." He huffed in frustration. "Look at him!" He pointed to Bryant, who clutched his injured hand. "If he can't fight, he is useless to this order!"

Bryant bit his lip, trying to hold back the tears that were welling, from rolling down his face.

"Is he crying?" Marius sneered. "Unbelievable!"

"That is enough, Marius!" Theodore said, his voice nearly a

shout. Marius's own peons suddenly went silent, aware that the game had got out of hand.

"What will you do about it, Theodore?" Marius responded. "We cannot fight—our own trial forbids it. So why don't you run off and take Bryant to the matron?"

Theodore's face reddened with anger. But Marius was right. If he were to strike him now—a week before their scheduled trial—then Marius would be declared the victor, for Theodore would have acted dishonourably.

Suddenly a new person spoke up, and everyone turned.

"It seems Theodore cannot fight you, but I can."

Kara's voice was soft and provocative, and her eyes met Marius's astonished gaze with mocking contempt. She pushed herself away from the wall and—to Theodore's astonishment—walked confidently toward him, all signs of weakness gone.

"A girl dressed in the white linen of an invalid?" Marius snarled. "I will not demean myself."

"If I am to fall so easily, then it will take little of your time, Marius," she replied. "Surely you can spare a few minutes."

Marius was struck speechless, and not knowing how to retort made him angrier still. He turned to walk away, but Kara would not let him go so easily.

"Come on, Marius," she said to his back. "Are you afraid to face me? Perhaps Bryant would be a better match."

The peon lowered his head again, fearful that he would be the victim of a new taunt. Kara noted his look, and her heart softened. By the time she had reached his age, she had hunted with the dwarfs in the blackness of the mines. But she was not malicious and she didn't want to cause him any more embarrassment. *Everyone has their hour*, her adoptive father had told her, and she hoped that Bryant's was yet to come.

Marius continued to walk away, his pace quickening.

"At least Bryant is honourable," she persisted, speaking loudly. "And he is brave, Marius—braver than you, for he is not afraid to acknowledge his weaknesses."

Marius stopped in his tracks and turned to face Kara, his face contorted in anger.

"Please, Lady Kara." Bryant said as he struggled to his feet. "You mustn't."

"Shut up!" Marius shouted, seizing a training sword from the closest boy.

"Marius! Kara! This cannot be allowed to continue!" Theodore cried out. "I forbid it." He stepped between them, his hands outstretched. But his rival shrugged him off.

"The girl's brought it on herself, Theodore. I am not interested in what you have to say."

"Theodore, please stand aside." Kara's voice was hard.

"Kara. Please—this is madness," Theodore said.

"She must learn her place, Theodore—women do not fight," Marius declared. He pointed his training sword straight at her. "They should be at home, scrubbing the hearth and nursing children." When he saw her anger at his insult, a look of smug confidence crossed his face.

"Let us see, Theodore," she said. "I wish to compare myself to the fabled Knights of Falador, and see how I fare."

Theodore knew then that he had lost the argument.

"Very well then, but it ends when I say it does. The first to draw blood is the victor." He retrieved Bryant's sword and handed it to Kara. He then clapped his hands and the peons withdrew, giving the combatants plenty of room. All looked on with a growing sense of unease.

And they were not alone, for their shouting had attracted the attention of many in the castle. From high windows, faces gazed down in silent watchfulness.

"You cannot allow it to proceed, Sir Amik." Bhuler pleaded.

"I need to see what this girl can do, Bhuler," Sir Amik said.

"But Squire Marius will injure her."

"I will not let it go that far, Bhuler," the knight replied. "And neither will Squire Theodore."

Marius was confident—she could see it clearly. He had spent years fighting in similar circumstances, training against other peons and then other squires. Now he was fighting a girl who could barely walk!

Perhaps he will be overconfident?

Marius laughed for a second, then struck first with a swift lunge. His feet were a blur on the stone as he launched himself forward. Confident his lunge would strike home, he went in low to stab her stomach.

But Kara moved with equal speed, dancing back a brief step, keeping herself only an inch from the reach of his wooden practice sword. She laughed now, and chopped down with her blade just as he began to withdraw it. They connected with a satisfying *clack*.

"Well done, Lady Kara!" Bryant called from the crowd and a murmur of agreement rang out from the spectators—even from some of Marius's own peons.

Kara ignored them. Her mind was focused entirely on Marius, above all on the way his feet were spaced, for his movements there would dictate his actions.

He closed in again, this time lunging and cutting several times, moving with swift intent. He was not inexperienced. He knew how to fight and how to hurt. But his leather armour slowed him, and each lunge was met by a parry from Kara's training blade.

Marius's breath came in gasps now as he forced her back.

"Do you not attack?" he cried breathlessly. "Is it all you can do to run?" He pressed her once more, his attacks still skilled despite the fact that he was showing signs of fatigue. Her best strategy was to let him exhaust himself, she knew.

With each step he advanced Kara took another back, keeping him at a suitable distance.

"The girl intends to tire him," a grizzled veteran observed from the onlookers. "Marius can't keep it up in his armour."

"Her speed is surprising," the man's companion replied. "And she hasn't even broken a sweat yet. Nor does she even appear out of breath. It is unnatural."

Marius made a sudden lunge for her, his face twisted in anger.

And Kara smiled.

Reaching out with her free hand she seized his wrist and twisted. At the same time she lashed out with her foot, kicking his ankle and forcing him to the ground.

Marius gave a startled cry as he dropped the training blade. Then he swore loudly as Kara shoved her open palm into his forehead, putting him flat on his back at her feet.

A cheer went round the courtyard as Marius lifted his head in surprise. Kara stepped away from him, quickly picking up his training blade as she backed away, her eyes shining fiercely.

"It is done!" Theodore shouted, stepping between the combatants. "I declare Kara the victor!"

The peons clapped and shouted, their applause echoed from many of the windows that had opened high up in the castle.

"It is not done!" Marius shouted angrily as he stood. "The victor was to be the first to draw blood. Neither of us is bleeding."

"That is true," one of the onlookers remarked cautiously.

"Do you wish to resume Kara?" Theodore asked.

She looked at Marius contemptuously.

"I am happy to, Theodore." She nodded in her opponent's direction. "But the boy should note that I've taken one weapon off him already. If he wishes to lose another, it is no trouble to me."

"You dare to mock me?" Marius shouted, enraged, his fists clenched.

"Calm yourself Marius" Theodore advised.

"Squire Marius!" one of his peons shouted from the crowd of onlookers, tossing a training blade to his teacher. Marius grasped it firmly.

Kara saw the hate in his eyes and knew that he perceived her not just as an enemy that day, but as a threat to all he had become amongst the knights. If he were to lose, it would severely damage his standing in the order.

He ran at her, his speed catching her off guard. There were no thrusts or parries this time, for her wooden blade was no deterrent to Marius's attack. A single cut would not stop him.

Kara's blade bit into the leather armour at his shoulder as he drove his fist into her stomach. She doubled over, falling to her knees in pain and surprise as Marius triumphantly stepped away from her. He raised his arm and pulled the training blade from his padded shoulder, ignoring the groans of disapproval.

"No blood! The contest is still in progress." he roared defiantly. "And I have taken my weapon back."

Kara rose to her feet slowly, her breathing sharp and painful. She had not expected Marius to behave like that. For some reason, she thought that the rules of this game of skill would prevent such brutal assaults. He had not even used the training blade in his attack.

"Are you all right, Kara?" Theodore asked. "You don't have to continue if you don't want to." He stretched out a hand to help her up.

"Do not touch me, Theodore," she said through gritted teeth. "I just didn't know Marius was allowed to do that."

"You can't play the same game as him, Kara. Marius's armour will cut your knuckles if you try to hit him—and you have no armour to impede his blows."

"I am not going to play the same game as him, Theodore."

"Are you rested enough yet?" Marius sneered. "Or perhaps you would like to return to the ward and your sick bed." Kara sensed his renewed confidence. She knew he had strength on his side, and she was certain he was going to use it.

With a final deep breath, she readied herself.

"When I am done with you, Marius, it will be you who sleeps in the ward, not I!"

Her words goaded him and he charged once more, his training blade held before him to parry any counter-attack that she might make. But she was not going to let him hit her again. As he swung his arm back, Kara ducked out of his way, getting behind him before he could correct his stance. She ran her foot into the joint behind his kneecap and with a cry Marius fell once more to the ground.

But he would not linger this time. With a roar of animal rage he stabbed back behind him in a wild thrust of desperation.

Again she seized his wrist as she had done before and he tried to push up, opposite to the direction in which she was twisting.

"Do you wish me to end it, Marius?" she taunted. "Or would you like another chance?" She drove her knee into his stomach, knocking the wind from his lungs as he had done to her only a minute before, and at the same time she increased the pressure on his wrist. The training blade landed with a clatter and immediately Kara kicked it away. "That's *both* of your weapons I've taken, squire!"

She released him with a smile and Marius fell back to the ground, his breathing loud and quick, his face red from exertion. Kara turned and walked away.

"Don't you dare turn your back on me," he cried, standing up, his voice trembling with rage.

She was several yards from him now and she made no effort to turn around.

"Look at me," he demanded. "I am a squire of the Knights of Falador, and you. You are nothing. A nobody."

His words stung Kara and she stopped in her tracks.

The courtyard was silent.

Kara turned to confront him, her face ashen. There was a truth in his words that hurt her. She didn't know *who* she was.

"Marius. Behave yourself," Theodore shouted. "Those words are beneath you."

"She cannot hide behind you, Theodore," Marius roared, laughing savagely as Kara's face fell. "But the contest isn't finished yet," he pressed. "Neither of us bleed."

Kara raised her head once more to peer intently at him, and for an instant his mocking expression faltered.

When she moved, she did so with unexpected speed, her hand bent back over her shoulder, and in a single movement she threw the training blade at Marius, slicing the air in a path directly toward his face. Only his swift reaction saved him.

He caught the blade in his hand and staggered back, laughing as he felt his fingers close securely on the wood.

"I have taken your weapon from you. Now I will draw your own blood with your own blade."

"It is over, Marius," Kara said, her eyes misting from the tears that his words had provoked.

Preparing to stride forward, Marius raised his hand to point the weapon at her.

Then, with a startled grunt, he stopped. For his hand was bleeding. The wooden blade had cut his fingers in several places, and wooden splinters had shredded his skin. Theodore stepped closer to investigate.

"The contest is over. Kara is the victor," he declared.

There was nothing else to be said. By all their laws Kara had triumphed. The actions of the onlookers prevented him from retaliating as the peons, without exception, swarmed to Kara, clapping her victory and shouting her name. Soon the chant, led by Bryant, could be heard from the courtyard, in celebration of the "Lady Kara".

Theodore fought his way to her, pushing the more eager peons to one side.

"You must shake hands with Marius, Kara," he said hurriedly. "The contest is over. There can be no ill thought between you."

She looked at Marius, standing alone, staring down at his hand as if it had betrayed him. She hadn't wanted to demean him so much, nor reveal her combat prowess to the knights. The contest had gone too far, but there was nothing to do about it now.

She nodded firmly.

"Very well."

She strode forward, her eyes still tearful. Marius had hurt her more than he knew, but peace between them was something she wanted.

She presented her hand to him, and waited.

But Marius did not move.

"If she were one of our order I would have no objection in taking her hand, Theodore," he said darkly, looking past her as if she wasn't even there. "But she isn't—she is no more than a feral cat."

And in the shocked silence that settled over the courtyard, Marius turned and marched away, leaving his bitter words to haunt Kara.

TWENTY-THREE

Darkness settled over Falador, bringing with it a vengeful rain that lashed against the windows of Sir Amik's high room.

"I am certain of it," Sir Tiffy Cashien said. He spoke as if he feared even the walls might be listening. "I have spent the last few days reviewing the records of the Temple Knights, translating the code that keeps them secure."

Sir Amik nodded in understanding. The Temple Knights were answerable to Sir Tiffy and charged with gathering intelligence concerning their enemies. Their secrets were impenetrable—or so he hoped.

"And have you identified the knight who went north with the Ring of Life in his possession?" Sir Amik asked. Like Sir Tiffy, he kept his voice low, despite the fact that they were alone.

"I believe so. I have recorded my findings for you."

Sir Tiffy opened his satchel and withdrew a document written on vellum.

Sir Amik read it in silence. Then he read it again, to be certain of what it implied. Finally, he sighed.

Justrain.

"We have not had any contact with him in over a decade," he murmured, lifting his gaze from the document. "A man like him would not abandon our cause. I fear he is long dead, as we had assumed."

"I was a senior knight back then," Sir Tiffy said, "when he volunteered to spy on the Kinshra. Kara's arrival has raised unanswered questions that have long lain dormant."

Twenty years ago Justrain, one of their boldest knights, had disgraced himself by accusing someone in their order of treachery. Such a charge, if not supported by evidence, led to expulsion. Sir Amik remembered the day vividly: the adamant Justrain resolutely clinging to his accusation and standing by his belief in the face of furious opposition.

While many believed and supported him, there had been no evidence, so he had handed over his sword and his armour, resigning from the order before he could be expelled. Sir Tiffy's predecessor, then in command of the Temple Knights, had offered him one of the Rings of Life, as a final acknowledgement of the man's ability and resolution. He was officially designated a Temple agent, charged to spy on the Kinshra, and sent to live amongst the foresters and the hunters near Ice Mountain.

For several years irregular reports had been sent back. Some hinted at his unwavering intent to prove his accusation of treachery at the highest levels of the order.

But then the reports had ceased altogether.

"How old is Kara?" Sir Tiffy asked.

"I think seventeen. Theodore has said that she herself is not certain. He told me her story: her village was the target of a Kinshra attack, and she was the only survivor. She has not yet revealed how she survived."

"That is suspicious."

"Theodore thinks she will tell him in the next few days. He did not want to force her to revisit the tragic attack."

Sir Tiffy shook his head.

"Does he have the stomach for this work?" he asked frankly.

"Kara-Meir is somehow important to us, and Theodore's approach is long-winded. Time may be of the essence."

"He will achieve the goals we have set him."

The silence that fell between them was uneasy.

Finally, Sir Tiffy spoke.

"Do you think that Kara is Justrain's daughter?"

"It is a possibility," Sir Amik replied cautiously. He knew the way in which Sir Tiffy's mind worked, and he was afraid of what he might suggest.

"If there is any truth to the accusations Justrain made all those years ago, then the traitor may still live." He seized Sir Amik's wrist, his grip strong in its fervour. "He may be in the almshouses in the city, even now."

Sir Amik peered at him doubtfully.

"It was twenty years ago," he said. "What could he hope to accomplish after all this time, even if he is still alive?"

"If a man has escaped justice this long, then it is our duty to ensure that he evades it no more," Sir Tiffy insisted. "Think, my friend. If it becomes known that Kara is Justrain's daughter, and that her father may have passed on to her important information, our treacherous knight would be forced to act."

Despite his doubts, Sir Amik's expression became more intense.

"You mean, Sir Tiffy, to use Kara as bait?"

The old man lowered his head, a dark expression clouding his face.

"I do," he admitted. "Yet I do not suggest it lightly, for Kara will be in danger. But in the years since Justrain's exile, events have indicated that he might have been right. Our agents have disappeared, knights have been ambushed, yet for no reason we have been able to discern. Often these things would have required information that could only have come from someone within our ranks."

Sir Amik nodded. It was something he had been afraid to admit, hoping that this treasonous knight—if indeed he existed—was long dead.

"Very well," he said, rising from his seat. "No one else must know of this, my friend—only you and I."

"Agreed."

The two men sealed their pact by shaking hands, and Sir Amik knew they were both uncomfortable with what they were about to do. Yet both were certain that it was the only way.

Bhuler led Sir Tiffy to a spare room, for the rain and the late hour prevented him from returning to the almshouse near the park. The knight had been withdrawn since his meeting, his expression strained, the valet thought, as he returned to Sir Amik's quarters.

Sir Amik was no better.

"Bhuler, I would like you to tell me something." His voice was tremulous. "I have always tried to do what is good for our order," he began.

The valet nodded, and waited for more.

"But sometimes such dedication demands a sacrifice." Bhuler noted a far-away look in his eyes. "What will they say of me when I am dead?"

"Sir Amik?" Bhuler asked, certain he had heard incorrectly.

"Have I been a good knight, Bhuler?" Sir Amik pressed. "Have I served our order with honour?"

"Undoubtedly, Sir Amik," the valet declared. "Your name will live in the hearts of those who come after us, and will be held high as an example to them all."

Sir Amik smiled wanly.

"Thank you, Bhuler, and good night."

The valet turned and left the room, closing the door quietly, his mind disturbed. What could have prompted such unnerving questions? His thoughts turned to Kara. Her coming was the catalyst for many things, and he recalled the sad look he had seen on her face that afternoon after her victory over Marius.

Something drew him to the ward, and soon he found himself outside the wooden door, his hand unwilling to open it at such a late hour. He stood silently for a moment, unsure of what to do, when a sound from within caught his attention.

It was the sound of someone crying.

He could not ignore someone in distress. Silently he opened the door. There was only one person in the room.

It was Kara. She had the sheet pulled over her, as if hiding herself from the world.

"Kara. It is me… Bhuler." The valet crept forward and spoke in a low voice as he reached out to pull the sheet back.

She didn't try to stop him, and instead tried to hide her face in her arms, clearly unwilling to let anyone see her in such distress.

"What is wrong, Kara?" The valet reached forward and pushed the girl's hands gently away from her tear-streaked face.

Her dark eyes met his.

"I am a nobody, Bhuler," she hissed. "Marius was right. I can never be a knight. I don't even know who I am!" Her words were wracked by pained sobs.

Bhuler unconsciously put his arm around her, drawing her into his comforting embrace.

"You fought better than any squire I've ever seen, Kara," he whispered to her, pulling the strands of blonde hair away from her face. "None have beaten Marius in such a contest before— and you did it so easily."

"It changes nothing," she said into his shoulder.

"It changes *everything*, Kara," he responded. "I do not know why, but the eyes of fate have marked you for a purpose. You have been granted a skill which few can equal."

He pushed her away and looked at her gently, his eyes sparkling.

"You may not know your own history just yet, Kara, but you must continue to do what is right for today, not what was right in whatever past you may have lived. We must learn from history, but we cannot be bound by it."

She looked at him and nodded. He kissed her gently on her forehead, and she lay back on her pillow, her sobs subsiding.

"You should sleep now, Kara," he said. "I will watch over you."

And with Bhuler sitting silently at her bedside, Kara-Meir slept as peacefully as he had seen since her arrival, calmed by the presence of her friend.

TWENTY-FOUR

"I have discussed Gar'rth's affliction with my coven and I do not think we can be of any more help to him." Kaqemeex's expression was pained as he made this confession.

"You have done more than we had any right to expect, my friend," Ebenezer said gently. The druids had developed a potion that had relieved Gar'rth of his ailment, yet it seemed his body was rebelling against it. Soon, the alchemist knew, the potions would be useless.

"There is another option, however," Kaqemeex offered. "There is a monastery northeast of here, close to The Wilderness. The monks there, under Abbot Langley, are worshippers of Saradomin. They may have the power to heal the boy."

Gar'rth was standing close by, his head lowered in unease.

"Then we shall go there, and soon," Ebenezer said, glancing at Gar'rth with a fond look in his eyes. "I am sure Castimir will accompany us—it will be useful having a wizard at our side with the monster still on the loose."

"The birds have told me of the beast, my friend," Kaqemeex said earnestly. "It is no longer at large in the wild. It went south and has passed beyond the limits of my spies. I think the east road to Varrock will be clear of any danger, for the Knights of Falador have sent many of their agents abroad to guard travellers, and even the Imperial Guard are helping.

"I would suggest that you make for the River Lum, and take advantage of the hospitality of the barbarian folk. From there the monastery is just a few days north, east of Ice Mountain."

Ebenezer nodded.

"Then we shall leave today to take advantage of all the time that may be given us. Have you prepared the potions for Gar'rth?"

"I have, but once they are gone, I feel certain that no potion we can make will be strong enough to help him. His only hope is the monastery." The druid bowed low, turned, and departed.

From an upper window which he had opened to let in the morning light, Castimir watched the druid go. He had heard their conversation, and he quietly feared for Gar'rth. They had developed a tentative friendship stemming from his willingness to educate the unfortunate youth in the common tongue.

The young wizard made ready to pack his belongings, securing his precious rune stones in their many pouches upon his belt. He preferred to travel light, with only two packs and a straight staff which glowed a fiery red at its knotted top.

"Ah well," he sighed as he found his yak in the stables. "Off I go again. Farewell, peaceful Taverley—until next time."

In fact, every inch of Castimir was itching to depart. He had nearly finished his year's wanderings, and he was eager to see as much as he could before he had to return to the Wizards' Tower. The tales of the barbarians and their hospitality had been an inspiration to him when he was young, so he was eager to experience it first hand.

"I wonder if what they say about the barbarian women is true?" he asked his beast as he slung the first pack over the creature's back.

The phlegmatic yak looked at him as if it thought him mad, and didn't bother to answer.

TWENTY-FIVE

"Crown Prince Anlaf, has he been having your dreams?"

Sulla spoke with authority to the sybil, who stood in the red-carpeted meeting hall of the Kinshra.

"He has," the hag replied. "He will soon be paralysed with fear, unable to make a decision, open to the suggestions given by our supporters in Burthorpe. Through his indecisiveness the Imperial Guard will be redundant."

Sulla turned to the men gathered around the table. They were the most influential followers of the Kinshra, and they had sworn loyalty to him after he had assumed command. He knew how little their oaths were worth, however.

"Are you sure of this, Sulla?" Lord Daquarius asked. Sulla despised him, but was too wise to make an enemy of him, for Lord Daquarius was a cunning man who was popular due to his well-known concern for his men. Sulla possessed no such weaknesses.

"I am," he replied. "All we require is the will. For long years we have held ourselves back from interfering in Asgarnian politics, and the Knights of Falador have grown strong, taking advantage of King Vallance's illness. The followers of Zamorak are persecuted throughout the kingdom. How long will it be before the blessed name of Zamorak is forgotten in Asgarnia, unless we—his sworn followers—do something to remind the people? Our ancestors helped found Asgarnia with King Raddallin. Will we dishonour their memory by letting our enemies consolidate their grip? I say no!"

Several of the men growled approval, and even Lord Daquarius nodded.

Sulla raised his hand to silence them.

"We have the weapons needed to break the walls of Falador, and we have spies everywhere. We have agents monitoring those who come and go from the Wizards' Tower in the far south. We have agents patrolling the greatest city of humankind, Varrock, in neighbouring Misthalin." He paused. "We even have the promises of the goblin chiefs, who are angered by the unfair treaties they have been forced to sign by the knights, requiring them to cede their lands to human farmers, driving them farther and farther north.

"For many years now I have worked toward this moment. I have been called extreme, and some have decried my methods as too violent." Sulla smiled as he noted the amused looks on the faces of the men seated before him. "But over the course of years we have exhausted diplomacy, and only war remains!"

His captains hammered their fists upon the tabletop, indicating their agreement, and Sulla looked with satisfaction into their feverish eyes. He knew they would back him, for it had been many years since the Kinshra had ridden forth to open battle against their hated enemies. Many years during which their anger had only grown.

Some hours later, when only Sulla and the sybil remained, his wandering mind focused upon the girl. He had continued to dream of her, and he knew not why.

"She is alive. I know she is," he hissed to the sybil, his fists raised in sudden hatred.

"Do you fear her, Sulla?" the old woman said in a crackling voice.

He didn't answer, ignoring her and her evil laughter, for she alone had the power to mock him now. Instead he spun and walked away.

But as he left the hall he knew with certainty that he *did* fear the girl. For he sensed in her a nemesis, someone as violent and angry as he was—someone who was set solely and absolutely upon his destruction.

TWENTY-SIX

"Does the name Justrain mean anything to you, Kara?"

Sir Amik stood in the ward, his back turned to the girl, his hands folded behind him.

"No. I have never heard that name before." Kara's face was open and honest, and Theodore was certain she was telling the truth.

Sir Amik turned to face her then.

"I would like you to tell me about your father," he said. "About what happened to you after your village was attacked, and how you came to possess the broken ring."

"The ring was my father's," she replied. "He was a woodcutter in the village. He would spend long periods away, sometimes travelling as far as The Wilderness. Once he left us for some weeks…" Kara's face fell. "When he returned he was badly injured. Shortly after that, in the winter, the man called Sulla came and killed everybody."

She raised her head to the knight, who looked at her with sympathetic eyes.

"My mother forced my father's pack into my hands before she was dragged screaming from our house by her hair," she continued, her voice strained with the effort. "I escaped from the village, evading their hounds and hiding in the woods. I found the ring later, when I searched the pack for food."

Kara's eyes were far away as she recalled the horrific events.

"I was found by a party of dwarfs. They took me back to their caves and I was adopted by Master Phyllis. I learned to craft metals better than any human smith in Falador. I learned to mine and how to fight. I was always fighting. Master Phyllis saw the anger in me and took it upon himself to educate me. I even learned to speak their language.

"Then a few weeks ago Master Phyllis became ill, and he made me promise to leave the mountain. He thought it very wrong that I should be kept away from other humans, and decided that I was old enough to find my way in the world. I took my sword and my father's ring, and sought out the men who had killed my parents."

Sir Amik listened carefully, and showed no sign that he thought she was telling anything but the truth. Yet to Theodore he seemed uncomfortable as he began to speak again.

"There was a time when we knights had in our service a powerful mage who shared our aims," he began. "He created the Rings of Life and we issued them to those men who undertook our more dangerous missions—men like Justrain, who went to live amongst the people of your village, in order to spy on the Kinshra."

Kara's expression suddenly changed, to show that she understood.

Could it be true? she thought furiously. *Could he have discovered the true identity of my father?*

"But, Kara, there is something you should know about Justrain," Sir Amik said. "He forfeited his knighthood when he accused some in our order of being treacherous, of passing information to the Kinshra. When he left Falador for the final time, he did so without his squire, without his armour, and without his sword. He went as a normal man with a sacred mission. That would allow

him to marry if he wished—and it seems as if he did, becoming a
woodcutter and having you as his daughter."

The tears rolled down Kara's face. Suddenly she felt as if she had
found something that she had been searching for her entire life.

"But you must listen to me, Kara," Sir Amik continued
urgently. "There is evidence that the traitor might still be alive,
and if he is, he must be brought to justice. I need you to think of
anything your father might have said to you about this person.
Promise me you'll think about it?"

Kara nodded her head in agreement, although she was too
excited to speak. Sir Amik smiled sadly as he squeezed her hand
and left her in the ward with Theodore.

For Sir Amik, the conversation had been one of the hardest
things he'd ever had to do.

He had lied to Kara.

Sir Amik had read Justrain's reports, and they mentioned
nothing at all about taking on the persona of a woodcutter.
The knight lowered his head in shame. Not only had he wildly
raised her hopes, he had set her on a path that would put her
in danger. Kara-Meir would try to remember something that
would incriminate the traitor, and Sir Tiffy would see that the
suspect knights in the almshouse would know of it.

"I am trusting in you, Theodore, not to leave that poor girl
alone," he whispered to himself as he returned to his quarters,
there to greet a suspicious-looking Bhuler. He would have to
watch his valet, for he knew how clever he was and that he
would object loudly to Sir Tiffy's plan.

It is for the greater good, he told himself as he sat down at his
desk. Yet, as much as he knew it was true, that sentiment didn't
make him feel any better.

TWENTY-SEVEN

The following day was uncharacteristically warm, and many of those who dwelt in the knights' almshouse ventured forth to take their places in the park for the first time in weeks.

Amongst them was Sir Pallas, an old man who was glad to get outside to take advantage of the warm day. He sat by Sir Tiffy's side, listening to his acquaintance of long years as he spoke of Kara. His eyes widened when his friend mentioned the possibility that she was Justrain's daughter.

"Sir Amik thinks it a possibility. I think it a certainty, however," Sir Tiffy said. "I am *certain* she knows something about Justrain's accusations." He turned to face Pallas. "You will recall that he believed there was a traitor amongst the knights. I think she can give us the evidence we need to solve the mystery once and for all!" He grabbed his friend's wrist and squeezed enthusiastically.

Sir Pallas winced from the strength of the grasp.

"You seem very sure," he said, his voice lower than that of his friend. "In my experience, things of this kind tend to drag on indefinitely, and always without answer." Sir Pallas wasn't really looking at Sir Tiffy, however. His gaze was far away, clouded in memories of distant youth.

"I am certain, Pallas. She did not know her father was a knight until yesterday, but she knew he was spying on the Kinshra. It is obvious that his efforts led him to some conclusion, but before he could communicate his information he was killed and the village destroyed. Only Kara escaped. It must be by the will of Saradomin that she was delivered to us, to lead us to the answer we have sought for so long."

Sir Pallas nodded doubtfully.

"But what if the traitor is still alive?"

"Then he must be brought to justice, my friend."

"You would have him hanged?" Pallas asked. "What if it turns out to be one of us? It could be Sir Erical, Sir Finistere, Sir Balladish or Master Troughton." He counted them off on his hand, one by one. "It could even be me!"

"Yes, Sir Pallas. For all I know it could be you." Sir Tiffy's grey eyes stared coldly at his friend, and his voice turned flat and menacing. "The men you mentioned, and yourself, are the only men left alive who are of the right age and station to have been capable of committing such a treason. I pray that whomever it turns out to be is already dead."

The words wounded Sir Pallas, and he left the spymaster to sit by himself, not wishing to spend such a pleasant day under a cloud of suspicion. As he passed by two other retired knights on a footbridge that arched over a small pond, the men made way for him.

"Lovely day, Sir Pallas," the one-armed Sir Erical said.

"Yes," he answered quietly, his eyes glancing furtively at both men, a distinct sense of unease growing inside him.

They continued on their way. Sir Tiffy raised his hand to attract Sir Erical's attention, and the one-armed knight walked briskly over to take a place beside him on the bench.

It was too much, coming at this time of life, Sir Pallas reflected. He did not want to spend his last years consumed once again by thoughts of treachery, as it had been all those years ago. He watched from outside the park as Sir Erical's expression mirrored his own. After but a few moments, he too left Sir Tiffy's side, wearing a dark look on his face, another unhappy receiver of the spymaster's news.

Not far from the park, Doric sighed bitterly.

He had moved to a rented room that had unexpectedly become available in The Rising Sun. He had also lodged his claim with the magistrate in an effort to recover some of his possessions, but he knew it would be many months before any result would be forthcoming. Still, he thought, it was a first step on a long road that he knew he had to take.

The dwarf browsed the markets in the city, casting his knowledgeable eye over the precious stones that some of the merchants sold. Several times he had to bite his tongue to stop himself from criticising the workmanship on the polished metalwork that was on display.

His eyes focused on the gems on one of the stalls, weighing up their quality and quietly dismissing their value. As he did, the trader spoke.

"You know the woman? The beggar?" the man said to his neighbour.

"I know her," came the answer. "She tried to take one of my silks last year. When I caught her she pretended to be insane."

"Mad I think she may be. Look at this—she sold this gem to me this morning. Have you ever seen anything finer?"

Their talk drew Doric's attention, and he was eager to see the stone that the trader prized so greatly, certain it could not compare to those in his own collection.

"I paid a small fortune for it!" the trader said, and he laughed as he noticed Doric's curiosity. "Here, dwarf, your kind are well-known for their skill and appreciation of such things. What do *you* think?" The man handed the gem to Doric, his eyes shining happily. He knew it was of a far better quality than any he had possessed before.

Doric took the gem in his hand, weighing it first before unclenching his fist to look at it, and when he did so the blood drained from his face and he let out a strangled cry.

"What is it?" the trader said with alarm. "Are you all right, my friend?"

"Where did you get this thing?" Doric demanded.

"An old lady sold it to me this very morning," the man replied. "Why, what is wrong with it?"

"It belongs to me!" the dwarf said loudly. "I would know it anywhere. It was taken from me several days ago, when my house was burned and ransacked by yokels who had been whipped into a fervour by those purple-robed idiots. Squire Theodore and I found their bodies a day later—the monster had killed all of them."

"That cannot be," the trader insisted. "It was an old lady who sold it to me. I promise you!"

"I am not concerned about the gem," Doric said. "The purple-robed men took the best of my collection and the monster, in turn, must have taken it from them. If it has been sold in Falador, then that means the monster is inside the city!" He peered around, as if he expected the creature to appear.

His shouting attracted the attention of the city guards, and several men clad in chain mail stepped close about him. One of them laid a hand on his right shoulder, gripping it firmly.

"That'll be enough, dwarf!" one of them said sternly. "Continue to alarm the citizens and you'll have to come with us!"

Doric tried to shrug off the painful grip. A crowd began to gather.

"The monster is inside the city!" he implored. "Don't you see?"

Anxious looks appeared on faces in the crowd, and some of the onlookers were repeating the dwarf's words. A young woman with a child held close to her breast looked at Doric in sudden fear.

"Is it true? Is it here?" Her face paled further and she swayed on suddenly unsteady legs. "Remember what they said it did to the gypsy caravan? My child…" Her words ended as she fainted and a man behind moved to catch her.

"That is enough!" announced the guard with his hand on Doric's shoulder. "Go about your business! The dwarf is under arrest for causing a public disturbance."

At that, Doric was seized by the guards. He struggled silently, his anger preventing him from speaking coherently. Although several of the crowd had dispersed, there was still a considerable gathering.

"Why does he say such a thing?" someone shouted from the onlookers.

"Who's to know?" the guard answered loudly. "The monster cannot be in the city. The gates are guarded night and day, and someone would have noticed if it tried to sneak in."

Many nodded in agreement, but not everyone. All had heard the rumours of the beast, and all had imagined what it must be like. The fact that it had killed a dozen men and ripped a gypsy caravan apart had many believing it was a bear-sized creature or bigger. And how could a bear possibly sneak unnoticed into the city of Falador?

Finally Doric found his voice.

"Send for Squire Theodore of the knights! He will verify my story," he demanded. Then, realizing it was futile, he ceased struggling.

"In good time, dwarf," the guard said. "You'll spend a night in a cell—that'll help you to cool down, and teach you not to make a nuisance of yourself."

The guards led the dwarf away as several men shouted from the crowd, accusing him of worrying their wives and children needlessly. A few voices even jeered at him for being a drunkard.

But the dwarf's conviction had got the gem trader thinking.

It was extremely odd, he realized, that the madwoman who was well-known on Falador's streets should have come by something so valuable.

Suddenly the thought of his wife and daughter alone at home made him uneasy.

TWENTY-EIGHT

"Kara can stay in the ward a few more days," Sir Amik said, feeding a scrap of meat to the huge falcon that sat beside him on a perch. "The matron is unwilling to let her out—despite her ability to beat Marius, she still insists our guest is not completely healed. Although there is no longer any need for Kara to wear the clothes of an invalid. She can wear the ones Bhuler had made for her."

Theodore was certain Sir Amik was hiding something. As if sensing the young squire's unease, the knight's falcon flapped its wings as it adjusted its balance.

"I want you to give Kara more of your time, Theodore," he said. "We must try to unearth what it is that she knows."

"And what of my other duties, sir?" Theodore asked.

"Your other duties can be delegated to other squires for now. Your challenge to Marius is important, I know, but that is five days away. Kara is everything right now." When the young man didn't reply, Sir Amik peered at him and continued. "Has she said anything about her father?"

"Nothing," Theodore responded. "She has no recollection that her father was a knight, and she hasn't recalled anything with regard to Justrain, which is probably just as well."

"Ah! So you know why Justrain's daughter is so important?"

"Everyone knows of his unfounded accusations—now that they've been reminded, it's all anyone can talk about." Theodore's belief in the knights prevented him from admitting even the possibility of treachery. "Some say that Kara might be the key to ending it all."

"You sound doubtful."

"She had never even heard the name Justrain before you told her," Theodore said. "She can barely remember her father, let alone any secrets they might have had. Even if there was a traitor she will be absolutely no help in identifying him. I have said so repeatedly, just today."

Sir Amik turned on him quickly, suddenly angry.

"You must not say that, Theodore! That is an order," he barked. "Such opinions must remain your own. I called you here because I want your help. You are to tell others that Kara's memory is getting better—that she is recalling more of her youth and of her father's conversations. Do you understand?"

Theodore was startled, and not entirely certain that he *did* understand.

"Then there *was* a traitor?" he asked uncertainly.

Sir Amik said nothing.

"And you are asking me to lie," the squire continued. "To Kara, and to others in our order?" This flew in the face of so much that he had been taught about the knighthood.

Sir Amik put a hand to his forehead in distress.

"I am doing exactly that," he said. "I know it goes against everything we stand for, but we cannot pass up an opportunity like this. To do so would allow a murderer to escape justice."

Theodore's brow creased in puzzlement.

"A murderer?" he uttered quietly.

"Oh yes, Theodore. Many of our order have perished under mysterious circumstances, and some had families who were targeted by Zamorak's agents. All of this happened long before you joined the knights." He paused for a moment, appearing to gather his thoughts. "In my position, Theodore, I must make hard choices, but I can truthfully say that putting Kara in harm's way is the hardest decision I've ever had to make."

"You believe her to be in danger?" Theodore's voice was suddenly very high, his words strangled in disbelief.

"If the traitor is still alive, then it could be so," Sir Amik admitted. "That is why I haven't moved her from the ward, and that is why you are to spend as much time as you can with her without arousing suspicion."

"I am to guard her then?" Theodore asked.

"That, and observe," the knight acknowledged. "Watch who comes to see her, and make sure she doesn't go out around the castle. She doesn't know that she is the bait for our trap, and therefore she cannot be allowed to break the illusion that what she knows is vital to unmasking the traitor. You do understand, do you not?"

Theodore nodded, suddenly feeling unclean.

"I do understand, sir. And I will obey your orders. But I take no joy in doing so. What I do, I do for the good of the order, and perhaps the ruination of myself."

Sir Amik had no reply. The young man bowed his head and left.

The old woman was restless. She chewed on her dirt-stained fingers, her eyes flashing nervously from left to right.

She stepped to the small doorway and looked through into the darkness within. Her lodger was sleeping, his body motionless in the shadows with his hands behind his head. He slept in absolute silence, and for a moment she hoped he might be dead.

"He is rich," she said to herself softly, for that same afternoon she had seen the contents of his pouch, the glittering jewels. "And he is sleeping. How can I lose this opportunity?" Her greed overcame her conscience. The knife felt heavy in her sweaty grasp. "It will only take a few seconds. He won't feel a thing."

She stepped through the doorway, careful to avoid the creaking and unsteady floorboards. Within a few seconds she was standing over her sleeping guest.

She raised the knife, breathing out slowly. And then she drove the knife downward into his body.

His cry was all the louder for the silence that had preceded it.

She pushed down with all her weight. But something was wrong.

There was no blood.

The knife pierced the skin easily enough, but there was something underneath that prevented it from going any further, something that gave a sound like sackcloth tearing.

And he stopped screaming. His arm was drawn across his face, his breathing deep. Then the hoarse laughing began.

"How utterly pathetic!" he sneered, his voice animalistic and inhuman.

"I'm sorry," she said, pulling the knife out quickly as if she thought that was enough to make him forgive her. Then, suddenly, she stabbed down again, trying to pierce his heart.

The blade hit his body and failed to penetrate the sackcloth-like coating that lay beneath his robe. He laughed once more. His huge hand seized hers and squeezed, causing her to let out a shriek of terror.

"You're hurting me!" she gasped, falling to her knees.

He tightened his grip on her hand and old bones cracked under his fingers. Her breath came out in rapid gulps, each one a grunt of pain.

"Have mercy on an old lady!" she wept. Never before had she felt such agony.

"I shall give you the same mercy you offered me," he growled.

With his free hand he pulled back the hood, his red eyes glaring in the darkness, his long teeth gleaming under his wide nose.

"No!" she gasped. "No!" Her heart was pounding in her chest.

"You humans are all alike." He released her hand and she could feel her old skin torn into strips by her broken bones, wet with her own blood. "I assume you are interested in my expensive jewels?"

She shook her head feebly, a last attempt to deny her greed.

He reached for his pouch, and plunged a clawed hand into it.

"You may have this one—the largest one!" He withdrew the hand, which held a huge opal between thumb and forefinger, bringing it just an inch away from her eyes. Then he grabbed her jaw with his free hand and forced her mouth open, inserting the opal before she could resist. Her attempt to bite seemed only to amuse him. Her soft gums barely tickled his thick skin, for she had lost all her teeth years before.

He shook her violently and she swallowed the opal in a single gulp, the large gemstone lodging in her throat. With a savage push the monster sent her staggering into the centre of the room, where she fell.

The old woman's hands reached for her throat as she began to choke. But nothing could dislodge the opal. Her last thought was to avenge herself on her murderer, to reveal his presence to the citizens of Falador, but she hadn't enough strength even to reach the door.

The monster watched her die without any satisfaction. He had suspected she might attempt something like this.

Yet killing her meant that he had to act quickly now. She was, he knew, well-known in the marketplace. It would only be a matter of time before she was missed. He needed to lure Theodore out of his castle for a lengthy and very private interrogation.

And he needed to do it immediately.

TWENTY-NINE

It was morning, and Doric was angry.

After a sleepless night in one of Falador's gaols, spent in the company of a flatulent drunkard, he was released at dawn with a warning from the guard who had arrested him.

"No more talk of the monster, citizen," the man said pompously. "We can't afford a panic in the city." With that, the self-important law-giver shut the door.

As he stood alone in the morning light, Doric shivered, and anger gave way to wisdom. He recalled the scene of the purple-robed men who had been killed in their sleep. It was no mere animal with a taste for flesh they were after; it was a callous assassin, a cunning murderer who possessed monstrous strength. Whatever it was, its intellect made it doubly dangerous.

His first plan was to alert Theodore. He made his way to the castle, and his mood darkened further when he was told by a guard that the squire could not take the time to see him.

"You have not even told him that I am here," he said angrily. "Tell the squire that the monster is in the city." His voice rose, and he tried his best to put fear into the man. "Tell Sir Amik to recall his men from the countryside. Tell him to bring them home to patrol the streets of Falador!"

But to no avail. The guard ceased even responding to his entreaties, and he left with a foul curse on his lips. With no other course to follow, he returned to The Rising Sun and retrieved his weaponry and helm, for he would not be caught unguarded. It was shortly after midday when he found his way once more to the gem stall in the marketplace.

The trader gave him a long look as he saw him approaching.

"You won't be disturbing my customers again, will you, master dwarf?" he asked.

"No disturbance today," the dwarf said quietly, swallowing his pride and leaning heavily on his axe. He couldn't let his temper get the better of him again. "But I am interested in the old woman. Do you happen to know where she lives?"

The trader pointed the dwarf toward a squalid quarter with narrow streets and dark alleys that people called the Dens.

"Most people in Falador know of her, my friend," he said, his tone almost conspiratorial now. "If you head that way and continue asking, then you should be able to find her."

Doric thanked the man and slung his axe over his shoulder. As he left the marketplace he ran his hand over the two sharp daggers he had secured in his belt, and the smaller throwing axes that hung from his hip.

He took comfort in his weapons, and he had a grim feeling that he would be glad to have them.

Theodore pulled back the cloth and smiled as Kara's eyes widened in happiness.

"I thought you should have it back." The words came surprisingly easy to Theodore as he watched her examine the adamant sword closely.

It is because I am telling her the truth, he thought to himself.

Kara should have her sword, and not just in case she might need it to protect herself from the traitor.

"Thank you, Theodore." She put the sword down and embraced him. The young man stiffened at her touch. She released him with an embarrassed look.

"You said you had received a message—was it important?" she asked suddenly, changing the subject to that of the anxious guard who had knocked nervously at the door some hours earlier.

"Not really," Theodore lied. The guard had told him how angry Doric had been at being denied entry to the castle, and how he had raved about the monster. Perhaps, Theodore thought, he had been drinking again.

And yet...

He went to the window and looked up at the ramparts. The day was cloudy. Sir Amik had invited the residents of the almshouse into the castle, and quite unexpectedly. He had requested their help in teaching the peons, for their training was suffering because many knights had been sent to hunt the monster in the countryside north of Falador. The old warriors had willingly agreed, thankful to be of use to their order once more.

Yet Theodore knew the truth. He knew it was a ploy by Sir Amik to bring the traitor back amongst them, to let him think he had a realistic chance of striking at Kara before he could be identified.

That was why the young squire refused to leave her. That was why he had ignored Doric's warning in the morning. Kara's safety was more important to him than anything else. He would not leave her side while the residents from the almshouse were in the castle.

The peon Bryant had been sequestered by the amiable Sir Balladish. The old knight needed the youth to run to the apothecary to purchase the ingredients for one of the many potions he consumed to ease the pains of an old body dented in battle.

"Make sure you get everything, young soldier," Sir Balladish told Bryant as he eagerly took the list. "We old war dogs need all the medicine we can get to keep us going. Isn't that right, Sir Finistere?"

"Indeed it is, Sir Balladish," the bearded man agreed, turning to add his own encouragement to the young man. "Run along, and be sure to get everything he requires."

Bryant ran all the way, his face beaming in pleasure that he had been chosen for the task. In his eagerness, he turned a corner swiftly and ran directly into someone who was coming the opposite way.

"I'm very sorry, sir!" he said as he regained his balance. The newcomer had hardly flinched. "It was entirely my fault!"

The tall figure in the red robes said nothing, and Bryant's face wrinkled as he caught a sweet smell from the man. He could feel the man's eyes, concealed deep within the cowl, watching him eagerly. After a moment he spoke.

"Are you one of the knights?" the man asked. "I am new to these parts, and I am eager to meet the warriors of Falador." He spoke in a guttural tone, an animalistic accent which Bryant couldn't place, emanating from deep inside his body.

"I wish to be, sir!" the young man said eagerly. "I am Bryant, a peon, under the tutelage of Squire Theodore."

"Squire Theodore?" The man said the words with a tone Bryant assumed was reverence.

"Yes, indeed—you have heard of him, sir? He's the squire who rescued the dwarf from the monster, and found the corpses of the human supremacists. He's the best of our order, and promises to be a great knight!"

"Indeed, I have heard it said so." The man spoke softly, his voice suddenly gentle. "I would like to meet him, young peon.

Do you think you could arrange that?"

Bryant shook his head.

"I am afraid not, sir. The squires are far too busy to meet with the citizens of Falador, especially with so many of the knights away hunting the monster!"

"That is unfortunate," the man said slowly.

For a second Bryant stiffened, suddenly feeling as if, for some unknown reason, he was in great peril.

"But I do understand," the man uttered finally, and his soft words diffused Bryant's concerns. He said nothing more, however, and stepped past, briskly disappearing into the crowds.

Aware that the delay had cost him time, Bryant ran quickly on.

A few seconds later, the red-hooded man turned the corner once again, this time following the peon's path, even though the young man was no longer in sight. He found his way easily to the apothecary several streets away, as if following an invisible trail that only he could see.

He watched the youngster through the murky pane as a list was handed over to the apothecary, and he noted, too, how the shopkeeper's eyes widen as he read the list.

"I hope your knight knows what he is about, master peon," the older man said grimly. "If he mixes these in the right doses, then he will come up with a rather nasty poison."

A look of confusion swept over Bryant's face.

"He does know—he must, for he often uses potions as a salve for his ancient injuries. Many of the older knights do."

"Be that as it may, master peon, you just remind your knight of what I've said." Then the apothecary disappeared, hunting amongst his jars and powders to fulfil the needs of the list in his hand.

Several minutes later, Bryant emerged from the shop, closing the door behind him and looking downcast. The apothecary had charged him more than he had expected, and Bryant had not had enough money to pay him. Knowing he was a peon of the knights, however, the kind apothecary had given Bryant all he had asked for, on the condition that he would return that same day to pay the outstanding sum.

"You have my word, sir!" Bryant had told him as he left.

In his disappointment, knowing he would have to make another trip and have to explain the embarrassing situation to his tutor, he failed to notice the tall man in the red robes who was concealed in the shadows of a large doorway, watching him depart.

"I trust you, boy," the figure muttered to himself, unheard by all. "You will return to the apothecary today and in an hour it will be dark. Then I shall have my bait!"

Red eyes glowed under the hood.

THIRTY

Doric had spent five hours asking about the "mad old beggar lady" and had narrowed down her place of residence to all but a few streets. But the deeper he got into the Dens, the less people were willing to volunteer information, for their poverty formed a bond between them that was hard for an outsider to penetrate.

It will be dark soon, he thought. He hefted his axe from his shoulder and leaned on it, deep in thought, and as he did so some coins chinked in his tunic.

They may not volunteer information to an outsider, he thought, *but they will very likely sell it.*

He considered briefly going back to the castle to see if Theodore had become available, but his mood soured when he remembered the morning guard.

I will go back to him when I have something conclusive, he decided. So he lifted his axe once more to his shoulder and approached the nearest door to renew his search.

Bryant arrived in the courtyard entirely breathless, his face bright red. He had wanted to return to the apothecary before the afternoon grew dark, but it seemed as if the low clouds and ailing sunlight were deliberately mocking him.

Sir Finistere and Sir Erical were touring the courtyard and reminiscing. The peon always thrilled at hearing their stories, for their words took him back to a glorious time.

"I remember the first time I ever stood here, Sir Erical," Sir Finistere said, casting his fond eyes to the daunting heights of the white towers. "First as a peon, then as a squire, and finally as a knight preparing for battle. We lost a lot of good men in those days." The men lowered their eyes.

Then Sir Finistere noticed Bryant labouring for breath nearby.

"Ah, boy!" he said. "Did you get everything on Sir Balladish's list? He does have some very odd requirements."

"I have it all here, sir!" Bryant's words tumbled out. "The apothecary said that he must be wary of mixing them, for they could be blended to make a poison! I promised to inform him."

Sir Finistere's eyes narrowed.

"That is interesting," he commented mildly. "I'll be sure to tell him when I give him the ingredients."

Bryant handed Sir Finistere the brown box that he had been given, and prepared to run to his trunk to retrieve the money necessary to pay back the apothecary. He dared not ask a knight as distinguished as Sir Finistere for the funds. But as soon as he turned to leave, the knight stopped him.

"Where are you going at such a rate, lad?"

Breathlessly, Bryant told him how he intended to make things right with the apothecary.

"A noble cause, but you should know this—knights do not run about the streets looking red-faced and desperate. We must take pride in our appearance. Here!" He flicked Bryant a coin and took him by the shoulder. "That should cover the expenses. But before you return to his shop, I want you to run some water over your face and have a ten-minute sit down. And when you do return, you will walk and not run. Not for a single yard!"

With that, Sir Finistere turned his back on Bryant, nodding to Sir Erical as he passed him. "I will deliver this to Sir Balladish. Good evening, Sir Erical."

The old knights exchanged genteel nods, and Bryant walked slowly away, intent on obeying Sir Finistere's words to the letter.

A quarter of an hour later, having washed himself down and regained his breath, Bryant walked confidently across the courtyard and out of the castle.

I shall wait a while, until the right moment, the man thought to himself. Deftly, he ducked from one doorway to another, following the boy expertly. *I am not so old yet that I cannot overtake a mere peon,* he thought. His right hand massaged the hilt of the curved dagger that he had tucked into his belt.

It will be quick, he mused, *but that is the only promise I can make, for the boy has learned enough to reveal my treachery.*

Even if he doesn't know it just yet.

The apothecary was about to shut the shop for the evening when he spied the peon crossing the street. He smiled and waved to him. It was good to know there were people in the world that could still be trusted. Whatever others might think of the knights and their fanatical devotion to Saradomin, he at least was thankful for their presence in the city.

The boy named Bryant apologised again for not having enough money in the first place, and then thanked him for his trust, even bowing as he left the shop.

How polite they are, as well, the apothecary thought as he watched the peon walk swiftly back the way he had come. Then he cast a wary eye skyward as he felt the first drops of rain on his bare face, and noted the hurried footsteps of all those citizens who were still out of doors as they rushed to get home before the downpour came in earnest.

He hardly noticed the tall figure in the red robes who stepped swiftly after the vanishing peon.

An ominous feeling crept into the traitor's heart. It was a feeling born of experience that had kept him alive and undetected throughout his long career.

He watched Bryant enter the apothecary's, and he observed the figure in the red robes standing on the opposite side of the street.

Something was very wrong. He did not know what it was, but his senses remained honed enough to detect another intelligence focusing on the boy. He stepped back into the shadows of the doorway and watched, waiting for a moment as Bryant paid the apothecary and emerged with a satisfied look on his young face. There had been too many people on the streets for him to strike during the journey so far, but he hoped that the winter darkness would give him his opportunity.

Now Bryant walked briskly across the street and back the way he had come.

The handle of the dagger was slippery in the traitor's grasp. The anxiety of what he had to do was causing him to sweat, despite the chill of the evening.

The red-robed man also turned to follow Bryant. The traitor watched with a growing realisation that this figure was the source of his ominous fear. He decided it would be best to watch, rather than to interfere. *Besides*, he thought, *Bryant's information is only useful if I carry out my original plan.*

Yet he knew also that if he did not act to silence Kara, then her knowledge of Justrain's investigation would see him hanged for treachery.

He gripped the dagger tightly. If the opportunity presented itself, then the peon would die by his hand. Once he was dead, Kara would follow, and no one would have the knowledge to incriminate him.

The rain gathered strength and Bryant held his hand flat above his eyes to prevent the drops from obscuring his vision. People were beginning to huddle under doorways and to take advantage of whatever shelter they could.

His hair was becoming soaked and his clothing dishevelled. He thought of Sir Finistere's words about taking pride in his appearance, and he knew he could not return to the castle in such a state. As he lifted his gaze to evaluate the rain, he decided its strength could not last. Surely it would exhaust itself in a few minutes. So he looked about for a place to wait it out.

Seeing that he was now nearly alone on the street, he identified several suitable shelters. He ducked into the nearest one available, beneath an overhanging rooftop that gave him easily enough room to avoid the inclement weather.

As he stood waiting for it to end, his thoughts turned to Lady Kara. He was envied by the other peons for having attracted her attention, and the title he had bestowed upon her had led many to think of him as one of her favourites. Although none would admit it, some were fervently jealous of his achievement. It was the first time in his life that he had actually outdone his fellow peons. Although they often were warned of the dangers of pride, he could not deny himself a congratulatory smile.

So caught up was he in his thoughts that he barely noticed the tall man in red duck under the overhang to share his shelter from the rain. Without a word, he moved along the wall to allow room for him.

Concealed behind a timber frame down the street, the traitor watched the two figures share their shelter. He observed the red-robed stranger step close to Bryant and noted with a feeling of sudden apprehension that the peon was in danger.

The rain suddenly sleeted toward him and he turned away

from the street in order to draw his hand across his eyes. Above him the first thunder sounded, echoing off the high white walls and bouncing across the city rooftops. He blinked to clear his eyes and turned to look back toward the two figures.

But no one was there.

Bryant had vanished, and the red-robed man was disappearing swiftly into the darkness, visible only for a second as he turned and hastened down the nearest alleyway.

I cannot miss this chance.

He cursed in the darkness, running out into the street to where Bryant had stood only seconds before. His legs ached in protest, unused to such exercise and enfeebled by his age, but he ignored the pain with an angry grimace. He rushed into the alleyway to see the red-robed figure stoop, a heavily-laden sack slung over his right shoulder.

The sack didn't move, but as the man disappeared amongst the buildings, the traitor saw a booted foot slip from the cover.

It was Bryant. The man had kidnapped him.

The traitor hoped that he was dead, but the fact that the man had taken him made it more likely that he was alive. Slavery had long been outlawed in Asgarnia, yet there were always rumours of children being carried off to the savage communities in The Wilderness, or even smuggled to Morytania by the wandering gypsy folk, where their fates were beyond the imaginings of even the darkest human mind.

The red-clothed figure moved quickly, from one shadow to the next, and the traitor had to run to keep up. It quickly became apparent that the kidnapper did not know Falador, for several shortcuts presented themselves which the traitor would have taken, if their roles were reversed.

As he followed the fleeing figure to the poorest quarter of the city, he knew it would not be long before the kidnapper's base was revealed.

Then he would have to decide what to do.

The rain interfered with his sense of smell and it always put him on edge. He was certain he hadn't been seen as he had pulled the sack over his unsuspecting victim and knocked the peon's head against the wall, yet he couldn't shake off the feeling that he was being followed.

The unfamiliar city further disconcerted him and he had decided that speed was the best option in making his way back to the old woman's house.

But as he neared the house he caught a scent that he had not detected since the night he had scaled the castle wall: it was the smell of the dwarf. Doric's odour lay heavily in the street, indicating he had walked up and down it several times.

"I have no time for that now!" the creature growled, his red eyes glowing in anticipation. He entered the house, bolting the door behind him. Then he tied the unconscious human down and gagged him roughly with a cloth scarf he had found in the woman's cupboard.

He wiped the dried blood clear from Bryant's temple. He had pushed his head into the stonework harder than he had intended in his rush to secure him, and he hoped he hadn't caused too much damage.

For he needed the boy alive.

Doric was lost.

The city looked very different in the darkness and the rain, even to his night-attuned eyes that had spent long years in the perpetual blackness of the subterranean realms.

He had found where the old woman lived, and after a half hour of uneasy watching had decided to find Theodore and inform the squire of his story, whether he was willing to hear it or not.

But since that time he had been going round in circles, unable to find his way out of the warren of old buildings that tottered forward on their foundations as if they were about to fall over. Every street looked the same in the dark, and there were very few people he could ask for directions now that the rain had become a torrent.

Finally, frustration getting the better of him, he banged on the nearest door with his fist tightly clenched. An uneasy voice called out from inside and the door opened a thumb's width, only enough to allow the occupier to peek out into the dim street.

"What do you want?" the man called out in an accent that Doric could barely decipher, and through a mouth that had long since lost all of its teeth.

"Just some simple directions," he replied, holding his ill temper. "I'll pay, of course." Doric huffed as he reached into his pouch, feeling the cool metal coins in his fingers.

He was beginning to hate Falador.

The traitor watched the house for only a few minutes. He debated whether to try and enter, to make sure that Bryant was no longer a threat, or whether he should return to the castle and deal with Kara.

She was the important one. Bryant was just an unfortunate witness.

He recalled the red-robed figure and knew he was afraid of him. There was something very powerful about the man who had seized Bryant—unnaturally so. That helped him make his decision—he would return to the castle right away. He relaxed his grip on the dagger and withdrew into the shadows of the surrounding dwellings.

Kara will die tonight, he promised himself, *and then I'll see if I have to bother with the boy.*

Bryant awoke slowly, unable to comprehend where he was.

Gradually he understood that he had been blindfolded. When he tried to cry out, he nearly choked on the gag that had been secured about his mouth.

He jumped when a guttural voice came out of nowhere.

"Understand, young peon," the voice said calmly, "that I mean you no harm. But understand this also: if you do not cooperate, then I will hurt you."

The voice drew closer. Bryant could feel the hot breath on his face, and suddenly he was glad of the blindfold. A rough hand removed the gag.

Bryant gasped for air before speaking.

"What do you want?"

"Nothing more than information," the voice replied calmly. "I have been sent to your land to retrieve something that is precious to my master. For some months it has evaded me, always running. Then very recently I chanced upon your Squire Theodore. He knows the whereabouts of the thing I am seeking, but he is unaware of its nature.

"It is a dangerous thing, young peon. It has killed several times and unless I can catch it, then it will continue to do so."

"The monster? Is that what you are hunting?" Bryant whispered in awe.

"You call it a monster, but I have another name for it. Regardless of that, the truth is that we are after the same thing—we both want it gone from this land. Will you help me?"

"Why then the subterfuge?" Bryant asked, at once curious and fearful. "Why not simply ask me?"

A low laugh emanated from deep within his captor's throat.

"I doubt the servants of Saradomin would be so quick to aid one who looked like this!" In an instant his blindfold was torn off, and red eyes glowed savagely as the wolfish maw with its long teeth and longer red tongue breathed a rancid odour into the peon's face. Only in his darkest nightmares had he ever encountered such a creature before—a werewolf!

Bryant cringed back in abject fear.

"Your kind are only legend!" he whimpered. A strong hand gripped his face, so hard that Bryant thought his skull would crack.

"We are very real, boy! But we do not come into your lands often and you should be thankful for that. I have been tasked with bringing back a traitor. Theodore knows where he is. If you help me, I will spare your life and his.

"But if you do not, you will suffer as none of your order has ever suffered."

"What guarantees do I have?" the boy asked, regaining a portion of his composure.

The werewolf looked at him with something new in its expression—something akin to respect.

"You are brave, peon," he admitted. "But I do not seek your death, not unless you give me no choice. If I were to kill you I would be hounded by your knights, making my search all the more difficult. Logic is your guarantee.

"All I wish to do is to call Theodore in your name, boy. I will write him a letter, telling him of an injury you have sustained, and you will make certain of its accuracy. Then, when he comes, I shall release you."

"I shall help you then," Bryant agreed. "If you promise me you will act as you have said." He bowed his head low in a defeatist gesture.

The werewolf smiled.

"You have my promise, boy. Now, the letter…"

THIRTY-ONE

Kara was looking out of the window.

Theodore stood near the entrance to the ward. Both of them had been silent for a time, and when he spoke, she jumped slightly.

"You should come away from there, Kara," he said. "I would like to see you practise with your sword."

She looked at him curiously.

"Why are you armed, Theodore? You have never been armed before, on your visits to me."

"It is the rumour of the monster, Kara. Doric left a message at the guard house, saying that it might be inside the city. I just wish to be ready in case we are called." He was getting better at lying, he thought grimly. He was armed simply to protect Kara in case the traitor decided upon a desperate attack.

A loud thump at the door drew their attention. Theodore's hand tightened on the hilt of his weapon, as if he expected to fight. But it was the same guard with whom Doric had argued that morning, and he saluted before handing the squire a rain-soaked envelope.

"It's just been delivered, Squire Theodore. By one of Emily's boys from The Rising Sun." The owner of the inn kept several street urchins on her payroll to run chores for her around the city, and they acted as Falador's couriers, at least for those willing to pay to have their messages delivered.

Theodore took the message and read quickly. A look of alarm spread across his face.

"It's from a citizen writing on Bryant's behalf! He's been hit by a runaway horse on a street corner near the apothecary." He continued to read. "Bryant has asked that I come to aid him." He hesitated—what was he to do? Go to Bryant and abandon Kara, or remain at her side?

She noticed his sudden anxiety.

"Well, Theodore?" she prompted. "What are you waiting for? Bryant is your peon, and he is under your care. You must go to him."

Sir Amik's words came back to him. He knew guarding Kara was the most important of his duties, yet abandoning Bryant would be against every rule of the order, and an insult to everything he had pledged his life to. After what seemed like long, agonizing moments, he came to a decision.

"Keep your sword close, Kara," he said firmly. "And do not leave the ward on any account!"

"I remember my orders, Theodore," she said, an irritated note in her voice. "I am to remain here until Sir Amik is satisfied about my health." Her brown eyes lapsed into deep thought. "But if Bryant has been hurt, then perhaps I should accompany you."

"No, Kara. You will stay here—and you will not leave the ward," Theodore insisted. "I shall not be long, Saradomin willing."

As he closed the door behind him, Theodore could not help but feel that fate was following closely on his heels.

Despite the promises made by his captor, Bryant was in pain.

His tormentor had sunk his claws into his left arm, and several times he had passed out. It was during one of his fainting sessions that his captor had hastened out to The Rising

Sun, passing along the message he had written in the guise of a concerned citizen.

Upon his return he had splashed Bryant with cold water, waking the peon in order to find out more about Theodore.

"So I shall become a werewolf?" Bryant asked him after a silence. His voice was taut.

The creature looked confused.

"Do you not pass on your curse to those you injure?" the peon elaborated.

"Of course! I had forgotten about the fairy tales that you humans whisper to one another before bedtime. You believe that if I bite you, then you will change at the next full moon." He laughed mockingly. "It isn't true. A normal human being cannot be infected in such a manner. Maybe a half-breed, but I doubt if your ancestors deigned to marry into any of my race—not after Saradomin's armies drove us back and cursed the River Salve to prevent us from leaving Morytania."

"Then how did you get out?" Bryant asked, growing bolder. "How did you cross over the holy river?" His voice was weak from blood loss.

"Holy places can be defiled by sacrifices and powerful magic. But it was still very difficult for me to do it, and the dark lord of my realm had to have a hand in it himself. It has put me in debt to him, and that has put me in danger should I fail."

Bryant fell silent, and the look on his face bespoke the pain he was enduring. Finally he gasped for air as he blacked out once more.

The werewolf was grateful for the silence, but he checked Bryant's breathing to ensure that he was still alive. He wasn't going to kill him just yet—for if Theodore proved to be as stubborn as his pupil, then threats would make little headway.

He would simply torture Bryant instead, until the squire complied with his requests.

Scant moments after Theodore rode across the moat, Doric rounded the corner.

"Not you again," the guard said, noting the dwarf's breathlessness. "What do you want this time?" He moved to stand on the centre of the bridge, his arms crossed tightly as if to dissuade the dwarf from any more nonsense.

Doric was angry. He was wet from the rain, he had been on his feet all day, and he was certain the monster was in the city and that the old woman knew where. A feeling in his gut had made him afraid of her house, as if he could somehow sense the monster's presence there. It was a feeling he would never forget.

He needed Theodore, and nothing would deter him now.

"I only want to speak to Squire Theodore," he replied.

"Squire Theodore is not here," the man responded. "He has gone out in response to a letter that came from a citizen in the southern quarter."

Doric's attitude changed at once. His face paled, and his voice shook.

"Not Dagger Alley, not the Dens?" he said.

The guard nodded. "It is in the Dens but I do not know the address," he replied. "Why should he not go there? Every citizen is entitled to the protection of the knights, no matter what their situation of birth or wealth. Saradomin is not an exclusive deity."

"But he is in danger!" Doric insisted. "I trailed the monster there today."

"Why would the monster want Theodore?" The guard's patience appeared to be at an end.

"It followed us on our journey south! If it does not want me, then surely the only alternative is Theodore? Quickly, man, you must send help!"

"I will not be ordered about like a common guard. I am a knight of Saradomin!"

"Then Saradomin take you!" the dwarf roared, and before the guard could answer Doric turned and ran, heading south.

For a moment the guard stood on the bridge, his mind racing as he wondered what to do.

Dagger Alley, was that what the note had said?

A deep echo of thunder rolled across the rooftops, prompting his decision. He turned and ran from the bridge, heading for the ward to retrieve the note he had delivered to Theodore, just a short time before.

As the storm rumbled overhead, the kitchens of the knights were busy. The visitors from the almshouse expected the best from those for whom they had spent their lives fighting, and the cooks were eager not to let them down.

Elise moved with purpose. She was keen to get out of the hot kitchens and return to the ward with Kara's meal.

"It is not ready yet, Elise," the cook told her. "I have prepared Lady Kara's drink. I have even mixed some chocolate into it for a treat. From the gossip going around the castle, I think she deserves it."

The woman sighed and looked at the retired knights. Eager to look in on the places where they had spent their youth, they had even invaded the domain of the kitchen. Two of them— Sir Erical and Sir Balladish—were standing close by, and as she waited she listened to their conversation.

"It's been a long time since I've been down here," the one-armed knight said with fond nostalgia.

"And for me, Sir Erical," his companion agreed. "I was taught to cook on this stove as a peon."

"And can you remember what you learned, Sir Balladish?" a voice called from the stairwell. Sir Finistere ducked his head under the lintel and entered the room with a broad smile, his eyes looking eagerly over the food that was on display. He noted the chocolate drink and darted toward it with a suddenly greedy look, scooping it up.

Sir Balladish laughed.

"Hand's off, Finistere. That is Kara's drink."

Upon hearing who it was for, the old knight handed it to Sir Balladish, who placed it on the tray close to Elise.

"I am surprised that Master Troughton isn't here," Finistere said. "I have not seen him for some time." Although he was not an actual knight, Master Troughton had served the order for many decades as a capable master-at-arms before handing the responsibility over to Nicholas Sharpe. He was not as friendly with the retired knights as they were amongst themselves, for he had not gone through their extensive training and had missed many of their shared experiences.

"He will be here shortly, for he has a good appetite," Sir Erical replied, laughing.

The group of old friends remained in the kitchen for several minutes, each poking their deft fingers toward whatever food came within their reach as they relived their youth.

Finally, Elise was called to take Kara's meal to the ward. Her eyes hovered enviously over the hot chocolate. It seemed as if everyone in the castle was eager to please Kara, and she thought how beautiful the young girl was, how strong and capable she had proved in her battle with Marius. Not like Elise at all, who slept on duty and felt awkward shuffling around in her frumpy robes.

Suddenly, in spite of herself, she was jealous.

A few minutes later, Elise opened the door to the ward quietly, eager to avoid Kara's attention.

But the room was empty.

"Kara? Where are you?" Panic gripped her stomach. She knew that Sir Amik had left the matron specific instructions that the girl should be kept in the ward. "Kara? This is not funny," she said, her voice high with alarm.

She put the tray down and explored the ward carefully. Stepping around Kara's bed, she saw a motionless guard on the floor. Her training took over as she knelt by the young man's side. She saw instantly that he was breathing steadily, though there was a dark bruise on his temple.

He moaned, his eyes fluttering open.

"The girl," he whispered. "She's gone after Theodore. She thinks he's in danger, that he's being led into a trap by the letter. She knocked me down to go to his rescue."

"What letter?" Elise asked.

"I asked her for it when I came up—said the dwarf thought it was meant to lure Theodore in. But she took it and she's gone… to a house in Dagger Alley!"

The young man tried to stand, but as he did he fell back into unconsciousness, his head dropping to the tiles.

Elise knew it was up to her. She would raise the alarm. She would tell the knights that their beautiful and headstrong visitor was pursuing Theodore to Dagger Alley. She would be the hero!

Calm yourself, Elise, she told herself. *Saradomin is the god of peace. I must be calm.*

She walked to the door, noting the hot chocolate on the tray. She hadn't had such a luxury since she was a child and the delicious taste came back to her in an instant.

She took a deep gulp of the hot drink, *to fortify myself,* she thought, and knowing that Kara was running from the castle she decided that she wouldn't need the rest of it.

On the third draught she knew something was wrong. A stinging pain erupted in her stomach and she dropped to the floor in agony, unable to cry out for help. Her tongue began swelling up, choking her, and she knew that there was only one way she could become so ill so quickly.

"Poison!" she gasped. "Someone's tried to poison Kara."

She made it as far as the door before she gave in to the darkness.

THIRTY-TWO

Kara ran across the battlements in the gloom. Two more guards had tried to stop her and she had left them both unconscious. She knew Theodore was riding into danger—she had grown up amongst the dwarfs and she knew their ways better than any guard who might write off their warnings as drunken ramblings.

But first she had to get out of the castle. The gatehouse near the moat would be too well-guarded, so she chose the only other way she could think of in such a short space of time.

She stood atop the battlements and looked down into the darkness below. Light glinted off the dark water. She whispered a prayer to Saradomin.

Someone shouted something in the courtyard. A sentry had found one of the unconscious guards. Cries of alarm erupted from the men at their posts as they drew their weapons.

Kara leapt.

She fell with astonishing speed and hit the ice-cold water. The shock forced her to fight her way to the steep bank. Voices shouted from the bridge. Her landing had drawn the guards' attention and she could see in the dim light a small body of armed men rushing out to investigate.

Kara was too far away for them to see, however. She climbed the bank, slipping twice on the muddy sides. She knew she had to get clear of the castle, aware that the knights had every advantage since the streets were unfamiliar to her.

A heavy carriage rolled by as she stepped onto the road. The driver gave the wet girl covered in mud a long stare of disapproval. As he passed, Kara jumped aboard the carriage, clinging close to its side as it carried her past the guards running in the other direction.

Within minutes the castle was in uproar. Sir Erical woke one of the unconscious guards by pouring a bucket of cold water over him. After a moment of sputtering he glanced around in alarm.

"It's Kara! She's the one who attacked me!"

"She must be found at once." The master-at-arms bellowed his orders as he hastened to inform Sir Amik. "Wake every knight, squire, and peon available. Send men out to watch the city's gates!"

Soldiers rushed across the bridge, seeking to reach the city's gates and to prevent Kara from leaving Falador. At the same time, a dozen guards rushed out to search the immediate vicinity.

"Kara does not know the city," Sir Amik said, looking intently at Nicholas Sharpe and Sir Tiffy. "That is our advantage."

"But we don't know where Squire Theodore has gone," Sir Tiffy observed. "One of our guards is missing, and two have been assaulted. Peons and squires have all poured into the city in a disordered mass. If we find her it will be by the will of Saradomin only." The old knight shook his head in dismay.

Hearing that Kara had fled, the traitor knew he had to take the opportunity. He gathered a weather-beaten cloak and headed across the bridge into the city, turning toward the Dens and Dagger Alley, to end the threat of Bryant once and for all.

As he turned a corner his unease grew, however. Something was wrong.

Was that someone following me?

He hesitated.

I cannot afford to be weak. I have lived so long and so dangerously. The boy and Kara have to die. Both of them.

As quick as he could manage, the traitor ran on, his mind set.

Theodore made no effort to conceal his presence, for he had no reason to be suspicious. He tied his white mare to the rusted strut in the wall, noting how everything in Dagger Alley seemed to reflect its reputation as a place of squalid destitution. Even the air seemed stale.

The mare was reluctant to be tied and he had to force her to the wall in order to secure her. It was unlike her to be so jumpy, he thought as he walked toward the shadowy door of Bryant's rescuer.

He knocked loudly.

"Who is it?" a man's voice called out.

"Squire Theodore, sir. From the knights. I received a letter regarding Bryant, a peon of mine?"

The door handle turned and the lock was opened from the inside.

"It is good of you to come, Squire Theodore."

The door opened, and before Theodore could react, a huge hand seized his shoulder and dragged him inside, forcing him to the floor as if he were a child's doll. He glimpsed Bryant tied to the chair, his arm bleeding.

Rolling free, he rose to confront his attacker, his hand on his sword.

A tall figure stood before him and Theodore could sense the power of his assailant.

"Who are you?" he demanded, his will faltering in the face of this enemy.

His foe made no attempt to answer. With a speed that confounded him, he hit Theodore in the stomach. As the squire cried out he saw red eyes glow deep within the hood, eyes that delighted in inflicting pain on others.

A monster's eyes.

Theodore drew his sword and lunged, the tip of the blade cutting deep into the red robe and glancing off something underneath.

Animal hide was Theodore's first thought as he pulled his arm back to deliver a second strike. But this time his enemy was ready for him. He sidestepped the blade and retaliated with a punch that Theodore could not hope to avoid. His vision blurred and his grip loosened on the sword hilt. With a groan, he knew he couldn't remain conscious.

Doric had tried hard to memorise the location of the house in Dagger Alley, knowing that he could not afford to waste any time in leading Theodore back there to confront the monster.

Now he ran through the dark streets, aware that each passing second reduced the chances of him finding the young man alive.

"If only my legs weren't so short," he muttered angrily to himself as he paused to read the street names carved into the stone walls. He ran as swiftly as he could, hopeful that he knew where he was going.

If he was right, he was less than a minute away.

The carriage driver was fond of Falador. He liked the white city's wide streets and clean thoroughfares, and he always felt a certain peacefulness settle upon him whenever he saw the castle at the city's centre.

He didn't like the city at that moment, however. The mud-stained urchin girl, dripping wet, had appeared next to him out of the darkness as silently as a wraith. She had forced him to change his route and to carry her to a part of the city about which he knew little. He prayed that his prestigious passenger, the daughter of a Varrock noble, didn't get curious and open the cabin's curtains.

"How long?" the little thief asked him.

He flogged the horses harder.

"We should be at the end of Dagger Alley in a few more minutes." He swallowed as he spoke, trying to sound calm.

"Be sure you are right this time! I cannot afford any more mistakes."

The glint in the girl's dark eyes scared him, and the sword that she held with a deadly assurance made him decide against any attempt to resist her commands.

"Yes, ma'am!" he said automatically, whipping his horses all the harder.

THIRTY-THREE

"Wake up, Theodore!"

The guttural voice penetrated his consciousness.

"Your peon needs you!" it persisted. "Wake up!"

He could just make out the shape of the tall figure standing over a whimpering Bryant. He tried to speak, but his mouth was gagged, and when he attempted to raise his hand to calm his pupil he found that he, too, was restrained in a chair.

The red eyes glowed sadistically in the darkness.

"So you are awake at last." He stepped forward, standing close. "We can do this in one of two ways, servant of Saradomin. You can willingly tell me everything I need to know about the man I hunt, or you can resist me. If you choose the latter path, then both of you will die, and neither quickly."

The single candle could not penetrate the black depths of the captor's cowl, but Theodore sensed that he was dealing with something unnatural, a foe beyond his power. He flinched as the creature's strong hands tore the gag from his mouth and the leather-like palm closed over his lips to prevent him from crying out.

"If you shout I will hurt you and kill the peon." The hand remained. "So what is your decision?"

Theodore nodded, and his captor loosened his grip, allowing him to speak.

"Let the peon go," Theodore insisted. "Then I will help you as best I can." Somehow his words sounded strong, reflecting a confidence he didn't feel.

Bryant heard the words and cursed into his foul gag, but the creature didn't appear to notice. Just before Theodore had arrived the werewolf had told Bryant that it was he who had carried out all the killings, and that he was going to kill them whether they cooperated or not. It seemed to relish the effect its words had upon him.

And now Theodore was making the same mistake he had. He was trying to bargain with something that had no intention of keeping its word.

We are lost, the peon thought. *We are both going to die here and this monster will continue to kill. Is there no justice?* Bryant was close to cursing Saradomin. Had all his years of diligent work been wasted?

And then the door shook.

The werewolf looked up at the sound, his attention drawn away from Theodore.

"Help us!" the squire shouted before the creature's huge hand clamped once more across his mouth, gripping him so tightly it was painful just for Bryant to see.

Then the door shook a second time. An instant later it flew open with a splintering *crack*.

"I've been looking for you!" Bryant recognised Doric's voice instantly.

"And now that you have found me," the monster sneered in reply, "what do you intend to do?" He thrust the gag into Theodore's mouth once more. Then he strode forward.

But Doric had years of experience behind him. He had fought numerous enemies, both underground and beneath the open sky, from goblins to trolls and darker nameless creatures. Before his enemy could take another step he launched his first attack.

A hand-axe sliced through the air toward the monster's face. Without waiting to see if it struck home, Doric yelled and charged into the room.

The traitor had only just managed to avoid the dwarf in the narrow streets that joined Dagger Alley, ducking out of sight as he observed Doric pat the white mare. He watched in surprise as the dwarf stood for a minute at the door and listened, noting how well he was armed.

He heard Theodore's cry for help and watched Doric force the door's lock with two heavy blows from his axe. Then the dwarf stepped into the semi-darkness, and the sounds of a vicious battle followed.

The traitor knew he was too old to fight either Doric or Theodore. He was turning away from the house, intending to keep watch from a safer distance, when he heard a carriage shudder to a halt on the main street. He watched in stunned silence as a blonde-haired girl jumped from the driver's seat, wiping back her wet hair and running with a confidence he had rarely seen in the most seasoned warriors.

He pulled farther into the inky shadows. The girl passed him by, unaware of his presence, heading as fast as she could toward the anxious mare that was now straining at its rope.

It wasn't going well for Doric. He was surprisingly fast, and his small stature allowed him to duck and avoid many of the creature's swift strikes, but he didn't have the chance to deliver a strong blow with his axe. He was reduced to jumping and parrying, using his weapon more like a staff to fend off the creature's frenzied claws.

The monster lunged at him and swung with one large hand. Doric stepped back and batted it away with the handle of his axe.

And he knew he had made a fatal error.

With superhuman speed the monster seized the axe-haft with its other hand and wrenched it toward him, pulling Doric toward his jaws.

Doric knew he had only one chance to avoid the knife-like teeth that were tearing at his face. He lowered his head and drove his armoured helm as hard as he could into the wide mouth of the beast, hearing it roar in frustration as one of its teeth broke.

But the werewolf did not let go of the axe. He lifted Doric from the floor, shaking the handle in an attempt to dislodge him. Then, with a second howl of frustration, he released the axe and sent Doric spinning toward the wall.

The dwarf felt glass and crockery break as he smashed against a tall dresser and fell to the floor. The dresser tottered and shuddered above him and he rolled away as it crashed over, knocking Bryant on his side.

The dwarf knew he needed help. With a single deft swing of his axe, he cut Bryant's restraints, breaking the back of the chair and giving the peon the slack he needed to get himself free.

"Run and get help, lad! Go!"

Bryant obeyed Doric's command, pulling out the small dagger that he always kept on his person to cut through his remaining bonds. The werewolf had not even bothered to search him after his kidnapping, so confident was he of his control.

And then he was free!

He ran straight for the door, ignoring the sounds of the fight behind him, ignoring everything as Doric was thrown back against the table, upsetting the sole candle and plunging the room into darkness.

The peon had escaped, but the monster cared not. He had Theodore and he only needed a short time to wrest free the information he needed.

"Can you see as well as me in the dark, dwarf?" the werewolf sneered. His own eyes worked perfectly, watching Doric as he stood wearily against the far wall, gasping for breath. He focused on the dwarf's eyes, wondering how long it would take for them to adjust to the complete darkness.

Doric could barely see anything, but while he waited for his eyes to become accustomed to the sudden blackness, he sensed the monster's rush toward him. Instinctively he raised his axe and made to step back, but his enemy had all the advantages now.

With a quick grab it seized Doric's axe with one hand and punched him hard in the face with the other. The axe was pulled from his grasp and thrown to the other side of the room. Doric tasted blood, and he couldn't hope to avoid the monstrous hand which seized him by his mail shirt and hurled him head first into the wall.

His helmet provided some protection and, still conscious, Doric stood, his hand reaching for the last hand-axe that hung on his belt.

"I can smell your blood, dwarf," the creature taunted. "Now I shall end your misery!"

Doric had little strength left to fight, and with a savage look in his eyes he lay back against the wall.

Let it end, he thought grimly, *but I promise you that you'll lose a few more teeth.*

His hand-axe felt suddenly very small.

Bryant fled into the alley, and ran straight into Kara. He saw the anger in her eyes and inadvertently stepped back, pointing toward the house as he reached for the mare's flank, preparing to pull himself into the saddle.

"It's the monster! It's inside with Theodore and the dwarf!" he cried.

"Take the horse and get help, Bryant," she instructed.

Bryant nodded, too weak with fear and blood loss to argue. He climbed into the mare's saddle and turned her away from the house, leaving Kara outside.

"Saradomin bless you!" he called as the mare began to trot away from the house. When he looked back, she had vanished, and the sounds of fighting had ceased.

He had gone only twenty yards when a voice hailed him in the darkness.

"Bryant? Is that you, worthy peon?"

He recognised the man's tunic, the four-pointed star visible on his white robe. The knight's face was hidden by a battered cloak that swirled around him as it was buffeted by the wind.

"It is I, sir!" Bryant said, dismounting and moving forward to make out the man's face.

"Come, Bryant!" The man reached out and grabbed the youngster by the shoulder, herding him into the darkness of an alleyway.

"But Squire Theodore…" he protested, suddenly on edge.

"I know!" came the reply. "Help is at hand. Now come on!"

THIRTY-FOUR

Kara was silent as she entered the room. She could hear Doric's groans, and the padded feet of an adversary stalking her in the darkness.

"A girl? They send a girl to fight me?" he sneered, and the voice was like that of an animal. She had never heard anything quite like it.

She said nothing, her dark eyes peering into the blackness around her.

The monster laughed, a deep, throaty sound. She guessed that he could see in the darkness as well as any human could in daylight.

"I have bested a squire and a seasoned dwarf tonight, my dear," he taunted from the safety of the shadows. "But I shall enjoy hurting you more than any of the others."

Kara stepped back toward the door as if she suddenly meant to run. As she did, she heard the monster move closer.

"Theodore? Are you all right?" She kept her voice steady.

The squire groaned, and she could tell that he was gagged.

"Run, girl," Doric urged.

"I came for Theodore," she replied calmly. "I will not leave without him."

Standing a few paces away, the monster was puzzled. He recognised the scent of fear on humans, knew what it did to people. But here, in this house, he sensed that this slight girl was totally unafraid.

Suddenly the girl stepped boldly forward, her sword held before her. The monster ducked backward, circling to stand a single pace behind her.

How to do it? he pondered, and licked his lips. Many decades earlier, his mother had taught him not to play with his food, telling him that he would be burnt by a mage or cut with a holy blade if he did so. But she had died a long time ago, and this girl who stepped blithely into the room did not know what manner of creature he was.

He decided to play.

He leaned forward, a claw hovering an inch from her skin.

The girl struck.

She spun on her heel, driving her blade into his body with all her strength, forcing it through the tough skin that had protected him from all manner of human weapons over the years.

He screamed with pain, his eyes widening as he felt his own blood pour from a deep wound and stream onto the wooden floor of the house. He reached down and grasped the blade with both hands, pulling it from his body, the sword's edges slicing deeply into his palms.

His strength was greater than hers, and she could not impale him further. So the girl stepped back and pulled the blade free, leaving two of his twitching fingers on the floor as she did so. Once again he screamed.

But still the girl hadn't finished her dreadful work. She brought the sword over her head and into his face.

At the same time he made for the doorway, knowing now that it was his turn to run. As he did so, the sword tip sliced across his forehead, severing his left ear. His hot blood flowed freely into his eyes as he fled into the alley, his hands pressed against his stomach to staunch the wound.

He ignored the few onlookers he passed, his face revealed now for all to see: the face of the werewolf. None dared to stand in his way, for no guard or peon was willing to confront him at the gates to the city.

Within a short time he was away from Falador, back out in the countryside, nursing his wounds in a deep hollow a good distance from any road, away from the eyes of men.

By the dim light that filtered in through the door, Kara released Theodore, while Doric retrieved his axe. The dwarf pulled a match from his cloak and held it up, giving them some more light.

"How did you do that, Kara?" the squire asked in shock.

"She can see in the darkness," Doric said.

Kara smiled wickedly.

"You are right, master dwarf," she said in his own language. "I have spent more time underground in the darkness of the mountains than above. My eyes have grown accustomed to seeing in darker places than this."

Doric bowed deeply with genuine respect.

"You saved our lives," he said in the common tongue. "I owe you a great debt."

"As do I, Kara," Theodore said slowly. Yet the change in his voice told her that he was deeply unhappy. "But you left the castle when I specifically asked you not to. You put yourself in danger."

Kara was in no mood for Theodore's lecture.

"I saved your life, as well, Theodore. The monster was after you—not me."

"I did not mean the danger of the monster, Kara..." Theodore's temper had got the better of him and he lowered his gaze in haste.

"Then of what?" She tried to look him in the eye, but he wouldn't allow it. "What else am I in danger from?"

Theodore shook his head and declined to answer. Doric lit the candle and immediately the room was illuminated with an eerie glow.

"Look at the blood!" Doric's eyes widened as he gazed at Kara's sword and the monster's blood which still dripped onto the floor.

"It is pure black," Theodore whispered, looking at it in disgust. "What creature was it? Could it be a werewolf?" His eyes turned to the dwarf.

"If legends are anything to go by, then surely so. A wolf in a man's body—ideal for hiding in a city of men," Doric said.

"We should find Bryant. He was here the longest, and maybe he can tell us more," Theodore advised, heading out into the alley.

The night air was cool on their flushed faces, the city of Falador was strangely quiet. A horse neighed and Theodore saw his mare wander into view.

"I told Bryant to take the horse back to the castle to get help," Kara said, her hand once again gripping her sword.

"Bryant is usually very reliable," Theodore said. Kara saw his worried frown. "It might be his injury—perhaps he's fainted?"

Swiftly the three companions moved to the junction of Dagger Alley.

It was the smell Kara noticed first, a sickly smell. Theodore turned his head away in sudden disgust and Kara stepped back to breathe the cleaner air.

Only Doric remained unmoved.

"It is blood." The dwarf spoke quietly, his eyes glaring intently at the narrow passage that lay before them, attempting to make out the silent shapes.

Suddenly, one of the shapes moved in the darkness, and a thin sigh sounded.

Theodore and Kara overtook Doric as they ran forward simultaneously, their weapons readied for any new foe that might assail them.

Kara knew something was wrong, terribly wrong.

The squire reached the moving shadow and gently turned it over. As he did so the small figure sighed once again.

Hot tears leapt into Theodore's eyes as he cursed in the darkness. Kara stifled a cry and dropped her sword, falling to her knees with her hands covering her eyes in despair. Doric averted his gaze and reverently removed his helm, shaking his head in anger.

It was Bryant.

His face was very pale, too pale, and Theodore suddenly realised that he'd knelt down in a dark pool of the peon's blood that flowed from a savage wound in his neck.

"I've failed you…" Theodore wept as he clasped his peon's cold hand. "I've failed you…"

Bryant tried to speak but he could not form any words, and yet another quiet sigh escaped his blood-stained lips. All he could do was to squeeze Theodore's hand with the last of his strength.

Kara raised his head and rested it on her lap, her tears falling onto Bryant's forehead.

"Lady Kara is here, Bryant," she whispered. "Lady Kara will avenge you."

His eyes took in her face, his expression suddenly happy as her golden hair teased his cheek.

"Who did this to you? Who was it?" Doric shouted at the boy. But the grip on Theodore's hand relaxed and the light in the peon's eyes dimmed.

Bryant was dead.

Theodore wept openly, and Kara held Bryant's still head in her arms, her head bowed next to Theodore's, the two young people united in their grief. Only Doric, who in his hundred years had seen death in many forms, looked farther into the alley.

He was about to speak when he decided to leave them to their grief, for another shape drew him onward. He knew what it was before he stood over it. It was a second body—a man who wore the white tunic of the Knights of Falador.

"Theodore!" the dwarf called, readying his axe, his eyes scanning the narrow streets nearby. Was there any chance the killer was still here?

The squire's sobbing subsided as he raised his head to look at the dwarf.

"It's another body! A knight!" Doric called.

At once Theodore stood, pausing only to place Bryant's hands neatly on his lap as if he were sleeping. Kara remained by the body of the boy, seemingly unwilling to leave him alone in the darkness, her hands still gently resting on his face.

"Do you recognise him?" Doric asked.

Theodore knelt at the dead man's side.

"It is Sir Balladish," he said. At his side, coated in blood, was a curved dagger.

Doric pulled the dead man's cloak aside to reveal a dreadful wound in his chest where the dagger had entered above the heart.

"What does this mean?" Doric asked in a hushed voice.

"Sir Balladish is an old knight who lived at the almshouse near the park." The squire examined the dagger closely. "And this is Bryant's knife! He was killed with my peon's weapon. Why would they fight one another?"

Their debate was silenced as several shouts echoed from the main street and the sound of running feet drew their attention. The voices were drawing nearer and in a moment the glare of torches held in the hands of a dozen men illuminated the alley and drove back the shadows. It was a group of peons and squires, alerted to the battle while in search of Kara. At their head was Marius.

"We have been scouring the city for you!" he said. "Are you all right?"

Behind him stood Sir Pallas and Sir Finistere, both wheezing heavily.

"Step with caution, Marius. We have two dead members of our order here." Theodore said.

"Who?" Marius asked, his face suddenly dark.

"Bryant is dead. My peon is dead. And Sir Balladish also." The tears came again to Theodore's eyes.

Marius clasped his hand on Theodore's shoulder, all signs of rivalry forgotten in their mutual sorrow.

"Sir Balladish is dead?" Sir Pallas asked in an awed voice.

"Slain with Bryant's own dagger," Doric said flatly.

The two old knights forced their way into the alley, holding a torch above them. Sir Finistere knelt to examine the body of his long-time comrade, then pulled something from the folds of the man's cloak.

"What is this?" he remarked in surprise, holding his hand out for the scrutiny of the onlookers.

"It looks like a Guam leaf," Sir Pallas answered. "And something is wrapped inside it. Are those Belladonna seeds?"

"I think so, Sir Pallas," Sir Finistere said, speaking softly. "Belladonna seeds—mixed with Guam leaf and other herbs—can be used to make a deadly poison."

"But why would Sir Balladish have such things on him?" Theodore asked.

Both men looked briefly to Kara with deep questions reflected in their eyes. She left Bryant's body and walked over to Sir Balladish.

"And why did he kill Bryant?" she asked, her voice edged with menace. Kara looked briefly at the man, and then her eyes looked deeper into the alley.

"We do not know that he did," Sir Finistere said. "You must return to the castle," he continued. "Everyone is looking for you. And you are not needed here. Sir Amik will have stern words for you. Theodore, take her back, for she is not safe."

"Not safe? What do you mean?" she demanded.

He brushed aside her questions by grabbing Theodore's shoulder.

"Take her back to the castle. And take a guard of men with you."

The squire took Kara by the arm and led her away, Doric following. Several peons and squires formed a cordon around them as a sombre guard. Still others remained behind to guard the bodies of Bryant and Sir Balladish.

No one spoke, for no words they knew could express the bitter emptiness they all felt.

THIRTY-FIVE

The two bodies were brought back to the castle under cover of darkness.

Theodore sat in vigil over Bryant's body in the castle's chapel, the young peon wrapped in a white cloth and laid before the altar. Soon after, he heard a noise and turned to watch the other squires walk quietly in to sit on the benches behind him, their faces downcast in grief and their heads bowed in respect.

As each passed Theodore they grasped his shoulder in a gesture of support. Never before had such a thing happened to any of them, and the event unified them in grief.

On searching the house, the knights found the body of the old woman, a well-known resident of the city who was a professional beggar.

Elise's body was discovered in the ward when the guard woke. Kara understood that the murderer had meant her to die, and not the nurse. Her chocolate drink was spilled next to the body and Theodore—his grief overwhelming him—finally told Kara the truth.

She knew now that Sir Amik had deliberately used her as bait, spreading rumours that she remembered more than she did in an attempt to draw out the traitor. She also knew that he had invited the almshouse residents to help educate the peons in place of the knights, in order to put the traitor in their midst and within range of harming her.

Kara lay in her bed, but she could not sleep. She went through the fight in her mind, wondering if she could have taken another course of action that would have kept the young peon alive.

Was I too hasty to prove myself? Was I too eager to fight, to show the knights that I am as good as they are?

In the small hours before dawn, she pondered the death of Elise and the morality of Sir Amik's actions in placing her in danger. An innocent woman had been killed by a calculating murderer. The poison's components had been found on Sir Balladish. She knew that it was accepted by many, without question, that he had been the traitor all along, and that while he was murdering Bryant, the peon had managed to deliver a lethal blow with his own dagger before collapsing to the ground of the alley.

Sir Balladish.

Had her father ever mentioned that name to her, all those years ago? If he had, she could not recall it. Of course, for all she knew her father wasn't Justrain at all.

Would they have lied about that also? Could they really be so deceitful? I have been a pawn in their game, used only to suit their purposes.

Suddenly she hated the knights and their hypocrisy. An innocent life had been taken—and she felt as if she was partly to blame. If she hadn't arrived at the castle, then Elise would still be alive. Was it her own fault that Sir Amik had used her as bait? Was it her fault that she had so swiftly and unquestioningly embraced the possibility that Justrain might be her father, thus letting Theodore spy on her on Sir Amik's behalf?

Theodore!

She thought of the young man and her affection for him, and the remembrance of how he had used that affection turned her heart bitter. He was Sir Amik's instrument. He had lied to her as much as anyone else.

Kara lifted her head from her pillow. She knew what she needed to do.

Sir Amik and Sir Tiffy analysed the situation. Neither man had visited the scene at Dagger Alley, so Sir Finistere's and Sir Pallas's reports were used to provide the facts from which they were to draw their conclusions. The two men had debated throughout the night, Sir Tiffy with his books spread before him, documenting the history of the traitor's existence since the revelations of Justrain had prompted a quiet investigation all those years ago.

"Does it add up?" Sir Amik asked. "Could Balladish have been the traitor?"

"Any of them could have been," Sir Tiffy replied sombrely. "Sir Balladish was in the right places at the right times; he had access to all of the necessary knowledge. It would not have been easy for him, however, and luck must have played a significant part in his ability to remain undetected for so long. That he should be brought to justice at the hand of his own young victim..." The old knight shook his head in wonder.

Sir Amik nodded.

"So you believe that Sir Balladish was the traitor."

Sir Tiffy thought for a moment before answering. The evidence was overwhelming. The man had been found with the components for a lethal poison on his person, a blood-stained dagger next to him, close to the body of a murdered peon. It had been Bryant's knowledge that had posed such a threat to him, for if Kara had been killed by the poison in her drink, then the peon would have come forward to raise uncomfortable questions. Only Bryant, who had delivered the herbs, knew of the deadly ingredients that came from the apothecary.

"Yes, I believe it to be so," he replied finally. "As a matter of caution, however, I suggest you send the residents back to the almshouse and away from Kara. She has suffered enough at our hands."

Sir Amik nodded, painfully aware that he had acted ruthlessly. He remembered Bhuler's long looks of reproach as his valet had guessed at the turmoil in his mind. With a pull of the red rope that hung over his desk, he summoned his valet, who waited patiently outside.

"Have them take the traitor's body away at dawn," Sir Amik ordered. "See to it yourself. Take it far away, out of the city, to a desolate spot south of here, and bury it deep in the earth in an unmarked grave."

Bhuler nodded and left to carry out the grisly instructions.

Guilt assailed Marius over how he had behaved to Bryant when the boy was alive.

Yet Bryant needed to be strong, he told himself, *and he needed to be goaded harder than the others.*

Was I wrong to do that? he wondered. *Is it wrong to drive the peons, to ensure they appreciate the harshness of life outside the castle walls? Even if it is right to do so, why did I enjoy humiliating him so much?*

He could not escape from the uncomfortable truth. He had singled Bryant out time and again to illustrate the weakness of the peon and to highlight what he perceived as Theodore's indulgent leadership. The knights were warriors. They were expected to give their lives in the service of Saradomin. They needed to be strong.

But then his actions toward Kara had reminded him that in his own way he was weak.

If I were truly strong, I would have taken her hand after our battle.

He recalled the tears on Theodore's face throughout the night as he had stood amongst his fellow squires. Theodore had been unashamed to show his grief. And Marius admired him all the more for it, for it showed his belief in himself, uncaring of what others thought.

Do I have such strength? Marius wondered inwardly.

He stood outside the ward as first light illuminated the eastern sky, unsure of how to apologise to Kara. Apologies did not come easily to him, but he knew he had to give one. He knew he had been wrong.

He knocked first and waited for a moment. When there was no answer he knocked again and the door opened under the force of his fist.

The ward was empty.

Kara was gone.

THIRTY-SIX

"Come lad, drink this." Doric held a steaming mug out to the youngster.

Theodore took it and drank without bothering to check what it was. His mind was far away and his eyes were still misty from tears.

The sound of running feet caught his attention, however. No one should be running in the chapel while Bryant lay there. Theodore rose in anger, his face flushing as his temper soared.

But it was no frivoling peon. It was Marius, and his face was full of alarm.

"It is Kara!" he cried. "She's not in the ward, and has not been seen for half an hour."

"She cannot have got out again, can she?" Doric asked, looking wearily from one young man to the other.

"Search everywhere, Marius," Theodore said. "She must not be allowed to leave the castle. Sir Amik still has questions for her." His voice faded as he issued the instruction. He didn't know exactly *what* Sir Amik wanted from her. She could provide no useful information about her past. But Theodore knew he didn't want Kara to leave, for she had become very special to him.

"Peons are scouring every room," Marius said. "If she were in the castle, she would have been found by now."

Theodore recalled how angry she had been with him at his deception, and he knew she had escaped from the castle.

"Then I shall go after her," he said. "She is my responsibility."

He moved forward, but Marius's hand stopped him.

"You cannot leave, Theodore. There is unfinished business between us. In a few days' time we have a challenge to settle. I called you a coward and you called me to answer for it by trial of combat."

Theodore met his gaze.

"I haven't time for this, Marius. Kara is everything at the moment." He made to go, but Marius's hand remained fixed against his chest. Theodore's eyes burned. "Let me pass, Marius, or I shall force you aside!"

"If you pursue Kara, Theodore, you will miss our trial and bring dishonour upon yourself. I cannot allow that."

"I am warning you, Marius. Stand aside!"

"I will not, Theodore. Another squire can pursue her."

Theodore smashed his fist against Marius's jaw and knocked him to the floor. Marius tried to stand but Theodore hit him again, bloodying his nose before racing past him, Doric following close behind.

Theodore grabbed the first peon he found and the boy looked up into his fiery eyes.

"What is the news of Kara?"

"A guard has come from the city gates. Kara stole a horse and headed east!"

Theodore ran to the stables, shouting instructions to those peons he came across. One was sent running for maps, another for a sword and shield, still another for food and water skins. He had decided to wear his leather armour rather than his full plate, for his mare would need all her speed.

Within five minutes he trotted swiftly across the courtyard, Doric hanging precariously behind him. He would not gallop on the stones. He would wait until he was out of the city before urging his mare on over the soft earth.

As soon as he recovered, Marius went to Sir Amik, and now the squire stood in the knight's study high up in the tower.

Sir Amik listened to his report.

"Theodore was right to pursue her, Marius," the knight said when he had finished. "They have a connection between them that neither understands, but they are both aware of it."

Marius shifted uncomfortably. He had not been able to stop entirely the blood that flowed from his nose. He had even wasted a few precious minutes attempting to hide his injury before reporting to his superior.

"Who broke your nose, Marius?" Sir Amik asked. Marius's eyes darted briefly out of the window, and then quickly back.

"Nobody, Sir Amik," he said earnestly. "I ran into a door in my haste to inform you of the news."

Even as he spoke, however, he knew the knight could tell that he was lying. He felt his face flush under Sir Amik's unflinching gaze.

"It has nothing to do with Theodore, does it?" Sir Amik pressed. "I know you two are scheduled to fight each other. If he struck you before the challenge, then he would forfeit the match. You would be declared right and just in the eyes of Saradomin."

Marius's face fell. He knew now with absolute certainty that Theodore was no coward, and that the grievance between them had been of his own making.

"Sir Amik," he said slowly, his head pounding and his eyes feeling a huge pressure swell up behind them, "Sir Amik, I must confess to a lie. The grievance between us was instigated by me. I accused him of cowardice, and I know he is no coward."

He breathed deeply, and the swelling behind his eyes relieved itself as tears on his face. Then he continued.

"I hadn't expected him to challenge me, but he did so, and now I admit my lie. I offer myself for the harshest penalty appropriate to my actions. I admit now what I think I have always known—I admit that Theodore is a better man than I." His words were broken by muffled sobs, and his hands shook at his sides.

Sir Amik's face softened slightly.

"A lie is a very serious offence, Marius. Deception is not a part of our order and is against what we stand for. You realise I could expel you for this?"

Marius nodded in miserable understanding.

"I have no wish to do that, however," the knight continued. "You are a good squire, perhaps as good as Theodore, but you shall have to do penance for your transgression."

"I will do it gladly, Sir Amik!" he declared.

"You will be confined to the castle; the city is off limits to you until I say otherwise. And you are to take over the management of Theodore's peons. You will train them alongside your own. I would advise you to adopt more of Theodore's methods, as well."

The squire bowed his head, and left without another word.

THIRTY-SEVEN

When he was young, Castimir had read with wide-eyed interest of the barbarian tribes that lived east of Falador.

Now he had spent the day with Ebenezer and Gar'rth, exploring the village's wooden huts and marvelling at the fine beauty of the pottery and metalwork. The barbarians offered the travellers food and ale in their great hall, an immense building with a thatched roof that stood so high that the beams were in perpetual shadow. Their belongings, left on Ebenezer's wagon, were protected by the barbarian code of hospitality to the extent that they did not even need a guard. Truly their word was their bond.

"You are quiet tonight, Castimir," Ebenezer remarked, readying his pipe.

The young wizard sighed and raised his eyes to look discreetly at the two barbarian women who stood several yards away. They dressed themselves in short fur skirts and leather brassieres that allowed the eager Castimir a good view of their midriffs. They adorned themselves with finely crafted jewellery, so subtly and intricately fashioned that Castimir could not recall seeing any finer. He examined the necklace of one of the women, the blue stone shining at its centre, and wondered how many years of practice it would take to craft something of such beauty.

He laughed quietly to himself when he recalled his first attempt to make even a simple ring while under the tutelage of his uncle. He had dropped the mould and the boiling metal had scalded him, ending his career as a craftsman that same day. Truly, he thought, the reputation of the barbarian women's skill in the art of crafting, from fine pottery to cunningly-fashioned bracelets and necklaces, was well deserved.

One of the women returned his gaze, direct and unembarrassed. Castimir choked on his drink and looked away.

"You might have insulted her, averting your gaze like that," Ebenezer chuckled.

"How did you know I was looking at her?" Castimir asked, for the alchemist was facing him across the table, his back to the two women.

"I may be old now, Castimir, but I was young once. Though I cannot remember when."

Castimir didn't respond. The journey from Taverley to the barbarian settlement had taken nearly three days. The entire way their minds were fraught with fear of the monster.

The young wizard glanced to his side and observed Gar'rth. The youth was trying hard at his lessons in the common tongue. He had mastered several dozen words that gave him a limited ability to communicate.

But his illness was getting worse. Castimir did not know what it was. It seemed as if Gar'rth sometimes became a different person. He would sweat profusely, his eyes staring at a fixed point whenever his ailment threatened to overwhelm him. Sometimes he would cry out for a minute or so, his hands clenched before him as he fought the dreadful influence of whatever it was that held him in its grip.

Years ago, when Castimir was a boy, a madman had wandered through their village. He'd had a wild look and would break into stretches of nonsensical dialogue with imaginary onlookers that only he could see, muttering about a fantastical realm called Zanaris which was ruled by a fairy queen. Castimir wondered if Gar'rth's illness was something similar—a disease of the mind.

Gar'rth was in full control of himself now, however. He also sat opposite Ebenezer, drinking water. The alchemist never allowed him to drink any ale or wine, and he had instructed Castimir that Gar'rth should never be given such, for fear that it would contribute to his ailment.

Castimir risked another discreet look at the girl whose blonde hair fell loosely down her back. His spirits fired by the ale he had been drinking, he stood up resolutely, left his empty mug on the table, and marched toward the women.

"Oh dear," Ebenezer whispered, smiling mischievously at Gar'rth.

The wizard was back in less than a minute, his face downcast and burning bright red.

"They don't like mages, these barbarians," he muttered. "They don't trust magic. I only introduced myself and asked them if they wished me to melt an iron dagger." He looked furtively at the table, avoiding the stares of his friends. "But they weren't interested."

The two women glanced over at Castimir several times in the next few moments, their faces reflecting their distrust of the blue-robed sorcerer. Castimir found himself another drink and sat down with a resigned sigh. He had taken his first sip when he saw one of the women gesture to him.

"What now?" he mused as he stood up.

"Him!" She pointed at Gar'rth who sat quietly, unaware that he was the subject of their conversation. "Is he a mage?"

Castimir shook his head.

"No," he said firmly.

"Good!" the woman said, before turning away and muttering in a hushed tone to her younger friend.

armed men searched the woodlands. He would have to leave.

It was on the western road, south of Taverley, that he had first encountered Theodore, who carried the scent of his quarry. Despite his failure to question him, he knew the best chance of picking up the trail that he had lost would be to head north, moving only at night, backtracking along Theodore's route.

He stood warily, his stomach protesting from the wound. He would remember the girl with the blonde hair. Before he returned east to Morytania and his dark lord, he would find her somewhere, alone in the wild, and have his revenge.

His hatred gave him the strength he needed to ignore the pain and slowly he made his way out of the overgrown hollow.

The wind was cold on Sulla's face, yet he could sense a change in the seasons. The daylight hours were lasting longer. It would soon be time.

Behind him stood several of his commanders, waiting.

"The monastery," he said. "Ever since I have walked this land it has always stood there, taunting us." Sulla pointed to the east, his arm stretched out across the cliff edge to a vista covered in dense woodland and bathed in the last embers of sunlight. A white tower was just visible, rising above the trees many miles away.

"You want us to sack the monastery?" Lord Daquarius asked uncertainly.

"They are our enemies!" Sulla spat back. "They are worshippers of Saradomin."

"Truly they are, but they are not worthy of our attention. They are old men in robes. If we attack them we will unite our enemies. If Misthalin becomes involved, if Varrock sends an army against us…"

"They will not," Sulla insisted. "We shall test our weapons on the monastery and then turn south toward Falador. Thorbarkin, are you ready?"

A hunchbacked dwarf made his way forward.

"Yes, Lord Sulla," the figure croaked, lowering his red cowl. His smile revealed sharp teeth that had been filed down to add to his terrifying appearance. His eyes shone eerily and were maniacally bloodshot.

"How many of our weapons do you think we will need to assault the monastery?" Sulla snarled.

He didn't like using the non-human races in his army but the chaos dwarfs who shared his faith were industrious. And they had given him new weapons that could hammer down the strongest walls and clear a path through the boldest army.

Weapons against which the knights had no defence.

"No more than five, Lord Sulla," came the reply. "Zamorak smiles on our cause."

"Then we will assault the monastery within days. We will test ourselves and our weapons against the faith of the monks of Saradomin."

"And after that, my lord?"

"After that we turn south. To Falador!"

Darkness fell over the barbarian village and several braziers were lit to keep the night at bay. From over the wooden paling that surrounded the settlement scavenging dogs could be heard, barking over the scraps of meat that some children had offered as bait to draw them unsuccessfully within range of their spears.

And it wasn't just the children who were disappointed. Returning to his wagon to gather his bedding from under the seat, Ebenezer found that one of the front wheels had cracked. It put an end to the early start he had hoped for. He knew the monastery would not be reached the night after tomorrow, as he had initially planned.

Swiftly, he returned to Castimir and Gar'rth, who were still sitting in the crowded hall.

"My wagon is going to need fixing," he announced. "The front wheel is splintered and won't last the journey north."

"I do not think we can take your wagon north with us anyway, Ebenezer," Castimir said. "The roads are non-existent and the dense woods will make it all the slower."

The alchemist sat down heavily on the bench. He hated being away from his wagon for any period of time.

The young wizard's usually humorous face darkened.

"And if our friend's condition is as severe as you think it is, time will not be on our side." He cast a swift glance to Gar'rth, who sat next to him, unaware of their conversation. "We need to find a guide, Ebenezer, or else we could find ourselves lost in the heart of The Wilderness."

Ebenezer raised his eyes and looked despairingly into Castimir's round and clean-shaven face.

"Tell me, wizard, which guide did you have in mind?"

"Well, alchemist," Castimir laughed, his eyes darting past the old man's shoulder, "do you see that woman over there? The one with the big…"

"Even I'm not so old as to miss her, young man."

"Be that as it may, it's not her, Ebenezer." Castimir exaggerated a sigh of despair. "It's the dark-haired girl who is standing next to her—the one in the pale blue gown."

"The one with the silver tiara?" the alchemist asked, glancing in the direction Castimir had indicated. "She doesn't look like one of the barbarian peoples. Who is she?" He was peering at the girl through his thick glasses, and his gaze caught her attention.

She turned her head uncomfortably.

"You're staring at her," Castimir hissed in alarm. "She's a priestess!"

Their conversation caught the attention of another traveller who had just entered the hall. A blonde-haired girl with a pale face sat quietly on a nearby bench, her back to the wall as if she were unwilling to let anyone out of her sight. She held her long sword carefully across her lap as if it was more precious to her than anything in the world.

She looked exhausted, and peered earnestly at the succulent meats that the barbarians cooked over the open fires.

"Do you think a priestess will know the way to the monastery?" The alchemist faced Castimir. "And if she does, would she be willing to help us?'

The wizard shrugged.

"That is the question we have to ask."

Castimir looked about him as if deep in thought and again noticed the young blonde who was staring enviously at their food. He watched her for a second, noticing how pretty and how sad she looked, as if she carried the troubles of the world on her shoulders.

He noted how Gar'rth watched her, too, and he was shocked to see a look of fear on his face. Or was it a look of hope? He knew so little of Gar'rth—where he was from, what his background might be—that it was hard for him to understand his expressions at a glance.

"Are you all right, Gar'rth?" he asked, placing his hand on the youth's shoulder, suddenly concerned that he was about to fall ill again.

Gar'rth closed his large hand around Castimir's in a grasp of friendship. Then he stood and made his way over to the girl in silence. She watched his approach with a distrustful stare.

He stopped before he reached Kara, taking a portion of meat that had moments before been cooked over a fire. Amongst the barbarian people a guest could eat freely in the hall, a tradition of which the girl must have been unaware.

"Food?" Gar'rth muttered, holding a clay dish out to her. He backed away, however, as he saw her eyes flash in sudden anger.

"I have no money!" she said fiercely, thinking he was taunting her.

Castimir rose to intervene.

"Young lady, I must come to my friend's rescue. He speaks only a few words of the common tongue, but you should know that guests of the barbarian tribes eat freely. As long as you do not abuse their trust, then you have nothing to fear."

The young man's round, smiling face disarmed Kara. Her flight from Falador and the theft of the horse had made her angry with herself. She was not a thief—she had never stolen in her life— but she knew she had to escape from the knights.

"Thank you," Kara said, bowing her head to the man with the plate.

He smiled at her, and returned the bow.

"It is not appropriate for a young lady to be travelling alone," the blue-robed man continued. "Forgive me, but I know my companions would be as happy as I if you would accept our invitation. Will you join us?" He extended his hand in exaggerated gallantry.

Kara accepted, and as introductions were made, she was confident that she had made a good decision. There was safety in numbers, they knew the tribe's customs, and Kara felt less threatened than when she had sat by herself.

But there was more to it than that. Castimir's joking and Ebenezer's scientific speculations were second in importance to the one called Gar'rth. She felt a bond with him, as two outsiders might come together in the face of common hostility or danger. It was as if they alone shared a secret knowledge that barred anyone else from coming between them. He could not speak the common tongue yet his actions spoke for him and his gaze never left her face.

Kara sensed a great strength in him that made him stand out against the fiercest barbarian warrior. When he returned from fetching travelling blankets from the wagon, he pushed open both of the double oak doors to the hall without pausing to muster his weight or gather his strength. It was a feat that even the largest warrior found difficult, yet here was a youth who had done it without strain.

The barbarian chatter thinned as the men saw him enter, a cold gust racing into the hall from the darkness outside. Some murmured in approval of his obvious strength, while others stared darkly at the youth.

Kara noted one barbarian woman gazing admiringly at Gar'rth and fiercely at her. She felt the woman's hostility from across the hall, cold enough to douse any warmth from the burning braziers.

She shifted her sword uneasily and tried her best to ignore her.

THIRTY-NINE

"How much longer?" Doric asked Theodore.

Theodore was not certain if the mare could go much farther. It had been a mistake to bring Doric at all, he thought, for the dwarf's grumbling was wearing down his own spirits.

His only hope was that Kara would have to stop for food and shelter, allowing him to catch up with her. He was sure his horsemanship was better than hers, and he hoped that would count for a great deal.

"Do you see those fires ahead?" he shouted to Doric, nodding his head forward to indicate the flickering flames of the burning braziers that stood either side of the main road leading into the barbarian settlement.

"Aye," came the reply. "Is that it?"

"It is. Only a few minutes now until we can rest for the night. We may even be lucky enough to find Kara here."

"Please," he said under his breath as they galloped into the village and passed the wooden paling.

Please let Kara be here.

It was the woman's jealousy that led to the fight.

She had watched Kara and Gar'rth for an hour, whispering

enviously to her friends about the blonde-haired outsider who sat with the mysterious youth.

And the woman's attention had not gone unnoticed by a young barbarian warrior who had worked hard to secure her affections. The barbarian's angry eyes focused on Gar'rth. His anger was fuelled by the mocking smiles of his fellow tribesmen.

So he emptied his ale and strode over to the travellers, his every movement revealing his hostile intentions.

He would see how well this lanky youth could fight.

Theodore lowered Doric to the ground, then dismounted. The dwarf grumbled quietly to himself as the demeaning spectacle was watched by several of the barbarian people, but Theodore was too tired to care.

"We can arrange lodging in the hall at the northern end of the village," he announced, handing the reins to the boy whose duty it was to look after travellers' steeds.

As they approached the hall, they could hear the noise of a contest within—men shouting either approval or condemnation at whatever was occurring. Then, as Theodore reached forward to push one of the oak doors open, the shouting abruptly ceased.

Something had changed.

He pushed the door inward. His presence drew no attention from those inside, and immediately he could see why.

In the centre of a chalk circle stood Gar'rth. The firelight reflected off his feverish-looking skin, which was coated in a glistening sweat. His eyes were large pools of black, and his nose was just beginning to bleed.

And above his head he held his helpless opponent.

With a roar of anger Gar'rth hurled the man into a table on which stood several men who had sought to better view the contest. The table shattered beneath the barbarian's flailing body and men and crockery fell about in disarray. In the confusion, the nearest brazier was knocked over and burning coals rolled onto the dry floor. That portion of the hall was plunged into a dull twilight, obscuring Gar'rth in the shadows.

A silence fell. Gar'rth's breathing was heavy and he slowly backed away against the wall. Much to Theodore's astonishment, Kara rushed over to him, her hand on her sword hilt, as if ready to fight anyone that dared to attack him. Beside her was Ebenezer, who placed his hand on Gar'rth's shoulder and spoke in soothing words as a father might do to his young child.

Gar'rth let out a long moan as if he were about to weep.

"What is wrong with him?" Kara whispered in fear. But the old man didn't answer her. Instead he turned to the young wizard.

"Castimir, run and find his medicine! Go!"

The wizard stood, and as he turned, he caught sight of Theodore standing at the entrance to the hall. Kara noticed his delay and followed his gaze to see the squire, illuminated by the torch that hung above the doorway outside.

Theodore was about to speak when the brazier was righted and light returned to the hall. Then he saw Gar'rth's face over Kara's shoulder.

"In the name of Saradomin!" he swore, drawing his sword.

Standing by his side, Doric grasped his axe in readiness for a fight.

Kara knew it was not her they wished to confront and she turned to look behind her, following their gaze to look directly into Gar'rth's bloodied face.

And immediately she knew why her two friends were so eager to arm themselves, for the blood on Gar'rth's face was not red. It was black—the same black blood that she had wiped from her sword just two nights before.

Gar'rth was no human. He was a werewolf.

FORTY

Ebenezer was the first to react. Before anyone could make a move or utter a cry, he covered Gar'rth's face in a wet cloth that he had held in readiness for such a task.

"Castimir! You must get his medicine at once!" The wizard, who did not understand the reason for Theodore's hostility, ran to the wagon, knowing that only the medicine could help Gar'rth now.

The blue-robed priestess approached Theodore.

"Why are you armed?" she demanded, looking angrily at Kara and Doric. "The warrior was wrong to challenge the young man but you have nothing to fear from my people."

"Did you not see his blood?" Theodore asked.

A murmur rippled through the barbarian onlookers. Gar'rth's injury had been visible only in the confused light as the brazier had been righted. That and their appetite for strong ale had caused many to imagine that the black blood was just a trick of the light.

"He is unwell!" Ebenezer said loudly. The barbarians had turned to lift the unconscious challenger from the ruins of the table, pouring cold water onto his bruised face. It was an advantage the alchemist would not waste. He guided Gar'rth outside, ignoring the suspicious looks of the barbarian priestess.

Theodore was waiting for him.

"Gar'rth is not human, Ebenezer," he declared. "He is an enemy of Saradomin."

"He is no such thing, young man. It is his choices in life that make him what he is, and by virtue of those choices he is not an evil man." Ebenezer gave the squire a contemptuous stare.

"He is a creature of Zamorak," the squire persisted. "He must be slain!"

Kara looked at him.

"Theodore!" she said tersely. "Do you not think he deserves mercy? He is no murderer—he is not like the other one." She lowered her voice as she stepped between them. "It was not his choice to be born as one of them."

"That means nothing, Kara," he said. "He cannot change his nature. He is evil, a creature from Morytania—a follower of Zamorak."

"Do the knights not believe in free will?" Ebenezer's voice was shaking in anger. "Are you nothing but simple zealots?"

"We *prevent* persecution," he protested. "We fight for the people of Asgarnia."

"At what cost, Theodore?" Kara countered. "Your precious Sir Amik was willing to risk my life for his own ends, and two innocent people died because of it!" She spoke angrily, and the painful truth in her words made Theodore's face pale.

"Now that I see Gar'rth," Kara continued, "despite what he is, I am willing to give him a chance. If anyone thinks otherwise, they shall have to deal with me." She levelled her sword at Theodore's throat.

Silence held sway. Kara did not move. Doric's eyes remained fixed on Gar'rth.

Theodore knew his principle goal was to bring Kara back.

He remembered Gar'rth from their meeting in Taverley, remembered how helpful and faithful he had been to both Castimir and Ebenezer.

Slowly he lowered his sword.

"Very well, Kara," he said. "But to encounter two of these creatures in as many nights surely means they are connected. He must know something about the monster."

"You are right," Ebenezer said quietly. "I found Gar'rth running from someone. He had been running for months, but he could never evade his hunter—not for long. I divined his true nature with the help of the druids in Taverley. Kaqemeex developed a potion that can keep his bestial nature from asserting itself, but it is not a permanent solution.

"Each time he uses it the beast returns stronger than before. Soon the potion will be entirely useless. We are heading for the monastery northwest of here. Gar'rth's only hope is that the monks of your god can quiet the demon within him."

"But why is he being pursued?" Theodore asked, returning his sword to its scabbard.

"I do not know. There are legends of Morytania that we've all heard, but we must wait until Gar'rth masters the common tongue and chooses to tell us himself."

Castimir emerged from the darkness, breathing heavily. He was not used to running and when he did so he found that his long blue robes got caught beneath his feet. More than once he had tripped himself up in this manner and now he ran with one hand holding them up above his knees.

"Here is the medicine, Ebenezer. I hope I am not too late?" He looked in concern at Gar'rth, who stood silently, as if focusing all of his concentration on keeping the growing pain inside him under control.

Ebenezer gave Gar'rth the potion, and quickly it calmed him.

His features were less contorted, and his skin coloured from its previous dusky pallor to a more healthy pink.

"Will you accompany us to the monastery?" the alchemist asked the squire as Gar'rth recovered. "Is it not for a worthy cause? A cause worthy of the knights?'

"I will come with you," Kara said, stepping back from Theodore but still holding her sword close. "Our journey lies together for some of the way and I would like to look once more upon the monastery where I was blessed as a child. It is a memory that is precious to me."

"Then I shall come also," Theodore said, resigned.

"As will I," Doric growled. "I owe you a debt, young lady. And I always repay my debts." He leaned on his axe. "But I will not take my eyes off your new friend, mind. Not for an instant!"

Ebenezer spoke, diffusing the tension.

"Thank you, my friends," he said. "Then let us return to the hall and take lodging near the fire, for it will be the last warmth we shall get under a roof for two nights."

He led the way back toward the hall, eager to avoid any more questions. For he was certain of one thing: Gar'rth's persecutor would not be far behind them.

FORTY-ONE

He stumbled through the night, oblivious to the rain and the cold, staying away from the road, stopping regularly to listen for any signs of pursuit.

He had left the hounds far to the west many hours ago, as they had picked up a false scent, following a path toward the great lake south of Taverley.

The wind had changed suddenly and he himself had picked up a fresh scent, the one he had been looking for. But it was going the wrong way.

In his hundred years of life he had grown to trust his sense of smell as a normal human trusted their eyes, and he knew at once what had happened. Gar'rth had come south, away from Taverley, passing along the very road where he had assaulted the gypsy caravan several nights before.

He cursed in his harsh language, aware that he was turning back into the country where guards and knights were still patrolling, knowing he was running back to face possible capture.

The cold taunted the stubs of the two fingers that the girl had severed. He was thankful that his body had healed itself, however Her thrust had missed his heart and vital organs, and the stomach wound had closed, leaving a vicious scar surrounded by bruised flesh.

Again he promised to make her pay for that.

A breeze stirred the undergrowth and he stiffened. A scent reached him, driven up from the ground by the rain.

He recognised it immediately and it made him very afraid. At the same time it stirred his blood.

It was the girl's scent, and she had left Falador.

He settled down into the darkness to think. He would follow Gar'rth, for the girl's scent was too weak for him to track—no more than a taunting whiff on the air. Was he becoming obsessed with her? Was the fear of her making him jump at shadows?

"I am the monster!" he called out into the darkness, shaking his fist angrily. "They fear *me*, and I fear no one!"

His words faded as he lifted his gaze to the clouded sky, and then he hid himself amongst the protective bracken.

He knew his words were a lie.

It was dawn. A fine mist had entered the village from the River Lum that marked Asgarnia's eastern border with the kingdom of Misthalin. The barbarians were forbidden by treaty to hunt on the eastern bank, for that belonged to the hunters of Varrock, the greatest human city in the world, which lay two days' travel away.

Theodore was tired. He had slept little in the warmth of the hall during the night, unable to relax while only a few yards away from Gar'rth. Doric had been the same, and they had exchanged uneasy glances many times, their hands never far from their weapons. Even the fatigue of their long ride was not enough to grant them the peace to rest.

"The barbarian trader has a mule for you, Doric," Castimir called. "I am taking my yak with me while I ride a horse. He carries my saddlebags and my books—diaries I've made of my travels. We have a good understanding and he's as sure-footed a beast as any other animal." The wizard patted the animal's flank with affection. The yak looked at him as if pondering just what trouble they were getting into this time.

"I, too, need a horse," Kara said as she took the muzzle of the one she had stolen in Falador. "I wish to return him to his master with suitable compensation. It is the right thing to do." Theodore nodded, approving.

But Doric spoke up.

"You have no money, Kara. You cannot pay for another horse, or for a man to escort this one back to Falador."

"I was intending to walk as far as the monastery, anyhow, and maybe this will be enough to buy the favour of a traveller to return the animal." She held her hand out and opened her palm to reveal the shattered remains of the Ring of Life.

"How did you get that?" Theodore asked.

Kara looked at him before replying, as if choosing her words carefully.

"A friend gave it to me, to ease my loneliness after he found me one night in the ward." She bowed her head.

Theodore knew of only one man who would dare incur Sir Amik's wrath by taking it upon himself to return the object.

"Bhuler," he rasped, but then his expression softened. "It must have been him. Saradomin bless him, for he is the true heart of our order." Tears leapt to Theodore's eyes as he contemplated the kindly valet who all took for granted.

"Kara, I shall not let you part with such an item," Doric insisted. "For it is obviously precious to you. I shall pay for your horse to be returned, as well as for a new animal to bear you." He tucked his hand into his belt, his pouch jingling with coins.

A barbarian guard strode forward before Kara could reply.

"We have chosen a guide for your journey." He pointed to where a sole figure stood obscured by the mist.

The person stepped forward, leading a horse by its muzzle. Castimir gasped, for he noted instantly the deep blue eyes and the silver tiara which kept her thick dark hair in place. It was the priestess. He felt her eyes focus on his before briefly flicking away to observe the rest of his companions. A second later and they were back on him, however.

"The priestess is to be our guide?" he asked in awe.

"She, too, has business at the monastery," the guard said. "Although Saradomin is not our deity, we respect the ways of our neighbours, and she is being sent there to learn how to write in the manner of the monks. The priestesses of our tribes are amongst the few who are capable of recording our histories and setting down our laws. She will spend the next few months learning their skills."

"And what is the priestess's name?" Castimir asked with reverence.

"My name is Arisha." She spoke softly, her blue eyes intent on the young wizard. "And I am a worshipper of Guthix."

Castimir bowed, aware that she was important to the people who had shown them hospitality, and his friends followed his example. Even Gar'rth, clearly still fighting the inner agony that seemed to grow worse by the moment, managed to show his respect.

"Once we find Ebenezer we shall be ready to leave," Doric said, taking possession of his mule and watching Kara climb easily into the saddle of her new horse.

"Where is he anyway?" Theodore asked, anxious to begin their journey.

"Here I am," the alchemist called, leading his own horse into the group. He was accompanied by a mule that he dragged behind, holding the reins firmly in his hands. The smaller animal was laden with saddlebags.

Castimir looked on despairingly.

"That's where you've been?" The young wizard clapped his hand to his forehead in exasperation. "You've been sorting out which chemicals to bring with you. Do you think that's necessary?"

"I have been sorting through my wagon for the last three hours, Castimir, as you lay dreaming in the hall. It is better to travel prepared." His eyes focused on Gar'rth, then he turned to the others. "Are we ready to leave?"

Kara nodded and turned her horse to the west, watching with a slight smile as Doric scrambled unceremoniously onto his mule, which tolerated his efforts with a stare that could be nothing but sarcastic. As the rest of the companions prepared themselves, Arisha rode past them toward the western gate.

"Dig your heels in," Theodore called to Doric, as the dwarf was in danger of being left behind. Even Gar'rth, whom animals normally feared, had taken command of his horse and goaded it westward. The youth was heavily cloaked, shivering in the cold morn.

Doric's mule had turned to face east. At a brisk trot it headed in the opposite direction to the others. The dwarf swore loudly in his native tongue.

"If he continues to shout like that, he'll wake the entire village," Castimir mused, passing Theodore on his horse with his yak's lead held tightly in his hand. Theodore turned his mare and rode swiftly after the dwarf. He took the mule's reins and guided the animal along behind him.

"He's obstinate! He's totally set against me, Theodore!" Doric protested. "No doubt he'll try and break my neck on some mountain pass." He fumed angrily as they trotted through the western gate.

"I think it a certainty if you continue to call her a he," Theodore chastised him good-naturedly, to the laughter of their friends.

FORTY-TWO

Once they were on their way, the party travelled more than twenty miles over the course of the first morning.

The land was one of gentle grassy slopes and widely-spaced trees, with hints of spring beginning to show. But a quick glance north to the hills beyond showed that the way would get harder as they progressed.

When they stopped to rest, Theodore stood silently, looking to the southwest in the direction of Falador. He imagined he could actually see the sun reflect off the white walls of the city, but he told himself that he was too far away to make it out.

He'd sent word to the knights with the man Doric had paid to take Kara's stolen horse back to the city. But still he knew they were alone, beyond any help, travelling into remote territory with a monster pursuing them.

As they took to the road again, Castimir made good use of the time by talking to the priestess. Arisha, Theodore noted, was willing to talk, eager to learn of different places and customs.

"But is it true, Castimir? Can the seers who live in Kandarin really see into the future?" she asked.

"I am doubtful, Arisha," he replied knowingly. "I never actually visited them myself. But the fishermen of Catherby seemed to believe it so." The wizard smiled. "But they also spoke of fish that could fly, and leviathans big enough to sink the largest vessel with a flick of their tail or a grapple of their tentacles."

By midday the travellers were famished and they made a halt. Each of them took the opportunity to stretch their legs and eat.

"The land will change from here on," Arisha warned them. "The afternoon will be tiring for our beasts."

It was during their break that Kara finally realised what it was that had caught Gar'rth's attention in the hall. She had unsheathed her sword and immediately Gar'rth's black eyes had focused on it. Curious, she handed it to him to see what he would do.

"It is very sharp, Gar'rth," she said softly as the youth raised it to his face, looking at the blade closely. Suddenly he lowered his nose to it and sniffed, his eyes widening in recognition.

It took her a moment to realize what that meant.

"Do you smell blood on the blade, Gar'rth?" she asked. "Is that what you recognised in the hall?" The blood of the werewolf had left a pungent scent that even she could detect, for she had not had a chance to clean her blade properly.

Gar'rth nodded.

"I wounded him, Gar'rth. He was hurt badly." She saw his eyes rise to hers in wonder. "It might be that he crawled somewhere to die."

The youth shook his head. He returned the sword to her reverentially.

The afternoon journey was as arduous as Arisha had said it would be. From the outset, the land rose steeply and the trail grew increasingly treacherous under the hooves of their steeds. Few words were spoken by the travellers.

Castimir felt weary now and spoke rarely, his concentration

set on ducking his head from any low branches and ensuring that the yak was safe on the often-sliding rock paths. Others on horses fared less well still, and Kara glared angrily at Arisha, as if blaming her for the route she had chosen. Theodore had said more than once how he wished he had brought a helmet with him to protect his face.

The alchemist, too, said nothing, his concentration fixed on the mule beside him, its saddlebags filled with chemicals.

It was after several hours, when Ebenezer urged the beast on and pulled on its rein to guide it away from a steep drop, that Castimir's patience finally snapped.

"Why on earth did you bring those things?" he demanded. "Our journey is not going to last us more than a week. Are they so important to you?"

"My chemicals are very important, Castimir," the alchemist replied calmly. "They are my life's work, and not a single hour goes by when I am not either thinking or dreaming about them."

"There's his chemistry again," Castimir said sarcastically to no one in particular. "What use are sacks of rocks when you've got magic?"

This time Ebenezer shot him a glance that made the wizard uneasy, but the old man refused to be drawn back into their ongoing debate.

They stopped near a still lake with crystal-clear waters, formed by the run-off from the melting snows high up on Ice Mountain. Unafraid of the travellers, large silver fish played near the surface.

"We should stop here for the night," Arisha announced. "It will be getting dark soon, and we have come far today. I shall gather some wood for a fire."

The priestess tied her horse to a tree stump and headed into the woods with Doric in tow, keeping within sight of the travellers.

Castimir groaned at the thought of food, his eyes on the silver flashes that caught the evening sun as the fish leapt out of the water.

"Do you think you could catch any of them?" Theodore asked, following his friend's gaze.

"When I was in Catherby I learned to fish," Castimir replied. "They look as if they could feed us all." He went to his yak and began to dig in his pack, emerging a few seconds later with a line, a hook, and several wood poles that screwed together to form two rods. "This won't take long, Theo," he boasted confidently.

Theodore's expression was doubtful.

"There's nothing like fresh fish!" Castimir yelled gleefully, running to the edge of the lake like an excited child. He handed a rod to Theodore and the two friends patiently cast out their lines.

Half an hour later their good humour had disappeared as the fish evaded all attempts to catch them.

"Maybe you should use your magic, Castimir," the alchemist said laughing.

The wizard turned to him.

"Can't you make yourself useful and light the fire?" he retorted.

Ebenezer made no reply, and busied himself preparing Gar'rth's herbal drink. Smugly, Castimir cast a quick look at Gar'rth and Kara, for the two were sitting huddled together, the young woman holding his hand in hers. Her face was etched with concern. He noticed also how Theodore avoided looking in their direction, instead staring stonily at the lake before them.

Poor Theodore, he thought. *I'd wager his duty has never felt more onerous than now. The death of the peon must pain him deeply, as must feelings for Kara that can never be fulfilled.*

Arisha and Doric returned, having gathered enough wood for their needs, and Castimir grinned as he watched Ebenezer's hesitant attempts to prepare the fire. It would not be long now until he could prove the value of his magic over the old man's science.

After a moment of watching Ebenezer's woeful attempts at starting a fire, Theodore gave a curt smile and left the lakeside to help.

"The wood is wet," the old man complained. "It won't catch."

Castimir hurriedly pulled in his line, aware that Theodore might well succeed before he'd had a chance to prove his point to Ebenezer. The wizard ran swiftly to his yak and pulled his staff from its leather straps. It glowed a fiery red in the dimming light.

Then he laughed theatrically as he approached the heaped kindling.

"Stand back!" he hollered, lowering the top of his staff to touch the damp wood. He furrowed his brow in concentration and the red light burned angrily in the knotted tip, a mysterious red flame threatening to burst from its wooden prison.

The heat rose from the glowing staff and suddenly, with a crackle and a hiss, the damp wood caught light, the fire roaring to life with unexpected ferocity.

Ebenezer jumped back with a yell.

"Get some water! He'll have the whole forest up!" The alchemist ran to the lake, wading in up to his knees before realising that he didn't have anything in which to gather the water.

"It's all right," Castimir laughed boastingly. "I have it under control now. It's a fire staff, alchemist—similar to my fire runes. I can light a room with a cosy glow or throw a ball of fire. The white wolves on the mountain near Taverley learned that to their cost."

The young wizard beamed a happy smile toward Ebenezer who, with an angry look, waded back to the land. He pointedly ignored his young friend as he moved to dry his feet near the now-roaring fire.

"Magic works where science fails." The wizard laughed

one more time for good measure, before stowing his staff and walking back to continue his fishing. His good mood was heightened by the smile Arisha gave him.

"Are you going to catch anything, Castimir?" Kara called. "We're all hungry, and the sun's warmth is fading."

"Have faith in a magician, young lady," Castimir called back, silently praying for a good bite.

"We have a fire, but nothing to cook on it," Doric mused, lighting his pipe.

"Patience, master dwarf!" Castimir called as Theodore cast his line back out

A chill breeze blew across the lake's surface, and the wizard shivered as the sun's rays failed to warm him. He cursed inwardly and wondered if any magic might persuade the fish to bite.

Ebenezer stood up and went to his saddlebags, where he hunted through the packs. After a moment his hands settled on a long tube. Gently he unscrewed the lid, releasing the faint scent of oil. He reached carefully inside.

"Stand back!" he shouted, withdrawing a thin silvery object and throwing it into an area of water where the fish were playing.

Neither Castimir nor Theodore had time to duck. A second after the metal hit the water a bright flash erupted, followed by a loud explosion that covered the encampment in a brief squall of water, as if a rain cloud had come and gone in an instant.

Castimir lost his balance and his flailing arms failed to prevent him from falling face first into the lake with a startled cry. Every onlooker stood up in amazement, Doric seizing his axe as he did so.

But the initial explosion wasn't the end of the alchemist's performance. Pieces of metal scattered across the lake, causing smaller explosions to ripple out as they reacted with the water, each in turn.

After only a few seconds the scene grew still once more.

"What in the name of the Abyss was that?" Theodore exclaimed.

"That was science, my young friend. A tube of sodium coated in oil to preserve it from the air. It explodes when combined with water. Now if you don't mind, you may gather the fish!"

Theodore glanced back at the water, and grinned in surprise. The explosion had stunned a dozen large fish that now floated close to the surface. Eagerly, he waded in and grabbed as many as he could, throwing them back to Castimir who, shivering from the cold water, laid them on the bank.

"Science, Castimir," the old man said firmly. "It has rules that are stronger than any magic. Rules that allow results to be anticipated and reproduced."

The wizard said nothing, his eyes burning angrily as he wrinkled his nose in disgust at the smell of fish on his robes and hands.

"My dear friend, Castimir," the old man added, "if the wizard thing doesn't work out, I'm sure you'll make an excellent fishmonger." The alchemist's words were followed by discreet laughter from his friends.

The young mage took a deep breath and clenched his fists tightly.

Ignore him, Castimir, he thought darkly. *Let the lunatic have his fun.* He bent down to pick up the last of the fish, and was surprised to see Arisha standing nearby. Her smile drove all ill thought from his mind.

"You'll catch a chill, Castimir," she said with concern. "Come over to the fire to dry off." He complied happily, and she handed him a bear-skin coat that was large enough to cover him from head to foot. "Wear that while your robe dries," she ordered with an amused smile. "The sun will be gone in a moment, and this high in the mountains the cold will be crisp. The fire will be the only heat we have."

Castimir accepted her offer without a word, hiding behind his yak to change. Wet from wading out to retrieve the fish, Theodore did likewise, borrowing Ebenezer's coat while his clothes dried next to Castimir's.

Later, after they had eaten their fill, drawn into a nostalgic mood by the sweet smell of Doric's pipe and Arisha's humming, the two young friends sat side by side leaning against a log in front of the fire, reflecting on their antics as children. They laughed at remembrances of the giant rats that lived to the east of Rimmington where they had grown up. Although the size of a pig, the animals had been uncommonly stupid and clumsy. Hunting them with rocks or arrows had been a frequent hobby of the children.

"They were happy times," Castimir said, and he yawned, weariness upon him. Theodore didn't answer, so he looked over to his friend, and smiled to himself when he noted the squire's low snoring.

Dreaming of the home he hadn't seen for a long time, he closed his eyes and fell into a deep sleep by the fire on the shores of the clear lake.

FORTY-THREE

Sulla sat in silence, his one good eye straining in the dim light of the torch.

He had led a small army of fifty of his horsemen and a hundred foot soldiers down from Ice Mountain the day before, but his swift progress had been delayed by the lumbering weapons of the chaos dwarfs. It had taken them all day to catch up and Sulla had used the time to issue new edicts to his troops, dispatching messengers to his spies abroad as well as liaising with the sybil.

His master plan was coming together. Crown Prince Anlaf, in command of the substantial Imperial Guard, was of great concern, but the sybil had assured Sulla of the prince's inaction. For months now she had sent terrible dreams that tormented him, making him fearful and paranoid. Without his capable command, the Imperial Guard would be unable to interfere.

Yet their neutrality was not enough for Sulla. He wanted them under his own banner, marching under his orders. The sybil, therefore, had changed her torments, offering the prince a solution.

"Zamorak," she crooned in the night time. "You must embrace him! He alone can offer you release." The words had haunted the crown prince, she insisted. He had withdrawn into his private chambers in the mighty citadel that dominated the skyline of Burthorpe, refusing to take any food and turning away his worried valets.

Sulla opened the most recent missive from the sybil and as he read it, his eye glinted in wicked delight. Tormented for many months and driven to near madness, the crown prince had succumbed to Zamorak. He had even erected a small altar to the god of chaos, secreted in his castle and accessible by hidden passages that only he knew.

Folding the document, Sulla considered the other steps he had put into motion. Kinshra ambassadors had journeyed to the neighbouring kingdoms of Misthalin and Kandarin, to ensure that neither kingdom would become involved in the coming war. The campaign would not be one of conquest, the ambassadors assured their hosts, but one designed to secure religious freedom for all. They would end the dogmatic Saradominist viewpoint that the Knights of Falador had forced on the ordinary people of Asgarnia. This was no war of plunder and revenge, and any intervention from neighbouring countries would simply endanger more lives.

Of course, Sulla thought to himself, *our ambassadors make no mention of the carefully recruited hordes of bandits and outlaws who bolster our numbers.* Nor would they divulge his plan to press the goblin tribes into action, as slaves to help in his efforts.

A movement interrupted Sulla's thoughts. The flap of his tent was pushed back by a black-clad guard.

"The dwarfs have caught up, Lord Sulla," he announced. "They will be in a position to assault the monastery the night after tomorrow."

Sulla said nothing for a long moment, his mind focusing on his new weapons and their one major drawback—they were entirely too slow.

"Very well," he said finally. "The night after tomorrow is good enough."

He had travelled as swiftly as he was able, ignoring the pain in his stomach that burned continually as he ran.

The wound was healing well—the pain was a sign of that.

The hunters who had pursued him had long been left behind. He noticed how the air had changed as he travelled northward. The scents that betrayed the humanfolk, which were usually so easy to perceive, were fewer. The population was sparser. He was back in the land of isolated farmsteads and lone woodcutters, where he knew he should feel more confident, for he was the hunter once more.

With every step he took north he swore anew that he would make the girl pay dearly for what she had done to him. No agony would be too much for her and no injury too little. He would dedicate his life to destroying her.

But without warning, the thought of the girl with the blonde hair caused him suddenly to stop. He was scared of her. For the first time in his life a human had made him afraid.

He raised his hand to the afternoon sky. The absence of his two fingers taunted him under the grey clouds, and goaded him into a savage outburst.

"I will destroy her! She shall scream my name before she dies!"

The forest's silence was the only response.

He put his head down, close to the earth, sniffing the currents that would betray any human nearby. The scent of men was present and he knew what type of men they were—barbarians. At once he realised he must have drifted farther east than he had intended, eager to be away from the men who pursued him. He recalled a map he had seen in the old lady's home after he had killed her. He had studied the map with interest, tracing the route he had taken since crossing into Asgarnia from neighbouring Misthalin. Near the top right corner, a small collection of illustrated thatched huts surrounded by high pale fencing had marked the location of the tribesmen.

There he would find his prey. Their trail betrayed them. *Both* of them, Gar'rth *and* the girl.

"I am not finished just yet," he swore. "I have both of your scents now."

He recognised the scent of the dwarf, as well, and of the squire, and it was the thought of revenge on all of them that gave him the strength he needed to overcome his pain.

"I am not more than a day behind them," he growled to himself, moving ever toward the mountain. His mouth watered in anticipation.

As their journey stretched into the next day, Ebenezer rode in silence. He ignored Castimir's jesting, which normally would have drawn him into a bout of good-humoured arguing. He had no doubt that the others knew something was weighing heavily on his mind.

But he didn't tell any of them what it was he had seen in the night, as they had slept. When Ebenezer had taken his turn at the watch, his gaze had fallen on Gar'rth, and the youth had looked more peaceful than he could ever recall, his hand resting gently in Kara's palm. The image disturbed the alchemist.

Gar'rth was suffering, growing from a boy into a man, and as such Ebenezer was certain that whatever natural instincts the werewolf race possessed, they would likely be far stronger than usual. The temptation to resign himself to his bestial nature would be near overwhelming.

And if he did, the alchemist thought sadly, would even Kara be able to destroy him? Stabbing a murderer in Falador was one thing, but he doubted that she could bring herself to destroy a friend and ally.

These dark thoughts consumed the alchemist until they reached the foothills of Ice Mountain, where the paths were seldom trodden by any folk of good will. Rarely did the barbarian peoples ever wander so far. The trees were wild and overgrown, frequently tearing at the travellers as they made their way in a north-westerly direction. Many times they dismounted to guide their steeds carefully through the long shadows of the forest, and many times they started at the sounds of creatures they could not see.

Once, a low moan echoed through the wooden boughs under which they walked and even Gar'rth paused, his eyes shining feverishly yet intelligently under the cowl that he kept permanently pulled over his head.

No one moved, and no one spoke for long, tense moments. Finally it was Castimir who broke the silence.

"What was that noise?" he asked in little more than a whisper. "Even the white wolves with their dreadful cries were not so chilling. I have never heard so unearthly a sound."

Arisha looked fearfully at the trees.

"My kin tell stories of the people who live in the trees, spirits that guard the forests and take any traveller they enslave into their magical world to serve them forever in a sleepless nightmare."

Doric grunted.

"Stories! Tales to frighten children." Nonetheless, his hand gripped his axe-haft as tightly as ever.

"Would you not have said the same about werewolves a few days ago, my old friend?" Ebenezer whispered.

No one responded.

They heard no sound like it for the rest of the day, but as the light faded, so did their mood. No one talked as they travelled, for under the trees it seemed as if the voices of men and women were unwelcome, barely tolerated by the dark gods of the woods whom men had long forgotten.

Arisha finally stopped them as the darkness became too dense for them to continue safely. When they made their camp, Theodore volunteered to take the first guard. Kara joined him, for Arisha advised that a single guard was not enough.

And to Ebenezer, who watched the two youngsters take up their positions on opposite sides of their encampment, it was obvious the relationship between them was heavily strained.

Something was wrong with Theodore. Of that, Kara was certain.

He deliberately kept himself away from her, pretending to maintain a sharp vigilance over their friends rather than let himself be drawn close enough to talk. She suspected it was only a ploy that gave him an excuse to avoid her, and after a few minutes she turned away from him, her face flushed with anger and hurt.

I will not let him see me like this, she thought as she stood at the opposite perimeter of the camp. *I have no reason to feel ashamed—his order deliberately endangered me.* But she knew her angry thoughts were just excuses. A gulf had widened between Theodore and her since their last days in Falador, a gulf built up of distrust and suspicion fuelled by his superiors' deliberate attempt to expose the traitor.

She knew Theodore had been powerless in their machinations and she wanted him to know that. But if he wasn't willing to listen, then he would have to wait a while longer before she told him.

The moment he had caught up with her in the barbarian hall, Theodore had known instantly that there was something between her and Gar'rth. As a result, he found himself resenting the cursed youth. Kara had stood between them, and even threatened to fight him for Gar'rth's life.

The squire couldn't understand it.

Yet while he was growing envious and wary of Gar'rth, he also harboured a deep sympathy for him. He knew it wasn't his fault that he had been born of a race that had behaved so wickedly and with such avarice that legend said they had become wolves. He recalled with sadness how happy Gar'rth had been, after he had thanked him when they had first met in Taverley.

So much had happened since then.

No, it wasn't Gar'rth's fault, nor was it truly Kara's. But in his current mood, Theodore had no wish to be the first to breach the gulf between them, which all the time grew wider.

FORTY-FOUR

It towards midday of the following day when the companions saw the monastery for the first time.

The walled building was shaped around a large rectangular courtyard which was dominated by soothing fountains and well-kept gardens. *If serenity dwelt upon the earth*, Castimir mused philosophically, *it did so here, even more so than in Taverley*.

The monastery had been constructed many years before. A long-dead king had built it as a civilized outpost as he sought to tame The Wilderness, but he had died before he could embark upon his expedition, leaving the monastery behind for the worship of Saradomin.

The brown-robed monks welcomed the travellers. A young man who introduced himself as Brother Althric led the companions into the courtyard.

"Is your friend unwell?" he asked, rubbing his hand over his tonsure to stave off the afternoon sun.

Ebenezer answered as he helped Gar'rth from his saddle.

"He is the reason we have come. He is ill, and I have here a letter from the druid Kaqemeex of Taverley, requesting your help. It is addressed to Abbot Langley himself."

Brother Althric took the note.

"The druid is known to us. I shall pass this on immediately."

Out of all the travellers, the most profoundly moved was Kara. Of that she was certain. She led her horse away from the others and looked about at the high white walls and blue stained-glass windows with an overwhelming sense of recognition. This was the place to which her father had brought her, years earlier.

"I have been here before, Theodore," she said excitedly, forgetting their feud, as the squire took her horse to lead it to the stables at the northern end of the courtyard. "With my father, when I was blessed as a child by Saradomin. I wonder if the monks remember him?"

"It was a long time ago, Kara," he replied. "Woodcutters and hunters in these parts regularly travel here to offer the monks fuel and food, and in return the monks care for the sick and dying."

Arisha had heard their conversation.

"Do you forget the reason for my journey, Kara? I am here to learn their art of writing so that I may record the songs and spoken histories of my people, else we stand to lose them forever. The monks at this monastery keep records of their actions, a skill I am here to learn."

"And you think they will have a record of my father bringing me here?" Kara gripped Arisha's wrist in sudden excitement.

"I think it likely," the priestess admitted. "The monks are assiduous in their duties, and a young child brought to be blessed would be a noteworthy occasion." Tears came into Kara's eyes, and Arisha placed a hand on her shoulder.

"They might have recorded my name." Kara wept openly in hope. "They might have recorded my true name and the names of my parents."

Was my father truly Justrain? Am I the daughter of a Knight of Falador?

Her thoughts were interrupted by Brother Althric, who had

returned to inform Ebenezer that the abbot was willing to help as best he could. Only when Kara's joyful sobs had subsided did she ask about the records.

"We do have records," Brother Althric said. "A girl brought to receive the blessing of Saradomin would indeed be recorded in our archives. It will not be a quick search, however, for our records are many and we do not know the exact year. It will require at least several hours." Kara thanked him sincerely.

What are mere hours, after wondering for so long.

The travellers were made welcome after that. They were invited to attend lunch with the monks in a large hall of stone that kept the heat of the day outside.

"They didn't ask us to relinquish our weapons," Castimir observed curiously. "I would have thought the monks of Saradomin would be against permitting any such things on their land." He mused as they stood at their table, waiting for the entrance of the abbot who would bless the food they were about to eat.

"That is true on the holy isle of Entrana, but here, so close to The Wilderness, it is wise to arm yourself," Theodore whispered as the holy man entered.

The abbot raised his arms toward the ceiling and began his prayer, a sonorous chant that lasted no more than a minute. As he concluded the monks took their seats amid a jostling of wooden benches that were moved from under the long tables.

All save Gar'rth were ravenous from their journey, but despite her hunger Kara was growing impatient. Her heart beat quickly as she realised that after years of not knowing her true name, she was finally within reach of discovering who she was.

Brother Althric sat with them, talking with Ebenezer about Gar'rth's deteriorating condition, and in the brightness of the dining hall it was exceedingly obvious. Over the course of their journey he had visibly altered. His skin seemed darker and his eyes more bloodshot and feverish.

"He is not an evil man, I can tell that," Brother Althric said earnestly. "This monastery is guarded against creatures of Zamorak, although that—alas—does not include his human servants."

"Gar'rth is not of this land, brother. He hails from Morytania." Ebenezer whispered the words. "And neither is he human."

Brother Althric looked suddenly fearful. He hadn't read the letter that Kaqemeex had sent and, to him, Morytania was very far away, its inhuman inhabitants regarded as legends and nothing more.

"Do not worry, my faithful friend," Ebenezer said slowly, resting his hand on the monk's arm to prevent him from acting rashly. "He is our friend. And like you said, creatures of Zamorak cannot gain entry here."

"He is s-still an innocent then," Brother Althric stuttered. "If he h-has refused to take an innocent life, then his pact with Zamorak is still unconsummated. His will is still his own, untainted by the influence of chaos."

Without warning Brother Althric seized Ebenezer's arm with sudden ferocity, his eyes glinting. "He could still be saved! We can deny Zamorak mastery over his soul. We must waste no time—after lunch we shall set about exorcising the evil inherent in him."

While Kara knew that Gar'rth's need was greater than her own, she could not help but feel disappointment as the travellers were led to a private room to speak to the abbot about the exorcism. Her mind was in turmoil over the records that she was certain held the key to her name, and that of her father.

The abbot confirmed what Brother Althric had said.

"We shall carry out the ceremony at once," he announced. "Brother Althric has already begun to fetch the necessary items.

It is indeed a blessed miracle that you were brought here." The old abbot's grey eyes looked affectionately at Gar'rth. "Never in all the annals of our order can I recall such a situation. Surely it is a herald of something greater happening in the heavens, something that we mortals cannot perceive. Such a triumph over Zamorak by our blessed lord!"

He took Gar'rth's hand in his own and rested his forehead on it, as if he were paying homage to a direct emissary from his god. Standing erect again, he turned to leave, proceeding down the hallway to a set of stairs.

They followed the excited abbot to the chapel on the second floor where the ceremony was to be carried out. Brother Althric was working with a younger monk, similarly attired in modest brown robes. The abbot spoke to the newcomer, and as he did Kara's heart leapt.

"Brother Jered, would you please escort our emissary from the barbarian tribes, and young Kara-Meir, as well, to the archives? They can begin the search in our records, for it will be good experience for the priestess."

"I shall not leave Gar'rth in the hour of his need," Kara said. Standing next to her, Arisha nodded in agreement.

"But what of your true name, Kara-Meir?" the abbot persisted. "What of your father's name? Do you not wish to seek them in our archives?"

"I will not leave Gar'rth," Kara replied firmly. "The records have been here for many years. They can wait several hours more." Her mind was unchangeable.

The abbot smiled knowingly. "That is good. Having his friends near will help Gar'rth in the exorcism."

Theodore leaned toward Ebenezer, his face dark.

"What if this doesn't work?" he whispered. "What do we do then?" His hand rested on the hilt of his sword. "He will only be a danger to himself and to others. There is no alternative."

Ebenezer lowered his head.

"You must have faith, young man. Faith in whatever god you believe in. Even a man of science knows that."

The abbot began his chant.

Gar'rth was restrained by thick ropes, bound to an iron chair that sat inside a holy circle drawn on the floor. He faced the stained-glass window with the light of the sun shining directly into his face. As a cloud moved across the chapel window, it seemed to the onlookers as if his face had suddenly become inhuman, twisted and savage, the visage of a true beast.

But a second later the cloud moved on and the sunlight revealed a weary and pale Gar'rth, but the Gar'rth they knew, wracked by pain and hungry for something he knew it was wrong to take.

The abbot's chanting continued as Brother Althric lit the incense and set it burning slowly from four golden stands. At one point the monk stepped forward and wiped a cloth soaked with holy water across Gar'rth's forehead, provoking a sudden change in him. He became a screaming maniac, his face contorted in a rage that was devoid of any reason or humanity.

This was the beast.

Gar'rth's rage lasted for just a minute before the holy water steamed off his forehead. As it did so, he returned once more to his former self, sweating profusely and gasping for breath.

"This will take some time," the abbot said sombrely, closing his eyes in concentration. "He is farther gone than we expected, and it may even be too late. When we continue none of you must step inside the holy circle—for Zamorak will try hard to maintain his hold."

"It will get far uglier from now on," Brother Althric said as the abbot began to chant once more.

FORTY-FIVE

Sulla watched the powerful figure dressed in torn robes that were so ill-kept they no longer had any distinguishable colour. The man stood alone, no more than a hundred yards away, on a small rise to the east, barring their way to the monastery.

Sulla was disturbed by the man's ability to appear seemingly at will out of the undergrowth, evading his scouts and bypassing his patrols. So far he had done no harm, but Sulla did not like to be made a fool of.

"We have been unable to catch him," the Kinshra scout said.

"Can't you shoot him with an arrow?" Sulla growled.

"We have tried that, my lord. But each time he vanishes again into the undergrowth. His ability to hide is unnatural—even the horses daren't go near him."

"Then I shall go to him alone." Sulla mounted his horse in a single deft movement and trotted slowly toward the lone figure who stood by a dense copse at the top of the rise. He didn't ride straight to him, but as if he meant to pass him by. As he began his ascent he closed the visor on his helmet. No man he had ever met had been able to suppress their surprise at suddenly witnessing Sulla's mutilated face.

The closer he got, the more he had to wrestle to maintain

control over his animal. The horse pulled to get away, but ultimately gave in to its master, its eyes wide with fear and foam flecking its lips.

The figure did not move as Sulla approached him, and the leader of the Kinshra did not call out. He rode within twenty yards of the man and still neither spoke. Sulla could sense the power emanating from the mysterious stranger.

"You are a follower of Zamorak?" The guttural voice sounded from inside the cowl, and the tattered man looked up to reveal two shining red eyes in the darkness of his hood.

For a brief second Sulla was uneasy, and his hand tightened on the hilt of his sword.

"I am Sulla, lord of the Kinshra, followers of Zamorak, feared throughout Asgarnia and renowned throughout The Wilderness."

"I have never heard of you. And I don't fear you." The words were said without malice or sarcasm.

The brutal honesty took him by surprise.

"Then I would say you are a fool. I have an army only seconds away."

"That is more than enough time for me to kill you, if I wish."

Again, the matter-of-fact tone disarmed the Kinshra lord. With a quick movement of his gloved hand he unclasped the visor on his helmet and raised it, staring at the robed man coolly as his marred features were exposed. He noted with satisfaction that the red eyes widened slightly in surprise.

"Many people have said as much," Sulla replied. "A few of the more foolish have tried. But you are no normal traveller. Why have you avoided my scouts and stalked my army?"

"To know who you are, lord of the Kinshra," the figure replied, his composure quickly regained. "I am not of this world and I have been hounded by the followers of Saradomin for several days now, driven from Falador while I pursued what

I was sent here to retrieve. It was important that I knew who you were before I approached you. But you have no reason to fear me, Lord Sulla, for I too am a follower of Zamorak. What I seek has taken refuge in the Saradomist monastery not far from here—a place I will not be able to enter."

"Holy barriers mean nothing to men, regardless of their god. Following Zamorak is a choice but not a destiny for us. You may join us, for we are marching on the monastery. But tell me where you are from, and let me see your face."

"I am from Morytania," the figure said, lifting hands which had remained hidden under the cover of his long robes. "My name is Jerrod."

Sulla noticed instantly the two missing fingers, the long claws and the hair covering the back of his hands. And when the cowl was pulled back to reveal his face, the lord of the Kinshra was greeted by the face of a fiend.

Sulla simply smiled in his peculiar way, and then, as he dismounted, he laughed.

FORTY-SIX

The exorcism had reached a horrific stage. A loud moan came from Gar'rth's open mouth, a chilling sound that had lasted for half an hour. A brisk hot wind swept up from inside the circle.

"It is the anger of Zamorak!" Brother Althric yelled against the wind. "He wants to keep Gar'rth for himself!"

The moaning grew. As it did, the wind roared and the light faded.

Theodore had never in his wildest imaginings dreamed of such a scene. To him, it represented everything he fought against—the domination of a being by Zamorak, the evil with which Gar'rth had been infected, the conflict in his soul.

"Fight it, Gar'rth!" he shouted. "Do not give in!" He was about to shout further encouragement when something *moved*… just beneath Gar'rth's skin. "What in the name of Saradomin is that?" he cried, glancing sideways to Castimir. He noted then how pale the wizard's face had become.

"This is not magic, Theo," Castimir said, his voice catching in his throat. "This is a contest between the gods about which I know very little." He gave a sudden cry and covered his mouth with his hand.

Theodore looked at once to Gar'rth. There *was* something

moving under his skin, pushing out from inside him, like a beast trying to escape. The shape of a large clawed hand appeared in Gar'rth's chest, beneath the stretching skin, before suddenly disappearing again.

And it was not alone. Dozens of other claws and wolf-like impressions were erupting across his body as Gar'rth's dark heritage fought back against the commanding chants of Abbot Langley. A thousand contorted visages in screaming agony were outlined in the youth's undulating flesh. Each disappeared as swiftly as it had come, only to be replaced an instant later like ripples on a lake in a rainstorm.

"What are they?" Kara asked, her fear evident in her tremulous voice.

"It is Zamorak's power," Brother Althric said hoarsely. "That is Gar'rth's heritage—it is what he is, and that is what we are trying to rescue him from." He spoke loudly, stepping to Kara's side. "You can do nothing but pray for him now, and give him words of friendship and encouragement." She reached out, and the wise monk caught her wrist in a suddenly tight grip. "But you must not cross into the holy circle. If you do that, he shall be lost, and so will you. You must promise me that, Kara. You must all promise me," he demanded, looking at each of them in turn.

They nodded their assent, and the abbot's voice rose still louder against the raging winds which threatened to extinguish the candles that Brother Althric had lit to aid them. As the abbot shouted, Gar'rth gave a hideous cry, straining at his bonds with all his strength.

But it was no longer a man who was restrained in the holy circle. It was a werewolf.

All about him lay pieces of human skin, as if they were discarded clothes in which the wolf had dressed himself in order to masquerade as a man. His entire body was coated in shaggy hair which hung wildly about his suddenly massive frame, for

the beast was nearly twice as large as Gar'rth had been in his
human form.

From his face, two huge red eyes glared out at the onlookers,
focusing on Kara in particular.

Kara could feel the evil presence conquering her will, and she
struggled to resist it. With a stumble she stepped forward, her
hands reaching out again to Gar'rth, offering pity and comfort.

"Oh Gar'rth! I'm sorry..." she began, but before she could
utter another syllable she was roughly seized and pulled back.

"It is not Gar'rth, Kara!" Brother Althric yelled. "That thing
is one of Zamorak's servants sent here to prevent us from saving
him. It is a creature from the Abyss, intended to lure one of his
friends across the holy circle and to their doom. And it would
be Gar'rth's doom also. For your blood would have driven him
beyond our power."

Hearing Brother Althric's words the wolf creature laughed
contemptuously, an animalistic sound that carried no humour.

"Fool!" it growled. "If I do not succeed, then another will
come. Even now he is near, and by nightfall he shall turn your
souls over to me." The creature gave another savage laugh and
then, as the wind suddenly slowed, they saw once more that
Gar'rth was at the centre of the circle, still bound to his iron
chair and still wracked by the endless agony.

Throughout the afternoon the conflict continued. No more
servants of Zamorak appeared after the wolf creature, and yet
the abbot became increasingly strained. It was early evening
when they ended the exorcism. A small pool of black liquid lay
at Gar'rth's feet. It was an oily substance and the abbot told his
fellow monks not to touch it.

"It has been expelled from Gar'rth," he said with an exhausted
sigh.

"Then it is done?" Ebenezer asked. "Gar'rth is cured?"

The abbot looked away, pity on his face.

"No," he said. "It is not done, my friend. Gar'rth is too firmly under the influence of Zamorak for me to drive out the beast entirely. But we have restored his will once more, giving him control over his nature."

"Yet how long will this last?" Theodore asked. "What shall we do when it comes once more to possess him?"

The abbot looked at Gar'rth, who was being untied from the chair by the gentle hands of the monks. He was exhausted, his eyes closed in deep sleep.

"It might never come to possess him again," came the response. "We might have driven enough of it from him that he can always remain in control of his actions. We will know nothing until he wakes." The abbot looked at each of them in turn. "Brother Althric shall guide you to your rooms." He bowed as they left.

The monk guided them through the dimly-lit corridors to a set of rooms in the eastern wing. Their belongings had already been laid out for them. Even Ebenezer's chemicals were displayed, but for once the alchemist showed no interest in them.

Yet Kara refused sleep. As soon as Gar'rth was resting under the watchful eyes of her friends, she sought out Brother Althric and asked about the records. Theodore went with her, and although the two had yet to make their peace, she offered no objection.

Despite his own fatigue, the monk took them to a room filled with books and documents of every shape and size.

"We have set aside records dating from the year 148 to 156 of the Fifth Age," he explained. "That should capture the time when your father brought you here to receive the monastery's blessing, when you were a child."

Kara could not resist a hopeful smile and for the first time in many days she looked happily at Theodore, forgetting her anger toward him. Theodore smiled back.

FORTY-SEVEN

Fatigue was the victor, and Theodore stumbled away to his bed, hardly able to stand.

Yet still Kara refused to sleep. She remained, alone throughout the night as the wind howled down from Ice Mountain and swept through the corridors of the monastery.

She stared at the pages for hours, rifling through the calligraphic records in awe at the skill of their authors, for each writing was the work of an artisan. She read and reread many of the pages. Never before had she taken such a simple joy in reading.

Once she nearly cried out, for she read about a local man bringing in his child for the blessing of Saradomin. But her hope was short-lived when she saw that the child had been a boy. With a patient sigh she turned the page to continue, her mind blocking out the four other volumes she had yet to examine.

But eventually reading the fine writing by spluttering candle light took its toll, and she found herself squinting heavily at the text before her. She pinched her eyes to drive away the fatigue, but it was not enough. With another sigh she stood up, stretching her tight muscles, deciding that it was time to return to her room—for it was already dawn.

Kara took the candle and left the archives, shutting the door firmly behind her. For several hours she had heard no sound that indicated any other living person, and the silence unnerved her. In such a place it was easy to believe in ghosts.

She had gone only a few yards when she heard the padded feet of a monk. He was followed by a second man, and Kara heard them speaking in low voices, their concern easily apparent from their anxious tones.

"Who are they?" asked the first man. "What do they want?"

Kara extinguished the candle before the light could give her away. There was something in their voices that made her uneasy, and somehow she suspected it was best to hide her presence.

"I do not know—but they have surrounded the monastery," replied his companion. "There are torches being brandished at every perimeter. We must wake the abbot!"

At once Kara's mind screamed a single word.

Kinshra.

It had to be them, she thought. Only they had the strength and daring to assault a monastery. The roving bands of thieves and outlaws who dwelt in The Wilderness were not organised enough. But the Kinshra, Kara realised, with Sulla at their head, were capable of anything.

She raced to wake her friends.

"We are ready, Lord Sulla," the chaos dwarf hissed with anticipation. He squinted up at his master in the semi-darkness of dawn, the light of the flames making him look even more deformed than usual.

"Then begin the bombardment!" the lord of the Kinshra ordered. "Let us see what these new machines can do."

The chaos dwarf gave the order and at once the five troopers standing above the heavy iron weapons lowered their burning torches onto the fuses.

Scarcely a moment later an immense roar perforated the silence of the night. Each of the iron carriages discharged a great plume of acrid smoke as they leapt, bellowing flames from their barrels.

Sulla's ears rang from the noise. He motioned the dwarfs to reload their guns and fire again.

Kara was entirely unprepared for the explosion. Before she could react, she was knocked to the floor as the roof collapsed, showering her with brick and timber.

"It must be a dragon!"

Castimir's voice reached her where she lay, and she groaned and coughed as Theodore, his leather armour already strapped on, came to her aid. He grabbed her by the hand and pulled her roughly to her feet. Their eyes locked. She was ready—even eager—for a fight.

"We cannot fight dragons, Theo!" Castimir yelled in distress.

"It is no dragon," Ebenezer shouted. "It is a perversion of science." All around them the many cries of "Fire!" increased in urgency.

"We must gather our horses," Arisha insisted.

"You would suggest we flee?" Theodore said, his face darkening.

"There are too many of them," Arisha told him. "And the monks are not warriors. We must save those we can and leave this place."

"She's right, squire," Doric said, his head appearing from behind the door frame to his room. "This is no mere band of outlaws—these men are organised. Sir Amik and Falador must be informed."

Before Theodore could speak a second eruption sounded from beyond the monastery's walls, and immediately several chilling whines came from the night sky.

"Get under cover!" Doric shouted, seizing Kara by the wrist and pulling her into his room, forcing her to shelter against the stone wall. The others followed and within seconds all were packed so tightly they could not move.

"If the shell comes through the roof and into this room…" Ebenezer looked fearfully at the low ceiling.

Feet sounded outside the door as a monk ran by. In the very same instant the corridor shook with an explosion and the door to Doric's room was wrenched off one of its hinges as dust and smoke swept inside.

"We have to get out of here," Castimir shouted. The wizard ran to the oak door, but its distorted shape meant that he could not move it an inch. Theodore moved to help, and the two youths put all their weight into forcing it aside.

It didn't work. The one remaining hinge, twisted by the force of the explosion, held the stout oak door in place.

"We'll suffocate with all this smoke coming in," Ebenezer shouted. The corridor was burning. Soon the flames and heat would finish them.

Gar'rth pushed past Castimir and gave all his strength to the door, with Theodore straining at his side. The squire coughed and brushed the tears from his reddened eyes.

"It is no good. We cannot get out."

"If I had room to swing my axe I might be able to break it," Doric muttered. "But there is not enough time."

"Castimir," Ebenezer wheezed, his head close to the wizard, "in the barbarian hall when you offered to melt that knife—can you melt the hinge?"

The wizard nodded grimly. He looked hard at the metal hinge that so completely denied them their freedom.

His hands delved into one of the many pouches at his belt. Kara noted how he had organised his pouches so that each one contained a different type of the mysterious rune stones that he

needed to control his craft. In a few seconds Castimir held five
of the small pebbles in his hand, four with a fiery red engraving
on them and one with an obscure green symbol that she had
never seen.

Castimir focused on the hinge, setting his jaw against the
doubt that flickered briefly across his expression.

His hand opened to reveal the stones in his palm, stones
that immediately began to dissolve into a viscous liquid which
blended together. Theodore, standing closest to the hinge,
pushed himself away with a sudden cry as heat radiated out
from it as if it were a coal in a furnace.

Within seconds it was glowing red. With a sudden *crack*, the
weight broke the weakened metal and the heavy door crashed to
one side, clearing their path into the corridor.

"You did it, Castimir," Theodore shouted gleefully. "We must
get to our horses."

They ran out into the burning corridor and were greeted by a
sight that destroyed their sudden burst of optimism. The monk
who had run past their room at the time of the explosion lay
before them, his lifeless body shattered and torn.

"If we had been out here when that went off..." Ebenezer
looked to Doric.

"It was just dumb luck," the dwarf said. "We should take our
weapons, for we may need to fight our way out," he suggested.

The company braved the flames to leap back into their own
rooms and collect their most prized possessions. Castimir
emerged with his fire staff and knife, Ebenezer the chemical bags
which he struggled to haul onto his back, as if he were the mule.
Kara took her father's broken ring and the adamant sword.

They made their way down the stairs and out to the
courtyard, where the monks were busy with buckets of water,
trying to combat the growing fires which so far were restricted
to the eastern wing. Though it was morning now, thick clouds

hampered the sun's attempts to light the landscape.

A desperate figure lunged toward them from the flames, his face blackened by the smoke. It was Brother Althric.

"Abbot Langley is injured," he said frantically. "He is unconscious. What are we to do?"

"I will go to the abbot," Arisha said. "The rest of you prepare to defend the monastery and gather the monks for a breakout." No one questioned the priestess, for she displayed a calm wisdom from which each of them drew a measure of courage.

The companions gathered the monks near the stables in preparation for a swift escape. But as Theodore finished explaining Arisha's plan, the weapons of the Kinshra sounded again. The fearsome whining from high above made everyone look up in cold anticipation.

"Here we go again," Castimir muttered grimly.

Everyone dove for cover.

FORTY-EIGHT

"The mine is ready," Thorbarkin hissed. His excitement was apparent in every facet of his person, from his wringing hands to his manic smile and shining eyes.

"Then detonate it," Sulla ordered without hesitation.

The chaos dwarf bowed and scurried away into the violent darkness. The wind had changed and the smoke of the burning monastery was blowing in their direction, carrying with it glowing embers and the smell of explosives.

"When do I get to join in?" The unearthly voice came from behind Sulla's shoulder.

Several of his bodyguards stepped fearfully aside. They hadn't even noted the werewolf's presence so close to their master.

Sulla remained unconcerned.

"We need to get you across the holy barrier, my friend. The raiding party have instructions to desecrate the entrance with innocent blood. Will that allow you entry?"

"It might. A holy barrier is usually associated with some structure or place, such as a wall or a river. If the wall is breached, then it might be enough. But remember, the youth is mine. Gar'rth is his name. He must not be harmed."

"Why is he so important to you?" Sulla asked.

Jerrod's eyes narrowed.

"Gar'rth is my nephew," he replied, his voice low. "He dishonoured his family and fled from our homeland, and it is my task to ensure that he is returned."

"And what of the others?" Sulla asked, eager to unleash his soldiers.

"The girl is also to be handed over to me, for she has caused me great injury." The werewolf held his hand in front of Sulla's face and again the lord of the Kinshra noted the missing fingers.

"She did that to you?"

"She got very lucky in Falador," Jerrod growled. "I was playing with my food, and she must have heard me in the darkness." He pulled his long sleeve over his hand. "She should not have been able to see me, much less strike as she did."

"I thought normal blades couldn't harm you?" Sulla asked suddenly.

"Not unless they are wielded by a strong or skilled enemy, but she doesn't wield a normal weapon. It is a stronger and sharper blade, and could cut through most armour with ease."

Sulla thought back to his encounter with the blonde-haired girl who had ambushed his men. She had fought with ferocity, and the sword she had used had easily cut through the armour of his soldiers. Could it be the same girl?

Could this be the girl the sybil has warned me against? he wondered grimly. *The one who invades my dreams?*

"Tell me, my friend, this girl—what exactly does she look like?"

Ebenezer's head pounded from the blast. His vision was blurred as he looked for his companions, peering through the murky light. One by one they crawled swiftly from under whatever protection they had found.

The alchemist himself had ducked behind one of the

fountains, for his heavy pack and his aged limbs had not allowed him enough time to find anything better.

And he had been lucky. He had been so lucky he laughed hysterically. A shell had landed a short distance from him, impacting in the soft earth of a once-pristine flowerbed, its fuse sputtering wildly. Ebenezer had done the only thing he could think of—he had suffocated the flame with a clod of damp earth, holding it tightly over the burning fuse. And it had not gone off.

A moment later, a second shell had landed directly in front of him, splashing into the fountain and spraying his face with water. It, too, had failed to detonate.

"I'm living on borrowed time," he breathed to himself as he attempted to pick up the shell that had landed by his side. It was heavier than he had expected, and *hot*. To overcome the heat he wrapped it in a discarded cloth that he retrieved from the nearby body of a monk who had been far less fortunate.

Castimir ran to his side and pulled him towards the safety of the stables.

"The monks are ready to go," the wizard shouted.

"The town of Edgeville is closest," Ebenezer answered. "If we can break out then we should turn east. It is a day's journey away."

Suddenly a huge explosion sounded from the southern end of the courtyard. The wooden gates were blasted off their hinges, sending deadly splinters flying in all directions.

As the smoke cleared a single rider appeared through the haze. A large black-armoured warrior on a heavy warhorse stared at the survivors. With a cry, he lowered his visor to shield his face, digging his spurs into his horse as he did so. At once the animal leapt forward and galloped into the courtyard. At least a dozen armoured warriors followed their leader, with as many men again running in behind them.

"What are we going to do?" Castimir asked in a panicky voice.

"Scatter!" Doric said quickly. The dwarf didn't wait for the others to respond—he swiftly ran to the cover of the stables, his efforts inspiring action in his companions.

Castimir's fear forced him to act quickly. Unconsciously his hand dipped into a pouch on his belt, then another. He hurled a ball of red flame at the foremost Kinshra warrior. His aim, although inaccurate, caused the man's horse to turn suddenly in fright, confusing the charge behind. His magic had bought them valuable time.

"They aren't attacking us," Theodore said, watching as the Kinshra rounded up two prisoners near the wreck of the gate. "What are they using the monks for?"

The answer came a second later. The monks were herded to the entrance. Although Theodore's sight was obscured by the Kinshra horsemen, he could tell by their savage cries and the vicious thuds of heavy axes that the monks had been slain. He held a hand to his mouth as comprehension sank in.

"We are going to have to fight for our lives," he shouted to his friends. "They have killed the monks near the gate—they mean to kill us all!"

"Then they shall have a heavy price to pay," Doric growled, his eyes burning in righteous rage.

The rest of the companions stood silently, their grim faces removing the need for them to speak. They all knew Theodore was right.

"The entrance to the monastery has been defiled by the blood of the monks." The man spoke to Sulla with breathless excitement, the heat of the raid instilling a passion that flared brightly.

Sulla smiled.

"Then take our friend to the monastery and allow him his fun."

"Is there any sign of Gar'rth, or the girl?" the werewolf asked the messenger. The man hesitated, peering suspiciously at the tattered figure, then answered.

"Yes," he said. "They have taken cover near the stables at the rear of the courtyard. The men have refrained from attacking them, as you instructed."

Sulla nodded.

"I would like the girl alive," he said, his hand resting firmly on the chest of the werewolf.

The creature drew back his lips in a gleeful snarl.

"I shall keep her alive for you, Sulla. Together we shall design a fittingly slow end for her!" Without another word he stalked toward the monastery's shattered gate.

The raiding party had lost what discipline it had once possessed. The leather-clad footsoldiers advanced toward the end of the courtyard to assault the monks who cowered near the stables.

There was a small paling near the stables, and the first soldier who advanced on it expected no resistance. He had no time to raise his guard as Theodore ran him through. The squire looked into the man's eyes as he died, sliding from Theodore's blade soundlessly.

"I killed him," Theodore said, his face suddenly pale. He turned to his companions. "I just killed a man! I've never killed anyone before." Suddenly he felt very sick.

"He would have killed you if you had not," Doric muttered, his expression grim.

Ebenezer caught his look and nodded discreetly. The alchemist turned to his friends, speaking in low tones.

"We must fight. All of us! And we can have no qualms about killing these murderers, for if any of you hesitate then you will die today." He turned to face the squire. "Theodore, you are a trained warrior of Falador—now is the time when all your learning will come into use. Castimir, you are a wizard in the real world now— your power is going to be important to keep the enemy at bay. Kara, you must ensure that Gar'rth stays close to us."

A faint moan from Abbot Langley caught their attention. He lipped toward them pale-faced, clutching Arisha's wrist for support.

"Gar'rth," he stammered, "you must not be afraid to fight. It is only the blood of innocents that you must fear to spill. These men are not innocent!"

The youth seemed to understand, and he nodded, moving forward to stand beside Theodore. Behind him stood Doric, his axe ready, and farther back, his runes ready, Castimir waited.

But now the Kinshra attack was renewed with increased ferocity. With terrifying yells, six of the leather-armoured foot soldiers charged amongst them, hacking wildly in their anger.

Theodore was the first to bar their way. With a cry he smashed the nearest with his shield and slashed at another man's hands, severing fingers and forcing his enemy to drop his sword with a scream. He heard Kara yelling wildly at his side as she fought the third, the ring of adamant on steel echoing as swords clashed, and he heard the sharp crack as the steel weapon was severed in two.

The Kinshra warrior cried out as Kara ran her blade deep into his chest, his armour no hindrance to her weapon.

Without pausing, she leapt to Theodore's side to confront the squire's two opponents, whilst from behind them Doric hurled his hand-axe at the first of their foes, stunning him. But the two men behind leapt over their comrade without slowing. As the dwarf readied his axe, a blazing red ball of flame struck the nearest attacker squarely in the chest, setting him alight.

The man ran wildly away, shrieking in horror, trailing the smell of burning flesh.

The last of the Kinshra, outnumbered, turned to flee, but Doric leapt after him, his axe cutting deeply into the back of the soldier's calves. The man howled as he fell and Doric silenced him with a vicious blow.

"That's the last of them for now!" Theodore called, for the squire's two enemies had fallen quickly and without mercy at Kara's hand. He peered at her strangely.

"Do not look at me like that, Theodore," she chastised. "These people deserve the same mercy they offered others. Others like my family." There was anger in her eyes, and a hunger for revenge.

"And what of him? Are you going to kill him also?" Theodore demanded, pointing to the man whom Doric's hand-axe had stunned. The man lay prone, unmoving, but he was still alive.

Kara put her sword to his throat and gritted her teeth.

"Don't do it Kara," Arisha warned. "Killing in battle is one thing, but what you are about to do is quite different."

A horn sounded in the courtyard, drawing their attention away from their unconscious enemy.

"We must ride out now," Theodore insisted, watching the Kinshra gather. "If we leave it any longer there will be too many of them."

"We are ready to go," Brother Althric said wearily. "Every man who is still able is ready to ride."

The wind changed suddenly, carrying the heat of the raging fires toward the stables. With a blistering crackle the flames found new thatch to consume.

"It is the archives," one of the monks moaned in despair. "The archives will burn. All our labours will have been for nothing."

The words felt like daggers piercing Kara's skin. Looking at the flames, she made a decision.

"I am going to get the records," she cried. "If you have to go, then go without me—but I will not let the Kinshra win again!" She gripped her sword and ran into the courtyard before anyone could stop her.

A Kinshra soldier shouted out in alarm and several men ran to intercept her.

"Come on!" Theodore yelled, running after her. The small group split, with Gar'rth and even Castimir refusing to heed Doric's cries of warning in their eagerness to help Kara.

"Impetuous youths!" the dwarf called out, knowing that her rash action had likely condemned them all. With an oath he followed them, leaving behind a fearful Ebenezer who watched discreetly from behind the wooden paling, deep in thought.

The first man who tried to seize Kara died before he could even touch her. He saw her blonde hair and noted her slight frame, and with a brutal arrogance he underestimated his foe. Her sword edge sliced across his throat. Without waiting for him to fall she ran past, Gar'rth following close behind her.

Then Theodore, yelling an ancient battle cry of the knights, charged into the midst of the invaders. He made straight for the largest of the enemy but quickly the Kinshra warrior parried his sword thrust, slipping his own blade beneath the squire's shield to stab him in the side.

Theodore screamed.

But even as the sword tip stabbed through his leather armour, the Kinshra warriors were put to flight. His blue robes flailing behind him as he ran, Castimir hurled red flames from his hands, scattering the enemy. Doric followed, hurling his hand-axe with unerring accuracy, felling a Kinshra foot soldier as the sharp edge embedded itself in the man's forehead.

And then there was Gar'rth, who carried no weapon. One of the Kinshra lunged toward him but he was too quick, sidestepping the foot soldier's thrust and hitting him with all his strength. The man went down at once, a sickening crack sounding from his jaw.

"Follow Kara!" Doric yelled to Gar'rth as he leapt toward Theodore, putting the wounded squire behind him so he could face the big warrior in his stead.

The dwarf ducked and parried the warrior's attacks, buying time for Theodore to overcome his pain and rejoin the fray. The squire's blade intercepted his enemy's thrust. Seizing the advantage, Doric drove his axe into the man's calves, felling him instantly.

Theodore stepped over the soldier, an angry glare in his eye.

"For Saradomin!" he declared, and ran the man through in a single thrust, putting his weight onto his sword to drive it through the man's armour and into the soft earth beneath.

"They are regrouping," Ebenezer called out in warning. He ran out to support a weary Castimir who had spent much of his strength with his magical fire and was clearly exhausted.

"I'm not sure if I can go on," the young wizard wheezed.

"You have to, Castimir," the old man said, squeezing his hand in support. "For all our sakes!"

FORTY-NINE

Sulla watched the battle from the saddle of his horse.

"My friend, your enemies are before you. Do you wish to avenge yourself upon them?"

He lowered his gaze to the werewolf who stood beside him and noted how haggard the monster looked. Perhaps the strain of forcing his way over the holy barrier had been too great an effort.

"Very well." The werewolf spoke slowly, pulling the cowl farther across his face and striding forward.

The heat from the fires radiated down into the courtyard, warming Theodore uncomfortably. He noticed with alarm how the roaring flames had swept dangerously close to the archives.

"Kara?" he called out, his voice unable to overcome the blistering cries of the wooden beams or the crackle of burning thatch.

It shouldn't have taken Kara and Gar'rth so long to rescue the archives. He was tempted to run in after her, but Doric's warning cry held him back.

"It's him! He's here!" The dwarf cried. His companions looked to the lone figure who was striding toward them—the one who had inspired the dwarf's terror.

"The werewolf!" Doric shouted.

The figure stopped several yards in front of them, standing absolutely still.

"You were lucky to survive last time, creature," Doric shouted, readying his two hand-axes.

"As were you, dwarf," came the guttural reply. "Only the intervention of the girl saved you. Tell me, where is she? And where is Gar'rth?"

No one spoke, and the werewolf reached up with his hands, pulling back the cowl to expose his face to the onlookers.

"You cannot win," the werewolf said. "If you give me Gar'rth and the girl, then the rest of you may leave here. Sulla has given his word."

"You would ask us to give up our friends?" Theodore spoke with disdain. "The reputation of the Kinshra is well-known to us. Sulla will not honour his word!"

"Very well," the creature said flatly. With deliberate slowness he pushed up his sleeves.

Theodore knew only Kara's blade had been sharp enough to pierce the unearthly hide, but now they had Castimir at their side. The squire was certain that the werewolf was not impervious to magic, yet he had seen how weak Castimir had become from his previous exertions.

He needed to buy the wizard time to recover his strength.

"Wait!" he uttered as the creature stepped forward. "If you intend to fight us, then you can grant me a moment to answer a question. Who is Gar'rth? Why is he so important to you?"

The werewolf halted, his eyes glowing in thought.

"You cannot understand the customs of my people, human," he growled. "Gar'rth has disgraced his family by his cowardice. He has refused to accept our way of life, refusing to be blooded when he came of age. The lords of our land wish him returned so he can be forced to embrace our ways and become one of us."

Theodore frowned, but did not respond. Nor did he back down.

"He is not royalty, human, but he is of minor nobility," Jerrod continued. "Even if he were not, if he were born the lowliest of birth, I would still pursue him. For amongst our race children are rare." His maw broadened into a twisted smile. "Our race is not as… prolific as your own, and every newborn is valuable.

"My offer still stands. I want the girl and I want Gar'rth. The rest of you are of no consequence."

"We have given you our answer," Doric stated, his voice barely audible over the angry fire that roared through the eastern side of the monastery, its black smoke drifting across the courtyard.

As if the smoke were a signal, Jerrod gave an eerie howl and ran forward, crouching low, ready to launch himself at the nearest of his enemies.

He had identified the wizard as the only threat in the battle, and sought to remove him first. He seized the dwarf and threw him toward the magician, knowing that the young man would not risk harming his friend with his magic, forcing him to jump aside to avoid colliding with his dwarf ally.

In doing so, the wizard forfeited his chance to use his magic effectively. He frantically hurled a ball of fire that only singed Jerrod's thigh.

The werewolf was upon him before he could ready a second spell. Jerrod hit him before deftly running his long claws across the young human's throat, intending to kill him outright. At the last moment he hesitated, however, thinking that it would be more amusing to keep the unconscious wizard alive for later, once he was defenceless.

With a swift strike from his dagger-like claws he tore the man's belt from his waist and hurled it into the burning monastery. Even if the wizard did regain consciousness, he would have no runes with which to wield his magic.

Casting his victim aside, Jerrod then occupied himself with the fun of revenging himself upon the dwarf and the squire. He took his time, dodging their attacks and pushing them away as a tutor might disdainfully parry a hot-headed pupil.

But then the wind changed. He caught their scent in the air, carried on the burning embers.

It was the girl and Gar'rth.

Kara knew she had made a mistake. Her eyes ran with stinging tears. Her lungs burned as she coughed feebly in an effort to breathe clean air.

"Come on, Gar'rth," she called weakly, the strength fading from her legs as the smoke threatened to overwhelm her. She had made it through to the archives with Gar'rth close behind her, but as they had entered, the roof in the passageway behind had come crashing down, cutting off their exit.

Kara seized the four books that she had put aside for later inspection and quickly they made their way out onto a narrow stone staircase that had thus far avoided the flames.

Yet when they reached the next floor, Kara's gut twisted itself in fear, for the only way out was back into the burning part of the monastery.

She knew her luck had run out.

The flames were engulfing the passage ahead, and the wooden floor had already collapsed in several places. There was no way they could cross.

But if they could not escape that way, she could at least divest herself of the cumbersome books. She smashed the stained-glass window with the hilt of her sword and prepared to push the weighty volumes through the small gap. But as she looked down she hesitated.

Her friends were losing the battle. She instantly recognised the werewolf as he lifted Doric straight off his feet with one hand while simultaneously fending off a thrust from Theodore. Then her eyes fell on Castimir in his blue robes, and she uttered a silent prayer, for the young sorcerer lay on the ground, his hand held to his throat, his face deathly pale.

"Get up, Castimir! They need you," she shouted, but her voice could not carry over the roaring of the flames.

There was only one thing she could do. Without hesitation, she hurled the books out into the courtyard, unsheathing her adamant sword as they fell. As Theodore was beaten to the ground and disarmed by his vicious opponent, she hurled her sword toward him and attempted to shout his name.

But she couldn't muster the strength to do so.

A wave of dizziness and despair overwhelmed her, and she knew they were trapped. Her arrogance and selfishness had killed them both—perhaps all of them.

Kara gave a despairing moan as her knees gave way beneath her, the smoke too much for her.

"Saradomin forgive me," she muttered as her eyes closed. "May my friends forgive me."

She felt Gar'rth's strong arms slip under her back as he heaved her across his shoulder. She felt weightless as he turned back toward the archive and the stairwell that they had just climbed, away from the burning passageway that was filled with black smoke.

Then all consciousness fled.

Jerrod's acute hearing picked out her cry, and he turned to look at her briefly as she threw the sword.

Instantly he knew—it was the sword that had harmed him in Falador.

The squire managed to grab the hilt of it before the werewolf delivered a vicious kick to his side. Theodore staggered, attempting a desperate lunge which the werewolf dodged easily.

He smashed a heavy fist into the squire's skull and took the adamant sword from his grasp. As Theodore knelt, dazed, Jerrod hurled the green-tinted blade toward the Kinshra soldiers.

At a distance, he saw Sulla nod in approval of his strategy.

"You won't need that," he laughed as he lifted Theodore from the ground only to dump him at the wizard's side. The squire felt limp in his arms, and Jerrod knew the human possessed barely enough strength to stand. He would enjoy taking his revenge on his enemies, a slow revenge that would last long hours. There was only one enemy left now who dared to fight him.

Jerrod turned his attention once more to Doric, who stood wearily.

The dwarf is strong, to still stand after so much punishment.

"Let's be having you," Doric growled, his voice quieter than usual, as if resigned to a fate he knew no mortal being could ever avoid.

Jerrod laughed. It had been so easy once he had removed the wizard and the girl's sword, for his two enemies had nothing else left with which to hurt him.

"Castimir," Theodore muttered, his jaw swollen from the crushing blows of his enemy's huge fists. "We need you, Castimir!"

The wizard gave a low groan and opened his eyes.

"There is nothing I can do, Theo," he wheezed. "He has taken away my runes."

"Not all of them, Castimir. Look, on the ground next to you. He must have torn through your pouches when he ripped your belt."

The wizard's eyes lit up in sudden hope and he struggled to his knees.

"Gather them up, old friend," he said. "Let us see what we can muster for our final moment."

Quickly and as discreetly as he could, Theodore hid Castimir from the werewolf's view, his hands working quickly in the damp earth. Within seconds he had thrown at least a dozen of the small stones back to the wizard.

"Can you do anything with them, my friend? Do you have enough?"

Castimir's voice sounded strong as he breathed deeply.

"I have enough, Theo. When I cast my spell we shall have one chance and only for a few seconds. Now listen very carefully."

Theodore listened silently to Castimir as Doric was once again beaten to the ground by a savage blow.

"I understand," the squire said meekly. Very slowly, as if he had no more to give, he rose, drawing the werewolf's attention.

Ebenezer returned his knife to his pocket. He had finished what he had set out to do. It had taken him a few minutes, sitting behind the fence near the stables, and all the time he had watched the battle unfold.

Carefully he slid lumps of the powdery cake-like element into several oil-soaked leather pouches, in which it would be protected from the air.

"What are you doing?" Brother Althric whispered urgently. For some minutes now the monks had been ready to ride out, to risk a charge past the waiting Kinshra and an escape out into the open country.

"I am nearly ready, young man," the alchemist insisted. "If you will prepare yourselves, then I will arrange our exit."

He gathered the small pouches in his arms as a hungry man would gather food. He knew that to get by the Kinshra they would need a distraction, and he was holding that in his hands.

"Come on, Gar'rth," he muttered to himself, his eyes pausing on the burning building above him. The fire had engulfed the window where Gar'rth and Kara had been seen, and the archives were now alight.

But in a malign twist of fate the flames swept up, engulfing the roof of the eastern wing and spitting hot tongues of fire from the windows. As Ebenezer stood, the last of the thatched roofing collapsed, crashing down into the library and the dry books inside. The wall of the building tottered dangerously.

"Kara!" Theodore yelled as he witnessed the destruction, certain that neither Kara nor Gar'rth would survive if they were inside.

"Theodore!" Castimir shouted suddenly. "Move!" The wizard leapt to his friend's side to confront the werewolf, who stood scant yards in front of him. He wore a look of determination that bordered on madness.

The werewolf reached forward to seize him by the throat, but it was not to be. His massive hand slowed, his long claws stopping a bare inch from Castimir's pale skin. As he snarled impotently, the wizard waved his empty hands in the air, ending his complex spell. For it had been cast and the werewolf could barely move.

"Quickly! The werewolf will only remain snared for a few seconds. Where is the adamant sword?" Castimir shouted to his friends with renewed energy. He followed Theodore's frustrated gaze toward the Kinshra, and immediately saw the green-tinted blade lying at Sulla's feet.

They would not be allowed to use that in their battle.

"Throw him into the fires then," Castimir shouted, aware that with each second the spell waned. "Drag him toward the wall." The squire bent low and rushed at the werewolf's knees. With a loud cry he lifted the massive figure onto his shoulder and stumbled forward. The wizard joined him, and Doric put his strength into helping them as well.

"What... are... you... doing?" the werewolf growled, his

mouth and tongue bound by the spell, making speech near impossible.

It would only last a few more seconds.

The companions dropped the ensnared creature at the foot of the wall of the archives—a wall that shook unsteadily.

It tottered above the werewolf. The magic was fading, it would last only seconds longer, Castimir knew. But not long enough for the wall to fall first. He had one chance to make that a certainty.

Castimir stepped closer, conjuring a ball of flame with the last of his runes. With all his concentration the young wizard hurled a single ball of fire into the final support.

The whole wall crashed down on top of the monster, burying him in dust and brick.

Sulla sighed inwardly. From the start the werewolf had performed exactly as he had hoped against such a diverse group of enemies, but the wizard had proved his undoing.

He had debated going to his ally's rescue, but the speed with which their opponents had acted had surprised even him. Besides, he told himself, if he had been defeated so easily, then the werewolf was of limited value to the Kinshra ranks.

But the time for games had passed. He was about to order a charge when the sounds of an approaching rider drew his attention. He turned and found to his surprise that he faced an old man.

"What do you want?" he called out. "Have you come to beg for a quick end?"

"Two of your champions have died today," said the elder. "If you do not let us pass, then many more of you shall follow them to the Abyss!" The man looked swiftly to the ground and Sulla followed his gaze, noting the half-filled buckets of water that stood next to the horses. They had been left over from the

monks' firefighting. Then the newcomer glanced furtively at the
fountain from which some of the Kinshra horses were drinking.

What can he be seeing?

Sulla looked warily at the old man, and for the first time
noted that he had blindfolded his horse. He held several small
pouches in his hands. Was he a wizard also? That might pose a
problem.

"My name is Sulla, old fool," he said angrily. "And it is a
name you will die cursing!" The black-armoured warrior
raised his sword.

The man paled, but he held his ground.

"Then you have brought this upon yourself," he uttered as
he hurled the first of his dozen small pouches toward the water
bucket close to Sulla's horse. A greyish cake-like substance fell
loosely from the leather packet and splashed into the liquid.

A sudden explosion flashed from the bucket. Sulla's horse
gave a wild cry of fear, rearing onto its hind legs then turning
quickly away from the violent reaction.

But the old fool had not finished. With a triumphant yell
he hurled several of the pouches into the fountain. At once the
water fumed as if it were boiling, sending bright flashes and
pale clouds of powder into the air as echoes of the explosions
rebounded from one side of the courtyard to the other in a
roaring cacophony.

Pandemonium reigned now. Sulla lost his grip on his horse
and fell to the ground with an impact that made him grit
his teeth in pain. He saw his horse gallop away through the
desecrated gateway.

The panic was contagious—some of the horses followed,
while others fled into the courtyard to escape the explosions.
Within mere moments, the disciplined Kinshra troops devolved
into a chaotic mass.

Sulla cursed, knowing that without a horse he was vulnerable.

He watched as his enemies, led by the old man, spurred their horses forward, toward the shattered gateway.

Knowing he was absolutely powerless to prevent their get away, Sulla leapt to one side to avoid being trampled.

"Come on!" Ebenezer yelled, leaning forward to pull the blindfold from his horse's eyes. As he did so he noticed Kara's sword lying forgotten on the ground. Moving quicker than he had for many a year, he dismounted to pick it up as the monks rode past him to their freedom, unchallenged by the panicked Kinshra horsemen.

Theodore and Doric came last with Arisha, for the priestess had prepared two horses for them in the stables. Following her was Castimir's faithful yak and the alchemist's mule, still laden with its saddlebags.

Saradomin bless her, he thought gratefully.

"And Gar'rth? And Kara? What about them?" Doric called as he rode by.

The alchemist shook his head.

"There is nothing we can do for them. And our dying here will do no good, either." He spurred his horse through the gateway. As he did, he saw the man called Sulla lurch to his feet.

"Get after them," the Kinshra leader roared.

Immediately a small group of riders who had managed to regain control of their steeds followed them through the gateway.

Ebenezer turned to Castimir, who looked so weak that it amazed the old man that he could retain his grip on his horse.

"I need you, Castimir!" he shouted, reining in his steed as they gained a small rise. "For the last time today."

"I cannot. I am so weak," the wizard responded hoarsely, his mouth parched and his throat stained with his own blood that had now begun to clot. "And I have no more runes left for an offensive spell."

"Your fire staff then. Quickly, Castimir, or it will be too late."

The sorcerer sat up, straightening his back with a visible effort.

"I do not have it, Ebenezer," he said, suddenly alarmed.

The thunder of the Kinshra horsemen, charging down a narrow path that led to the rise, grew. They were seconds away.

"I have it, Castimir," Arisha said with surprising calm. Her wide eyes looked sadly at him as she handed him the staff. Upon seeing his unharmed yak by her side, the wizard managed a sudden grin that looked entirely out of place on his blanched face.

"I don't know what I would do without you, Arisha." He slurred the words, his voice cracking.

Suddenly he swayed in the saddle.

"Do it, Castimir. Do it now!" Ebenezer spoke urgently.

Castimir held up the staff, and the knotted end glowed fiercely with its inner flame. Ebenezer removed the unexploded shell he had retrieved when he had taken shelter behind the courtyard fountain.

"Light the fuse," he said briskly.

As soon as Castimir's staff touched it, the fuse came to life with a loud sizzle.

"Ride now, my friends," Ebenezer instructed them.

Arisha took Castimir's horse by the reins and galloped swiftly after the disappearing monks.

"You must go too, Theodore," he said. "And you, Doric. We have no time left." He held out the adamant blade for the squire.

Theodore shook his head, taking Kara's sword and wearing a vicious look on his face. Doric, too, said nothing, but goaded his horse away from where he knew Ebenezer would throw the spitting explosive, just where the pathway ended.

The alchemist kept his keen eye on the fuse until the first of the Kinshra rode out onto the rise, yelling in triumph. Ebenezer did not need to think, for he had rehearsed the action in his mind. As soon as the spitting shell left his hand he dug his heels into his steed and lowered his head, yelling at the horse.

"Ride! Faster—"

The explosion silenced his words, shattered men and ripped through horses. He saw Theodore and Doric gallop at full speed into the suddenly disorientated enemy. But he could hear little, for the noise of the explosion had near-deafened him.

As he turned back to see the dozen contorted bodies of armoured men and horses that lay scattered like broken toys, he could barely hear the screams of the injured. Even Theodore's war cry sounded far off.

Theodore's timing was perfect. The first of the Kinshra who rode from the now smoke-filled path was unarmed, his hands pressed against his helmet in great agony. Theodore didn't hesitate. The man was a follower of Zamorak. He had helped to violate the monastery and desecrate a peaceful place of worship.

He had to die.

With a practised move the squire brought Kara's slender blade across the man's throat. With shocking ease the adamant bit through the armour and cleaved deeply into his neck. Giving only a sudden cry the man fell from his horse and crashed awkwardly onto the grass where he remained, utterly motionless.

He was dimly aware of Doric, guiding his horse directly into a black-armoured warrior who staggered aimlessly on foot, stunned by the blast. The man screamed as the dwarf's horse charged into him, knocking him violently off his feet and trampling him underfoot.

For the Kinshra the battle was lost. Most of the pursuers had been killed outright by the blast or stunned and knocked from their horses. Those who hadn't, who had waited near the back, were not the bravest of men. Theodore's vicious war cry and the yells of their dying comrades made them swiftly turn their horses away, toward the monastery.

For Theodore there could be no mercy. With each of the men he killed he thought of Kara—of how he had failed to protect her, of how he had betrayed her in Falador, and of not having the opportunity to make his peace with her before she was killed.

"Theodore!" Doric called as the squire leaned forward in his saddle to run through one of the few remaining Kinshra. The man screamed as he died and Theodore withdrew the sword, already looking for another enemy to feed his passion for revenge.

"Theodore, stop! We need a captive," Doric cried. "We need to know what the Kinshra are planning, and how many of those weapons they have."

The squire halted upon hearing Doric's words. His eyes were bloodshot with anger and he breathed deeply as he fought to regain control of himself. Rage was not the way of the Knights of Falador, and with a grim look at the carnage all around him, he lowered his sword in shame.

"You are right, my friend," he muttered, reminding himself that it was Kara's own anger that had ultimately resulted in her death. "No good can come of revenge."

A low moan attracted his attention. It was one of the Kinshra—an officer of minor standing, judging from the man's insignia. He was lying upon the smouldering grass, pinned beneath his dead horse. He had removed his helm to tend to his injuries. His face was blackened and he held his hand across his eyes.

"He'll do," Doric said, gesturing to the man with his axe.

"I beg for mercy!" the wounded man pleaded when Theodore dismounted. "Please! I am unarmed!" His voice shook with fear.

Theodore looked at him in contempt.

"You Kinshra deserve only the same mercy you offer to others. But I shall spare your life today, for you are coming with us to Falador. If you cause me or my companions any problems, we will kill you."

"We should search him thoroughly," Doric said, carefully looking over the man.

"He will not need his armour—it will weigh down our horses." Theodore forced the man to his knees and carefully cut the straps with Kara's blade, mindful not to injure him. With a loud clatter the man's heavy breastplate fell to the ground, followed by the rest of his cumbersome plating.

They bound the man's hands and sat him on one of the Kinshra horses that had survived the attack, tying him to the saddle and ensuring that the reins were secured to Theodore's steed.

"Where is Arisha leading us?" Doric called as they rode to catch up.

"To the east, to Edgeville, I think. It is a full day's journey, and the monks have little food with them." Theodore spoke as if he disagreed with her decision.

"Then where are we headed?" Doric asked, knowing that only one destination could be important for the squire.

"We will catch up with them and make our farewells. Then we will ride on to Falador. The Kinshra will not be far behind."

It was fully daylight by the time they galloped away, leaving the cold light of the cloudy winter morning to illuminate the colder faces of their dead enemies.

FIFTY

"Dig him out!" Sulla shouted across the courtyard. His temper mirrored the weather, for it had started to rain heavily and he was in ill spirits.

He looked toward the east wing of the monastery, which was smouldering now that the fires had been dampened. *It seems the chaos dwarfs' weapons have worked*, he mused with a hint of satisfaction. He relished the idea of turning them against the crowded city of Falador. He imagined the streets running with the blood of innocents. Of women shielding their young, of the sheer helplessness of the knights in trying to protect their city from the falling shells.

His reverie was interrupted by the yell of a soldier who stood over the collapsed wall. Sulla stalked quickly over as they shifted enough of the debris to locate their demonic ally.

"Get him some water!" he spat. The nearest of his men ran to a fountain and filled one of the buckets abandoned by the monks. With a nod from his superior he emptied it over the werewolf's dust-covered face.

Instantly an agonized howl caused all but Sulla to back away.

"It burns me!" the werewolf bellowed. "The water had been blessed by the priests of Saradomin."

Sulla glared at Jerrod furiously. He contemplated leaving the creature there, or perhaps emptying several more buckets of water onto him and putting the bricks back, abandoning him to starve to death.

The werewolf struggled to free himself, pushing upward with a sudden strain. The bricks on top of him shuddered slightly in response.

"Free him!" Sulla ordered, before leaving to commandeer a room for himself in the western wing of the monastery, all of which was untouched by fire and undamaged from his bombardment.

"Wake up, Kara!"

The voice sounded far away. She opened her eyes slowly, unsure of what she saw. The last thing she remembered was the stinging smoke in her lungs and the searing heat on her face.

"Am I dreaming?" she asked, her voice weak. Somewhere nearby a man laughed, finding amusement in her confusion.

"You *should* actually be dead. Both you and Gar'rth."

At the mention of his name Kara looked wildly about, but she was alone on the side of a red mountain under an eerily dark sky which obscured the stars.

"Where is Gar'rth? Where am I?" Panic filled her voice.

"Gar'rth is not required, not yet anyway," the voice answered calmly. "It is you with whom I wish to speak. And do not be afraid—you will not be kept here very long."

"Who are you?" She found herself staring at a diminutive figure swathed in red robes. His eyes gleamed cunningly and his bent frame caused him to look up at her, a smouldering orange glint in his pupils. The man's face was misshapen, his forehead swollen, and red sores were prevalent over his pale skin. He drooled somewhat, as if he were a fool.

Yet Kara feared him.

"Just an old friend," the hunchback replied. "You do not know me, but I have watched over you for a long time. Since the day you were born, in fact."

"Are you saying that you knew my parents?" she asked, hope in her voice.

"Alas, I did not," came the answer. "But I do not wish to speak to you about the past. It is the future I am interested in. Look, there, to the east."

The man pointed, and she followed the direction of his hand. Then she gasped.

The entire horizon was swarming with an army encamped. Never had she imagined such a mass of men and weaponry with their thousands of campfires, more numerous to her than the stars in the night.

"Who are they?" she asked, awestruck.

"They are your followers, Kara-Meir. If you wish them to be."

"Mine?" Suddenly she was afraid.

"Yes, my dear. Yours. Think, Kara, about the past." The voice was seductive, compelling. "The world cannot go on as it is. You feel hatred against the Kinshra for what they did to your family, and rightly so. But where should the true blame lie?"

"With Sulla?" Her voice was faint, unsure.

The small figure in the red robes shook his head patiently.

"No, not with Sulla—for he is just a man. A victim like yourself. No, who has waged war on the followers of Zamorak for generations? Who strives for domination in the world at this time? Think, Kara—who has betrayed you?"

Realization dawned as she understood what was being said.

"The Knights of Falador used me," she said slowly. "It is they who…" For some reason she could not bring herself to finish the sentence.

"They have hounded the followers of Zamorak for decades, Kara—and yet still they permit the Kinshra to live. The deaths of your family occurred not because of Sulla, but because of the Knights of Falador. Do you not see? They *need* the Kinshra to remain a threat to the people of Asgarnia—they need an enemy to justify their own existence. They could have destroyed the Kinshra years ago, if they wanted.

"But they didn't, and because of that your family are dead and you are alone. You know their lies and their hypocrisy— they endangered you to achieve their own ends. They are attempting to take over Asgarnia, making the people believe them indispensable by letting the Kinshra continue with their savagery. This is their plan."

Kara lowered her head in thought.

"Let me show you something, Kara," the man said, his mouth twisting into a macabre smile.

And suddenly she was amongst the huge army of black-clad men, standing next to a column of horsemen who rode under a black banner. As they drew parallel with Kara their leader raised a hand and the column halted.

"What are they going to do?" Kara whispered.

"Just watch, Kara-Meir. They cannot see or hear you."

The leader spoke and Kara recognised the voice. For it was her own, although different somehow, harsh and impatient.

"Where is he?" her voice said, as the figure removed her helm, shaking the blonde hair that fell loosely about her shoulders, her dark eyes flashing in the light. Kara gasped in amazement, for it *was* her—at least ten years older—who commanded the many thousands of men.

"Here he is, my lady," a guard shouted, dragging a man who wore a torn white tunic and whose long unkempt hair hid his identity. He was thrown before her horse.

"Have you considered my proposal?" her older self asked, and to Kara's ears there was a definite malice in her words.

"I will not take up the sword again," said the man whose voice was alarmingly familiar. "I vowed to Saradomin never to do so."

"Do not speak his name!" She spat the words, her face contorted in sudden rage. Her expression softened after a moment however, and even appeared gentle. "Tell me you will reconsider," she ordered.

"I will not, Kara," came the reply. "You have kept me prisoner for years, ever since my order fell at your hands. My mind is fixed."

The prisoner suddenly wept and Kara, looking on, realised with a cold shock who it was.

"It is a shame, for I had hoped you would join me in forging a better world. But I see it is not to be. I can no longer waste time on you." She tugged on her horse's reins. "Goodbye, Theodore, last of the Knights of Falador."

With a dark look she rode past him, nodding briefly to the guard who stood behind the kneeling man. She did not bother to turn her head as the guard brought his axe down, and she did not bother to look as Theodore breathed his last, his eyes looking to her as his life left him.

"I would never do that! I will never become that!" Kara shouted in outrage. "This is a nightmare. No one can see the future." She stared at Theodore's corpse and began to sob.

But the robed figure seemed not to care.

"It is only one of many possibilities, Kara," the hunchback said. "Think about the power you could wield—the power to change the world, to stop all this war and needless death. The world needs a saviour, Kara-Meir, and I am offering you the chance to accept."

Kara bent over to hide her tears.

"Think about it, Kara-Meir. That is all I am asking. I shall come to you twice more before you need to give me an answer.

"Farewell, Kara-Meir, for now."

And with a sudden gasp, she awoke.

FIFTY-ONE

The werewolf stood above the collapsed wall, covered in the dust that the stonework had left on him. Sulla's men stood back, suspicious that he might require an infusion of human blood after the battle.

"Lord Sulla wishes to see you," one of the captains called, a hint of fear in his voice.

The werewolf sniffed the dawn air. The scent of blood stirred his appetite.

"There are some captives, or corpses, if you need to eat," the captain continued, gesturing to three injured monks who had been unable to escape, and near them several lifeless bodies.

"It must be fresh," the werewolf said, looking at the monks in contempt. They were small and bony men, and would not make for a satisfying kill. He said nothing more as he went to answer Sulla's summons.

"I have to say, my inhuman friend, that I expected more from you." The words were said calmly, for Sulla had no doubt there were limits to the monster's patience.

"It is this place, Sulla. The power of Saradomin enervates me."

"Then why do you not eat, and build your strength back up? We have some captives."

As if on cue, a low moan sounded from the adjoining room, drawing the werewolf's attention. He ducked under the low doorway and found himself in Sulla's makeshift hospital, where two of his footsoldiers lay badly injured. The two men were young and strong, and the werewolf stared.

Sulla noticed his greedy look.

"I doubt very much either will live long. Take your pick but keep it quiet, for the men would not like it. And know this—the boy Gar'rth and the girl were last seen running into the inferno. I doubt very much they could have survived. It seems your mission is finished, so we will have to work out a new purpose for you." He paused to allow what he had said to sink in.

"If you wish, you can join the Kinshra, for your strength and abilities would be an asset." Sulla stared at the two men who lay in contorted pain. "Think about it, while you eat."

The lord of the Kinshra walked silently away, pulling the tattered curtain across before returning to his planning. He tried to block out the sound of the powerful maw crunching a man's bones into powder.

Moments later the captain came bursting into the room in obvious excitement.

"We have located more survivors, Lord Sulla!" he said. "It is the girl and the boy, Gar'rth. They are alive—trapped in a cellar under the archives."

"Take me to them," Sulla said gleefully. At long last he would force the mysterious girl to tell him who she was, and why she had plagued his dreams.

Gar'rth could not lift the beam that had shielded them from the falling debris. Now it prevented them from escaping. Kara had seen the black-armoured men look down into the pit and she knew they would return in greater numbers.

"Kara! Help me!" Gar'rth said, straining at the beam once more.

"I cannot reach it, Gar'rth," she moaned, still weak from the smoke that she had inhaled. She looked upward to the grey daylight behind the charred black rafters that hung precariously from the burnt ruins. Her mind was numb and she was overcome by sudden terror. If the Kinshra were still there, then what had become of her friends?

And what would become of Gar'rth and her?

Suddenly she wept. She wept because the Kinshra had won yet again. They had destroyed her life years ago, they had defeated her in her first quest for vengeance, and they had sacked a monastery and murdered innocents—and still they went unpunished!

"Is this what you want, Saradomin?" she asked, a futile whimper in her voice. "Is this all you can promise those who follow you?" She ignored Gar'rth's stare and pulled her legs up under her chin and cried, overcome by the injustice that seemed so prevalent in the world.

Suddenly a harsh voice intruded upon her sorrow from above.

"It should teach you the value of worshipping false and weak gods." Kara knew to whom it belonged even before she raised her tear-stricken face. Whether heard across fire or ice, the voice remained the same.

It belonged to Sulla.

"I will enjoy finding out about you, for there are many questions that I need to have answered," he continued, sneering at them from above. "But it will not be easy for you."

He turned away.

"Get them out. But mind the boy," he added, impatiently.

"The boy will not be a problem," a voice said from out of

sight. "Not while I am here." This voice, too, was familiar.

From behind Sulla the shadow of a large man emerged, his cloak and features stained in fresh blood, his red eyes staring triumphantly at Gar'rth.

Theodore stopped again, attracting the frustrated attention of his companions.

"Is there something wrong with your horse, squire?" Doric called uneasily.

Theodore glanced grimly at Kara's sword, and then back over his shoulder in the direction of the monastery.

"You cannot go back, Theodore," Castimir warned him, strength returning to his voice in his eagerness to prevent his friend from acting foolishly. "If you go, you will die."

"Castimir is right," Ebenezer added. "Kara and Gar'rth were trapped in that inferno. They could not have got out."

Theodore looked hard at the old man whose determination and science had saved them. Gone was the fool of an alchemist who experimented with chemicals and challenged wisdom passed down through the ages, replaced by a quick-thinking old man who had known instinctively what to do. He knew it was wisdom that training alone could not provide.

Still...

"How do you know, Ebenezer?" he asked. "Is it not possible that Gar'rth could have carried Kara to safety?"

"I have thought long on that possibility but it is unlikely, Theodore," he said ruefully. "The Kinshra had guards on all sides. If they had escaped the fires, they would have been caught."

It was an answer that Theodore could not accept.

The old man continued. "There is another reason we must return to Falador, Theodore. The knights must be warned of Sulla's new weapons. The walls of Falador were built to withstand marauders and cavalry—but not this new technology. If Sulla can make his way south in the next few weeks, then the city will be in danger."

Theodore nodded.

"The knights must be warned," he agreed. "Take this to Sir Amik." The young squire handed the alchemist Kara's sword. "It shall convince him. Tell him everything. Mention Doric and me by name, and Kara. Tell him about the werewolf, also, for he shall be happy to know that the monster walks no more."

Without waiting for anyone to speak, the squire turned his horse around.

"Theodore, this is madness," Castimir despaired. "We only just escaped from that place!" He seized Theodore's reins to prevent him from going any farther, but the squire took them back.

"Goodbye, old friend."

Theodore turned away from Castimir to look at Doric.

"You know my answer, squire," the dwarf said. "I promised Kara to fulfil my vow after she saved me in Falador." He nodded in the direction they had come. "Let us not waste any time."

And without another word, the two companions goaded their horses back along the path.

Castimir gave Ebenezer an awkward look.

"I should go too," he said, knowing with a grim certainty that he could be of very limited use now that his runes were near exhausted.

"I understand," Ebenezer nodded, smiling grimly. "But let me give you something first." He reached into his saddlebags and handed over a pouch. Castimir groaned inwardly, wondering what chemical he would pull out this time.

"Here, you will find them of more use than I ever did," the old man remarked with a subtle expression as Castimir opened the pouch. The wizard gave a yell of happy surprise, for inside were several dozen runes.

"Where did you get these?" he asked, feeling the tears come into his eyes.

"I am an old man, Castimir, and I have spent years travelling the world, attempting to unlock nature's secrets. But I was not always a scientist, you know. When I was your age I tried my hand at wizardry—I just wasn't terribly good at it."

Castimir cried in gratitude at the precious gift. He pulled his horse close, and the two friends embraced.

"And take this also." The alchemist handed over a small but heavy case. "It is a spyglass. It will help you see your enemies from a safe distance." Castimir noted a warning in his eyes. "Just remember, Castimir, it is a rescue mission only—you are not riding into battle. Make certain Theodore knows this also."

"I will." The wizard bowed to his friend for a final time. "When I come back, Ebenezer, I look forward to continuing our debates on your science—especially in the context of this latest revelation." He managed a smile.

Then he turned his horse to follow after Theodore and Doric. As he did, his eyes fell on Arisha. The barbarian priestess was watching him, her large blue eyes reflecting the hopelessness of her thoughts.

"Goodbye!" he said with a wave and another smile. "Please look after my yak." His voice broke as she lowered her head and turned away, her long dark hair hiding a tear-streaked face. All humour in Castimir's soul died instantly.

He tried to speak again, but the lump in his throat prevented him from forming the words. In silent agony he mouthed a single word to her, *Goodbye*.

Finally the wizard spurred his horse to catch up with his friends.

FIFTY-TWO

Sulla's heavy steel-tipped boot smashed into Kara's ribs and lifted her off the sodden ground. She rolled onto her front and lay still, breathing deeply, knowing it was pointless to try to run or to fight back. She had already tried both, and her body bore the bruises of her captor's anger.

"Tell me who you are—why do you want to kill me," he demanded. Then he leaned in close and whispered menacingly in her ear. "That is all I want to know." So far she had only revealed the name that Master Phyllis had bestowed upon her, but it wasn't enough to spare her from Sulla's brutality.

Now she mustered the strength to respond. Her lip was swollen, her face was bloodied and bruised, and her wrists were bound. Nearby a fire sputtered and flared.

"Why?" she asked weakly. "Why is it so important?"

"Because I have dreamed about you, Kara. Before I ever saw you I fought you in my dreams—and you always won! I want to know why."

"Then I have bad news for you, Sulla," she said. "I don't *know* who I am." Somehow she found the strength to stand, her legs shaking from the effort. "I came here to trace my family in the archives, and now that those archives are gone, I have no hope of discovering my identity." She paused and peered directly at him. "But I will die with the comfort of knowing that you fear me." Her defiant speech had taken nearly all that remained of her strength, and she collapsed to her knees once more.

Sulla bit his lip in thought, and an idea occurred to him.

"I have news for you also, Kara-Meir. The archives weren't all destroyed—you and Gar'rth saved four volumes that my men have recovered." He moved closer, until his eyes were inches away from hers. "Do you wish to see them?" His scarred face betrayed no sign of emotion as he watched for her response.

Kara hung her head in defeat.

Sulla knew what her silence meant. He rose and walked swiftly away, returning with two of the heavy tomes, one held in each hand.

"Here they are, Kara," he said. "There is a problem though..." His eye glinted in undisguised malice. "My men need to keep warm!" He hurled the first book into the fire. The soldiers who had gathered to watch jeered as Kara slumped in despair.

He laughed at her as he picked up the second book and threw that onto the fire, as well.

Then he held the last one in his hand.

"Is there nothing you can do to stop me?" he taunted.

She said nothing, turning her face from his hideous glare, and Sulla hurled the last of the archives into the flames. Then he knelt down close to his mysterious enemy again.

"Why don't you just kill me?" she asked, exhausted.

Sulla sneered in triumph, knowing his next words would damage her more than a thousand beatings.

"Oh, Kara—do you think me a savage?" he mocked. "No, I am not going to kill you."

Kara raised her head from the ground to look at him suspiciously.

"No, Kara. *I* am not going to kill you. But *Gar'rth* is."

Sulla stepped away from her to reveal the robed figure of the werewolf she had nearly killed, standing nearby. In front of him Kara could see Gar'rth, his body as battered as hers, his eyes black and his skin darker than she had ever seen it.

Gar'rth's hunter had beaten him, forcing his bestial nature to the surface, and she was to be the innocent who would be sacrificed to secure his loyalty to Zamorak.

She was to die by Gar'rth's hand.

Kara gave a strangled cry and hid her face, sobbing in despair as Sulla looked on in triumph.

"Can you see them?" Castimir asked from the shadows of the trees that grew to the north of the monastery.

Theodore nodded.

"Kara is there, but there is no sign of Gar'rth." He gazed through the long telescope, the grey daylight making his spying easier. "But there are at least fifty Kinshra, as well as Sulla." He groaned suddenly. "And the werewolf is still alive!"

Theodore scoured the monastery once more. He saw the red-cloaked chaos dwarfs, who were busy cleaning the iron weapons that had been dragged into the courtyard.

"Now that I see those devices in the daylight, they are less of a riddle to me. They are some new sort of artillery."

Doric grunted impatiently. Knowing the dwarf wished to look, Theodore handed the spyglass across.

"What do you make of the red-cloaked dwarfs?" the squire asked his friend.

"It makes sense now," Doric said. "The new artillery are mortars, and they have cannons there also. I have seen them demonstrated by my people, and the red-cloaked dwarfs are chaos dwarfs. Just as you humans have followers of Zamorak, so do we dwarfs—and these chaos dwarfs have been a constant source of strife to us for many centuries."

"What can you tell me about the cannons?" Theodore asked, knowing that Sir Amik would insist on a full report of his enemy's capabilities.

"The walls of Falador won't stand against them, if Sulla has more." Doric's voice trailed off as he pressed the telescope closer to his eye. "It *is* Kara!" he suddenly hissed, seeing her for the first time. "She has been badly beaten. They are moving her to the stables near the fencing." His voice went suddenly faint as he looked on powerlessly.

"What is it?" Theodore asked.

"I have found Gar'rth," Doric said, lowering the telescope to look at his friends. "But he is no longer human."

Kara's hands and legs were bound tightly to the iron struts that were normally used for securing the horses to the wall outside the stables. Wracked with pain, she took comfort in the thought that she would shortly be dead and away from all worldly agonies.

Before her, secured by a chain, was Gar'rth. He had crawled into the shadows to hide from her as if he were ashamed.

Sulla and his werewolf companion looked at her critically.

"I will cut her," the hooded figure suggested. "Gar'rth will pick up the scent of her blood and will not be able to resist." The fiend stepped forward, his hand held out toward her face.

"Wait!" Sulla said. "I'll do it." He put his knife to her throat, and deftly cut her skin, but not so deep that she lost consciousness. "I want her fully aware of what is happening," he sneered gleefully as the blood dripped from her wound and onto her bare shoulder, revealed through her torn clothing.

"Get up, Gar'rth!" the werewolf growled, grabbing him by the nape of the neck and throwing him to the ground in front of Kara. "Drink in her scent—know her fear!"

Gar'rth did not reply, his expression contorted with pain. But he began to sniff the air, and instinctively turned toward her.

"This time you will not escape, my nephew," the hooded figure continued. "You have brought embarrassment on our family by refusing your first blooding. I will make sure you are blooded today, make certain you feast on the blood of an innocent so that you can give your life to Zamorak. I don't care how you kill this girl, but she *will* die by your hand.

"I will starve you until you can no longer resist the scent of her!"

He hit Gar'rth hard on the back of his head, causing him to yelp in surprise and cringe away.

A circle of Kinshra warriors had gathered to watch. When Gar'rth failed to act, a groan went up. With a frustrated cry one of them hurled a brick at him, hitting him on the shoulder and forcing him to crawl away.

"Do not damage him too much, men," Sulla admonished. "He will be useful to us once he has accepted the spirit of Zamorak."

"It will not harm Gar'rth to goad him on," the werewolf said, peering from man to man. "Indeed, it will increase his frustration and anger, and he will lose whatever control he has left. Just make certain that you are all beyond the reach of his chain."

The men of the Kinshra avoided his stare, but they nodded, eager to see the youth exact a hideous revenge on the girl who had slain their comrades.

Gar'rth gave a despairing moan as he crept as far away from Kara as the chain around his neck would allow. He lay with his hands pressed against his ears, blocking out the taunts of the onlookers.

"Well, Kara-Meir, you have gone from one bad situation to another!"

The old man's face betrayed a savage smile that said he found her predicament amusing.

"Where am I?" she asked. Her wounds were healed and all the pain was gone. She was standing beside the small red-cloaked man on the parapet of a black castle built in the middle of a great city. It was all strangely familiar.

"You are in Falador, Kara," he said with a wave of his hand. "A Falador as it might be if you accept my proposal. Gone are the knights, for their righteousness and arrogance destroyed them. Your armies have overrun the known world. Your empire is the largest there has ever been, your laws are upheld, and men fear to utter your name. There are no more pointless deaths, no more wars.

"Look at all you have achieved."

Kara looked at the dismal faces of the people who had become her subjects. The people of Falador walked about their city under the hard stares of dozens of black-armoured guards. In this new world, constructed over the bodies of impressed citizens worked to death, the people were no longer free. Suddenly she was certain who it was who offered her such power.

"Zamorak!" She turned to face him. "Why am I so important to you?"

The hunchback gave a childish giggle.

"I am a mere servant of the power, not the power itself," he said. "When I lived, many centuries ago, I was an able pawn. You would best think of me as his high emissary. One of many."

His burning eyes stared deeply into hers.

"The world cannot continue as it is, Kara. A new system must be found, a leader who can unite all men for the new age. Under his guidance you can create a world in which no family will be destroyed as yours was!"

"And what of my friends?" she asked. "The last time you

came to me you showed me a future in which I had Theodore killed."

She stepped away from the man, looking down into the courtyard where an execution scaffold stood on permanent display, its wooden deck stained a darkish brown.

"Your friends have abandoned you, Kara," he said in a matter-of-fact way. "For you to achieve the destiny that was meant for you, you do not need friends."

The execution stand attracted Kara's gaze again.

"Send me back," she demanded. "For I refuse your offer. A world ruled by fear is not a world I wish to be part of."

The old man laughed once more, but his eyes glinted in annoyance.

"Very well, Kara-Meir, but I shall appear to you one last time before my offer is withdrawn. In the meantime, you must save yourself." Suddenly she was paralysed, and as she tried to move she found herself back in the monastery, restrained by the thick ropes and subjected to the cruel jests of the men, her body once more bruised and aching.

But this time she did not despair. For if Zamorak's emissary was to visit her again, then she knew she would somehow survive.

That thought gave her the strength to think clearly, and to plan.

She looked at Gar'rth, and the chain about his neck gave her an idea. With a solid resolve she turned to the Kinshra onlookers. Mustering herself, she laughed back at them, and from their expressions she knew that her sudden change unnerved them.

She knew she had to play upon their impatience now, and draw one of them close enough for Gar'rth to reach.

"How 's it, Jerrod, that you are able to speak the common tongue and Gar'rth isn't?"

"My people only learn it after adolescence, after their blooding and when their true form is set. Gar'rth is simply too young."

Sulla turned his attention to the captives.

"You know, some of the men resent me giving Kara to Gar'rth. But she is too dangerous to be left alive, and the men will be content with the spectacle as he devours her."

Jerrod bowed his head in acknowledgement, aware that Sulla, like his men, was growing impatient for Gar'rth to act. Worse, Kara was mocking them, and the men's tempers were becoming strained. If one of them slew Kara themselves, then Gar'rth's blooding would have to be postponed, *again*! Jerrod turned to caution Sulla about his men, but as he turned to speak a hideous cry carried across the courtyard. It was followed immediately by yells of alarm and the scrapes of swords being drawn.

One of Sulla's men, angered by Kara's taunting and tired of Gar'rth's inaction had stepped toward the girl to beat the laughter from her. As soon as he strode within the range of Gar'rth's chain, the werewolf leapt, dragging the man down as his teeth found his throat and the warm blood within. Jerrod could smell it, powerful, near irresistible.

And he knew of the danger. He knew the power fresh blood instilled in his kind, even if it did not belong to an innocent. He knew that Gar'rth might now have the power to break free from the restraining chain. With a challenging growl he hurled himself at his nephew.

They spun viciously in a swift battle. Gar'rth attacked with a mindless fury, yet Jerrod was a far more experienced fighter and his movements were unhindered by the rage that consumed his nephew.

But Gar'rth was strong. He ignored the blows that Jerrod heaped upon him. With a frenzied cry he seized his uncle by the legs, lifted him into the air, and hurled him into the Kinshra warriors who stood with their weapons drawn, afraid to enter the fray.

Jerrod rose from the damp earth, his muscles already aching from the fight. Subduing Gar'rth was going to be more difficult than he had thought.

FIFTY-THREE

Doric hated hiding. He preferred to face his foes in open battle rather than jumping from one shadow to the next. But the three of them were no match for the Kinshra and their werewolf ally.

The squire had decided that the dwarf should remove the Kinshra horses to buy them time enough to escape, once they accomplished their goal.

If they accomplished their goal.

The horses were tied near the entrance to the monastery, in the care of a single tired guard. Doric knew he didn't have long until Theodore and Castimir launched their attack, but if the Kinshra still had their mounts then escape would be impossible.

He held Theodore's long knife in his right hand. He had left his heavy battle-axe with his friends, knowing it would be unsuitable for the task. He crawled forward, his movements concealed by the charred remains of the once-peaceful dwelling.

Suddenly, from close by, a wooden beam fell into the rubble, kicking dust into his face. Doric held his breath, his hand tightening on the hilt of the knife, aware that the guard must have heard. Finally he peered out from between the fallen beams.

If the guard had looked, he hadn't seen Doric. No doubt he was tired of jumping at every sound the wrecked building made.

Ignoring the sound, he had stepped away from his post, eager to see the outcome of the fray.

Swiftly Doric jumped out of the ruins and ducked behind a horse. Still the guard's back was turned.

He took his opportunity.

The two combatants smashed into the wall close to Kara and Jerrod broke away again. Twice Gar'rth had cut him, and both times it had been near his eyes. It was a sign that he was mastering his anger, for he was thinking tactically.

"Gar'rth!" Kara hissed into his ear, uncertain whether he would understand her. She saw his eyes narrow. "Cut the ropes on my wrist."

Gar'rth lowered his hand, feeling his way toward her arm but never removing his eyes from his uncle. The Kinshra jeered, unaware of what he was doing.

"I shall enjoy hunting her down, Gar'rth," Jerrod growled, perceiving his nephew's subterfuge. "I can smell her fear!"

Gar'rth said nothing as he cut through Kara's bonds. With a satisfying snap the first rope gave way and Kara's right hand was free. Then he moved away—it would be up to her to try and free herself now. As he renewed the attack on his uncle, she turned her attention to the knots that still held her.

Without warning, a bright ball of fire flew from the shattered entrance, and Castimir rode straight toward Kara at full gallop. A Kinshra warrior screamed as the fireball exploded on impact with his breastplate, sending flames to torment his nearest companions, who immediately fled to avoid the wizard's deadly magic.

As the men broke, Castimir threw a knife toward Kara, which she caught with her free hand. A second later and the wizard returned his attention to the Kinshra.

Like all of his men, Sulla had been drawn to the fight and

his guard had slipped. But it only took a heartbeat for him to recover from his surprise.

"Get the horses!" he roared, knowing that on horseback their opponents had a great advantage.

Kara watched as Theodore rode down a single red-robed chaos dwarf before reaching the artillery and the wooden crates that contained the explosive shells. Without dismounting, he bent down to reach inside.

At the same time Gar'rth threw himself at his uncle, keeping him from Castimir, letting the wizard drive the Kinshra back, whilst Kara, both hands now cut free, knelt to sever the ropes that bound her ankles.

As with their demonic ally, magic was something the Kinshra warriors feared. Castimir wisely kept his distance, and every time one of them rushed him, the wizard deftly directed his horse a few steps out of range before hurling a ball of fire at his attacker. Several of the Kinshra had fallen at his hand by the time Theodore reached his side.

"Are you ready, Theodore?" Castimir asked with feverish excitement.

"I am!" The squire held something out, and Kara saw that it was one of the explosives he had removed from the crate.

Castimir leaned across with his fire staff. As soon as the wood touched the fuse it hissed into life. Theodore rode toward the nearest group of Kinshra warriors, brandishing the explosive. As soon as they caught sight of him they ran. Two of them fled into Sulla's commandeered quarters, and Theodore knew by their concerned cries that there were at least a dozen others inside.

Kara watched as he rolled the shell through the open door. Then he swiftly turned his horse back toward Castimir. He didn't even bother to look as the explosion blew the door outward and silenced the men inside.

"Where's Sulla?" he asked.

"I don't know," the wizard shouted. "Pass me another one of the shells." As he took it from Theodore, he reached into his pocket and drew his hand out with a set of prepared runes.

"Gar'rth!" the wizard shouted. "Get Kara. Get her out of here."

Taking advantage of the distraction, Jerrod slammed his fist into his nephew's face. Then he turned.

"Wizard! This time I shall make certain of you," he said, stepping toward Castimir's horse and hunching low to leap at him.

But Castimir showed no fear. With a swift action he hurled a ball of fire toward his enemy, forcing the werewolf to jump to one side to avoid it.

The flames sailed harmlessly past him. Jerrod laughed.

"How much strength have you left, wizard? How many times can you afford to miss?"

But Kara saw that Castimir was *smiling*, for he had not missed his target. Behind Jerrod, the chain restraining Gar'rth had been blasted from the wall and lay idly on the ground. With a knowing growl, Gar'rth turned his attention to cutting the remaining bond on her ankle.

Castimir didn't reply to Jerrod's taunt. Kara watched as he cast his next spell as soon as the werewolf renewed his advance.

Immediately the werewolf halted, and visibly strained forward. He was unable to move.

"This... won't... hold... me..." he muttered, his voice restrained by the snare spell.

"For no more than ten seconds I should imagine," Castimir agreed as he lowered his fire staff onto the fuse of the shell he had taken from Theodore. "Kara. Gar'rth," he shouted, "run!"

He dropped the shell directly at Jerrod's feet.

"But this will explode in no more than five."

Without looking back, he turned his horse and dug his heels deeply into the animal's flank, goading it into a fast gallop. He reached the gates of the monastery where Doric was waiting for

Kara and Gar'rth with the Kinshra horses. At the same time, Theodore helped the three monks who had managed to slip away from the Kinshra in the confusion, telling them to make for Edgeville.

Kara looked back and smiled grimly at Jerrod. She needed to be sure that the werewolf would not walk away from this battle.

For he was too powerful to leave alive.

But Jerrod was not alone. Sulla had witnessed the deadly trap that the wizard had laid. He knew he had only scant seconds to act, and with a cry of determination he ran the short distance to his ally.

The fuse had burned out, disappearing into the shell.

Instinctively he hurled the explosive into the nearest fountain, pushing Jerrod roughly to the ground. He heard the splash as the shell hit the water and then the sound of a great explosion followed, emptying the fountain's pool and blasting apart the stonework.

"You saved me," the werewolf gasped, his voice restored. "Why?"

Sulla shrugged. He didn't know what force had made him save Jerrod—he rarely lifted a hand to save *anyone*.

"Somehow I think you will be of extreme importance to me in the days to come," he replied. "I will need a warrior of your strength at my side."

Jerrod stood first, extending his hand to Sulla and dragging the lord of the Kinshra to his feet in one easy pull.

"Then I shall join you. Until such time as my revenge upon those adventurers is complete."

FIFTY-FOUR

It was midday when Theodore signalled to his companions to slow their pace. They had taken nearly all the Kinshra horses, turning them loose when they were far enough away to make any pursuit worthless for their enemies.

"We have no food, Theodore," Doric muttered. It was a feeling they all shared, for every one of them was hungry and exhausted.

"A day's journey should bring us into more civilised lands where we can beg or buy something to eat," Theodore said. "It will take us at least three days to get back to Falador if we cut across country to the southwest, and then we can have all the food we can eat."

"I cannot last three days, Theo," Castimir lamented. "The magic has exhausted me for now, and I feel faint." The wizard's miserable face drew concerned looks. He was paler than usual, and he sat uncertainly on his horse.

"We could rest for a while," Kara suggested, and she wheezed, still in severe pain from her beating. "The Kinshra are unlikely to catch us now."

Theodore looked at Doric and the dwarf nodded. They could afford to rest.

"Very well then," he said reluctantly. "We shall stay here for an hour—but no more. I shall keep a watch along the trail behind us." The squire directed his horse back to the north, to keep an eye out for any sign of pursuit.

Both Kara and Castimir fell into a deep sleep as soon as they found themselves a suitable spot amid the warm ferns, while Gar'rth curled himself up with his knees beneath his chin. Doric did not want to examine the youth too carefully, for although he was no longer in his wolfish form, nor was he back to his human self either. His eyes were still dark pools devoid of hope, his jaw distended too far, his skin an inhuman grey.

The dwarf sat watching his companions with a sudden affection. They were so very young and yet already in their lives they had seen so much violence. It was not right, he thought as he tightened his grip on his axe. It was not right at all.

His thoughts turned to the artillery that the Kinshra had used. He imagined Falador besieged, the knights powerless against the technological advantage of their enemy. He knew the walls of Falador, built to protect the city in previous decades, would not withstand Sulla's guns.

Doric had thought on this for twenty minutes when a high-pitched screech sounded in the forest. His body went cold, for he knew it was a creature in its final moments. Looking north toward Theodore, he was comforted to see him come galloping back down the path.

"What was that?" the squire asked. "And where is Gar'rth?"

Doric glanced nervously about him, but Gar'rth had vanished into the forest.

"He was here a few minutes ago," Doric said, amazed that anyone could have crept away so silently through the dense undergrowth.

A loud crackle sounded nearby and the thick vegetation shook, betraying the signs of a large animal moving underneath.

"Gar'rth?" Theodore asked, his hand tight on the hilt of his drawn sword.

The undergrowth parted and Gar'rth crawled out from the shadows. In his clawed hands he held three dead rabbits, a gift to assuage the hunger of his friends.

It was on the third day of their journey that they crossed the grassland that lay to the north of Falador. Theodore knew instinctively that something was wrong. He had travelled along the east road many times, but never before had he seen the country folk so worried. Not even when the monster was at large had they been so dismayed, and it was not long before they found out the reason why.

They stopped to let their horses rest before making a concerted effort to reach the city. Theodore listened to the conversations of two ragged travellers who looked woefully to the north.

"It's the Kinshra," one said, and Theodore noted immediately the northern accent of the dour forest men. "They are driving everyone south, seizing people as slaves and burning property."

"It is not just the Kinshra," the other said bitterly. "I have heard that large groups of men are heading out of The Wilderness, bandits and murderers. And some of the men are talking of unrest in the goblin tribes—another new leader promising change and glory."

"It is an ill wind that blows in the new season," the first man added. "I will head south and put Falador between my family and the north."

"Aye, I shall do the same," the other remarked, raising his cup in response to Theodore's inquisitive stare. But he did not look welcoming.

Within a few hours, the companions passed through the high gates of Falador and over the bridge to the castle. They were unchallenged, for all recognised Theodore and Kara, and

Doric's hard stare dared anyone to try to bar him as before.

"I am aware of your news, Squire Theodore," Sir Amik said as the companions stood before him and several senior knights. In the corner Bhuler stood quietly, away from the others. "Just last night we received a missive from a priestess of the barbarian people, Arisha, in which she recounted your actions in the monastery. She made it through to Edgeville with the monks and immediately dispatched a messenger to Falador on the fastest horse. You have all acted courageously."

A murmur of approval sounded from the knights.

"Your friend the alchemist is also here." Sir Amik turned his head to meet Bhuler's gaze, his face reflecting some brief exasperation. "Somehow he got back with your prisoner intact. I do not know what magic he wields, but I have never seen a Kinshra soldier so humbled." The knight shook his head in bewilderment. "He has taken a room at The Rising Sun, where you should go to meet him after you've made your report."

He turned to address the entire group.

"You should each take the opportunity to be with your friends in the days to come, for soon such happiness will be scarce in the world."

The knight knew his ominous words would darken the hearts of the companions, and blunt their happiness at knowing that both Arisha and Ebenezer had made it to safety. Yet he saw no sense in presenting the situation as any less dire than he knew it to be.

Sir Amik and the knights listened intently to Theodore's report. When Gar'rth's true nature was revealed to them, they looked at the youth with a mixture of concern and awe. Before them stood a being from the unholy realm of Morytania, and yet he had been able to enter their sacred fortress.

They nodded in understanding when the squire told them of

Abbot Langley's belief that Gar'rth would remain pure unless he consumed innocent blood.

"His control over his true nature will make him an invaluable warrior," Theodore added, placing his hand on Gar'rth's shoulder. "He possesses strength akin to the greatest of our order. If the Kinshra are coming south, then we can ill afford to turn away such help."

"This is true," Sir Amik agreed, aware now that the Kinshra artillery was unlike anything the knights had faced before. "And that reminds me—I have something for you, Kara."

The old man motioned to Bhuler, who held an item wrapped in a blue cloth in his hands. He stepped forward and held it out.

"Take it, Kara," the valet said.

"My sword!" she gasped. With a swift movement that seemed to drive the aching pains from her arm she seized the hilt and raised it above her head, as if it were a symbol of everything she believed.

"You must take care of that blade, Kara," Sir Amik said. "And I must insist that you remain in Falador now, for if the Kinshra do come south, then there is no need for you to run to meet them. Do I have your word?"

"I will remain in Falador at your request, Sir Amik, but on two conditions," she said, looking him in the eye. "The first is that I train with the knights, for I am not arrogant enough to believe myself beyond the need for learning. The second condition is that I take a room at The Rising Sun, for the remembrance of your hospitality is still bitter to me."

"I will accept those terms if you will allow me to impose one of my own—upon Gar'rth. I believe that he has so far refused his nature, that he has fought against it with a temerity that can only be praised. But I cannot let him loose in the city, amongst a scared and suspicious population made more fearful still by the threat of war.

"Thus *he* will remain here in the castle, where we can keep him safe and secure. Do you understand?"

Kara and her companions shared angry glances, and when she turned to Theodore, the squire avoided her gaze.

"If my friends agree then it will be so," she replied. "But I insist on having unrestricted access to him."

Sir Amik nodded. He had no wish to imprison Gar'rth, but rather to separate him from the bustling city and customs that would be totally alien to him.

"I would suggest that you all return to The Rising Sun tonight. You may go too, Theodore, but you shall return here with Gar'rth when your revels are concluded. Some of the castle guard shall wait for you at the tavern to escort you both back.

"There are many new faces in Falador now—refugees, travellers, and vagabonds. If the Kinshra come south, then no doubt they will have sent their spies before them, and the streets may no longer be safe for anyone of our order to walk alone, squire or otherwise."

As they filed out of the chamber, a cold shiver took hold of Theodore. Falador was a very different city from that which he had left only days before, and he pursed his lips in apprehension at the change in atmosphere.

Falador now reverberated with grim expectation and dreadful inevitability. It was a city preparing itself for war.

On seeing the weary group enter The Rising Sun, the proprietor waved her hand in their direction, calling them over through the fug of smoke and beer.

"You are Squire Theodore, aren't you?" she asked. "I am Emily." Her admiration of him was read by all on her enthusiastic and smiling face. "Ebenezer told me to look out for you. He has taken a private room upstairs where you can eat. Follow me."

She conducted them up the staircase and away from the crowd. As they went, Theodore could feel inhospitable eyes watch him intently.

The people are scared, he thought, *and their fear will lead to anger that may be directed at the knights, if they are blamed for not preventing the coming storm.* Civil unrest inside the walls of Falador, while an enemy camped outside, could spell his order's defeat, he knew.

The smell of a pipe and the crackle of a roaring fire greeted them as Emily ushered them into a room at the top of the stairs. Ebenezer stood gazing thoughtfully out of the window and into the darkening evening. When he saw them his eyes shone with happiness.

"So you are all here then?" he said cheerfully as Castimir was the first to cross the room and embrace his dear friend. "You are all safe?"

No one replied, for their very presence answered his question. Suddenly, spontaneously, each of their faces erupted in a smile. They had faced danger and triumphed and now the danger, still in a place far away and many miles from the white walls of Falador, was forgotten. At least for the moment.

They drank and ate more than they needed. The rumours of war and their shared hardships over the previous few days made them ravenous, and they were aware that such revelry would be unlikely to come again for a long time. As they ate, each of the companions questioned the others about their experiences. It soon became apparent that the question on everybody's mind was how Ebenezer, an old man with little strength, had come to so dominate his aggressive prisoner.

"I thought he would strangle you," Castimir confided, the drink making his face shine. "I did not expect you to be able to control him. Tell us, alchemist, how you did it?"

Ebenezer smiled mischievously.

"Watch!" he said. With a sudden mysterious gesture, as if he were casting a spell, he waved his hands in the air, murmuring. Suddenly, with a shout, his eyes opened and a bright burst of white flame erupted near the window, setting the curtain alight with its vigorous heat.

With a cry of alarm, Castimir ran forward with his full tankard of ale, smothering the flames with the dark liquid. The wizard turned to face Ebenezer.

"That wasn't magic, alchemist. That was a trick! We wizards are trained to spot charlatans, and I saw right through your sleight-of-hand. You threw something on the floor when you raised your voice and opened your eyes."

Ebenezer laughed heartily.

"So I did. It was a trick. My voice and my eyes were the distraction. In reality I used science again."

Castimir refilled his tankard and sat again while the old man continued.

"As soon as I left with my prisoner, allowing you to head back to the monastery, I knew I had to employ a deterrent or else I would wake up with his hands around my throat one night. And so I set my mind to how best I could use my chemicals to achieve that end. Fortunately he knew nothing of science, and he didn't pay me any attention as I prepared my mixture.

"I did not need much—potassium and magnesium powder are a dangerous mix, needing little friction to set them off. At the right moment I threw my compound at his feet and the heat singed his eyebrows! After that I had no trouble from him at all."

"So he believed you were a wizard?" Doric asked with a grin. "Brilliant!"

All save Theodore broke out in laughter. Even Gar'rth, though largely ignorant of the words, shared in their humour, for the atmosphere was contagious.

With a low sigh Theodore turned to the window, his face etched with concern as he looked at the burning lights of the city he had come to accept as his home. His mood affected his companions and with sudden sobriety they returned to their chairs, each aware of what was on his mind.

"You have proved your worth time and again to us, alchemist," he said, choosing his words carefully. "Is there anything you can do for my city? Can any of your chemistry or your science give us an advantage over the Kinshra?"

Ebenezer shook his head.

"Since I returned to Falador I have been occupied with no other question but that one," he said. "But I must be truthful, Theodore. I have few chemicals at my disposal, and those I do have were prepared over many long months, with the help of my associates in Varrock. I'm afraid I do not have enough of them to turn the tide in our favour. I am sorry."

The alchemist's expression was pained as he watched the young man's head fall. After a moment's silence, he spoke again.

"But there are other ways I may be able to help. The people of Falador must be kept busy—they must not be allowed to dwell on the possibility of defeat. They know that the Kinshra are likely to come, and no doubt the agents of the Kinshra are spreading rumours of their strength before them. *This* is the war that must be won now—this is the immediate threat. The people must be rallied, and they must be convinced that the knights will protect them."

Theodore knew he was correct. The knights could not afford to ignore the people of Falador this time, not when the threat was so close.

"They must be managed, Theodore," Ebenezer continued. "The people must be turned into a service for the city. We may not have cannons, but we can still use artillery. Catapults! Trebuchets!"

"The enemy will sit beyond our range and smash the high white walls to dust with their guns," Doric said despondently.

"But Ebenezer is right," Kara countered. "The people need to be kept occupied, lest their idleness work against us all."

Theodore looked at his companions, and renewed conviction shone in his eyes.

"You should check the city walls tomorrow, Doric. Your knowledge of the cannon and your engineering experience should give us a good idea of just how long they will stand up to the Kinshra bombardment." He turned to Ebenezer. "And you, alchemist, in your infiinite wisdom, shall find other ways we can prepare, and in doing so boost morale. We will not let the enemy defeat us before he has even arrived."

Theodore hoped that such thoughts would bolster his friends as they considered the future.

Outside, it began to rain.

FIFTY-FIVE

A week passed, and each day a herald of the knights passed through the gates carrying messages to the crown prince in Burthorpe—messages that so far resulted in no promises of action.

"The crown prince wants a diplomatic solution," Sir Amik announced. The tone of his voice told the listeners how much faith he placed in the suggestion.

"If the reports are correct, then Sulla has managed to amass an army many times larger than anything we can hope to deploy," Sir Tiffy offered. "He has recruited the goblin tribes to his cause. Our scouts think their armies will meet within two days." His long fingers were clasped to his chin as he spoke.

"But most of his army are bandits from The Wilderness, drawn to his banner by the promise of plunder," master-at-arms Sharpe said. "The Kinshra themselves are no more numerous than us. If we can strike at the core of Sulla's army before it attacks, then it might be enough to scatter his followers—the majority of his army is an undisciplined rabble who will not fight in the face of organised resistance."

A murmur went up at this glimmer of hope.

"We cannot do that," Sir Amik said immediately. "If we initiate hostilities then we will have lost our moral imperative.

In a pitched battle they are more numerous than us, but if it turns into a siege of Falador, then we will have the city guard to help us fight on the walls. His advantage in numbers will be reduced, and his new cannon will be incapable of working so well in such close fighting."

Sir Amik let his words sink in amongst the small circle of men. As doubt crept into their faces, a single voice dared to speak what they all knew. It was Bhuler's voice.

"Your strategy will sacrifice Falador, drawing us into a siege!" he said loudly. "Do you expect every citizen to fight?" His hand slapped down upon the oak tabletop, the sound reverberating around the room.

"Remember who you are speaking to, Bhuler!" Sir Amik snapped, his anger boiling over. "We have no other choice. We shall fortify the city and gather as many provisions as we can. Shortly I will address a delegation of citizen leaders. King Vallance himself has refused to flee—even though he lacks the strength to stand, he hopes his example will inspire others. Notably his son." Another murmur, but the comments were not kind, nor were they hopeful.

The listeners knew the meeting was over. Without a word each man stood and filed out, leaving Sir Amik to pray to Saradomin that he had made the right choice.

But peaceful prayer eluded him, for he knew something was wrong. The crown prince was being evasive and Sir Amik knew he was doing it deliberately.

He just couldn't understand why.

The shadows were long in northern Burthorpe, for the town lay encircled by dark mountains in all directions save the south. And it was cold, due in part to the hard granite stone that had been used to build the famed citadel at its centre. It was an imposing sight, unlike the white towers of Falador in every sense, and it was a common legend that beneath the citadel there were many miles of tunnels and vast secret chambers.

But that morning a sight more imposing than the citadel had come to Burthorpe. The embassy of the Kinshra had ridden through the night, composed of nearly a hundred men, all well armed. With Lord Daquarius at their head they rode unchallenged through the dark streets.

It was only at the entrance to the citadel itself that he signalled his men to stop.

"Is the crown prince ready to receive our embassy?" he asked, aware of the disturbing dreams that had been conjured by the sybil to make sure the crown prince would bend toward his will.

A pale-faced elderly man barred the way, and he bowed discreetly. His fine black clothes were decorated with all the hallmarks of privileged birth and high rank. As the most senior advisor to the crown prince, Lord Amthyst was entrusted to ensure that the Imperial Guard kept the nation safe from the trolls in the mountains.

"The crown prince is unwell," he said nervously. "Nonetheless, he will see you at the earliest opportunity."

Lord Daquarius bowed in acknowledgement. Sulla's orders came back to him: *You only have to delay him, Daquarius—even you should be capable of doing that!*

"They will not hold for more than a week."

Doric had spent every waking hour inspecting every yard of the walls. He had lost count of how many times he had walked around the entire city, as his aching feet constantly reminded him.

"They will last longer than a single week, dwarf," Captain Ingrew of the city guard said. Doric knew the man was tired of his pessimism, and each had become increasingly hostile toward the other. "You've condemned the work of my engineers along every yard of the wall. I will not take it any longer. We shall go to Sir Amik with your comments."

The dwarf turned away and looked down from the parapet in despair. He saw Ebenezer issuing directions and shouting orders. Some of his men pulled hard on a rope and a wooden contraption was raised into the sky—it was the first of the alchemist's trebuchets.

Doric shook his head. He had expected Ebenezer to be the first to understand the power of the cannons and how hopelessly outmatched the antique weaponry of Falador would be. And yet here he was, wasting his time.

Bidding a surly farewell to the captain, he marched down the stairs from the ramparts wearing a dark scowl and, ignoring Ebenezer's wave of greeting, he approached the enthusiastic alchemist.

"Has Sir Amik thought any more on my suggestions?" he barked.

"I do not know," the old man replied. "He appreciates your work on the walls, true enough, but I would imagine he doubts that there will be time even for your plan to work."

"There may be less time than we imagined." The dwarf took the alchemist by the arm and led him away from the citizens who were constructing the trebuchet. "The walls won't stand for more than a single week. If the Kinshra concentrate their fire, they will be breached. We need more men!"

"Or more dwarfs," the alchemist observed.

"Is it such a stupid idea?" Doric growled. "The enemies of my people have already joined the ranks of the Kinshra—why should we not enter it on your side? I could be back in the halls of my people within three days."

"I think it is a good idea, my friend, but you must talk to Sir Amik." The two stared at each other. "I hope you are wrong about the walls, Doric—I most sincerely do." Peering quickly back to the trebuchet with a sudden expression of defeat etched on his face, Ebenezer turned and left Doric alone.

"As do I, old friend. As do I," the dwarf whispered to himself.

Every day before dawn Kara woke and made her way to the castle where she joined Theodore in constant training. On her first day there, as she had wondered nervously how difficult it would be, Marius had walked over to her and offered his hand. She noted the silence that fell over the courtyard, the expectant hush that seemed to still even the air, and without any bitterness she accepted it.

"Thank you, Kara," he said loudly so that all could hear. "You truly are a better warrior than I."

True to her concerns, the training *was* hard. At times Gar'rth joined in. He was an awkward pupil, however, for his superior strength made him a powerful combatant and the fact that he spoke few words of the common tongue meant that his mistakes could not easily be corrected by his tutor. Still, he had taken to his detention better than Kara had hoped.

Knowing how hard it must be for the youth, Theodore had taken to sleeping in the room next to him. It was a gesture Kara appreciated.

The week passed the slowest for Castimir—of that he was certain.

The knights summoned as many wizards as they could find in Falador, even those junior apprentices who at that stage of their training always accompanied a seasoned wizard in relatively safe lands. Castimir remembered his own such experience.

It had lasted only a few months one summer and his master had insisted on sleeping under a roadside elm for long hours, listening to the babble of a brook or watching the farmers in the fields. That had been five years ago, when he was just twelve. Looking at the youngsters who were following their masters now, he knew they were too young to be of any use in a war.

"We should send them home, Master Segainus," he told the most senior wizard present, a frail old man who could barely stand unaided.

"We will not, Castimir! They took a vow to learn and practise our ways, and I can think of no better way to teach the apprentices the true ways of magic than in battle. Look at what it has done for you."

Castimir hung his head, aware that in an instant he had gone from being a feted hero to a youthful mage—and a mage still in training at that. With a sinking heart he listened as Master Segainus spoke with the master-at-arms, suggesting where best to focus their efforts in the coming battle.

No one asked him for any of his ideas.

"There is no time to strengthen the walls now, and I don't think you are giving our engineers a very fair assessment," Sir Amik said as he looked Doric in the eye and pretended not to notice when Captain Ingrew smiled victoriously at the dwarf.

"As for the other matter, we shall discuss that. Alone." The smirk vanished from the captain's face when he realized that Sir Amik wished for a private meeting with the dwarf.

Both waited until his footsteps had faded in the stairwell outside. Then Sir Amik spoke again.

"I will accept your offer to seek out the aid of the dwarfs," he said. "We need the help of your people in this war. I shall give you several carrier pigeons to take with you so you can keep us informed of your progress."

"Then I shall leave tonight," Doric announced. "In another two days the goblin army and the Kinshra will meet, and the way northward will be blocked."

"But you won't be going alone, Doric. You must go with someone we can trust, someone who also knows the ways of the dwarfs, and their language." Sir Amik looked intently at the dwarf, knowing that one person would immediately come to mind.

"I will take Kara," Doric replied. "She knows our ways and is apparently famous amongst my people. Theodore, too, and Castimir and Gar'rth should come. We have endured much together and it seems right that we should try and see it through to the finish." He shifted the helm that he held precariously under his right arm, a sudden agitation gripping him.

"And the alchemist?" Sir Amik asked. "He's been with you since the beginning."

"That is true, but his skills will be of more use here. We will likely have to fight our way to Ice Mountain. It will be a swift journey through enemy lines and the alchemist isn't suited to it." Doric lowered his eyes. "I shall speak with him first, but I think… *I hope* he will understand."

The dwarf found Ebenezer drinking water greedily from a wooden goblet, hot and exhausted from the day's hard work.

"It has taken people's minds off the imminent threat. Citizens from all different backgrounds are lending a hand—they are actually hopeful, Doric!" The alchemist's eyes smiled from above the rim of the goblet.

"There is even more good news. Sir Amik has approved my suggestion, Ebenezer. I am leaving tonight." The dwarf stood with his feet wide apart, hands on the axe before him, willing himself to be as immovable as stone.

"And who is to go with you?" The old man gazed into the goblet.

"Kara and Theodore will both come. As will Castimir and Gar'rth." The dwarf's voice trailed off and Doric lowered his eyes to the ground. "It will be a hard journey, Ebenezer."

"I understand, Doric. I am not a good rider—my bones are too old to withstand the jostling of a horse beneath me. I think I will be of more use here in Falador than battling my way through enemy lines. But I do insist that you promise me one thing."

"Anything," the dwarf said earnestly.

"Make sure they all come back."

Doric took Ebenezer's hand in a tight grip but said nothing.

For it was not a promise he could make.

Night had fallen. To the north of Falador, no more than a two-day ride from the city, Sulla sat hunched over a map. His one eye squinted in the candlelight as he read the details of his army's deployment.

Behind him, standing silently in the dark shadows, was Jerrod.

"Our picket lines are watching every approach to the camp, whilst the goblins are securing our western flank," Sulla said. "Tomorrow they should join with us."

"And what then?" Jerrod's voice was even harsher than usual, for he was impatient for the war to start.

"Then we will move to within sight of Falador's walls. The goblins will be used for the manual labour—digging trenches to secure our positions. Depending on how well they perform, we could use them as a diversionary force.

"My guns will make short work of the walls of Falador. The chaos dwarfs think that within a few days—perhaps sooner—we will have opened a fissure large enough to exploit." Sulla leaned away from his desk, his face a macabre picture of wicked humour. "The knights have no way of countering my guns.

"For generations the people of Falador have mocked us," he continued. "For decades we have been despised in Asgarnia." He turned to face Jerrod, a dark glint in his eye. "Soon Falador will fall. Its streets will run with blood and its ruins will be ploughed into the earth. Let the people of Falador believe in peace, let them pray for a diplomatic resolution. But know this, Jerrod—there will not be one. Falador is in its final hour!"

"And then, Sulla?" Jerrod asked, his curiosity aroused.

"I will seize the throne of Asgarnia and the worship of Zamorak will enter a new age. We shall both have our revenge against those who have stood against us."

Outside, under the blanket of cloud that concealed the stars, the wind whipped through the camp, taking Sulla's dark promise toward the south.

FIFTY-SIX

They rode through the starless night, the long shadows concealing their movements. Theodore carried a map, given to him by Sir Amik, with several locations marked to the north of Falador.

"We keep a number of hideaways for our scouts," Sir Amik had said. "In case they should be cut off from the city. You will hide in the daytime and travel at night. When you reach Ice Mountain you will be in Doric's hands."

The squire also carried a small cage with several pigeons. The birds would fly back above the besieging armies, bearing any message from Theodore.

To the west of Falador lay a swampland where an army could hide, concealed by the treacherous terrain through which only the knights knew the correct path. Dead branches and buzzing insects harassed the companions, and several times they saw bright lights bobbing up and down, as if a man were signalling to them.

"What are those lights?" Kara asked.

"Some think they are spirits of the dead," Theodore answered. "Whilst others claim they are just a natural phenomenon. I heard Ebenezer say that they were most likely caused by marsh gas."

"He places too much emphasis on science," Castimir said,

swiping the air in front of his face to deter a cloud of midges.

"Maybe, Castimir, but I would feel more comfortable with him here," Doric observed.

"He is more use in Falador, Doric," Kara said. "He admitted that himself when he came to see us leave." Few people had been present to watch them go, for their mission was secret.

Overhead, the leather wings of several bats sounded and Castimir instinctively ducked.

"I'm not sure how much more I can stand of the swamp."

The prisoner sat with his hands in his lap, shivering in the darkness. The knights had made him deliberately uncomfortable: he had been left in the dungeons, below ground, kept in cold and darkness.

I should have tried harder to escape the old man, he thought, recalling his journey back to Falador under the watchful eye of the man they called The Alchemist. Zamorak was not a forgiving deity. If he ever returned to Sulla's army, his capture would likely mean his death.

He had believed he would die in Falador, executed by the knights as a murderer. As his mind dwelt on that, he wept in the lonely darkness, cursing the fate that made him a prisoner. And then he felt the draft of cool air through the iron bars, and knew he wasn't alone.

"Eat," the newcomer whispered from the darkness. A hand appeared between the bars, holding a wooden bowl with fruit and recently-cooked meat. "Do not leave anything for the guards to find."

The bowl was upturned and the precious food dumped upon the stone. But the prisoner didn't care, for he was ravenous.

"I will come again tomorrow night," the voice continued. "Keep your strength up, for you shall soon be leaving here. I need you to give some information to Sulla."

And then the man vanished back into the darkness, making no sound as he went. The prisoner smiled bitterly for the first time in several days.

The next night the man came again as promised. As before, he brought fresh fruit and cooked meat with him.

"Tomorrow night you escape." The man had held out his hand, revealing two keys in his open palm. "One for your cell and the other for the guardroom at the end of the corridor. After the guards change their watch, you will count to one hundred ten times. Then you must make your move. There will only be a single guard in the guardroom—and he will have been drugged. Behind the door you will find the uniform of a messenger. There are dozens of riders coming and going each day and at all hours—no one will think it suspicious.

"With the uniform, there will be a satchel with a suitable pass to get you out of the castle and the city. My message to Sulla is concealed between two sheets of paper—a map of Falador and one of Asgarnia. It describes how I will communicate with him once he begins his siege.

"Also in the satchel you will find a guide to the stables of the castle. There, a swift horse will be waiting for you.

"Do you understand?"

The prisoner swallowed hard, his mouth still full. It was a lot to take in.

"I do," he said, his words distorted as he chewed greedily.

"There is one other thing I need you to do for me."

"What?"

"You must kill the guard. Although he will be drugged, he needs to die by your own hand to give your escape veracity. Else he could identify my presence here and I would be under suspicion.' "

"I will do it," the prisoner hissed, knowing that his situation

was radically altered, aware that he would return to Sulla's army
as a hero.

"What is your name, prisoner?" the man asked as he made
ready to leave.

"Gaius. And you?"

The traitor laughed in the darkness.

"Just do your job, Gaius. Make certain the guard dies
tomorrow night!" Without waiting for an answer, he left as
silently as he had the night before.

And now it was the night of his escape.

From his cell Gaius could hear the sound of chairs scraping
on the stone floor and the friendly remarks as one guard arrived
to replace the other. When the prison went silent again, he
began to count.

One... two... three...

A moment passed. He heard the sounds of two men talking.
The guard sounded surprised at the appearance of another man.
The prisoner continued to count, disregarding the talk to make
certain it did not interrupt his concentration.

Seventy-four... seventy-five... seventy-six... he counted for the
third time.

A dull thud sounded from the room, followed immediately
by a clatter as a chair was overturned.

There was nothing more as he counted the minutes away.

On the ninth count his mind was made up. He could no
longer restrain himself. The key was unsteady in his hot hand
and he wasted precious seconds getting it into the lock. With a
savage turn, the door fell open.

He seized the key and rushed into the corridor. There were no
other prisoners, for the knights rarely detained anybody other
than the agents of their enemies. He ran toward the guardroom,
the second key ready in his hand.

Silently he listened at the door before attempting to open it. There was no sound from within.

Swiftly now, and calmer than before, he placed the key in the lock and turned it easily, pushing the stout wooden door open.

The guard was lying on the flagstones, his food half-eaten on the table where he had sat. He was breathing quietly.

Gaius knew what he had to do. He took a hammer from the bench at the far wall and with several hard blows he made certain the guard would never open his eyes again.

The uniform was where the traitor had said it would be and in a satchel with it he found the pass and maps which concealed the traitor's message. Within scant seconds he was changed, making sure the cap was pulled low over his forehead. He knew the chances of anyone recognising him were small, and at this hour—when many of the men would be retiring—he knew his escape was near certain.

But he wasn't so sure when he opened the door of the prison house. As he crossed the courtyard he passed two knights deep in conversation. Both ignored him.

It was the same in the stables. No one bothered to challenge a messenger. Several men were tending to their steeds, each looking as exhausted as their animals. Gaius ignored them as he looked for the horse the traitor had promised him.

But it was not there. A panic gripped him.

"Are you looking for your horse, sir?"

He jumped, then glanced down to see a stable boy yawning sheepishly.

"I am," he answered. "You have moved it?"

"Yes, sir," the boy said. "I had to move her, as we are running out of room in the stables now that Sir Amik has commandeered the citizens' horses. But I will take you to her."

The youth led him to a brown mare, already saddled and prepared for immediate use. With a vicious look at the boy,

Gaius mounted the animal and rode out into the courtyard, a sudden elation gripping his stomach. He could feel the smile tugging at his lips and he had to resist the urge to laugh.

He was so nearly free!

The guard at the end of the bridge took a single look at him and didn't bother even to read his pass, waving him on with an impatient look.

The second guard was different, however. As Gaius trotted over the bridge the man moved to intercept him.

"Where are you off to this time?" he asked without suspicion. "Varrock? Burthorpe?"

"Burthorpe," Gaius said impatiently, as if he were eager to start upon the three-day journey to the town north of Taverley. The guard looked up to speak, but Gaius interrupted him.

"… again!" he added.

The guard nodded in understanding.

"Is it true what they are saying? Is the crown prince unwell?"

"I am just a messenger, my friend. And a very tired one at that."

The guard nodded and stepped back, gesturing for him to continue. He headed north to the city's gate, where several guards glanced at him without even attempting to question him.

With a widening grin he rode out unchallenged onto the open road north of Falador and finally gave a triumphant laugh.

For he was free.

FIFTY-SEVEN

"The people are already speaking of defeat, Sir Amik," Nicholas Sharpe said. "You must pass the order, for the security of Falador is at stake!"

The knight raised his eyes, glancing first to Sir Tiffy, who nodded very slightly, and then to Bhuler, who turned away.

He knew he had no choice.

"Then it shall be done," he said. "If it is not, panic will overrun the citizens, before the enemy." He leaned forward, his quill scratching the parchment. "Any dissenters and seditionists will be arrested. There are to be no gatherings of more than fifteen citizens. Any mob is to be instantly dispersed."

An uneasy silence settled over the four men. Sir Amik knew that for the people of Falador, their ancient and hard-won rights were of great importance.

"The people will not like it, Sir Amik," Bhuler said plainly. "The policy could backfire, further convincing them that we are desperate."

Sir Amik raised a hand to stop him.

"The security of Falador outweighs all," he said. "We must be under no illusion. Crown Prince Anlaf has been manipulated by the Kinshra and will not side with us. We cannot wait idly by, not any more. We have already arranged our plans depending on the actions Sulla takes.

"If he comes south and starts a siege then we will break out in an attempt to disrupt his cannons, attacking from the swamplands where we will gather our strength. He will not expect that." He yawned, exhausted and suddenly feeling very old.

The master-at-arms spoke.

"We have commandeered a great number of horses, so every man who can fight will have a mount. For the plan to work we will need to assault the Kinshra with Falador's full strength—a combination of both the knights and the city guardsmen." Sir Amik nodded in agreement.

"Then call in all able men, even those from the almshouses, for every one of them will be needed." He smirked suddenly as he spoke. "I have seen Sir Erical wandering around the castle in recent days, as well as a few of the other retired knights. Let us hope they still know how to wield a blade and ride a horse."

The daylight was reduced to a sickly twilight under the gnarled trees that grew north of the swamp. The companions had spent an uneasy night, sleeping fitfully as they listened to strange and haunting sounds. Only Gar'rth seemed comfortable in that dismal place, for he had grown up in Morytania, a land of swamps and mires, where the dead did not rest.

They had been travelling again for an hour when Theodore raised his hand to signal a stop, betraying a sense of urgency which made his companions freeze.

He pointed to the east, where a large body of mist rolled gently over a calm lake. The companions could see several bodies on the shore.

"Goblins!" Doric hissed.

"And druids, too," Castimir said quietly, a pained look on his face. "Why would the goblins kill druids? What is the point of it?"

"Goblins kill for the sake of killing," Doric grunted, readying his axe. "If they are patrolling this far south, it might mean that Taverley has been attacked."

"But why would Sulla waste men and resources assaulting Taverley?" Theodore pressed. "Why destroy a place that holds no consequence to his war?"

"That's goblins for you, squire," Doric muttered. "Besides, occupying Taverley means that none of our messengers can get to Burthorpe. It means Falador is alone."

"Then we must make a decision," Theodore said. "Taverley is a day's journey away. If it is occupied, we will find it difficult to break east and make for Ice Mountain. Instead, we could start eastward now and skirt around the south of the lake."

"That could lead us straight into the Kinshra army north of Falador," Kara warned.

"Then we take our chances with Taverley," Theodore said. "And pray it hasn't fallen."

The crown prince woke to find both his valet and his Imperial Guards replaced by Kinshra warriors. He demanded first to see Lord Amthyst, and when he was told that his most senior advisor was under arrest for treason, he demanded to see the person on whose authority it had been done.

That was Lord Daquarius.

"Where is Lord Amthyst?" Anlaf's voice rose as Lord Daquarius entered his bedchamber. The prince's knuckles clenched, bleaching his fingers white.

"Lord Amthyst is in several places, my lord," Lord Daquarius said coldly. "He was executed this morning—in the manner befitting a traitor. It transpired that he had been systematically poisoning you over some months. Documents seized from his chamber prove this. Therefore, we have taken steps to ensure that you are protected."

The crown prince gasped. Lord Amthyst executed? But Amthyst was his oldest and most trusted advisor, the closest thing he had to a friend!

He fell to the plush vermillion carpet, biting his clenched fist and weeping uncontrollably.

"My lord, Asgarnia needs you," Daquarius said firmly. "You must be strong!" The prince felt the Kinshra commander's hand on his shoulder and he knew Daquarius was right. His nation needed him. Slowly, his tears and wails subsided.

He stood unsteadily.

"You are right, Daquarius," he muttered. "What must I do to ease the burdens of my realm? Who is to blame for this ill fate?"

"Is it not obvious, my lord?"

The crown prince glanced wildly from one wall to the other. He shook his head doubtfully.

"Surely if anyone is to blame, it is the Knights of Falador," Lord Daquarius said. "Has not Sir Amik Varze tried to entrench his order in Asgarnia? Has he not always been in competition with your Imperial Guard? Has he not always sought to confine my own order to the barren wastes of Ice Mountain, where we are permanently assailed from The Wilderness, while he sits like a fatted calf supping on the milk of Asgarnia's greatest city?

"Is this not all true, my lord?"

"It is!" A fever gripped him now. "I have always thought so, by Saradomin!"

Suddenly, his mood changed. He felt sure he could trust Lord Daquarius. Had he not dreamed of riding to war with the Kinshra in the service of their dark god?

"Yet I have never really worshipped Saradomin, for I was taught that a ruler should wield balance. The ways of Guthix appealed most to me, but recently, in my dreams, another has spoken to me. You do understand, Daquarius?"

"I think so, my lord."

He turned his back on Lord Daquarius and moved quickly, waving for his guest to follow. He climbed into a large cupboard and pressed the back panel forcefully, revealing a secret door. It led to a narrow passageway that disappeared into the darkness, and into that blackness he plunged.

The two men walked briskly in silence. When finally they halted, Lord Daquarius knew that the sybil's magic had worked its poison, far better than he had imagined.

They stood before an altar of Zamorak, stained with the blood of several animals. Lord Daquarius had never seen such a crude shrine. He had to restrain an urge to laugh.

With a sudden reverence, Crown Prince Anlaf knelt before the altar and began to pray to Zamorak, the god of chaos.

And unwilling to disturb the man's tormented mind, Lord Daquarius knelt at his side.

By late morning the Kinshra army sat encamped only three miles north of Falador, their scouts riding unconcerned and unopposed just beyond the range of a bow. Just beyond that range stood Sulla, looking south toward the city.

"Can we see the house from here?" He asked the officer, Gaius, who stood close at hand.

"I believe it is that one," Gaius said, pointing. "It is one of the few houses that stand higher than the walls. Each night he will send a signal by torchlight. In his letter he explained the code that he will use."

"And what house is that?" Sulla growled. "Who does it belong to?" He was still unsure whether this might be a ploy of the knights to deceive him. He had debated this point with his officers, but none of them believed the knights would willingly let the prisoner murder a man in order to escape. Their code of honour would not allow such a bloody move.

"Some of our spies who returned from Falador have told me that it is the almshouse of the knights."

"Then the knights have a spy in their ranks," Sulla chortled. "Make sure that every hour of every night we have keen eyes trained on the house, for we must know what he is telling us."

Gaius nodded enthusiastically, and left to make the arrangements.

"Should you not secure the camp, Sulla?" Jerrod asked. "That would seem to be the first priority."

Sulla dismissed his concerns with a wave of his hand.

"The goblins are going to dig a trench around our position, my friend. As we journeyed south you will have undoubtedly noted how my men have hacked away the trees?"

"I did notice," the werewolf replied. "I thought they were eager to fight, or simply enjoyed the random destruction."

Sulla laughed.

"They are, my friend, and they do. But they have also been cutting stakes as we have marched south. Those will be hammered into the ground to form a perimeter about our camp."

"And the goblins?" Jerrod asked with an amused grin.

"The goblins are to stay on my western flank. They will form their own defences. Five hundred of them have gone to secure Taverley, which no doubt means they will destroy it, for they have argued with the druids over land rights for generations. But the goblins are my tactical advantage over the knights—they are the expendable soldiers I can use to tie down my enemy."

"The goblins won't stand very long against the knights," Jerrod observed.

"Only long enough for my Kinshra pikemen to come up on their flanks, and for my cavalry to hem the knights in from behind. Then…" Sulla's smile widened as he spread his fingers apart and pressed both hands together, his fingers interlocking. "Then we simply squeeze!"

It was afternoon when the companions emerged from the swamp. The landscape had turned from bleak mire into verdant groves where the song of the trees swaying in the afternoon breeze seemed deceptively calm.

Doric, more used to a life underground, looked cautiously from side to side as if expecting trouble. He had been unnerved by what they had found at the lakeside.

Suddenly, Kara stopped in her tracks.

"The birds have stopped singing," she warned, drawing her sword.

"Can you smell that?" Castimir asked, turning his head. "It is smoke."

Theodore turned his mare quickly off to the right, climbing a small hillock where a parting in the trees gave him a good view to the north. As he mounted the summit he gave a startled cry that brought his friends to his side

For to the north a column of black smoke rose into the sky.

Taverley was burning.

From as far south as Falador, the citizens on the walls could see the smoke rising from the direction of Taverley. They knew that war was inevitable. Men shared dark looks with one another, comforting their wives, who in turn held their children.

Some of the citizens had already left with their families, but now Sir Amik had sealed the city, and those who were left were trapped. From his chamber the leader of the knights looked toward the dark column with a peculiar sense of relief. His course was now clear—war had been declared on the citizens of Asgarnia and he had a duty to act.

He turned from the window.

"Our decision is made for us," he said firmly. "Are the knights gathered?"

"The army slipped out before first light," Sir Tiffy replied. "Over a hundred of the city guardsmen went with them. Our total numbers are eight hundred strong. A small reserve of old men and young peons are now all that is left of our fighting strength here in Falador."

"Then I shall join the army in the swamp this evening," Sir Amik said. "At first light tomorrow, under the cover of the mists, we shall attack from the west, taking them by surprise. No one except us knows the paths through the swamp. Sulla must believe that it will guard his flank." He thought for a moment. "Perhaps that is why he has left his weakest troops there—the goblins—for his cannons point to the south and the east."

"You are certain the Kinshra do not know of the hidden pathways?" Bhuler asked, his expression troubled.

"I am certain. A swift attack will restore the confidence of the citizens and take advantage of the Kinshra position. If we delay even a day, then they will have fortified their encampment, making any subsequent attack harder. Even now the goblins are digging a trench to the south of their position."

The three men looked to Taverley once more, their faces grim.

"At least the waiting is over," Sir Amik remarked quietly.

Campfires burned on the plain. The sounds of the goblins working under the direction of the Kinshra officers could still be heard, for Sulla was aware that his camp was vulnerable and he was driving his men hard to ensure that their defences were erected as soon as possible. Already a long trench ran the entire southern length of his camp, several yards deep and as many yards wide. Its northern bank was coated in sharp stakes that had been hammered into the firm clay ground.

Behind them stood his cannon, ready to turn the field south of the trench into a killing ground, should anyone be foolish enough to launch an assault. Tomorrow his men would start work on another trench, to the east of the camp.

Accompanied by Jerrod, who had become his constant companion, Sulla rode three miles south in the darkness, toward the small group of men who kept a watch on Falador, looking for a single light in the high window. Dropping to the ground silently, he crept up behind their leader.

"Well, Gaius?" he said. "Has our mysterious benefactor had anything to say?"

The young officer glanced at his commander with a sly smile.

"He has said something very interesting, my lord," he answered in a low voice. "Something you will be extremely glad to know."

For a long moment Sulla said nothing. He listened to Gaius's report, thinking hard. When the officer had finished, he smiled, pointing to the west and to the swampland.

"We shall redeploy the men tonight. They shall be armed and ready before first light, waiting in suitable positions."

"Are you sure that you can trust this source, Sulla?" Jerrod asked doubtfully. "Could it not be a ruse to lure you into a trap?"

"If it is, it is not a very good one, my friend. If they come from the east we will see them in plenty of time to redeploy. From the south they would be forced to brave the trench and our guns, and they cannot come from the north, for our scouts are watching the roads. If they can indeed negotiate the swamps then the west makes perfect sense."

He mounted again, flicked his reins, and turned his horse back toward his encampment. He had long hours of work to do before the dawn.

FIFTY-EIGHT

It was dark when the companions reached the outskirts of Taverley. The town was eerily silent and as they moved through the streets, they passed several corpses, their outlines just visable in the shadows.

"There are fewer bodies than I expected," Theodore observed.

"Is it safe for us to proceed?" Castimir asked.

"I can't see anyone," Doric said. "But I can feel it—we are being watched."

"I can feel it too," Kara agreed, drawing her sword.

A small blackbird flew down into their midst, chirping a few inches in front of Castimir's face. It flew back to a nearby branch, chirped again, and nodded its head.

"Bold little chap, isn't he?" Castimir said, grinning.

The bird once again ducked off its branch and landed on the wizard's shoulder, chirping more urgently. It flew back to the east, landed, and again nodded its head.

"I have never seen a bird behave with such intelligence," Doric said.

Suddenly Castimir stopped grinning.

"Kaqemeex the druid! He could talk to the birds. Remember, Theo?"

Theodore nodded, realising what the bird had been trying to tell them.

"We must follow him. He will be our guide, for he and his friends see everything that occurs." The squire took his mare by the reins and led her quietly forward, travelling to the east. His friends followed.

Within an hour, with no sign of either goblin or druid, they came upon two lines of great oak trees whose boughs formed a natural arch. At its centre a bubbling spring cascaded from some ancient rocks that rose from the gentle turf as a cathedral might have an altar. In the grove were many druids. At their head was a man in a green cloak, his fraught countenance etched with a smile.

"So you have come," Kaqemeex said, smiling at Gar'rth especially, and the youth bowed his head in respect. "Many of us are here. The goblin attack was known to us beforehand and a few dozen of our older members volunteered to stay behind to satisfy the attackers' need for violence."

Theodore frowned in disbelief.

"They volunteered to wait for the goblins, knowing they would be killed?" Such bravery was rare, even amongst the knights.

"Yes. The goblins would have continued to hunt us if there had been no one there. Now their anger is sated and they have left Taverley, for a Kinshra messenger demanded that they head south to rejoin the army." The old man's eyes focused on Kara. Suddenly he looked more fraught than ever.

"Then the way to Ice Mountain is clear?" Theodore asked, hoping that another day's journey northeast would see them safely within range of the dwarf mines.

"Not quite," Kaqemeex said. "Supplies are being moved to the south. It will not be easy crossing the road to get to the mountain. Without my help, you are doomed to failure.

Therefore I offer you my aid, and the aid of my many friends." The druid pointed to the nearest oak, where a dozen birds perched on the heavy branches.

"Why help us, druid?" Doric said, curious. "I thought you were followers of neutrality, worshippers of Guthix."

"We *are* neutral, but neutrality requires balance, and the balance has been upset." Again his eyes focused on Kara. She blushed and avoided his gaze. "The gods are playing their little games again, and it is we mortals who suffer the consequences. Therefore, we must take the side of Saradomin to ensure that the balance is restored."

No one spoke as Kaqemeex bowed to listen to the chattering of a small thrush. When he straightened again, there was a look of urgency on his face.

"We must leave now if we are to cross the road before daybreak. We haven't much time."

FIFTY-NINE

The ground rumbled beneath them as they charged out of the mists in the west, blue banners flying, the dawn's eastern sun catching their polished armour. Eight hundred horsemen rode in three waves, with Sir Amik at the head of the first.

Following him in the second wave were three hundred knights, including Master Troughton, the former master-at-arms.

Behind those, in the final wave, were the city guards, the lightest of Falador's cavalry.

A packed column of goblin archers stood directly before them, a thousand strong, caught totally by surprise. They shouted angrily amongst themselves, aware that their infantry battalions to the north and south were too far away to defend them, while to the east a steep ditch they themselves had dug cut off any escape.

The archers had nowhere to run. They were trapped.

They only had time to loose four volleys of hastily fired arrows, without any organisation. Of those, very few reached the oncoming cavalry, and those that did were not powerful enough to pierce the heavy armour of Sir Amik's foremost line.

When the bright line of knights clad in heavy white armour ploughed into the panicking goblins, there was nothing that could prevent the onslaught. Sir Amik hacked to his right and his left, cutting through the resistance as his sword bit deep into green mottled flesh. He drove his horse onward, trampling those who were caught beneath the heavy hooves of his trained steed.

Panic overtook the goblins as each individual jostled his way over his comrades in an effort to escape. Their short daggers were of no consequence to the armoured enemy. They fled east into the steep ditch, or to the north and the south in a desperate bid to reach the infantry.

But to the north the goblin battalion lost its nerve. Upon witnessing the savagery of the knights, the nearest ranks turned and pushed back against those that stood behind. Amongst them were the five hundred goblins who had sacked Taverley, and that effort had totally exhausted them. They did not have the strength to fight such a battle.

Cutting down the last goblin archer who stood between him and the ditch, Sir Amik looked to the south, sensing victory in his heart. Sure enough, his second wave of cavalry had reached the southern goblin infantry, spreading chaos. He looked back to the north where the fleeing enemy was pursued by the city guards of Falador.

The goblins had fallen as easily as he had expected.

But where were the Kinshra?

With a roar, Sir Amik stood up in his saddle, beckoning his men south to deal the final blow against the goblin horde.

"The goblins have been defeated quicker than I could have imagined," Sulla noted bitterly. "And the city guard are loose on the field." He sat on his horse behind the ditch, watching the rout. The three cavalry lines of his enemy had spread themselves out to deal with the three goblin battalions. To the north a hundred guardsmen of Falador were driving over a thousand goblins before them. He hadn't expected them to split up.

Still, it is the knights who are the real enemy. The city guard

*will make the mistake of all ill-trained cavalry: they will pursue an
enemy from the field and abandon the true battle.*

"Send the first signal!" he ordered, watching the second line
of Sir Amik's cavalry cut their way deep into the southern goblin
infantry.

A second voice repeated the command and a burning fuse
was lowered. The cannon crashed backward, sending a roar
across the field. Sulla turned to the northwest, toward the
outlying woods less than half a mile behind Sir Amik's cavalry.

Out of the forest shadows they came—the Kinshra cavalry.
Four hundred strong, they were armed with lances that would
give them a greater reach than the swords of their enemies. He
watched as the black-armoured warriors rode forward, gaining
speed as they closed the gap.

But still his plan wasn't complete.

"Send the second signal!" he shouted.

Again a voice repeated his words, and a second and a third
and a fourth cannon roared in quick succession, the sounds
echoing off the white walls of Falador.

Sulla looked north to an area of ground just beyond his
encampment. There he had positioned half of his infantry, each
man concealing himself by lying down. At once the men rose
up and ran to the west. Their route would move them into a
position just north of where the goblin infantry had stood, and
once there, they would form a line.

To the south the other half of Sulla's infantry cut across a
small bridge of land that had been left between the two defensive
ditches. They raced to form a line south of the goblin infantry
which currently occupied Sir Amik's first and second waves.

Within minutes Kinshra were assembled to the north and
the south. With terrifying precision, they moved to close the
gap between them.

Sir Amik and his army were trapped.

The Kinshra horses went from a trot to a gallop, careening into the knights' unprotected rear. The long steel lance tips pierced the armour of their enemies, causing the rear ranks to crush in upon those in front.

Gaius shouted, throwing his bloodied lance to the ground and drawing his sword. He understood Sulla's plan—all he had to do was keep the knights from escaping so that the two lines of pikemen could get close enough to finish the work.

A man screamed below him. Gaius looked down to see a Knight of Falador stagger against the flank of his horse, a lance point protruding through his chest. Even in death the knight raised his sword. But Gaius was quicker, and with a savage hack the edge of his blade cut deeply into the man's exposed face. As the knight dropped his sword, Gaius struck him again.

Now the Kinshra cavalry and the knights fought at close quarters, exchanging sword blows, while goblins ducked and assailed the knights wherever they could.

Sir Amik leant forward to decapitate a foe, and his outstretched hand was seized. Another goblin leapt onto his horse behind him, a curved dagger glancing off the knight's visor in a desperate stab at his throat. Sir Amik heaved his sword arm back and then unexpectedly lunged forward, his blade stabbing goblin flesh. The grip on his arm slackened.

The goblin behind him cut the leather saddle, his blade biting into the horse's flesh beneath. As the horse reared up the saddle loosened, and both goblin and knight fell to the ground.

"Sir Amik is down!" Sir Vyvin cried. At once, the knights nearby hacked their way to their leader and surrounded him in a protective circle.

"We are surrounded—we are trapped!" Master Troughton called. His old body bore the signs of several wounds. "The

Kinshra cavalry have closed in behind us and there are hundreds of pikemen sandwiching us in."

The words cut through Sir Amik's daze and one thought above all pounded in his mind.

The Kinshra were prepared for this attack. We have been betrayed!

He could see the full extent of Sulla's grim tactics, how the goblins had been left deliberately exposed in order to draw out the knights while the pikemen took up their positions.

And then the pike bearers began their butchery. Each line of Sulla's pikemen was five deep, and each man was armed with a ten-foot pike. It seemed as if two walls were being pushed closer together, each lined with deadly spikes. And the knights were trapped in the middle.

Sir Amik knew it was unlikely that any of them would emerge alive from Sulla's jaws of death.

Captain Ingrew had never ridden into battle before, but he found the experience exhilarating. The goblin infantry had broken and fled before the city guards had even reached them, and now that they were running, unarmed and scattered, they were easy prey. He had already slain fourteen of them using the same tactic, riding swiftly past them as he delivered a sweeping cut.

If the knights were doing as well as he, the captain thought, then the goblin presence was as good as removed from the enemy's battle line.

Suddenly a call drew his attention, and he turned to see his fellow guardsmen mustering a hundred yards to the south. He cantered forward quickly, and as soon as he was within range he noted the horror-stricken expressions on the faces of his comrades.

"We have to go back," Colonel Payne insisted. "If we do not, the knights will all be killed! There should be enough of us to break through to Sir Amik's standard. Then we can withdraw from the field."

Captain Ingrew glanced again to the south. As far as he had been aware they had been winning. But one look was all it took to banish that illusion.

"We're running away?" a young officer cried in disbelief.

"We are extracting Sir Amik from that butchery, and whoever else may still be alive. We will withdraw back to Falador through the swamp."

With that, the colonel goaded his horse southward, and his men followed his example.

Hundreds of knights fell to Sulla's pikes. Even the goblin infantry succumbed. Knights and goblins had given up fighting one another in an effort to escape the deadly trap.

Sulla looked on approvingly. The knights could do nothing.

"Send in the berserkers!" he ordered. "Let us have some sport with our enemy."

Behind the lines of pikes, several ladders had been erected, and climbing them were savage humans. The berserkers were a chaos-worshipping people who lived in The Wilderness, practising cannibalism on any traveller who strayed into their clutches. They filed their teeth and their nails to a deadly sharpness and rarely used any weapons, for their savagery was weapon enough.

Sir Amik raised his banner at the centre of the trap, calling his men to gather around him in a last effort to break out. Then the first berserker leapt into their midst over the tops of the pikes. Others followed, leaping directly onto the horses of their enemies and dragging both man and beast down into the crimson mud.

Sir Amik turned to face one of the cannibals and was

shocked to see that it was a woman. He saw a green flash leap at him from his right, and instinctively he swung his sword up, parrying the goblin's thrust. But he could not protect himself from the frenzied woman who stepped in toward him with her teeth bared.

As he staggered back, a battle cry reached him through the confusion of the mêlée. It was Sir Vyvin, fighting at his side. Sir Vyvin hesitated before the berserker, and she took the initiative, leaping at him, her teeth finding his face, biting at him like a rabid animal. With a cry he stabbed her, finishing her off with a swift backhand swipe that cut her throat. Then he groped his way toward Sir Amik in their ever-shrinking space, his hand pressed over a wounded left eye.

The enemy's drumbeats quickened. As they did so, the Kinshra infantry moved in with a terrible haste, pinning back individual knights with several pikes at a time.

"Gather to me, men!" Sir Amik roared. "Under my banner we shall make a stand that will inspire a hundred generations of men!" His eyes were tearful as he drove his standard into an earth made soft not by rain but by the blood of men and goblins.

With a great shout his host charged the northern flank, hacking and slashing and dying on the impenetrable pikes, cutting down any berserker that landed amongst them.

Master Troughton, one of the most skilled of all the knights, was slain as he ducked in under the pikes, cutting down three of the Kinshra warriors before falling.

Nicholas Sharpe died also, saving Sir Amik from being impaled in an area where the two Kinshra lines had come close enough for the end of one pike to touch the end of its opposite number. And it was here that the real slaughter began.

The knights had thinned out as they had been squeezed, and now each man fought desperately to keep the pikes from stabbing at his front and his back. It was a battle that could only end in one brutal way. The men could only hope to delay their deaths.

Sir Amik was stabbed viciously in the side, and as he staggered another pike rammed into his calf. He dropped his sword in agony and seized his banner for support, and he knew the end could not be far away.

He looked at the men he had led to their deaths. With a feeling of pride he noted that none of them begged, that no one cursed him for his leadership. They were true Knights of Falador. They would die as they had lived.

Yet suddenly a panic seized the northern line of Kinshra infantry. Sir Amik watched as Colonel Payne and his sixty guardsmen crashed in upon the rear, forcing the pikemen to scatter across a wide front.

"Sir Amik Varze! Knights of Falador! To me! To me!" The colonel rode amongst the pikemen, mercilessly cutting them down as he perceived the carnage that they had wrought. Such was the ferocity that he and his men exhibited, Sir Amik was able to rally his troops.

"Knights of Falador, we must retreat!" he called. "Back to the city! Back to Falador!" Every man that could, took to the nearest horse, some even seizing steeds of fallen Kinshra warriors.

"Here, Sir Amik, take my horse," a young squire shouted, helping him up.

"Run, boy!" Sir Amik cried faintly. "Save yourself—and our banner!"

But the squire seemed not to listen. As the Kinshra cavalry pushed their way through their panicked infantry to finish the last few knights left, he gave a savage slap to the horse's flank that sent Sir Amik on his way to life and freedom.

The youth had no time to run as a steel blade swept down on him in a deadly arc.

———◆———

"Hold them off!" Colonel Payne cried, riding at full speed into the Kinshra cavalry, preventing them from pursuing the fleeing knights.

But his luck had run out. The Kinshra soldiers surrounded him, hacking at him from all directions. He fell from his horse into the soft earth.

"Shall we pursue them?" Gaius called to Sulla.

"No. Let them go," Sulla replied. "Let the people of Falador see their beloved protectors run. Let them know there is no one who can save them."

He turned to look at the city walls, visualising the weeping of men, women, and young children.

He imagined their fear. And he revelled in it.

SIXTY

Their journey was one of utter silence.

Once, just after crossing the southern road that led to Falador, Kaqemeex had hastily instructed them to lie their horses down behind a small embankment covered in ferns. Within a minute a troop of goblin infantry clattered past only yards away.

The druid left the companions at the foot of the mountain with Doric to guide them the rest of the way.

The dwarf led them further east, up onto the slopes of the mountain, heading always toward the snow line. After three hours of climbing, the atmosphere was noticeably cooler. Castimir took his fire staff and warmed them all in the red glow from the knotted tip when they paused to rest.

All of them were sombre, and seemed to become more so as they climbed.

"It is not far now. Another hour at the most," Doric said loudly, intending to instil some confidence into his friends. "We must travel along that ledge above us. It is wide enough for three men to walk side by side, and it will lead us to the entrance on the western face of the mountain." He noted the look of fear on all their faces, and admitted to himself that he didn't much like the ledge, either, with its terrifying drop of hundreds of feet.

"I do not recall this entrance," Kara said, "but I spent most of my time on the other side of the mountain. There is even a village above ground on a plateau to the south."

"All of that is true," Doric said, breathing wearily. "But this entrance is the most secure, and one which I am certain I can locate. Better this than spending hours searching for one of the hidden entrances near the valley floor, where the goblins would certainly find us." Without waiting for any further discussion, he urged them upward toward a flat plateau which led onto a narrow ledge.

"Here we should blindfold the horses," he said. "It will prevent them from panicking."

Doric led the way, with Kara and Gar'rth following closely. Behind them stumbled Castimir, his face an ill shade of green. Theodore remained several yards behind, making sure they weren't being followed.

"Don't look down, Castimir," the squire urged his friend. "Get in against the rock face and hug the wall."

But the treacherous path was not as long as they had feared, and as they rounded a corner, a plateau similar to the one they had left moments before presented itself. Doric led his horse confidently forward and removed the blindfold. His companions followed his example.

"We are nearly there. The entrance is hidden nearby, carved into the rock and under the frozen ice sheet." His voice echoed amid the natural walls above them. He was about to continue when Gar'rth hissed a warning.

"What is it?" Kara asked, her hand finding her sword.

"Battle."

It was one of the few words Gar'rth had learned in the travels with his friends, and it was a word none expected to hear so high up, so isolated from the rest of the world.

"Battle!" he said again, pointing to the ice that lay ahead.

And sure enough, faint cries and the crash of steel could just be heard.

The dwarfs were badly outnumbered, fighting on the ice against goblin soldiers who had studded their boots with iron nails. The three wolves that the goblins used in place of horses had also turned the battle in favour of their enemies, for the small dwarf patrol had no cavalry of their own.

And it wasn't just the goblins they were fighting.

The trap had been a simple one. A group of chaos dwarfs had been seen, wearing the red robes of Zamorak. The patrol had chased them across the frozen glacier... and straight into the arms of the waiting goblins.

Instantly the battle had become a disaster.

Commander Blenheim knew they were losing. The dwarfs had been unprepared and the wolves were taking a heavy toll on his men.

"Stand together!" he cried, raising his axe and gesturing for his men to gather close to the chasm that stood behind them. Yet that very same chasm cut off their retreat.

The three wolf riders grouped together to the north of the dwarf warriors, their commander barking out orders. The goblin commander pointed his sword and gave a harsh cry. The three wolves leapt forward, their yellow eyes focusing on their prey.

The gap had nearly closed when a spitting ball of red flame exploded in the face of the foremost beast, causing it to turn from its path and forcing its two companions to halt their charge. As they did, new sounds reached the dwarf patrol—hooves crashing on the ice, a battle cry of the Knights of Falador, and the familiar cry of a dwarf warrior calling his fellows to arms.

Theodore and Kara careened into the nearest of the wolves—the one Castimir's fire strike had wounded. They trapped it between them, each hacking from different sides. The goblin yelled as he swung his curved sword at Kara's face. Her adamant blade intercepted the thrust, shattering the goblin's weapon as she stabbed through his breastplate with enough strength to penetrate his black heart. As the rider died the wolf leapt at her horse, forcing Kara to jump from the saddle as her steed collapsed.

She thrust her sword into the beast's body as Doric and Castimir rode by. The wizard's second ball of flame went wide, passing between the two remaining goblin riders to burn a hole in the ice which rose like a wall above them.

But the enemy were scattered now. Shouting, the dwarf commander charged forward, closing the gap with the nearest of the wolf riders. Several of his men followed and with vicious hacks they felled the wolf and dispatched the rider.

Kara watched as the third wolf leapt at Doric, forcing him from the saddle with a blow of its forepaw. He landed hard upon the ice, cracking the frozen surface with his head, where he remained still. Above, the goblin rider raised his sword and lunged, his blade plunging toward Doric's unguarded back.

I cannot reach him in time! I cannot save him!

But then she saw that she didn't have to.

At the last second a strong hand seized the blade, its edges cutting the flesh of Gar'rth's palm deeply. With a cry the youth fell from his horse, landing atop the stunned Doric yet still holding the weapon in his bare hand.

The goblin rider dared to laugh. With a brutal wrench, he pulled his sword free from Gar'rth's grasp. But his savage laugh evaporated when he noticed the black blood on the blade.

The wolf caught the scent and let out a startled yelp, taking a step back as Gar'rth threw back his hood. His face was not human. His skin had turned grey, his eyes were two pools of blackness and his teeth and fingers had extended into bestial fangs and talons.

The goblin rider raised his sword in challenge.

The wolf leapt forward, obeying its master's command.

And Gar'rth stood his ground.

With snarling rage the two locked themselves in a dreadful embrace, Gar'rth ducking beneath the flailing maw and fastening his arms against the wolf's shoulders. With a chilling roar he dug his feet into the ice, which cracked under the strain.

Taking one miserable step after the other, Gar'rth pushed the wolf and its suddenly fearful rider back, yard by yard, closer to the chasm that yawned behind them. On they went, the goblin rider swinging and missing, shrieking at his mount, and urging it forward with the most virulent curses he could muster.

But it was no good.

Kara watched in awe as Gar'rth gave his enemies a final shove. With a despairing wail, both goblin and wolf fell into the black abyss. They spiralled into the darkness, their cries reverberating off the icy walls.

The werewolf's triumph spelled the end of their enemies' resistance. The dwarf patrol—with Castimir riding ahead of them—attacked the goblin troops and the chaos dwarfs who remained. Between the wizard's sorcery and the vengeful axes of the dwarfs, none escaped their wrath.

Far to the south, Bhuler watched as the Kinshra bombardment began. The trebuchets attempted to return the fire, only to find that their range fell woefully short of the enemy cannons.

As the first shots splintered stone and crushed wood, Sir Amik and the few survivors of his army returned to the city. They rode straight for the castle, ignoring the desperate looks of the people.

Sir Tiffy's face paled when they appeared in the courtyard. Turning to Sir Finistere and Sir Pallas, both of whom stood close by, he spoke, and Bhuler heard every shocked word:

"Of every ten men who rode out, only one has returned." And

for the first time he could remember, the ancient knight wept.

Sir Amik was shouting as he fell from his horse.

"We were betrayed!" he bellowed. "They knew we were coming." With a cry of impotent rage he threw his banner to the ground.

"Get them off the horses and to the ward," Bhuler instructed the squires and peons, who stood watching them in open-mouthed shock.

Only Marius failed to heed the command, for he was overcome by grief.

"I should have been with them, Bhuler. Many squires went, and few enough have returned. I should have gone... I should have died with my brothers..."

"Come, Marius," Bhuler said sternly. "It was by Sir Amik's command that you were confined to the castle. You are now a Knight of Falador, for too many of our order have fallen for you to be anything less! Don't just stand there—help me get Sir Amik to his chamber."

"Where is my banner?" Sir Amik cried as they dragged him toward the stairwell. "Where are my knights?" he called, gasping in pain from the wounds that had pierced his leg and side. "Where is Saradomin? Why does he not help us? Why? Why has he forsaken us?"

Bhuler hid his tears. He knew very well that the wounds Sir Amik had sustained would likely prove fatal, and that the shock of leading the knights to defeat had driven him to despair.

SIXTY-ONE

The way was lit by the torches of the dwarf patrol and the glow of Castimir's staff.

Doric's head had been hastily bandaged, but he had not stirred since he had struck the rock-hard ice, so Theodore's mare carried him on her back.

"He will recover, Kara-Meir," Commander Blenheim said, for of the remaining companions only she could speak the dwarf tongue.

"We are aware of the Kinshra," the commander continued. "The council has ordered our soldiers to be ready, for Zamorak is stirring again."

"Then you will go to the defence of Falador?" Kara asked hopefully.

He shook his head.

"There are some who would have us fight by your side. Others believe it would only endanger dwarf lives needlessly."

"And what do you think, Commander Blenheim?" Kara asked as they entered a large chamber.

"If the Kinshra win, then they will turn their attentions to someone else—maybe Kandarin, maybe us, but do it they shall," he answered. "And after that, it shall be someone else again." The dwarf warrior lowered his head. "Better to have an uneasy peace with Falador than deal with an ambitious enemy."

He spoke loudly enough that the entire patrol could hear, and a grim cheer went up, showing their approval. Kara knew then that his men all agreed.

The dwarfs were ready for war. They just needed a leader.

The summons instilled rising curiosity in Ebenezer, and he rushed to the guildhall. A group of men had preceded him, and he was surprised to discover that one of them was Lord Tremene, a wealthy merchant who controlled the city's bank and enjoyed good relations with the knights. By his side stood a young man of Theodore's age, wearing a squire's armour.

His inquisitive look prompted the armoured figure to speak up.

"I am Squire Marius, sir," the young man said. "Your actions at the monastery are known to me, and have been widely praised. In this dark hour, such initiative is to be commended."

A silence fell and Marius looked uneasily at Lord Tremene, who in turn looked expectantly at Ebenezer.

The alchemist did not know what to say.

"Thank you," he stuttered finally.

"I am instructed to offer you command of the city militia, sir," Marius announced slowly, as if unsure of how to proceed. A murmur of approval rippled around the room.

At last, something that will make a difference, Ebenezer thought, his mind beginning to race.

"Then I accept, Squire Marius," Ebenezer said. "How many men does the city militia have?"

Marius looked darkly at Lord Tremene, and his reply caused the alchemist's heart to drop.

"None, sir, for it is a new organisation." He turned to face Ebenezer. "It is to draw upon the average citizens of Falador to bolster our defences within the city. The population of Falador is usually forty thousand, but it has swelled to nearer twice that now the refugees from the north have taken shelter here. Therefore there is a large reserve of manpower upon which to draw."

Ebenezer nodded, and shook off his concerns. This was an opportunity for him, and he was going to make the most of it. Indeed, the more he thought about it, the more he relished the challenge this presented. So he took a seat with the other men and began to pepper them with questions. When he was satisfied with the answers, he rose and shook hands with Marius and Tremene.

The room cleared then, save for Marius and an older man. When the door shut behind the merchants, the newcomer stepped forward and introduced himself.

"My name is Sir Tiffy Cashien, Master Alchemist."

Ebenezer had seen him before, when he had returned from the monastery with his captive. Sir Tiffy had sat silently at Sir Amik's side, listening to his account of his journey. He was obviously an important knight.

"We have a traitor in our midst, Master Alchemist," explained Sir Tiffy. "We thought we had resolved the problem some time ago…"

Ebenezer held up his hand.

"This is not new to me, Sir Tiffy. On my journey north with Kara and Theodore I was entrusted with that knowledge, for it lay as a heavy burden between them. And the manner in which we were defeated this morning has indicated the possibility of further treachery."

"That is one of the reasons why we wish you to take charge of the militia. You are a new face in Falador and already beyond reproach. People trust you and they have faith in your science." Sir Tiffy looked briefly to Marius. "In fact, many may be more inclined to place their trust in science than in Saradomin."

"And how can I be of help in locating this traitor?" Ebenezer asked.

"We are certain he is a high-ranking knight—one of only three possible candidates. He could be more dangerous to us than a thousand Kinshra outside the walls."

Sir Tiffy rose and rested his fists on the table, leaning close to the alchemist.

"We cannot allow him to continue," he said grimly. "We must uncover him while there is still time."

"Then why not just lock all three up?" Ebenezer replied.

"These are senior knights!" came the reply. "The hopes of the people rest on my order. If word got out, then the citizens would abandon all hope. Their faith is already waning, but if they knew their betrayer was…"

He could not utter the words.

So Ebenezer finished his sentence for him.

"…If they knew it was one of you," he muttered in disapproval. "Then the knights would lose their trust, perhaps never to regain it." The knights were risking everything, just to protect their reputation. Ebenezer wondered if they had deserved it in the first place.

But as he looked into the old knight's eyes, he knew Sir Tiffy Cashien had a plan. Thus, with a resigned nod, he sat down at the table and listened.

As the dwarf commander led them on, the sounds of activity grew. Soon the rock caverns reverberated to the noise of hammers and picks, punctuated by the hiss of steam as smiths cooled their metal in ice-cold water taken from the underground streams.

"I was raised here," Kara said wistfully, looking across the immense cavern that was as big as any room Theodore had ever seen. "Tell me, Commander Blenheim, how is Master Phyllis?"

The dwarf's face darkened as he led them south through the cavern.

"Master Phyllis is old, Kara-Meir. He is too old to leave his bed. From what I have heard his illness has worsened."

"I would like to see him," she said, "for I owe him much."

"You shall see him in good time, but first you must address the Council of Elders. We must make a decision."

Though he could not understand what was being said, Theodore listened to their conversation with deep interest. He had not realised that Kara was so skilled in their language. After a time, he spoke up.

"Kara, you must make sure they attend to Doric. He hasn't stirred at all since he fell, and I fear for him."

Kara nodded and spoke briskly to the commander. He gave a brief nod, and three dwarfs took the reins of the surviving horses. Swiftly they departed, leading the horses west with an unconscious Doric still balanced on the saddle of Theodore's mare.

Commander Blenheim noted the concerned expressions on the faces of the travellers.

"He will receive the best of care, and you will see him again soon," he promised in the common tongue. "But now we must advise the council."

The Council of Elders was made up of the most experienced dwarfs in the mountain, Kara explained to her friends. It represented all aspects of dwarf society. Although the settlement was a recognised part of Asgarnia, neither the Knights of Falador nor the crown prince wielded any political power over their internal policies. Interaction between the two races was severely limited.

As part of the dwarf nation, the colony under Ice Mountain was allowed to take action to address any threat to their realm. It was because of this that the Council of Elders had met several times in recent weeks, even issuing orders to enlist all able fighters into a standing army. A request had been sent to the nearest colony, which was located under White Wolf Mountain to the west, beyond Burthorpe and Taverley. Two hundred additional dwarf warriors were expected to arrive, travelling via the secret passages beneath the earth, away from any spying eyes.

The dwarf council knew of the destruction of the monastery, the siege of Falador, and the burning of Taverley. They knew how the chaos dwarfs had stolen their own technology and delivered it into Sulla's hands. Such acts were not to be tolerated.

As the council meeting continued, all eyes turned to Kara-Meir and her companions, for she was known to them as a fearsome fighter and an equally skilled smith.

"What say you, Kara-Meir?" an old dwarf croaked from his chair on the plinth. "Should we intervene?"

Kara stepped confidently toward the chairman, and spoke the words she had rehearsed in her head.

"The walls of Falador were not built to withstand such weapons," she announced. "If Falador falls, then the whole of Asgarnia will become enslaved to Sulla, and he will have far more resources to use in future conquests. How long will he ignore the lure of the wealth that comes from these mines? With the help of the chaos dwarfs he will come for you. He will know your ways and your secrets, and you will be enslaved here to mine coal for his furnaces and gold for his treasury."

She paused to allow her words to sink in, then continued.

"If we act today, then victory can be ours. If we delay, then Falador will fall, and we will follow."

A murmur ran through the chamber. Unused to being the centre of attention, she had to force herself to keep her head held high and her expression stern, to show the dwarfs she was sincere in what she had said.

Yet not everyone agreed, and a small cry of disapproval sounded. The chairman called to the leader of the dissenters, asking him to explain his outburst.

"If we fight, then what will the humans of Falador give to us in gratitude?" he demanded. "The earth under their city is rich in resources, but for many years they have opposed any attempt by our kind to exploit them. I say that our efforts and our blood should be rewarded—in an agreement with the city to open our own mine there!"

"And why should we care if Sulla dominates the surface?" a second voice cried. "More likely he will wish to trade with us, rather than engage in another costly war."

A number of voices rose in heated debate. Leaning in close to Theodore, Kara quietly exchanged a few words with him. Then, as the argument threatened to grow out of control, she held up her hand.

"Listen to me!" she said as the voices eventually stilled. "My companion, Squire Theodore, is highly regarded by the Knights of Falador. He has the ear of Sir Amik himself. He has pledged to recommend your proposal to the highest authority, but this will only be possible if Falador can be saved. You know enough of the knights to know that his word is his bond."

The members of the council exchanged uncertain glances. Kara knew they needed more.

"Sulla would not trade with you, even if you offered him the fairest bargain. He is a conqueror, a worshipper of chaos! He will permit no other government to exist under his rule—and you will find yourselves slaves to the chaos dwarfs, who will give him whatever he needs to further the goals of their deity." Kara felt her face redden from the effort of her debate and she had to calm her rising anger before she could continue.

"I know this because I know Sulla," she added grimly. "He is the man who destroyed my home and killed my family."

In the sudden silence, an old dwarf priest stepped toward Kara, his quarterstaff bearing his weight and his free hand stretched out to guide him, for he was blind. The reverence the council showed him prevented any from shouting out. All waited for what he had to say.

"Guthix weeps, for the world is in flux and the balance is threatened," he said. "You, Kara-Meir, have been touched by the gods. It is you who must seek his guidance."

A murmur of surprise ran through the chamber. Never had a human been selected to attempt such a task.

Kara's eyes widened at the thought. Before she could speak, he continued.

"If you have been chosen by Guthix to lead us, then you must prove your worth. You know how Guthix favours the chosen— his words are spoken in the smith's hammer and his wisdom is revealed to us by the wielder's skill."

Kara knew what the priest referred to. Dwarf culture prized the skill of metalworking above all others, and in dark times it was customary for a leader to demonstrate his skill and thus reveal the will of Guthix.

She had no choice.

"What is the task?" she asked, aware that Falador's fate now depended on her.

"The amulet of King Alvis's queen must be repaired. For centuries it has been kept in our sacred care, waiting to reveal the mind of Guthix in a time of great adversity. The hands of a leader must be deft and skilful, for a leader must be a healer and not a destroyer."

The priest bowed and turned away, his proclamation complete.

Murmurs rippled throughout the chamber. None could doubt the ramifications of what had been said. Finally the chairman raised a hand and spoke loudly, quieting the assembly.

"Go now, Kara-Meir," he said, "and prepare for your task. When the priests are ready you shall be called. If Guthix so wishes, then you shall lead our armies."

SIXTY-TWO

At dawn, the southern gate of Falador opened and several wagons rolled out, escorted by thirty men.

"I hope this works, Sir Tiffy," Ebenezer said as he watched them go.

"One way or the other," came the reply, "we find out which of the two remaining suspects it is."

"You are certain Sir Pallas is not the traitor?" Ebenezer asked.

"The traitor who slew Sir Balladish had to be able-bodied. I have watched Sir Pallas discreetly, arranging some tasks for which he has needed to use his strength." Sir Tiffy shook his head. "The old man is not strong enough to be the traitor, and he could not have defeated Sir Balladish. That's not the case with the other two suspects however—even with one arm, Sir Erical is still a strong man."

"So you have leaked the story of the gold to just one of them?"

"That is correct," the knight said. "If the wagons are attacked, we shall know who the traitor is."

Perhaps at the cost of the unfortunate men who drive them, Ebenezer thought, but he held his tongue.

Their attention was drawn by a cry from the sentry above the gate. A hundred Kinshra horsemen had appeared on the crest of a hill, levelling their lances before charging down toward the wagons.

"Send out your riders!" Sir Tiffy barked to Captain Ingrew.

For the second time, the southern gate opened and two hundred armed city guards rode out to defend the wagons.

The skirmish was short and brutal. The Kinshra warriors had expected an escort, but as they rode toward the wagons the covers were ripped off, revealing a dozen crossbowmen in each. Their powerful bolts penetrated armour and felled horse and man alike.

Then, as the surviving Kinshra lancers reached the wagons, they were forced to discard their lances and use their swords, for the wagons had been modified with wooden slats to prevent lances being used effectively.

Captain Ingrew and his two hundred surrounded the attackers, as many of the crossbowmen in the wagons resorted to swords. Swiftly, the Kinshra were overcome. It was a minor victory for the city of Falador.

Once the skirmish was over, the men abandoned the wagons and retreated back to the southern gate, with Captain Ingrew's cavalry guarding them.

The men on the southern wall cheered and Sir Tiffy smiled grimly as he signed the document that rested on the battlement.

"Here is an arrest warrant," he said to a soldier who stood nearby. "Find Sir Erical and bring him to the castle immediately. He must not be allowed to see anyone until I get there."

Doric was sitting up in bed, grumbling to an exasperated Theodore about the dangers of horses. Castimir slept nearby.

Gar'rth sat next to the squire and Theodore examined his injured hand. The wound had nearly closed. The squire shook his head in envy of Gar'rth's regenerative powers. Though a look into the youth's sad black eyes made him dismiss such thoughts, for he knew that the turmoil Gar'rth suffered far outweighed the benefits of his inhuman nature.

"Those goblins were stronger than any I have fought before," Theodore said, interrupting Doric's complaining.

"Ah, squire, that's because the only goblins you've fought have been pitiful creatures driven from their homeland by their more vicious brethren," the dwarf explained. "You must think of them as beggars and thieves, mere nuisances throughout Asgarnia." He laughed bitterly. "No, my young friend, the goblin *warriors* are more deadly, although they aren't any more intelligent than their troublesome exiles."

A loud knock at the door disturbed a slumbering Castimir, who awoke with a start. Theodore looked up to see a breathless dwarf gesturing wildly for them to follow. Without a word the companions jogged behind him, wondering what could be so urgent. After several minutes, they found themselves in the company of Commander Blenheim and several of his soldiers.

"Squire Theodore," he said, bowing. "An army of soldiers is encamped in the foothills, nearly six hundred strong. We think they are a gathering of the Imperial Guard. Our scouts report they have little food and are debating what to do, for it appears the Kinshra have already siezed Burthorpe and have ordered the Imperial Guard to stand down. But they are still equipped for war."

Theodore glanced at his friends, unsure of what this could mean. Then he looked back to the dwarf.

"Get me my horse!" he said, and the elderly dwarf motioned to a soldier. "I shall ride down and speak with them."

As he said it, he wondered at the wisdom of his words.

Kara sat by Master Phyllis's bedside, listening to his weak breathing.

"Please don't die," she whispered, holding back the tears. "I don't want to be alone. There is so much I want to tell you!"

She had said these words many times, yet they had not stirred the old dwarf from his deathly slumber. But this time he gave a start and his eyes fluttered open, the orbs clouded with age. He watched her intently for a minute, and then he laughed carefully, though doing so seemed to cause him pain.

"Kara-Meir?" he asked. "What are you doing here, girl? Am I dreaming? Or am I dead? If you are here before me at Guthix's side then I am sorry indeed!" He squeezed her hand with a surprising strength.

"You are not dead, Master Phyllis," she replied. "And you are not dreaming. I have come back to the mountain to enlist the help of the dwarfs against the Kinshra, for they lay siege to Falador. But that is something for later. Tell me how you are feeling, Master Phyllis."

The old dwarf smiled, and caressed her blonde hair.

"I am ready to meet Guthix, Kara-Meir. I have dreamt of him much in the last few weeks." For a moment he looked into the distance, as if remembering something. "He told me you would come back. He told me to prepare something for you! Look under my bed, girl, in the iron box."

She pulled out the box and opened it with a fervour she couldn't explain, and when she saw what was inside she gasped in wonder. For it was a banner, resplendent with a golden Ring of Life and the flower of the White Pearl through its middle. Lying on the banner was a crystal vial strung on a necklace, with a blue liquid glowing unnaturally within.

"Men will rally to your banner, Kara-Meir," he said. "And the vial—you must wear it with pride. It has been in my family for more than a hundred years, since my father journeyed far south and was granted permission by the great serpent herself to take some of the holy tears of Guthix." Master Phyllis sighed, as though relieved of a great burden.

His grip on her hand slackened suddenly.

"Please don't die, Master Phyllis," she pleaded. "You are the only family I have." She rested her head on his chest and wept, barely aware of the dwarf's hand stroking her hair.

"We can't always have what we want, Kara-Meir. We must make the best of what we have. I am grateful to Guthix that I have known you. You gave my final years a great purpose."

His voice faltered and his eyes closed. After a moment his hand fell limply from her head.

Kara didn't move. She remembered how he had found her on the mountainside in the snow, years ago, and recalled the long days in which he had taught her how to mine and smith, and how to fight.

Her thoughts were interrupted by a loud knock on the door. Kara turned to see a messenger of the council and a member of the priesthood.

"Squire Theodore has gone into the foothills to parley with the Imperial Guard who have fled Burthorpe," the priest said. "Now it is time for your test, Kara-Meir. You must follow me."

She stood briskly, placing the crystal vial about her neck, her eyes on the body before her.

"Rest in peace, father. I will not forget you."

And then she left, following her escorts deeper into the earth.

SIXTY-THREE

Ebenezer was inspecting the new city militia when he heard shouts coming from the battlements.

Squire Marius and a dozen peons were drilling two bodies of four hundred men each, transforming them into fighting units capable of holding back the invading army. The men had been armed with pikes and trained to form an impassable column, which could force the enemy back into the breach.

As part of their training they remained in a perpetual state of readiness, sleeping with their weapons, never more than one hundred yards from the walls.

Yet concerns continued to plague Ebenezer. Even though Sir Erical's treachery had been uncovered, the old knight had disappeared into the mazes of Falador. All day he had been at large, and still dangerous, but the knights could not spare the men for a search. Thus Marius drilled his men all the harder and planned for every contingency.

The panicked shouting of the guardsmen was accompanied by a series of explosions.

That could mean only one thing.

A crack in the north wall had been made. A cheer went up from Sulla's line as they witnessed the beginnings of a breach. Like hounds scenting blood, every one of the Kinshra guns turned on that same area and within moments the firing resumed.

The alchemist knew the walls would not stand for long.

Kara wiped the sweat from her forehead and examined the blue ingot of metal that lay in her hand. She ran the point of her sword across the surface and, when it failed to even draw a scratch, her suspicions were confirmed. It was rune metal, stronger and heavier even than adamant, and far rarer.

Few were the smiths who could fashion it.

Her eyes focused on the forge and the red coals, and the image of Master Phyllis came back to her. She recalled the first time he had taught her the art of the smith, years ago. She had mined her own tin from cassiterite, smelting the metal on a fire of her own making, moulding the tin into the shapes of weapons. She had never made decorative necklaces or attractive trinkets. Always they had been the tools of violence, a symptom of her anger.

Now she pressed the bellows, blowing air into the forge. The coals responded greedily, glowing ever hotter. The colour of the forge began to turn from red to a bright yellow, hot enough to melt steel.

Her first time at the forge had also been under Master Phyllis's watchful eye. She had smelt bronze from copper and tin that she had mined herself, using the alloy to smith her first true sword. It had taken her days to complete and she had spent long nights hammering and heating and polishing the weapon. She had loved the work and Master Phyllis had been proud of her dedication.

Kara stirred the coal toward the centre of the forge where the heat was greatest. It would not be long now.

◆━━◆━━◆

It was dark when Theodore dismounted in front of the Imperial Guard.

A dark-haired man strode forward, his hand outstretched in greeting.

"I am Lord Radebaugh, leader of these men," he said.

"I am Squire Theodore." He grasped the hand firmly. "My dwarf allies told me of your presence here, and I come to ask for your help. Falador is under siege and the walls cannot last against the Kinshra guns. Together, however, we can have a chance of victory."

Many of the men who surrounded them nodded in eagerness, looking to Lord Radebaugh, but he avoided their stares.

"We are loyal to the crown prince in Burthorpe," he said. "Lord Amthyst was our captain and when the Kinshra embassy seized control of the citadel they executed him in the manner of a traitor."

That yielded an angry rumbling amongst the men as Lord Radebaugh continued.

"The Kinshra have the crown prince now, and he is their puppet. Our orders are explicit—we are to return to our homes and disarm."

"We must join the fight!" a desperate voice called from the back. "The Kinshra will burn Falador as they did Taverley."

"But we are too few," Lord Radebaugh sighed, looking to his men wearily, and it was clear they had discussed this before.

"By yourselves, that is true," Theodore agreed. "But we have help. Even now a hundred eyes rest upon you, for I have come from the dwarf mines where an army is mustering to go to Falador's aid. If you and your men side with us, then we may yet achieve victory."

A hush descended on the Imperial Guard. The men looked expectantly to their leader.

"For many years our orders have opposed each other,

Theodore, yet today I fight not as an Imperial Guard but as a citizen of Asgarnia," Lord Radebaugh said, and his voice reverberated with growing conviction. "I will fight with you."

A stunned silence descended over the soldiers. Somewhere nearby a horse neighed. Suddenly there rose a cheer from every man present.

"I shall fight with you!" a man pledged, stepping forward.

"As shall I!" another declared, drawing his sword and holding it high.

And then, six hundred swords were raised in unison, and again the men cheered.

Theodore held out his hand and Lord Radebaugh took it in a tight grasp.

Kara used the rune metal sparingly. She had only ever worked with it once before, and she had not been successful then. And this time it was not a simple blade she was making. The amulet of King Alvis's queen was a delicate thing of beauty, of subtle skill with hair-thick strands forming cascading rings emanating from the polished diamond that was embedded in its centre.

Three of the amulet's rings had been broken and it was Kara's task to rejoin them.

Kara was scared. She had never attempted to smith something of such subtlety before, and never when so much depended on the outcome.

She closed her mind to the sounds in the chamber, her concentration set on the task before her.

The tools felt strange in her hands. She held her breath as she leaned forward, her eyes focused entirely on the break.

"I can't do this," she sighed, panic gripping her. "It's impossible! How can it be right for the fate of a city to depend on a broken amulet? Perhaps I am not worthy of this task?"

Her face fell as she turned from the amulet and moved to a

bench. She sat in silence, her mind in a tumult as she regarded her failure.

It was the dripping of water that calmed her nerves. She searched for the source, high up in the shadows, away from the light of the forge.

As she did so she gasped in surprise. For the vial about her neck had begun to glow, strong enough to drive back the darkness of the cavern.

She held it before her, recalling Master Phyllis's tale of how it had come into his possession.

"The tears of Guthix!" she whispered. "Can it be true?" As she spoke the water in the crystal vial responded. The blue light grew in intensity, lighting the chamber all the way to the ceiling, high above her.

She recalled what she had heard of the legends, of the calming influence of the tears, of how they appeared to lead lost dwarf miners out of the darkness and back to their homes. Of how they gave hope to those who believed.

With a new sense of destiny, Kara raised the vial to her lips. And without a thought, she drank.

Throughout the long night, the citizens of Falador stayed awake, listening to the unending roar of the Kinshra guns and the crash of masonry as the walls of the city shivered and cracked. Children cried in their beds and pulled the blankets farther over their heads, while young couples, knowing that their future looked increasingly uncertain, spent the time clutched in tight embraces.

A light burned in Sir Amik's chamber. Bhuler pressed his fingers to his eyes to ease the weariness. He had worked tirelessly throughout the day, ensuring that his ailing master was made as comfortable as could be.

"There is nothing more I can do for him, Bhuler, and I have

many others to attend to," the matron told him. "It is for his mind that I fear most."

Sir Amik was lost in a delirium brought on by his defeat, but the loyal Bhuler refused to leave his master's side, working unceasingly to give whatever comfort he could.

He was disturbed by a knock at the door. Without waiting for an answer, Sir Vyvin entered, and peered at the figure on the bed. His own face was grim, for his wounded eye—although covered by an eyepatch—was causing him considerable pain.

"How is he, Bhuler?" Sir Vyvin asked. "Many of our order believe that he will not live to see the dawn."

As the highest ranking knight who could still fight, Sir Vyvin had taken command of the castle. He needed some good news to bolster his men's fading morale.

"He will live to see the dawn," Bhuler said quietly. "But he will not be able to lead the men. I fear his wounds are so grievous that he will never again wear his armour." The valet pointed to the crimson-splashed white armour which lay around the chamber. His attention focused on Sir Amik's banner, which rested in the corner as if forgotten.

"He *must* ride, Bhuler," Sir Vyvin pressed. "Without Sir Amik, our men are fearful. They and the citizens of Falador need to rally. At first light, I shall lead a body of squires and peons to the ramparts to repel the coming assault."

Bhuler raised his head in sudden alarm.

"Do you think it will be so soon?" he asked, silently shocked that the walls of the city could be breached in so little time.

"Sulla's goblins are mustering north of the city. Tomorrow, if the walls break, they will come."

The council members were uneasy. The amulet of King Alvis's queen was one of the finest ever examples of a smith's skill. Three dwarfs in the last two hundred years had attempted to repair it, and all three had failed.

Few expected Kara to succeed.

"She will fail, and then Falador will fall," one muttered angrily.

"But if Guthix calls her, then she shall lead us," an old dwarf said hopefully. He was a long-time friend of Master Phyllis, and he knew Kara well.

Before the doubter could reply, the door to the forge swung outward. From the chamber, with the red glow of the forge lighting her way, walked Kara-Meir. Her eyes shone with unnatural fervour and the crystal vial that hung around her neck was empty.

"It is done!" she said, her voice stronger and more commanding than before.

The blind priest gestured to her, his hand outstretched to feel the amulet. They all dared not breathe while he examined it in silence. Then he turned to them.

"She has done it!" he announced. "Kara-Meir has received the blessing of Guthix!"

They all clustered around to witness with their own eyes the miraculous workmanship. Murmurs of admiration rippled through the group.

"Then we shall fight under the banner of the White Pearl," Master Phyllis's friend said with pride. "And we shall be victorious!"

Ebenezer had not slept. He knew that if the goblins could get inside the city, then the Kinshra would follow quickly behind. Therefore, he planned to trap the first invaders in the breach, using his column of pikes as a second wall. But he knew the goblins were too numerous, and his four hundred strong body of city militia would not stand forever. He needed to impede the goblins' entry, so that even if they could get inside the walls, they could not do so in a single wave of overwhelming force, but only in small units where they could be cut down.

It was because of this that he now stood in front of thirty

large pigs. Standing next to him, Lord Tremene raised an eyebrow quizzically.

"How can pigs help to separate the ranks of the enemy, Master Alchemist?"

Ebenezer put his finger to his lips.

"The enemy has many agents within our walls. I would advise you to be more cautious." He motioned to a dozen men drawn from his militia who he knew had families in the city— men he could trust.

"By first light I want each of these thirty hay bales coated in pig fat and then carried to the ramparts and the artillery." Ebenezer noted the uncertain look on Lord Tremene's face. "Do you have so little faith in me, friend?" he asked the merchant.

"I have plenty of faith in you, alchemist," came the reply. "But using pig fat to fight a war?"

"Sulla uses goblins, we will use pigs. I'd say that gives us an advantage."

His humour gave his men strength, for laughter was no longer a common sound in a city that was preparing for death.

The traitor had sent his signal from the now deserted almshouse, for all the retired knights had been pressed back into active duty after so many had been lost in the battle.

He knew Falador was a city ready to fall, and when it did he needed to be sure he had an escape planned so he could avoid the butchery. And with the signal sent, he had arranged both his escape and a gift for Sulla. For the traitor had promised that he would deliver the knights' spymaster—Sir Tiffy Cashien himself.

As he reached the street he pulled his cloak tight about him, walking swiftly westward in the direction of the castle. He prayed silently to his true god, Zamorak, that he would not be caught in the open.

Kara-Meir looked to the south, her gaze followed by Theodore and Lord Radebaugh. Behind them stood several dwarf captains and Castimir, the wizard shivering with cold from the mountain air.

"It looks quiet from here," Theodore muttered.

"It will not remain so for long," Kara replied. "You must send your message, Theodore. We shall come to Falador at dawn, the day after tomorrow."

The squire nodded, turning to the small cage of pigeons he had brought with him. He had already composed the message with her, written in code so only the knights could understand it.

The birds didn't struggle as he took two of them from the cage. With a silent prayer to Saradomin, he threw them both into the air, and watched with satisfaction as they instinctively gained height and headed south. It would take them only a few hours to reach Falador from Ice Mountain, but still he prayed that it was time enough.

Two hours before dawn, a terrible rumbling stirred the citizens of Falador from what little sleep they had managed to take. It ended with a crashing echo that shook the earth and that could only have one single, terrible meaning—the northern wall had been breached.

It was the moment Sulla had been waiting for. As the dust rose into the dark sky, blotting out the lights of the city and the shivers of moonlight on its white stone, he smirked.

"Send in the goblins an hour before dawn!"

As he spoke he clenched his fist greedily, imagining the massacres that would follow his conquest of the city. The goblins had been angered by their defeat at the hands of the knights, and many more had hastened south to swell their ranks to nearly five thousand, in answer to their leaders' clamour for revenge.

The city would be turned into an abattoir.

SIXTY-FOUR

Thousands of goblins charged the breach, climbing over the wreckage of collapsed stone. They ignored the arrows that flew from the ramparts, as if they were pebbles thrown into the sea to stop the rising tide.

Even the frail Master Segainus and his fellow wizards who threw fire down into their midst, could not turn them back, for leading the charge were goblin warriors whipped into a suicidal frenzy by their more cunning masters.

Within moments, ladders were pushed up against the wall and more goblins climbed to storm the ramparts, in order to distract the defenders there from hindering the main thrust of their attack.

Even as Master Segainus blasted a third ladder from the wall, Sulla's artillery moved in behind the goblin hordes, sending shells over the wall and into the city beyond.

In the castle Sir Amik woke to hear his city in tumult.

"Has it come, Bhuler?" he asked, his face pale. "Has the end of Falador come?"

The valet was about to reply when the door opened. Sir Vyvin stood framed under the lintel.

"The goblins are outside the walls, Sir Amik," he announced. "If we do not go to the aid of the city guard and militia then they shall break through." His grim face, made all the grimmer by the black eyepatch he now wore, was resolved.

"Then go with my blessing, old friend," Sir Amik replied. "But do not allow the knights to leave the city—you are too few to face Sulla."

Sir Vyvin bowed his head and left the chamber hastily.

Bhuler looked down into the courtyard in the light of early morning, and the sight that greeted him made him gasp. For every man or boy who could wield a sword had been summoned, from the lowliest peon to the oldest knight. Even Sir Finistere of the almshouse was present, his face pale as he practised a thrust with his sword.

Sir Vyvin emerged and addressed the men.

"Knights of Falador, our city is endangered," he said, his voice loud and strong. "As we speak, the city militia are losing courage and men that could fight have fled, believing that we have abandoned them to hide behind the walls of our castle.

"Each of us took an oath when we took service in our order. The foremost of our responsibilities is the protection of this city. We shall join our citizens on the ramparts and in the streets, and we will fight with a courage that will instill all men with the will to take up arms to defend their homes. We shall drive the goblins out!"

He drew his sword and held it aloft, and the assemblage cheered.

"Sir Amik was injured, but he is very much alive. I have just seen him, and he gave me the order to fight!"

The men cheered again, and suddenly a young peon cried out, his finger pointing to the very window through which

Bhuler stared. The valet turned to find Sir Amik leaning wearily on his banner, his grey eyes looking over the men below.

"Sir Amik lives!" a voice shouted. The cry was taken up by every man, and some bashed their swords onto their shields in martial salute.

With a bow Bhuler moved to the side. Then with deliberate and calm slowness, Sir Amik raised his hand for silence, and a hush fell instantly.

"I do live, and Saradomin does, as well," he said, and all strained to hear, for his voice was weak. "The last few days may have made many of you question our faith, but know that we are his chosen people and Falador is a blessed city. So go now. Go forth to fight, and to avenge our fallen friends!'

Standing behind Sir Amik, Bhuler saw how much of an effort his speech took, and he noted how the old warrior's knees suddenly sagged. He ran forward to support him, out of sight of the men below who had begun once more to shout in eagerness.

"For Sir Amik!"

"For Saradomin!"

"For Falador!"

Sir Amik raised his hand in salute and the gates of the castle swung open to reveal the burning city beyond.

As the last of his men marched out, he collapsed in weariness.

The first faint rays of dawn broke through from the eastern horizon, yet they did little to raise the hopes of the defenders. Ebenezer's voice was hoarse from shouting and his militia, while holding back the goblins in the breach, needed constant leadership. He knew it could not have been done without Squire Marius's bravery. Even though he was the youngest present, he led the citizens of Falador time and again into the burning breach.

Side by side fought the blacksmiths and the ironmongers and the labourers who made up the militia—rich men and poor men alike, who all saw it as their duty as husbands and fathers to die protecting their families.

"There can be no retreat from here!" Marius yelled at them after the first of Sulla's shells had felled a dozen men. "If we run, then we shall die and our families shall die. If we stand and make them pay in blood for every yard they gain, then it is they who shall lose spirit!"

Yet even Marius's leadership could not keep the men at their posts forever, and Ebenezer knew he had to act. He turned his horse away from the breach and galloped toward his waiting trebuchets.

"Now it is time for the hay bales," he said. "Our archers will set light to them from the ramparts, with the help of the wizards if necessary."

Working briskly, the city guards prepared three of the bales. Within a few moments they were hurled over the wall and onto the goblins massing below.

"Send them all over!" the alchemist cried, riding back into the fray and signalling to the archers on the ramparts, who had lit their arrow tips in preparation.

The three hay bales, heavy though they were, had done nothing to stop the goblin surge, and the invaders laughed at the desperate measures of the defenders.

Then the archers loosed their burning arrows and the wizards, under Master Segainus's deft direction, poured fire at the bales that had been soaked in pig fat.

The goblin jeers died on their wide lips as the fat ignited, burning ravenously and uncontrollably, billowing out choking black smoke. As they yelled and screeched, the trebuchets fired again and three more stacks fell amongst the goblins and were ignited by the arrows and sorcery of the defenders.

Swiftly the flames spread, cutting the goblin army in two. Those goblins nearest the flames to the north were pushed mercilessly forward by those behind, screaming as they were jostled into the roaring fires. Meanwhile, the goblins to the south of the firewall found themselves trapped between the vengeance of the city and the uncompromising pyres. There could be no retreat for them, either.

Hundreds began to climb, so many that the defenders on top of the wall began to despair.

A wicked barbed arrow bit deep into the shoulder of Master Segainus's pupil, who collapsed in a faint.

"Take him to the city and tend to him," Segainus ordered the remaining members of the order. "But give me all your fire runes—I will hold them here." Swiftly the blue-robed mages carried the wounded youngster away, leaving their master as the last of the wizards on the wall.

"I am too old for this," he said to himself, breathing deeply, reflecting on the many years of happiness that he had spent in Falador. He tried his best to ignore the pain in his chest and the heavy pounding in his skull. Never before had he summoned so much power or fought so many enemies.

He held his remaining runes in his hands, calming his thoughts before continuing to muster his energies. Yards away, a ladder rested against the battlement, shaking as the goblins below began to climb.

He knew he didn't have long.

The runes in his hands responded to his concentration—he felt the power surge through him and threaten to break free from his restraint.

"Not yet," he said to himself through gritted teeth, his heart straining.

The runes twisted and warped in his hands, melting and

merging under his concentration to prepare the largest fireball he had ever conjured. He could feel the heat gathering as he fed the runes with his will, and he knew the magic demanded to be discharged.

"Just a few more seconds," he wheezed.

Then his breath left him as his chest twitched in agony, disrupting his concentration and making him stumble. The runes fell from his grasp and rolled out into empty space like a red flare falling in a dark chasm, fading from sight as they burned ever weaker.

Master Segainus knew he was defenceless. He was alone on the rampart with goblins overrunning the battlements on either side of him.

His knees gave way as he tried to breathe, and still the pain roared in his chest, but he knew it was too late. He had tried to summon too much power in defence of a city that he loved.

By the time the first goblin stood above the old wizard with his sword drawn, Master Segainus was already dead.

Even though Sir Vyvin wore an eyepatch he saw the danger clearly. One look at Marius and the pikemen of the city militia told him that they had successfully driven the goblins back to the breach, and that for the moment they required no help.

It was the ramparts that had fallen. The invaders had been forced to open up a wider front after Ebenezer's burning hay bales had disrupted their assault, and with sheer weight of numbers they had taken the battlements. It was up to the knights to take it back.

With a flourish of his sword, he leapt to the nearest stairs and ran purposefully upward.

To Ebenezer's eye, the battle was going well. The enemy had been prevented from flooding into the city, and keeping them trapped in the breach had removed the one advantage the goblin horde possessed. They had been unable to bring their thousands into battle against Falador's hundreds.

But the battle was shifting. The ramparts were filled with knights and goblins in a desperate struggle, yet for every goblin that was hurled down, another two leapt up to take his place. Swiftly, Ebenezer rode over to Marius, who was at the edge of the wall, shouting encouragement to the men next to him.

"We need to clear the ramparts," the old man called to him.

Marius nodded, thinking fast.

"Captain Ingrew!" he called, gesturing for the soldier to come closer so they could speak above the sounds of battle. "You must take fifty men from the breach and aid the knights on the ramparts. Use your pikes to prevent any more of the scum from climbing up."

The captain nodded and ran to obey. Ebenezer peered at Marius curiously and was about to say something when an arrow, fired through the breach, struck his horse in the neck. With a neigh it reared up and Ebenezer fell to the battle-marred earth, his face contorted in pain. With a hair-raising scream the horse galloped off into the city, forcing people to jump aside to avoid being trampled.

Marius was by the alchemist's side in an instant, helping the old man to his feet.

"Is anything broken?" the squire asked.

"I don't think so," Ebenezer wheezed, his face pale from the shock.

"You have done enough here for any man, sir," Marius said. "You should retire now to recover your strength. You will be needed later on." The squire's face was honest and concerned, and Ebenezer knew he meant no malice in his advice. Still, it hurt him to hear the words, and it hurt him more so as he realised the boy was right.

He nodded in agreement.

"I shall do so, Marius. But promise me one thing—promise me you won't let them break?" The alchemist nodded to the militia who were straining at the breach, successfully preventing the disordered goblins from gaining entry, and in spite of the pain, he smiled with paternal pride.

Marius nodded and his face brightened in an uncharacteristic smile.

"I won't need to make that promise, sir—for they have made it for me!"

On the wall Sir Vyvin was fighting savagely, with Captain Ingrew guarding his back. The pain in his mutilated eye made him angry and each goblin he hewed down seemed to bring him slight relief. But he was still thinking clearly, and he ordered his men to focus not on the goblins themselves but on the ladders—for once they were pushed away from the edge, their foes on the ramparts would be trapped in a city full of enemies.

A ten-year-old peon was cut down by a goblin soldier, drawing Sir Vyvin's wrath. With a raging cry he smashed at the nearest enemy with his shield, forcing the goblin back over the battlement and clearing the way for him to exact his vengeance. The goblin killer turned, his red eyes unblinking, and each leapt at the other with a single dreadful intent.

A sword swung and clattered on Sir Vyvin's shield. At the same time, the goblin stabbed forward with a curved knife in his other hand, the tip etching a line across the knight's breastplate.

With a stab of his own, Sir Vyvin forced the goblin to jump back, close to the rampart edge. A sudden swing of his shield made his foe lose his balance and sent him screaming into the city street below. Sir Vyvin saw Sir Finistere, followed by a host of youths armed with clubs and hammers, surge forward and batter the goblin down.

As Sir Vyvin drew breath, he saw that the militia had placed their long pikes at every point above the ladders, preventing any enemies from climbing up. Very swiftly, the goblins who remained on the ramparts fell to the vengeful swords of the defenders.

The goblins had lost heart for the battle. The cries of those trapped in the breach and behind the flames soon ceased, for none were spared the vengeance of the militia or the indiscriminate choking fumes of the fires. At least a thousand had been trapped and destroyed. As many again had been slain attempting to storm the walls, falling victim to the stoic magic of the wizards, the precise eyes of the archers, and the strong arms of the knights.

A signal was given shortly before midday. The goblins withdrew northward, exhausted and angry. The last hour of the battle had seen their assault reduced to simple archery, the very type of warfare the walls of Falador had been designed to withstand. For every defender who fell, at least five of the attackers perished.

"Continue the bombardment, Thorbarkin," Sulla said. "I want at least two more breaches in the northern wall before we try again."

Within an hour, the cannons resumed their ominous music, and the walls of Falador shuddered again.

"If they come again we shall not be able to hold them back," Sir Vyvin said, finishing his bedside report to Sir Amik. "The men are exhausted and desperate, and if the walls are breached elsewhere then Sulla will be able to get into the city. We do not have enough men to plug another gap."

"Then we must take the fight to the enemy." Sir Amik spoke softly. "We must prevent him from breaking the walls."

Sir Vyvin looked uncertain. Sir Tiffy sat nearby at a desk, writing furiously. The old spymaster made no reply, so intent was he on the message before him.

"Sir Amik will ride out tomorrow at dawn and charge the guns of the enemy," Bhuler explained. "If they can be seized and broken then it will buy the city time."

Sir Vyvin bristled at his words. "It will be a suicidal mission," he remarked, shaking his head.

"Possibly not," Sir Tiffy said from the desk, speaking with a hopeful tone that seemed out of place. The old knight stood up to explain, holding a piece of paper in his hand and motioning to Sir Amik's hawk. The bird stood on the ledge of the chamber window, shifting its weight from one talon to the other as it gorged itself on a pigeon it had seized from the skies above the battle. On the pigeon's leg was a small cylinder which had been opened.

"That's one of ours," Sir Vyvin remarked suddenly. "The murderous bird has killed one of our messengers!"

"It was a worthwhile sacrifice. The communication is from Squire Theodore. I have examined it against a copy of his handwriting, and it matches perfectly. The code he has used is a recent one and I have decoded it accordingly." He looked mischievously at his friends.

"Well?" Sir Vyvin said eagerly. "What does it say?"

"Kara is coming south. She will arrive tomorrow at dawn. She has several hundred dwarf warriors with her, and Theodore has recruited six hundred of the Imperial Guard. Together they number just fewer than one and a half thousand!"

So unexpected was the news that silence descended as each man looked at the others with renewed hope. If Kara could make it to the city then the Kinshra would not prevail against so many.

"It is tomorrow, then, that the fate of our city shall be

decided. And it is all in the hands of the woodcutter's daughter," Sir Tiffy said as he burned the message. "Speak to no one of this, for Sir Erical has not been found and he may be watching our movements. Tell the men an hour before dawn to prepare for battle. Only at the last minute will they be told that we intend to ride out."

Sir Vyvin nodded in understanding. When he left the chamber he was more hopeful than he dared to admit.

SIXTY-FIVE

The guns were relentless. By midnight, a second breach had been opened, wider than the first and several hundred yards to the east.

Some citizens collapsed on seeing the fissure, weeping in dreadful certainty that they and their loved ones would not be spared the Kinshra savagery. Brave men who had stood in the breach only hours before hurled their weapons down and cursed their gods for abandoning them. For, with two breaches, the defenders could not hope to defend the city.

Ebenezer had known this would occur and throughout the day he went along the northern wall, shouting encouragement and positioning barricades in the streets to impede the coming offensive. In the first breach, the defenders filled the gap with masonry and heavy timbers, stripped from those houses damaged in the mortar bombardment. They would prevent the enemy from making a surprise rush, but it would not keep them out.

To Sulla, watching from the plains, the walls were weaker than he had anticipated. They had been built generations ago by men who had never conceived of black powder and cannons.

Suddenly he detected a movement behind him. It was Jerrod, back from his hunt.

"Did you find anything interesting?" Sulla asked. "Perhaps a farm girl and her tasty young child?"

Jerrod wiped his hand across his mouth.

"No such luck, Sulla. I had to make do with some outlaws from The Wilderness who marched with the army."

"Just so long as you don't harm my Kinshra, for when the third breach is made we shall assault all three simultaneously, and I shall need them at their best." He placed his gauntleted hand on the werewolf's shoulder. "We'll find you a girl of noble birth, my friend—something soft and pale and very, very tender!"

His good humour went unnoticed by Jerrod who watched the bombardment with interest. He peered out over the battlefield.

"Why do you not turn your guns on the wooden gates, rather than the stone walls? Would it not be quicker?"

Sulla shook his head.

"Behind each gate the road will be built to favour the knights. They will be able to pour boiling oil on us, or trap us between portcullises. It is better this way. It makes them fearful, makes them gaze in horror at their fate!"

Inside Sir Amik's chamber the noise of the cannon and the wails of despairing citizens was inescapable. Bhuler was still awake and keeping watch, and he helped the knight to sit up.

"How long until the dawn, my old friend?" Sir Amik asked, his voice stronger than before. "How long until the darkness ends?"

"Another six hours," Bhuler said. He had spent the time in prayer, pleading for the knight's life and offering his own in its place. He knew that Falador needed staunch leadership now, more than at any other time in its history.

"Wake me at first light and help me with my armour." Sir Amik's eyes rested on his torn and bloodied standard, still leaning in the corner. "Everything shall be decided then," he sighed, lying down to sleep once more.

The third breach was made an hour before dawn, and it heralded panic amongst the people of Falador. From the window of his merchant house Lord Tremene watched in dismay as the wealthier citizens hurled their valuables into the moat about the castle.

The people have turned into animals, he thought. He saw a man push his wife to the ground and stand ominously over his daughter.

"It is a better end—to die here and now!" the man cried, tears running down his face as he raised his axe above his daughter's head.

"No, father!" she cried in horror, realising his intention.

But the axe never struck. Lord Tremene watched as Squire Marius pushed the girl aside and parried the blow with his sword before kicking the feet out from under the hysterical man.

"Do you call yourselves men?" he roared. "You are citizens of Falador—of the greatest city in the world! And look at you now. Sacrificing your women and hiding your gold, driven mad by your fear! Where is your pride?"

He gestured wildly with his sword at the crowd and immediately a strange calm settled over them. Men stopped shouting and the women ceased their laments. Swiftly the city militia broke the group up.

"Squire Marius!" Sir Vyvin called from the castle wall. "Bring the women inside the castle. They will be safe here."

If the Kinshra don't come soon, Lord Tremene thought, *the city will destroy itself.*

Ebenezer looked with disappointment bordering on despair at the men gathered near the westernmost breach, where they had successfully held the goblins before. Of his total strength of six hundred remaining men in the city militia, less than half had responded to his orders summoning them to the wall. The others had fled, to spend what they believed would be the last few hours of their lives with their loved ones or to hide themselves in the lowliest corners of the city.

Marius stood next to him, sharing his disappointment. The alchemist could sense anger in the squire, who felt betrayed by the citizens his order had defended for so many years.

Lord Tremene rode up behind them, and dismounted.

"Where are the reserves?" he asked as he stepped closer.

"There are none, save the city guard, and those number less than two hundred," Ebenezer said. "They are stationed at the gate under the command of Captain Ingrew." He spoke softly, his fingers caressing the runes in his pocket. He had retrieved them from the body of Master Segainus. He knew he could not wield a weapon with any degree of skill, so he had decided that resorting to magic was his best option.

At least, he thought wryly, *Castimir would approve.*

The alchemist looked grimly at the desperate men before him. He knew they could only hope to defend one of the three breaches that now perforated the wall. He cast tired eyes to the east, where he knew dawn would be lighting the streets of Varrock in neighbouring Misthalin. For a moment he wished he had fled before the siege had begun.

Anywhere but here, he thought.

Tremene laughed bitterly, catching the others off guard.

"Suddenly wealth doesn't seem so important anymore." He smiled ruefully at Ebenezer.

The alchemist smiled knowingly back.

"No," he said. "No, it doesn't."

"Permission to join your militia, Master Alchemist, to stand in the breach and fight by your side?"

The two men shook hands.

"Permission granted, my friend. Find yourself a suitable

position and send to the Abyss any enemy who crosses your path!"

The two dozen followers of Lord Tremene rode up and dismounted, checking their weapons and armour and finding places alongside his men. All the citizens of Falador were represented in the remaining militia—rich men stood alongside poor men, all of them *free* men who had offered to fight for their city.

Ebenezer looked into their faces—they knew that only death awaited them. As the drums of the Kinshra started to signal their advance, he felt very proud.

"Do you hear that?" a young peon said, his youthful face deathly pale from lack of sleep. "It's the drums. The Kinshra are coming!" The boy turned fearfully from the castle ramparts to face the man by his side.

"Courage lad!" Sir Tiffy looked unflinchingly into his young companion's eyes. "It is just a noise—and a noise cannot harm you." He ruffled the boy's hair playfully, looking northward across the city and over the shattered wall to the plain beyond. There was just light enough to see by, and on the plain he saw the black massed ranks of Kinshra soldiers march steadily forward, the sounds of the drums growing with each step.

"Soon they will be within range of our trebuchets," Sir Tiffy said loudly, "then their drums won't sound so confident!" His efforts were rewarded by the fleeting smiles of sudden hope on young faces.

The old knight left the ramparts a few moments later, walking swiftly across the courtyard to his horse. Without a word he climbed awkwardly into the saddle and rode toward the gate. He stopped to speak to Sir Vyvin, who was supervising the massed ranks of men who stood patiently in their armour next to their horses.

"Is Sir Amik ready to lead you out?" Sir Tiffy asked.

Sir Vyvin looked upward to Sir Amik's window.

"Bhuler is readying him now," he replied. "When he comes down we shall ride out into the city and Captain Ingrew's men will open the gate. With any luck we should be able to reach Sulla's guns before they can intercept us."

Sir Tiffy's eyes rested on the peons who sat nervously on their horses. There were only three hundred men and boys.

"They are too young for this, Vyvin," he said quietly. The other knight nodded gravely.

"They either die out there or in here, Sir Tiffy. If we ride out, we can buy time…" He lowered his voice even further. "… Time for *her* to come!"

The two men said nothing more, each praying that every minute brought Kara-Meir closer. Finally the old knight extended his hand to Sir Vyvin, shaking it firmly.

"Then good luck, my friend," he said with finality. "I doubt if we shall meet again. I shall go now, to visit the park for the last time and await the end, then to help where I may."

"Several of the old knights have gone out to help the city militia," Sir Vyvin said. "If you wish to fight, my friend, then you might be best employed there." He stepped away from the horse.

"Then I shall," Sir Tiffy promised, "after I have taken the air in the park one last time."

With a nod he rode out through the gates of the castle and across the moat, ignoring the despairing cries of the citizens as he galloped north.

SIXTY-SIX

At dawn they came. The Kinshra charged the three breaches simultaneously and raised ladders along the length of the wall. So swift were they that Ebenezer's trebuchets overshot their mark.

In the easternmost breach there were too few men to resist the enemy. Within minutes those few citizens and guards brave enough to stand had been driven off by the sheer weight of enemy numbers.

In the centre breach the same was true. Long arrows from the foresters who had fled their homes before the Kinshra advance were not enough to halt them, despite the fearful accuracy that felled scores of the enemy before they reached the streets.

In the western breach, where Ebenezer and his militia still fought, the Kinshra advance was briefly checked. The men of the militia fought with a suicidal desperation that overcame their better trained foe.

As the Kinshra hesitated in the breach, Marius's youthful passion asserted itself over his tactical training.

"Push them back! Drive them out of the city! Force them into the breach!" he yelled, waving his blood-stained sword above his head in a courageous frenzy.

His men cheered and the Kinshra gave way, their front ranks

turning to push aside the men behind. Into the breach the defenders rushed, shoving the Kinshra before them. They thrust with their pikes and slashed with their swords and yelled with an animal ferocity that even the followers of chaos had never heard before.

Sir Tiffy Cashien called to Ebenezer, aware of the danger Marius was falling into. He had ridden hard from his park bench, barely escaping the Kinshra soldiers who had stormed through the central breach.

"Ebenezer! You must pull your men back or we shall be surrounded," he shouted. "The enemy are in the city. If we linger here we shall be trapped!"

The alchemist knew he was right, yet he couldn't dismiss the thought that if they were victorious at the breach then the rest of the city would rise to follow them. Even if it were to mean their deaths, it would be worth it.

Sir Tiffy saw his friend's indecision.

"According to Theodore's message, Kara should arrive soon," he said. "We have a chance, Ebenezer. Sulla's force will be divided—some in the city and some outside—but we need your men to make it a reality. We cannot delay!"

The alchemist looked toward the breach, shrouded in smoke and echoing to the sounds of battle. After their brief hesitation, the Kinshra were rallying.

"And what of the city guard in the gatehouse? Do we abandon them?" Ebenezer asked, knowing that his retreat would leave them unguarded.

The old knight nodded.

"We have no choice. They can seal themselves in the building for a few hours. Besides, the gatehouse won't be the target— once the enemy get into the city they will look for plunder and forget the battle."

With a sigh, Ebenezer gave the signal. Swiftly his men

abandoned their position, running south toward the castle.

As they ran, Ebenezer counted the men. Three hundred had gone into the breach and now they were only half that number.

"The Kinshra have broken through the wall, Sir Vyvin!" a messenger announced breathlessly. "There are hundreds of them at each of the breaches."

"Does the gatehouse still stand?" Sir Vyvin asked calmly.

"Yes, sir—though for how long is anyone's guess."

"Ten minutes will be enough, my friend." He turned to the men under his command. "Gather your weapons, for we shall leave here as soon as Sir Amik joins us."

Sir Vyvin noted their courage lift at the very mention of the name. He smiled into the hopeful faces of the peons who had donned their armour and stood waiting to be led into a battle they were still too young to fight.

He thought back upon his last visit to Sir Amik's chamber. He had opened the door to find Bhuler struggling to help Sir Amik from his bed. In a fit of sudden anger the valet had shouted at Sir Vyvin.

"Shall I tie him to his horse as well?" he railed. "Will that satisfy your damnable honour?"

Sir Vyvin had said nothing, for there was no answer he could give that would pacify Bhuler's righteous anger. But Sir Amik's presence—riding in his armour and under his banner—was the only thing now that could give hope to his men. Sir Vyvin had closed the door, and as he had done so he heard Sir Amik fall to the floor while Bhuler uttered a curse.

He decided now to go back into the tower and drag Sir Amik from his bed himself. As he moved to do so, a door opened and a cry went up from his men.

For Sir Amik was standing there in the courtyard, holding his banner. With a sudden shout of encouragement, made all the more terrifying because it issued from behind his white visor, he raised the banner above his head and limped to his horse, which stood at Sir Vyvin's side. As he made his way through the men, they clapped and cheered and beat their swords on their shields with renewed fervour, while the peons wept unhidden tears at their leader's courageous sacrifice.

"I wish I had the strength to ride with him," an injured knight said as he, too, wept openly. "To go with him on the final ride of our order, and to commit indelibly to history the courage of our friends."

Without a word, Sir Amik drew his sword, pointing to the north where their enemy had begun to burn the city.

The guard on the gate looked to the north also, waving his flaming torch. The man next to him blew a long signal on a horn. It echoed across the city, gaining strength as it overcame all other sounds, until it reached the city guards and Captain Ingrew on the northern gate of Falador.

An answering torch was lit and a second horn was blown. Sir Amik dug his heels into his horse's flank, leading every man still capable of fighting out of the courtyard, to the north and to the war.

The Kinshra had driven all resistance before them, but now they were in the city their minds turned to plunder. Swiftly their discipline broke down and many, drunk on the rage of battle and their thirst for violence, fought amongst themselves.

It was the mistake that the defenders had prayed for, for it gave them time. With each passing second, Ebenezer and Sir Tiffy exchanged desperate yet hopeful glances.

When would Kara come?

Marius formed his men into a thin line across the street that led to the south part of the city, where all the inhabitants of Falador had fled. Dozens of others joined them in the retreat south. Some were bowmen from the northern forests who had fought the Kinshra at the central breach, others were young men who finally realised there was no other option but to fight in order to protect their families. Still others were old men who had decided to die with honour rather than whimper their days away, dwelling on their youth and what might have been had they had the courage to act.

Every citizen had been given a second chance, to face death with courage and prove that they deserved the right to call themselves free men. Sir Tiffy sat on his horse, looking to the north of the burning city. The Kinshra had made no attempt to engage in pursuit, and that worried him.

"Sir Tiffy Cashien? Is Sir Tiffy here?" a young voice shouted. Ebenezer turned to see one of Emily's messengers as he ran toward him.

"I have a message, sir! It is from Sir Finistere, from the almshouse." The boy looked furtively into the man's eyes. "It is Sir Erical! He has been seen. He is being watched even now."

The knight sat silently on his horse, his mind in turmoil. The man who had caused them so much damage over so many years was within his grasp, in the very hour his city was collapsing into anarchy. Was it all his fault? Had their defeat come about because of just one individual?

He raised his head, and his eyes filled with angry tears.

"He must be destroyed!" Sir Tiffy declared, his words shuddering. "He has caused so much death. He, above all others, must be destroyed!"

"I shall come with you," Marius said, before the old man had even asked him. "Many of my fellow squires perished by his treachery, and I could happily die today if I knew he was in the ground before me."

"I shall come also, if you will permit me," said the alchemist. "This man tried to murder my friend. I would like to look him in the eye and to ask him what reason he has for such treachery. I shall inform Lord Tremene that he is to take charge. He has proved himself more than capable."

The three rode to the north of the city, each burning with the desire to confront and punish this one man who had wrought such destruction upon them all. Their minds were so focused on their task that they did not even notice the horns sounding on the breeze, echoing above them off the high white walls.

For the knights had ridden out of their castle.

SIXTY-SEVEN

Sulla heard the horns.

Then he saw that the gates of the city had been opened. It could only mean one thing—the knights were riding forth. Instantly he recognised the danger, for his army was packed up against the breaches, trying to storm the city.

His men were not expecting an attack from behind.

He signalled his cavalry chief and saw Gaius raise his lance tip in acknowledgment. His four hundred horsemen would ride to intercept them.

The knights would come, but they would not find Sulla so easily caught.

No one barred their way. No spearmen attempted to hem them in, no arrows fell amongst them and no cavalry rode to intercept them.

They had taken the Kinshra by surprise.

Out they charged, following Sir Amik. The old knight's tattered banner waved above their heads and he brandished his sword before him. Through the gate they rushed, onto the plain. Their white helms and burnished shields reflected the bright morning sun from the east, blinding their enemies and filling them with panic.

The Kinshra infantry outside the westernmost breach had no time to react. They were too disorganised to repel an attack from an enemy they believed they had already beaten. Into the loose body of black-armoured men the knights charged. They smashed the invaders aside, trampling them under the hooves of their warhorses and driving their way to the centre of the group before any pikes could be levelled.

Sir Vyvin fought at Sir Amik's side, cutting the arm off the nearest enemy and parrying the panicked thrust of a pike.

"Sir Amik! We must charge the guns!" he yelled.

But Sir Amik pointed to the east, where Gaius's cavalry was approaching.

Then Sir Vyvin knew what Sir Amik intended. The lance points of the Kinshra horsemen would be deadly, and to remove the danger the knights had put the Kinshra infantry between them. So if the enemy cavalry chose to fight, they would have to ride through their own soldiers and sacrifice their tight formation. And if they did that, swords rather than lances would hold the advantage in close quarter fighting.

Ebenezer gripped the runes tightly. His heartbeat quickened. He knew Sir Tiffy and Marius shared his excitement, for both stared fixedly before them. Sir Finistere greeted them and sent away the messenger with a gold coin in his hand.

"He went this way," the old knight said, pointing to a culvert at the base of the wall—one which was large enough for a man to duck under.

"That way leads to the sewers of the city," Sir Tiffy said quietly. "If you know the way, you can actually get under the wall and out into the woods beyond. It may be that the traitor is attempting to run." He and Marius looked darkly at each other and Ebenezer knew that neither was willing to give up the chase, not even if it meant abandoning their city.

"He only went in a moment ago," Sir Finistere said. "He stood outside for several minutes before disappearing. Could it be that he is expecting somebody?" He, like the others, held his sword tightly.

"I know the way through the culvert and under the wall," Sir Tiffy said. "We should go after him now—just us, for we have no time to spare."

He looked briefly to the three other men. No one spoke. With a grim nod he drew his sword.

"Then let us go," he said, running briskly toward the culvert.

Across the road, in an abandoned town house, the man smiled grimly as he watched the four figures run to the culvert. He had known of the hidden entrance for many years.

He watched as the group disappeared under the wall, seemingly into nowhere. With a heavy sigh, he loosened his sword in his scabbard and ran after them as swiftly as he was able.

The Kinshra infantry was broken. The men closest to the savage onslaught of the knights turned their backs on their enemy, pushing their way through their comrades in an effort to flee.

Gaius watched as Sir Amik gestured with his banner, rallying his men behind him for a sudden charge that would direct the fleeing infantry into the path of the oncoming cavalry.

At the same time, another knight took charge of a dozen horsemen, riding out ahead of Sir Amik to the north. They prevented the Kinshra infantry from spreading out, herding them back directly toward their own oncoming cavalry.

Gaius saw exactly what his enemy were up to and he cursed bitterly, knowing there was nothing he could do. If he broke off his attack to avoid the fleeing infantry, then the knights would have the advantage and the speed to close in on them. Yet if he were to continue, then the infantry would be crushed by his own horses.

Yet that would give him a small chance to keep his formation intact and a slim possibility to enter the battle with speed and weight behind him.

With a cruel snarl Gaius made his choice. He raised his hand in command and the Kinshra cavalry gained speed, their direction unchanging.

They were going to ride down their own men.

The militia moved toward the gates of Falador, Lord Tremene at their head. The sounds of plunder were accompanied by the roaring flames that consumed the houses nearest to the breached wall. Yet their advance went unchallenged. It was as if the enemy had melted away. For the charge of the knights had cleared the western breach—those Kinshra who were not caught by their onslaught had hastened east to join with the rest of their army.

Lord Tremene saw Captain Ingrew watch them from the gatehouse, where he and his fellow guards had barricaded themselves in the hope of holding it long enough for the knights to ride out.

"Lord Tremene! How goes the war?" the captain called down from the fortified height.

"It appears the Kinshra fist has fallen upon the northeast quarter of the city," Lord Tremene called back. Even as he spoke he looked warily toward the nearby houses and cast an expectant eye up to the high walls. As the commander of the militia he would be the first target of any archer. The thought made him uncomfortable, and unconsciously he gripped his reins tighter, until his knuckles paled.

There was the sound of the barricades being ripped away from behind the stout doors, a testament to how far the city guard had gone to seal themselves in. Captain Ingrew emerged from the gatehouse.

"I have forty men with me," he said, blinking in the darkening sky as the wind carried the plumes of black smoke from the fires in the east.

Nearby, a house that had been burning since the Kinshra onslaught collapsed. The men nearest to it stepped back, away from flames that even from thirty yards were uncomfortably hot.

"Then what shall we do?" Lord Tremene asked the younger man.

"I suggest we march out onto the plain with the knights. That way Sulla will have to call his men out of the city, and our fellows still fighting in the northeast will have fairer odds."

Lord Tremene looked at his men sorrowfully. It would be a suicide mission. Carefully he turned his horse toward the open gate and rode slowly forward. As one, the men of Falador marched out after him.

The Kinshra cavalry had mercilessly ridden into their fleeing infantry, crushing them and ignoring their cries in their eagerness to engage the knights.

Yet the infantry had severely impeded their charge. Many of the Kinshra foot soldiers had sought only to save their own lives, and swiftly they had dug their pikes into the soft earth and stood resolutely before the black-armoured horses charging them down. In the end the infantry had been destroyed, but the Kinshra cavalry had lost its momentum and many of its foremost men.

That, in itself, would have been enough to give the Knights of Falador a fighting chance of victory, but Sir Vyvin chose to make it a certainty. As the Kinshra cavalry charged through the last of their own infantry, he urged his horse on and his men followed his example.

In he charged, intercepting the Kinshra and driving his warhorse into the flank of their formation. He and his men forced the enemy to press up against one another. This destroyed the Kinshra charge, for his flank attack had been perfect. The horses they had struck turned in to the horses next to them, and so on, rolling up the line as if it was an oriental blind from eastern Al Kharid.

Suddenly Sir Amik stood in his saddle, signalling his counter-charge.

Where can he have found such strength? Sir Vyvin wondered in awe. *Only a true commander can draw such energy from battle.*

In the knights shot, their white armour piercing the black formation like a bolt of lightning across the darkest night sky. Swords parried lances, pushing the deadly points aside before driving their polished tips into the now-vulnerable foes. Wherever sword met lance it was the same, for at close quarters the lance was an unwieldy weapon against an experienced blade.

Sir Vyvin hacked wildly at the face of the horse nearest him. As the animal turned away, its rider was vulnerable to a vicious stab that cut into his back.

The Kinshra horsemen knew they were losing, but only one man refused to run. Sir Vyvin guessed that he was the commander, and that he knew he had led his men into a humiliating defeat. With a courage born of despair he harangued his men from the saddle, bullying them into fighting.

"Fight, you cowards! Fight—or Zamorak take you all!" Gaius roared, driving into the ranks of his enemy with a bestial rage.

A flash of white armour on his left made him turn, but it was too late. With a precise lunge a defender drove his sword into his body, avoiding the black armour and finding the softer leather beneath his arm. It was a mortal wound.

Gaius screamed as the blade was withdrawn, his hands losing their grip on rein and lance alike. He could feel his life seeping from him. With a feeling of hopelessness, he turned to look into the face of his killer. It was a boy, a peon of the knights who was no more than twelve years old.

"A boy! Killed by a child!" he cried, falling from his saddle to the stained earth.

He was dead before he hit the ground.

"Send a message to the goblin commander," Sulla raged. "Tell him to move south toward the city." He had watched as half his cavalry had been destroyed by an inferior force. He cursed Gaius with the blackest words he knew, for the fool had lost a fight which he had started with every advantage.

But at least Falador has offered itself up for battle, he thought. Now he knew he had the city's last resistance before him.

"Tell the artillery they have a new target!" he called to the nearest messenger and issued new commands to the man, who immediately galloped to the north, where Sulla's cannons were stretched in a line facing the city.

The goblin mass reluctantly began to move south from their position. Since their defeat many had deserted, yet still they were two thousand-strong. But they were a rabble, he knew—undisciplined, exhausted and unwilling to be sacrificed in order to give Sulla another chance at victory. They might turn south, but they would be in no hurry to battle the knights.

Sulla knew the goblins would be incapable of winning and he knew that his own army, split between those inside the city and those outside, was in danger of being destroyed. Controlling his anger lest he make a decision he would regret, he sent another messenger with new instructions.

"Recall the men from inside the city. Have the remaining cavalry form up for a charge," he ordered calmly, knowing that he needed to concentrate his army before he could hope to smash his enemy once and for all.

SIXTY-EIGHT

The smell in the narrow passageway was nauseating, for they were wading through the sewage of the city. Ebenezer fought hard to stop himself from retching.

"It's not far now," Sir Tiffy said. "He can only be going to one place from here on. There are several cellars hidden down here, so old that I'd nearly forgotten them. We had a plan years ago to use them as hidden armouries but, in fact, we decided we didn't need any inside the city itself.

"Come on!" he urged.

The four men trudged onward, the pungent smell growing as they approached a stagnant pool. A faint draft blew down the tunnel toward them. Within a few seconds they entered a large chamber, walking knee deep in dark water.

"The entrance to the cellars is behind that door at the top of those steps," Sir Tiffy whispered. They crossed the chamber quickly and climbed the steps, moving in absolute silence. Marius and Sir Finistere drew their blades and Ebenezer stood nervously by.

"There is a light inside," Sir Tiffy whispered after peering around the open door. "It comes from the next room. I shall put out our lantern and we will go in."

The light was extinguished. Silently Sir Tiffy drew his blade and handed the lantern to Sir Finistere at the rear.

"We must take him alive if we can," the spymaster said. Ebenezer knew it was a decision not influenced by mercy, but rather by the idea of lengthy punishment.

Marius went first, followed closely by Sir Tiffy and then Ebenezer. Sir Finistere, the oldest of the group, came last, the excitement he felt reflected feverishly in his usually calm eyes. With eager steps they approached the room from where the light was shining, taking care not to brush against the unlocked iron gate that hung open against the wall.

Sir Tiffy clutched suddenly at Marius's shoulder, pulling the squire back.

"We shall rush him," he mouthed, raising his hand as a signal. Each of his friends nodded, and he lowered his hand. At once they rushed into the room.

There, in the glow of a lantern and hunched over a crooked desk, sat the man they had sought for so long—the man who had lived treacherously amongst the knights for so many years, who had betrayed Sir Amik's battle plan, and who had come so close to destroying their entire order. There sat the traitor, alone and strangely silent.

Sir Vyvin knew that the roar of the Kinshra guns signalled an adversary against which the knights had no defence. Horses and men were obliterated as the round shot drove deep chasms into the packed formation. But still Sir Amik rode ever eastward toward the centre breach, forcing their enemies to come streaming from the city for one last battle.

At the front of their charge, Sir Vyvin crashed to the earth when his horse was shot from under him. As his steed fell, he rolled instinctively, despite his armour, and his reactions saved him from breaking any bones.

Whilst ahead, Sir Amik was mercifully spared as a single shot passed only a hairsbreadth above his head.

The toll of the guns was terrible. Dozens lay crippled or dead.

Sulla watched the knights with contempt.

Standing by him, Jerrod seemed uneasy, and Sulla knew that his ally's snarl masked his fear.

He is a solitary hunter, not used to open warfare—though he would kill without hesitation, such carnage unnerves him.

The Kinshra lord motioned to one of his messengers.

"Form the infantry into two bodies. Have the cavalry prevent the knights from making any escape."

Behind his visor Sulla smiled suddenly, realising that this was the successful conclusion of his dreams. It had never been about Falador—rather his hatred had been for the knights themselves. Now, outside the walls of the city with his five hundred cavalry and two thousand infantry stretched before him, he vowed to erase them from history.

"Say something!" Sir Tiffy shouted, his passion overwhelming him as tears streaked down his face. He ran to the unmoving man, shaking him violently.

Marius rushed to his side.

"Wait, sir!" he shouted, pulling Sir Tiffy away. "Look!" the squire said, pointing to Sir Erical's stomach and away from his strangely ashen face.

Sir Tiffy pulled aside the man's cloak, which had fallen across his front. And as he did so he realised what a fool he had been.

For Sir Erical was dead. He had been dead for at least a day, murdered and abandoned to the rats by his killer.

"It is not him," Sir Tiffy gasped as he suddenly realised what that meant. "Sir Erical is not the traitor!" He looked vacantly to Ebenezer in shock.

Then, as one, they turned. Suddenly alert to the danger.

But it was too late.

The iron gate slammed shut, and from outside dreadful laughter sounded through the strong bars that had now become their prison.

The man rode as swiftly as his horse was able, guiding it toward Sulla. In his hand he clutched a Kinshra missive from the camp, marked with Sulla's own personal seal.

"Read it!" Sulla told the man. That it bore his personal mark enraged the Kinshra leader, for he had authorized no such thing.

But the messenger was terrified, and seemed unable to find his voice.

"What does it say, man?" Sulla demanded without attempting to conceal his anger.

Wide-eyed the messenger looked up, swallowing hard before commencing.

"It is addressed to you, Lord Sulla. It is a demand for your surrender. It says that if you turn yourself over to them as a prisoner, then the rest of us shall be spared. If not, then none of us shall end this day alive."

"Who dares?" Sulla laughed mirthlessly. "Where is the knight of Saradomin who is foolish enough to demand our surrender in his city's final hour? Has he nothing better to do than send impotent words against us, now that he has lost his sword?"

Sulla's men smirked at his confidence, but a whimper from the panicked messenger drew their attention once more.

"It was no knight... my lord!" the messenger said. He gestured back to the north and the men of the Kinshra looked toward their camp.

Sulla's single eye strained to focus. Then the faint flicker of orange flame caught his attention.

His camp was burning.

Swiftly he placed his foot in the stirrup to lift himself up into the saddle, lowering his visor in preparation for battle.

"It was a woman who surprised the camp, my lord… a girl!" The messenger cringed, as if he feared he would be struck down for uttering the words. "I was spared by her to deliver this to you, but few others were as fortunate."

The messenger's quivering explanation made Sulla stop.

"Is the letter signed?" he demanded, his heart quickening in anticipation.

The man's mouth moved, but no words came out.

"*Is it signed?*" Sulla repeated.

"It is, my lord," the man said. "Kara-Meir."

The Kinshra guns roared again, tearing their way through the knights, felling dozens.

"Why has Saradomin abandoned us?" a young peon cried despairingly.

Riding a horse he had taken from a fallen knight, Sir Vyvin could offer no answer. He had hoped to charge the guns in a last-ditch effort to wreck the Kinshra advantage. Yet Sir Amik had led them into the enemy infantry instead. Now they were paying for his hasty judgement.

"Can nothing silence those guns?" he shouted in impotent rage.

Then another sound echoed across the plain—a loud explosion, far louder than even the guns of the Kinshra had been, loud enough for the men near the walls to feel the vibrations on the air itself.

To the north, above the burning Kinshra camp, sat a huge cloud of smoke—vast enough to hide the mountain peak behind it—like a squat demon, intent on devouring the city and all those who fought on the plain.

"Is it the end of time?" a peon asked fearfully. "Is it the end of the world?"

Sir Vyvin shook his head, hope welling in his chest.

"Not for us!" he said. Then he let out a cry of savage hope, pointing to the northeast with his sword. For there an army marched under a white banner—and at its centre shone a golden ring with a white flower through its middle.

"It is her!" Sir Vyvin roared. "Kara-Meir has come!"

At the mention of Kara's name a new energy ran through the tired knights and their forces, and men who had been so near to admitting defeat rallied under the battered walls of their city, gaining fresh strength from the knowledge that their struggle and sacrifice had not been for nothing.

For the fortunes of war had shifted at last.

Kara-Meir had come.

Marius threw his whole weight against the iron gate. His efforts were rewarded by another cruel laugh as the strong barrier barely shook.

"Why?" Sir Tiffy said, his voice worn.

Sir Finistere stepped into the faint light of the lamp, making sure he was beyond arm's length of the gate.

"And how?" Sir Tiffy continued. "How did you know about our ruse with the gold, for only Sir Erical had been informed?" He sat resignedly on one of the crooked chairs, suddenly despairing, hiding his face in his hands.

"You ask me why, old friend?" Finistere replied. "I shall tell you. When I was as young as Marius and still a squire I accompanied a knight on his travels. It was winter, fifty years ago." His eyes were lost in reminiscence.

Suddenly he looked at Sir Tiffy.

"You would have been a peon then, a few years younger than I, yet you probably remember the uncertainty of those times. We had suffered the worst winter for a decade. Only a few years had passed since Misthalin had been invaded by the undead army from The Wilderness, and the city of Varrock was near destroyed. It was a time of fear—when old values were threatened and old securities failed. The wizards had no answer and there were rumours that they had reduced the size of their order, leaving the three human kingdoms unprepared to defend themselves. Some said they had spent their magic in the defence of Varrock. Whatever the reason, people knew they could no longer be counted upon to protect them."

"This is common history, Finistere," the alchemist said. "The turmoil of those times forced men of enlightenment to turn to more methodical and scientific ways to guarantee humanity's progress. That cannot be used to excuse your treachery!"

Finistere laughed bitterly. "Yes, alchemist. It signalled the growth of a new movement in science, but it did not change my views. I had become disillusioned with the knights but I was still faithful to Saradomin. It was when my knight and I fell into enemy hands that the fallacy of my belief was made clear to me. We were captured, lured into a trap by starving peasants we had helped only days before. They sold us to the Kinshra for mere alcohol they would use to further degrade themselves.

"Eventually they killed the knight but they spared me any agony," Finistere continued. "Rather, they showed me an alternative. They knew that in my youth I had been misled, inveigled into the service of Saradomin—a god who did nothing to protect my knight from the outrages committed against him. For a full year they kept me as a prisoner but treated me like an honoured guest, lifting the veil of falsehood from my eyes.

"They showed me how a man was meant to live—by the sword, with strength and passion!" His eyes glowed fiercely.

"You cannot imagine the liberation," he continued. "I had power to decide whether people lived or died. *Real* power under Zamorak!

"Eventually they released me, and very few of them were aware of my existence and loyalties. I found my way back to Falador and worked my way up the order over the years that followed. Never did I imagine, however, that I would be so successful in my role that I would bring about the destruction of the city and the order, living to see them in their final despairing hour."

Ebenezer coughed gently, afraid to interrupting the rant.

I cannot allow him to leave, he thought silently. *Not yet.* In his hands he held several of the magical runes and his mind raced as he attempted to summon the power that he had turned his back upon so long ago.

But he felt only the faintest connection.

Not enough, he knew. *Not nearly enough.*

"Falador will not end today, Finistere," Ebenezer said. "The city might burn and its citizens might flee, but it will continue nonetheless. It will endure a simple battle and an assault from a host of misguided men. History has proved that our race is not so easily brought low—not even the gods in the time of their wars could do it, and you shall not do it either. Even if you did triumph today and sack the city, in a few generations it will be only a footnote in the history of Falador. It will be but a dark hour measured against long years of light, and your name will not be remembered in any book or by any man."

Finistere ignored the alchemist.

"And how did I know about the lure of the gold? I have many spies in the city. They told me Sir Erical had received an important order from a messenger, and I proceeded to find out the details. It was not hard when I was living on the same corridor at the almshouse."

As the traitor turned to leave, he added a last mocking comment.

"To think I had to risk everything because of a mere woodcutter's daughter," he said. "It is an amusing thought now the game has ended!"

The words stirred Sir Tiffy.

"Why do you call Kara a woodcutter's daughter? All our stories were based around the probability that she was Justrain's daughter, and he never mentioned being a woodcutter in any of his reports."

The words seemed to catch the traitor by surprise, and he thought for a moment, then a new light appeared in his eyes.

"I see it all now." He spoke with the voice of a man savouring the ultimate victory. "You deliberately endangered her life in an effort to make me act."

He laughed, delighted by the knowledge of how desperate his enemies had been to find him.

"But Justrain *is* Kara's father, for he did pose as a woodcutter. I know this because the Kinshra informed me that their agents had intercepted a letter from a village woodcutter who matched Justrain's description." He waited for a moment to allow them to comprehend what he had said. "And when I signed my reply, I signed his death warrant and orphaned Kara, as well."

"So it was you who killed Bryant?" Sir Tiffy asked. "And Sir Balladish?"

"It was. I added several requests to Sir Balladish's list before it was sent to the apothecary—he did not know the exact details, but it is a routine we had established over many years in the almshouse. I made certain I was available in the courtyard to await Bryant's return, intending to destroy the list and remove my items before anyone knew exactly what I had ordered.

"But the apothecary had told Bryant of the possibility of using the herbs for poison, and the peon told me so. I knew that if Kara died from my potion, then Bryant would be suspicious. Therefore he had to die. Sir Balladish trailed me to Dagger Alley, however, confronting me after I slew Bryant. I do not know why he suspected me, but he died before he could make his suspicions known."

Again Finistere turned to leave.

"I have heard everything I n-needed to hear," a voice stuttered in grief from the entrance of the cellar. "And still I feel no triumph."

It was a voice every one of them knew. It was Sir Pallas.

With a grim look on his face, the old knight of the almshouse stood before the traitor, his unsteady hand holding a sword.

Sulla wiped the sods of earth from his face. He had been thrown from his saddle by the force of the explosion that had destroyed his camp.

"Someone must have lit the black powder!" Jerrod roared angrily as men and horses attempted to recover. "I can smell it!"

Nearby, the messenger groaned.

"The black powder is lost to us now. Soon our guns will exhaust their current supplies and they will be entirely useless," Sulla said grimly. "This is a failure that cannot go unpunished, and as you are the only survivor of those who failed me…"

He nodded to Jerrod, who stood over the messenger. The werewolf reached toward his throat before the man could defend himself. The messenger gave a brief cry before he died.

Sulla did not even bother to look, for he knew he had to rally his men.

"We must abandon the cannons," he said. "We cannot get to them in time now. We must concentrate on the knights first, for they are exhausted. Then we will turn our attention to *her*!"

He clenched his fists at the thought of the girl who had dared to interfere with his plans so many times, and he promised himself that—one way or another—it would not happen again.

SIXTY-NINE

Kara rode at the head of her army, which marched in a line. Under Theodore's direction, the cavalry remained hidden behind the burning encampment.

They had travelled south via ways unknown to any Kinshra patrol, under the earth, following Commander Blenheim. When they had come suddenly upon the enemy, they caught them totally by surprise.

Upon taking the camp, she had written her message to Sulla on his own paper and sealed it with his own crest, knowing it would enrage him. Then she had ordered everything else to be burned.

"Now is your hour, Kara! Now is the hour in which you will recognise your own power and take up my offer!"

The voice was one she had heard twice before. *His audacity is growing,* she mused. Before his words had made her fearful, but this time she was unmoved. Without even bothering to look at the ghoulish hunchbacked figure cloaked in red, she replied.

"So you have come to me again, Emissary, as you said you would." Her voice was calm. "Have your say, for there are more pressing things I must do."

"The way of the warrior is not the way of Saradomin, my dear," he said seductively. "I am offering you a place as commander of Zamorak's armies. Will you accept?" The High Emissary stepped toward her and held out his hand.

Kara looked at him for the first time.

"I have made my choice, Emissary. I will never follow your teachings. Nor will I follow Saradomin. I have suffered much at the hands of his followers, but I have suffered worst from your own. For me, the way is that of Guthix, the god of balance who exists in all things."

The figure stared at her for long moments before responding.

"Very well, Kara-Meir. If you survive this day, then I am certain we shall meet again." He turned his head at the sound of a horse galloping toward them. When his eyes settled upon Theodore he smiled evilly. "Know also that you have upset the balance. The Kinshra upset it first by marching on Falador and defeating the knights, but your refusal of my offer has made the pendulum swing yet again. This time the balance is too far toward the light. A sacrifice shall have to be made."

Before she could reply the High Emissary had vanished and Theodore was at her side. The Emissary's threat had found the one gap in her armour. Kara was not overly concerned for herself, but her friends were a different matter altogether.

"The cavalry is deployed as you instructed and the men are ready," the squire reported.

"Theodore," she said, as if she was seeing him for the first time in days. "I must tell you something, Theodore, before we go into battle." For a second she avoided his stare. "I just wanted to thank you for all you have done for me, in case I do not get another opportunity." She swallowed hard as she gathered her thoughts.

Theodore spoke before she could say anything more.

"You should not think like that, Kara," he said firmly. "We have fought together before, and you are as capable a warrior as I have ever known. Today is just another battle, and we will live to celebrate victory."

"Today is different, Theodore," she corrected him, desperate to tell him of the Emissary's threat.

"No, Kara. It is the same as any other. Only you have changed," he continued, drawing a curious look from her. "Do you know what the men say of you behind your back?"

Kara shook her head.

"They say you are touched by the gods. They all know your story, Kara. They have built you into a legend—and legends cannot die."

Kara lowered her head, fighting sudden despair. The army had made her into something she wasn't, yet she knew she had to take advantage of their fervour if they were to triumph.

She raised her head to Theodore once more and noted the bright look in his eyes.

"Then let us be about our business," she said, pushing her concerns away. "Let us save Falador."

She signalled to Commander Blenheim, and the dwarf army began to march.

"And what are you going to do, Sir Pallas?" Finistere asked. "Falador is dying, old friend, and yet you use your last hours to confront me rather than attempting to flee." The traitor shook his head, a mocking smile on his triumphant face. "Do you intend to kill me?"

The ancient knight stood resolute, though his sword hand continued to tremble.

"Release the prisoners first," he said firmly. "Release them and then surrender, for I promise you I will not let you leave here alive!"

The ferocity in the old knight's voice wiped the smile from Finistere's face.

"Do you think you are a threat to me?" he sneered. "You are a weak old man. Whatever glory you may have had has long

passed, abandoning you along with the vigour of your youth."
He drew his blade from his scabbard. "You cannot resist me."

Sir Pallas hung his head for a moment, acknowledging that
his defeat was inevitable. But then he straightened and looked
his opponent in the eye.

"You might be right," he replied. "But I am willing to sacrifice
everything to stop you. Are you as determined?" The old knight
breathed deeply and his sword ceased to shake.

Sir Tiffy nudged Marius and whispered in the squire's ear.

"If Sir Pallas charges him it might knock him against the
gate," he said. "If that happens then we must seize him through
the bars."

Marius nodded.

"So be it, Sir Pallas!" the traitor said. "But if we both die here,
then your friends will starve—and that will be an agony slow
to end." Then, with a growl of anger, the traitor threw himself
upon his enemy.

Sir Vyvin was knocked off his horse. The Kinshra pikemen
pressed in against the knights, pinning them and Lord Tremene's
militia against the wall of the city. They were trapped.

A Kinshra soldier ran forward to take advantage of the
situation. He put a foot on Sir Vyvin's sword arm and raised
his weapon to stab downward. Suddenly a horse neighed in
challenge.

The soldier turned just in time to see Sir Amik guiding the
tip of his banner toward his face. He did not have time to scream
before he died.

Sir Vyvin stood and began fighting on foot next to Sir Amik,
driving back the bolder warriors of the Kinshra army and giving
others cause for hesitation.

Lord Tremene shouted over.

"We are ready, Sir Amik! The cavalry has been kept back

behind our infantry. But we must go soon."

The leader of the knights surveyed the situation. The Kinshra had driven them against the wall in a horseshoe shape, and the enemy advanced from all sides, leaving only trampled corpses as they closed.

But Sir Amik had foreseen this, Sir Vyvin knew. He had played a desperate gamble to lure the Kinshra army in. He had ordered his cavalry to be held back, to keep them away from the enemy so they could be used to punch a hole in the Kinshra formation that was growing ever smaller.

He was just waiting for the right moment.

Sulla watched in satisfaction as his infantry hacked their way into the mass of white-armoured knights. As long as he could keep Kara from reaching them he was confident of victory, and the goblins had been ordered north to delay her.

"Lord Sulla?" a messenger called. "Word has come from one of our scouts. The goblins are in danger, for the newcomers have hundreds of cavalry. They have hidden themselves behind our camp and are preparing to charge."

The news stunned Sulla to silence. It was too late to warn the goblins now. A concerted cavalry charge would smash them in minutes.

Finding his voice, he cursed as he shut his visor once more, hiding his face from the uneasy looks of his men.

Kara-Meir had surprised him yet again.

Zamorak curse her!

The dwarf lines halted a hundred yards from the goblin rabble. A few dozen arrows had been fired half-heartedly by the enemy, yet they had failed to dent the dwarf resolve.

Kara sat on her horse at the head of the army and raised her sword. As she did so, the dwarf soldiers beat their axes upon their shields. The goblins jeered, attempting to drown the dwarf war ritual with their own. None of them knew the true purpose of the dwarf hammering.

But Theodore heard it and understood. He was at the head of the Imperial Guard, by Lord Radebaugh's side, hidden from the enemy's view.

The leader of the Imperial Guard turned one last time to his men.

"This is it!" he cried. "We must give Kara a quick victory! We must brush aside these goblins and move on to the city!"

The men cheered in anticipation, and from somewhere in their midst a cry was heard.

"For Falador, for Asgarnia and for honour!"

Every man shouted, raising his sword into the air, urging his horse on at a swift trot to answer Kara's summons.

"For Falador, for Asgarnia and for honour!"

Castimir clutched at Theodore's arm as they moved forward, and the squire turned to see tears in his friend's eyes.

"We read histories of the heroes when we were young, Theo. To think that in years to come children will read our stories!"

Beside them, a growling voice replied.

"So long as they are not our obituaries, Castimir. Then I shall be satisfied," Doric muttered.

The friends fell silent as the command was given to increase the pace, for speed was now of utmost importance.

Kara held her lines back, ignoring the goblin soldiers who called out to her and made obscene gestures.

"Keep up the drumming!" she instructed. "Let it hide the sound of Theodore's cavalry until it is too late for them."

The goblin horde had spread out to mirror the deployment of her army, for they knew how important it was not to become surrounded by an enveloping line. But in so doing, they had fallen for Kara's trap. Their formation would make Theodore's cavalry charge far more effective.

The first they knew of the six hundred-strong cavalry was the cloud of dust that appeared to the east. A cry went up, but by that time it was too late for their commanders to do anything.

From the northeast came the Imperial Guard, driving headlong at full gallop into the spread-out goblin line and cutting them down as if they were blades of grass under a scythe.

Castimir was the first to fell an enemy. He rode on the edge of the charge, intending to break off and use his magic from a distance rather than engage in close combat. Fire arced from his fingers and spread fear and confusion throughout the enemy ranks.

Then it was the turn of Lord Radebaugh and Theodore, who led the charge into the breaking goblin horde. There was no wall of spears to resist them, no packed column of disciplined strength to drive them off.

It was a massacre.

Theodore's mare trampled the first goblin under her hooves, while he beheaded another with a single stroke. The squire felt hot blood splatter his face through his visor. The scent of battle drove him on as he cut down another and guided his mare to ride over those who turned to flee.

"Fire!" Kara shouted. Five hundred carefully aimed bolts swept into the goblin mass. It was the only shot the dwarf crossbowmen would get, for they had no time to reload the bolts before the cavalry swept their enemy away.

In less than a minute, the entire goblin horde of two thousand had been put to flight. Those who had not been killed fled the field, abandoning their weapons and tearing off their armour in an effort to run all the quicker.

SEVENTY

The traitor parried Sir Pallas's blow with ease.

"This is pathetic," Finistere spat scornfully as the old knight stumbled, breaking off his attack to catch hold of the wall for support as he wheezed heavily. "I have kept my sword arm honed, practising in secret in case I might have to fight again. You don't have a hope."

"Let him go, Finistere," Ebenezer shouted. "It is murder now."

"It was murder a long time ago," Finistere replied.

Their swords sang as the two men exchanged several swift blows. The traitor was careful to stay away from the gate, ensuring that he was well beyond the reach of his prisoners.

"It is fortunate that I am in no rush," the traitor mocked. "I shall let the fighting end in the city before joining the victors in a satisfying plunder of Falador. None shall be spared!"

Sir Pallas lunged desperately, and the traitor sidestepped, leaving the old knight to gather his strength again.

"Come to us, Sir Pallas," Sir Tiffy cried. "Come close in to the gate. Finistere won't dare come so near to us."

"I cannot," Sir Pallas responded.

Then suddenly he grinned. "Evil must be fought, Sir Tiffy. We must all make sacrifices to that end!"

With a speed that surprised the traitor, Sir Pallas rushed him, his sword cutting a wide arc. But the traitor's patience had ended. He didn't even bother to parry the blow. Instead, he stepped forward, his sword darting in a single deadly thrust.

Sir Pallas gasped as the blade entered his body. He dropped his sword instantly and uttered a low moan of agony, collapsing to his knees, grasping at the traitor as if his killer would suddenly offer him a reprieve.

"Get your hands off me," Finistere said, reaching down to push the old knight away. But still Sir Pallas clawed at his killer as if his hands were weapons, tearing at his cloak and belt.

"Get away from me!" the traitor yelled, throwing the old man to the ground. He watched in contempt as the mortally wounded knight crawled with agonising slowness to the iron gate, where Sir Tiffy's outstretched hands were reaching for him, ready to offer what little comfort they could.

"My dear friend," he said with affection, his face dark as he observed the wound. "What could you hope to achieve by this brave act?" His hand lay on the shoulder of his friend, and he frowned as he saw Sir Pallas stretch his mouth into a pain-filled grin.

The traitor noted it, too, and was suddenly afraid.

"What are you laughing at, you old fool?" he demanded.

The dying knight smiled still.

"I have achieved a victory today, Tiffy," he gasped. "It has cost me everything, I fear, but it has been a just sacrifice to bring low a wretched enemy."

Finistere opened his mouth to speak, but as he did so the sound choked in his throat. For Sir Pallas's hand had fallen open, and a key dropped to the dusty stone within an inch of Sir Tiffy's hand. It was the key to the iron gate. Sir Pallas had ripped it from his belt.

The hunter had become the hunted.

With a cry of rage Finistere kicked over his lantern and fled into the darkness as Marius put the key into the lock.

He knew he could not outrun the Squire. It was in the darkness that his salvation lay.

Sir Vyvin followed Sir Amik's gaze north. Surely, he thought, it was time for them to begin their breakout? In the distance the goblins were fleeing as Theodore regrouped with the Imperial Guard in preparation for a second assault.

"We must go now," Sir Amik spoke for the first time to Sir Vyvin, who turned to reply, but his words were lost amongst the clamour of the Kinshra soldiers nearest the wall.

We will talk of this before the day is done, my friend, he thought, as he turned his attention to more pressing matters.

For the citizens of Falador had entered the battle. Hundreds of them lined the ramparts above the surrounded knights. Men hurled stones and bricks onto the heads of any Kinshra within range, while women emptied buckets of boiling water into the thickest concentrations.

At the same time, the knights' leader raised his banner, and the cavalry of Falador charged the thinnest point of the Kinshra horseshoe. Sir Vyvin was at Sir Amik's side, shouting to him in support. The great knight shouted back, urging them on, using his banner as a lance.

To the matron, who watched from the ramparts of the castle, it seemed as if the advancing enemy was simply biding their time, occupying themselves with plunder. She cast a dark look down into the courtyard. Pale, frightened faces looked expectantly up at her—injured men, unfit for battle, roused from their beds only to await the end.

"He should be here on the wall with us," she said to herself before turning away and marching across the courtyard. She ignored the whimpering of hungry children and weeping mothers who had taken shelter in the castle's protective walls.

She climbed the stairs and knocked upon the stout door.

"Bhuler! It is me. Open up!"

She listened at the door, expecting to hear the crackle of burning papers, the documents that Bhuler had said he would destroy to prevent them from falling into enemy hands.

"Have they come?" a voice responded. "Is it the end?"

As it spoke the matron opened the door.

"Not yet, old friend," she said, "for Sir Amik has..."

Her words died in her mouth. For sitting before her in his bed was Sir Amik Varze himself, his grey eyes regarding her coolly. He looked stronger than before, and with a gasp of sharp pain he pushed himself out of his bed and stood up.

"Where is Bhuler?" he asked calmly. "And where is my armour?"

The matron stifled a gasp as a cold realisation dawned on her. She remembered seeing Sir Amik ride out under the gate at the head of the cheering knights to face the Kinshra, and how his appearance alone had raised their spirits.

"It is Bhuler, Sir Amik!" she said. "It must have been him all along."

Before the walls of Falador, Bhuler knew he had been right. All those years of hard work and quiet determination had been worth it. Saradomin had spared him for a greater purpose.

He urged the men on, driving into the Kinshra formation and scattering them with his ferocity. Behind him the knights charged, their sudden rush surprising the enemy who had begun to assume an inevitable victory.

Horses and men screamed as sharpened blades stabbed through armour and flesh. The knights had focused their attack intelligently, and the Kinshra line could not contain them.

Out onto the open plain he rode, the first to break through. He circled wide to keep his men in formation as he turned back to drive into the rear of the Kinshra horseshoe. Now pikemen faced horsemen.

The offensive started a panic in the enemy lines. Very quickly they began to retreat, attempting to regroup into compact formations to resist the enemy cavalry. As the invaders turned their backs, the men of the city militia and those knights without horses exacted a terrible price, taking advantage of their disarray to fell many of their enemies.

Bhuler wept behind his visor.

"For Falador! For the knights! For Saradomin!" he shouted, raising Sir Amik's banner above his head and urging his horse forward into the mêlée.

"Over here!"

Finistere heard the squire's voice echo in the tunnel mouth as the sounds of two men wading through the shallow water of the sewer reached him in his hiding place. Finistere could hear the wheezing of Sir Tiffy and Ebenezer as the two older men caught up with the squire.

They only have one lantern between them now, the one I left in Sir Erical's chamber. I made sure of that when I sent the boy to lure Sir Tiffy here. How long can it last?

"He cannot be far away. He must be hiding," he heard Sir Tiffy say.

"We must not separate," Ebenezer replied. "We have an advantage in numbers."

"Finistere! You know you can't escape, " Sir Tiffy cried. "We'll find you sooner or later. Give it up!" he yelled. "Come out and I promise you will be treated fairly."

No one moved for a long moment, each waiting for the other to make the first sound that would give them away.

"We must flush him out." Ebenezer's voice echoed as the low glare of the lantern flickered alarmingly in the chamber.

It cannot last for much longer. The lantern will die soon, and then I will be able to make my move in the darkness.

"There are only two ways he can go from here—back to the city, or under the wall and outside," Sir Tiffy continued loudly. "Let us be patient, for we are the hunters now."

The lamp flickered again as a cool draft of air swept through the chamber.

No one moved.

SEVENTY-ONE

Sir Amik stood in the highest room in the castle, looking north, a spyglass to his eye. He watched as the cavalry regrouped itself and rode back to the dwarf line, which was moving south.

To the east he saw Sulla's remaining cavalry, several hundred strong. The horsemen were riding west to prevent the armies of Falador from combining with the dwarfs.

He lowered his head in grief.

"Bhuler, I pray you know what you are doing. If not, you have condemned us all."

But there was nothing he could do save watch.

Sulla had hurled the last of his men into the battle. His cavalry had been dispatched to keep the dwarf forces occupied while his infantry moved to annihilate the outnumbered knights. Even Jerrod had been forced into the battle. Sulla's one instruction to him was chillingly concise.

"Bring me Sir Amik's head! Fell him and the rest will follow."

The werewolf growled in acknowledgment. He had never fought in a pitched battle before. His fights had always been ones of hunting and ambush, never amidst hundreds of desperate, well-armed men. Feeling suddenly vulnerable, he moved to obey Sulla's command, knowing that his best chance for survival was to stay close to the Kinshra lord.

Kara's crossbowmen reloaded as they marched. She had ordered Theodore to keep himself between her and the Kinshra cavalry, aware of the threat they posed. She knew she had to beat them, for she could not enter the battle with the cavalry still at large.

She raised her hand as they reached the abandoned artillery. Commander Blenheim's engineers inspected the weapons.

"How long?" she asked.

"Just a few minutes," he said with certainty. "But the guns will only have one shot each." Kara nodded, examining her army.

"Bring the men together on a narrower front. That way our crossbowmen will be able to concentrate their fire. It will also make us look nervous in the face of the cavalry."

Commander Blenheim returned her nod, but she knew he was uneasy. His men were armed with axes and crossbows but no pikes. If the Kinshra charge reached them it would be a massacre.

"Get those guns ready," he whispered to his engineers urgently. "Do it quickly, but make sure you do it right."

Theodore kept his cavalry close to the enemy, barring their view of Kara's engineers, who were realigning the guns. Lord Radebaugh rode next to him, watching for her signal.

"This could be a disaster, Theodore," he said. "If the Kinshra reach the line…"

Theodore stopped him with an abrupt wave of his hand.

"Kara-Meir is touched by the gods," he said vehemently. "We must have faith!"

Lord Radebaugh made no reply, watching as Kara waved her sword.

"She's giving the signal," he cried suddenly.

Theodore stood in his stirrups and raised his sword. As one, the cavalry turned south, heading for the enemy.

Now it was all a matter of timing.

As Theodore turned his men toward the Kinshra cavalry, Sir Amik watched, transfixed. It was a move of which the enemy horsemen must have been wary, for the Imperial Guard were on slightly higher ground where they would benefit most from a sudden attack.

Seeing their foes make their move, the Kinshra rode to meet them. As the two forces approached each other, Sir Amik muttered under his breath.

"Saradomin help you, Theodore. If you fail, then Kara's line will be crushed."

The knight watched helplessly as the Imperial Guard charged in amongst the Kinshra. Despite the distance, he heard the crash as the two packed formations collided. They pressed against each other like tired fighters in the final desperate stages of a vicious match, but it was only a minute before one of them broke.

Sir Amik despaired as the Imperial Guard rode back to the east, away from the enemy cavalry and away from the city. At their head he could make out the white armour that distinguished Theodore from the black-clad Imperial Guard.

"How could you, Theodore?" Sir Amik moaned, knowing Kara's line was vulnerable now. "How could you?"

The Kinshra cavalry took a moment to regroup in preparation for their charge. Kara was defenceless. Her dwarf soldiers were arranged in several lines, one behind the other on the slope, those behind overlooking those in front.

Yet a cavalry charge would break any line, Sir Amik knew.

Sulla's bodyguards cheered as they watched their cavalry charge toward Kara's troops. The anticipation calmed the fighting before the wall, for all knew that the outcome of the charge would decide the fate of the battle.

Sulla grinned beneath his visor, confident his army would smash through the thinly-spaced enemy and trample their bodies into the earth. But then two things caught his eye and his smile vanished.

He noticed the dwarfs standing beside the cannons, foremost in Kara's line. And he noted also how the fleeing Imperial Guard had rallied and turned, with the knight at their head, riding back toward Kara, to intercept the Kinshra horsemen.

Their flight had been a ploy. They had lured his cavalry in, making them think that the infantry was vulnerable and unprotected.

It was all a trap. And his men had fallen for it.

Kara stood with her sword clutched anxiously. The earth shook as several hundred horses galloped toward her. The entire horizon seemed composed of black-clad warriors.

"Castimir?" she asked weakly, her mouth dry from fear.

"I am here," the wizard said. After his attack on the goblins, both he and Doric had chosen to stand by her side in the line.

"You haven't opened your eyes for two minutes," Doric noted, looking at the pale-faced sorcerer.

"I think if I did I would run," Castimir said over the growing thunder of hooves.

"Commander Blenheim?" Kara said, her voice threatening to falter.

"Do not worry, Kara-Meir," the dwarf said with a stern face.

The cavalry were two hundred yards away. It was nearly time.

"Wait!" Kara yelled, finding strength as her eyes chanced upon her banner. The charge had closed to within one hundred and eighty yards, and Kara noted how the dwarf crossbowmen blinked nervously as they raised their weapons to aim.

"Wait!" she yelled again, as the pounding of horseflesh at full gallop drowned out all other sounds.

She held her sword high above her head. She could feel the tears on her face as she adamantly refused to look elsewhere, not even risking a glance toward Theodore, who was riding swiftly back toward them.

If he times it right, she thought, *he should reach them seconds before they reach us.*

Gar'rth's hand rested on her shoulder and she grasped it for comfort.

The horses were one hundred and twenty yards away when she gave the signal, lowering her sword with a savage yell.

In that second, the thunder of hooves was wiped out by the roar of the guns that rolled backward on their wheels and obscured the Kinshra in white smoke. The shots ripped through the tight cavalry formation. The cries of horses and men and the crashing of metal-armoured soldiers falling to the earth followed immediately.

Then the first of the dwarf lines fired their crossbows, aiming purposefully at the horses to impede the ones behind with the bodies of the fallen. Castimir, meanwhile, hurled bolts of fire into those riders closest to him. Seconds later the second line of crossbowmen fired, followed by the third, and then the fourth. Finally, as the Kinshra horsemen closed to within thirty yards of the line, the fifth and last rank of dwarf crossbowmen fired. Their steel bolts hissed through the air to penetrate armour and horseflesh with ease, amid the screams of man and beast alike.

The several hundred bolts the dwarf soldiers had loosed destroyed the cavalry formation entirely. From a compact line of men riding shoulder to shoulder, the charge had been decimated. Those in the rear ranks had noted the approach of

Theodore and had broken off to either engage him or to flee.

A dozen riders did make it to the line dwarf. One horse, driven mad with pain, attempted to throw its rider, who grimly held on, directing the animal toward Kara's position. It reared up scant yards before her, its forelegs threatening to crush Kara's skull. Gar'rth stepped forward instinctively. His hands seized the stallion's forelegs and his body bent low as he dug his feet into the soft earth. The horse was pushed forward on its hind legs, the rider swearing. Within a few seconds, the horse fell onto the screaming rider, who was crushed beneath his steed.

"There will be no prisoners," Kara said resolutely. "They will be treated with the same mercy they offered those who fell into their hands—only it shall be quick for them." Her eyes were cold and hard.

Commander Blenheim looked to his men to see if anyone wished to argue. No one did.

Theodore struck seconds later. Those riders who had reached Kara's line were dispatched by the dwarf soldiers, and those who had broken off to confront him were too few to resist for long. Within moments, he had surrounded the last group of horsemen who had attempted to fight back, crushing them against one another so they could not even turn. He and his men struck at their enemy from every direction, outnumbering them three to one.

None were spared.

Lord Radebaugh hacked the arm off a Kinshra lancer as an Imperial Guardsman stabbed him from behind, and the same story was repeated on all sides. The Kinshra found themselves trapped, and their pleas for clemency were ignored.

Nearly two hundred of them managed to flee, however, galloping westward. A Kinshra officer rode swiftly to intercept them, but his shouts were ignored. Without stopping, they rode from the battlefield.

Theodore watched in satisfaction. The Kinshra will was breaking.

A few hundred yards away, Kara gave the order to advance.

The two men were alone in the central chamber, listening for Marius, who stalked the nearby passages in silence.

"You have no alternative but to reveal yourself," Sir Tiffy said loudly. "I shall send Ebenezer back to the city to return with more men, and then you shall be found. If you surrender to us, we shall not execute you. I cannot promise that if others join us."

The old knight exchanged a questioning look with the alchemist. For all they knew, the city might have fallen already. But neither dared say so.

"I have an idea, Sir Tiffy," the alchemist whispered, raising the lantern as he spoke, and motioning for his friend to come closer.

The breeze buffeted the lamp again and the light flickered once more.

The battle was going badly for Bhuler. Sulla's force had joined the fighting in front of the wall and by sheer weight of numbers had driven the knights back again. Soon they would be trapped in a second horseshoe, larger and more aggressive than the first. Now the Kinshra were fighting for their lives, knowing that Kara and her army would also have to be faced.

Bhuler knew he had to act. He raised the banner of Sir Amik, shouting to his riders to follow him in a desperate charge to buy time for Kara to come to their aid. He knew it could only result in one outcome, but he also knew with absolute certainty that this was the hour for which he had lived his whole life.

He wept behind the visor, hot tears of rage and fervour. Saradomin had accepted him. With a cry of determination he held the banner aloft and urged his horse forward at a gallop, charging Sulla's line.

But the pikemen were ready, standing shoulder to shoulder in an immovable formation with their pikes facing the oncoming enemy.

It was a formation no horse or rider had ever penetrated. Yet still Bhuler rode on.

The light guttered, leaving them in total darkness.

"Quickly, relight it," Sir Tiffy urged with a hint of panic in his voice.

"I can't," Ebenezer said desperately.

Now is my chance!

Finistere was no fool. He moved silently, knowing that if he did run he would reveal himself.

"What is wrong with it?" Sir Tiffy asked, his voice still unsettled.

"The fuel is gone," Ebenezer said. "We will have to listen for him in the dark."

It was the news he had been straining to hear. Silently he advanced until he stood at the chamber's edge, listening to the two men only yards away from him as they struggled with the lantern. The darkness was so black that his sight could not grow used to it.

He clutched his sword tightly, stepping down from the tunnel and into the knee-deep water on the chamber floor. But his foot slipped. Stifling a cry, he grabbed at the tunnel mouth to steady himself, his scabbard scraping against stone.

Immediately, the chamber filled with a sickly light.

"Well, Finistere, we have reached the end game," the alchemist said, smiling grimly as he pulled his cloak away from the lantern and opened a small hatch to allow the air to flow in and fuel the flame.

The traitor stared in hatred at him as the flickering light grew stronger.

"Clever trick, old man. Very clever!"

Knowing that all hope of stealth had gone, he launched himself in a desperate attack on men who had once called him friend.

SEVENTY-TWO

The plume of smoke parted in a ragged tear, like an invisible knife cutting down the centre of a silk veil. Through the gap, Sir Amik watched as Bhuler pulled his horse back at the last possible second, then urged it on in a jump that took it over the first line of pikes and into the men behind.

He smashed them aside, causing a ripple-like shudder to travel along their entire length.

"You valiant fool," he moaned, certain that his friend was doomed.

But Sir Amik was wrong. Even as he wept, he noted a dozen other horsemen follow Bhuler's example, each crashing into the Kinshra line that was still reeling from his valet's assault.

On the city's ramparts were the foresters who had fled before the Kinshra advance, a people who wielded bows before they could talk. They launched their lethal arrows now, and thinned the pikemen, leaving gaps in their formation large enough for the knights to drive in with all their armoured weight.

Sir Amik watched as—impossibly—the Kinshra line broke in two, severed at its centre as the knights before the wall rushed upon them, their determination now a fanaticism inspired entirely by one brave man.

Bhuler continued his merciless charge through the Kinshra rows, his banner adding another enemy to the grim toll as he drove its tip into a Kinshra helm. He urged his horse on, pulling the banner free, finding himself alone on the far side of the Kinshra line.

Only one enemy dared to challenge him.

Jerrod lowered his hood slowly, anticipating the fear that his nightmare visage would inspire. He stared at the knight across thirty yards of open ground.

He saw Sir Amik's horse neigh nervously as it tugged at the reins in an effort to make his master find another foe. But the knight was steadfast.

He raised the banner to his head, touching his white helm against the torn four-stared symbol.

The werewolf paused. There was an absence of the scent in the air that he found on nearly all his enemies.

It was the absence of fear.

His enemy was not afraid of him.

Jerrod hesitated.

The knight charged.

The traitor lunged. As Sir Tiffy parried, Finistere stepped past him, intent on extinguishing the lantern.

I need to hide! I need the darkness again.

Marius shouted, slogging through the knee-deep waters toward them. Finistere had seconds left. He drew his sword back behind his shoulder and hurled it toward the man who had outwitted him, at the same time pulling a dagger from his belt to parry Sir Tiffy's blade.

The sword span toward the alchemist's face, forcing Ebenezer to jump aside.

Marius leapt into the chamber.

The traitor's spare hand closed over Sir Tiffy's blade, cutting his flesh deeply. But now, free of the need to parry his foe's weapon, he thrust his dagger into the old spymaster's shoulder.

The room went dark as Ebenezer and his lantern crashed into the stinking waters.

But it was too late, for Marius was upon him.

Bhuler galloped toward his unworldly enemy. He understood the power of fear and the evil it could drive men to do, but he knew that he was a Knight of Falador who was chosen by Saradomin.

Guiding his banner, Bhuler guessed that his unarmed foe would try to jump aside. As Jerrod leapt, just as Bhuler had anticipated, he struck the werewolf. It was only his foe's incredible speed that saved him from being impaled through the heart. The tip of the banner pierced the werewolf's right shoulder instead, lifting him off his feet and carrying him several yards until he managed to break free.

The werewolf cursed violently as his black blood stained the earth. Bhuler turned his horse once more toward his enemy. Vulnerable now, the creature had only one option. With his red robes flailing behind him, he fled.

Bhuler watched him run and knew that to let such a creature live was to deny others life, for the werewolf would kill again. He readied the banner of the knights that had been passed from one leader to the next for more than a century, blessed by monks of Saradomin and held in reverence by their order. Some even believed that the tip of the banner had been used as a lance by Saradomin himself in the God Wars.

He prepared for a final charge, but the sound of hooves thundering on the ground caught his attention. He looked up to see Sulla and his thirty-strong bodyguard galloping against the remainder of his men who were fighting before the wall.

If Sulla rode in, the knights would be destroyed, for they were too few and too spread out to resist.

Bhuler turned his horse. The werewolf would have to wait. If he could divert Sulla's bodyguard for a single moment, then Theodore and Kara would enter the battle at his side.

Sulla's attention was focused on the knights near the wall. Several arrows fell amongst his bodyguard, fired by the foresters from the ramparts, but it was too little to prevent them entering the fray and demolishing the last of the resistance.

One of his officers gestured urgently. Sulla looked to his left.

It was Sir Amik, leader of the Knights of Falador, alone and unguarded.

Sulla broke off his charge, amazed that so important a man would isolate himself on a battlefield. It was a moment he had dreamed of.

"Zamorak could not have given a better augur of our victory!" he cried, raising his sword and pointing toward the armoured man. As one, the Kinshra surged forward.

Incredibly though, and foolishly, Sir Amik readied his banner and thundered towards them, alone.

The last thing Sir Tiffy saw before the light vanished was Marius leap toward Finistere, his blade lunging toward the traitor's abdomen.

He felt the traitor's blade pierce his shoulder as the hand holding his sword went suddenly limp. With his remaining strength he freed his weapon from the traitor's grasp and lunged, hearing a gasp in the darkness as his own blade entered an unseen body. He tried to withdraw the sword, but suddenly he was too weak to do so.

Unable to support his weight, he fell backward with a groan, his head slamming against the brickwork.

The only sound was a faint wheezing.

"Sir Tiffy? Marius?" Ebenezer called faintly. "Are you there?" His hand found the lamp in the water. It was broken and he knew it would never light now.

No one answered.

He needed light and he knew he would have to use magic to illuminate the chamber. He reached into his pocket and pulled out a fire rune.

Someone groaned nearby. Still no one spoke.

With a deep breath, Ebenezer concentrated on the single rune in his hand.

The thought of retreat did not enter his mind. Bhuler had only one aim now, only one goal to achieve.

Through tear-filled eyes he watched as the Kinshra rode into him. He focused on the tip of his banner and he thrust it into the chest of the nearest enemy.

He did not feel the blows of the Kinshra blades as Sulla and his guard surrounded him, hacking at him from all angles and cutting the banner in two.

Finally he fell from his saddle to the soft earth, putting himself beyond the range of their hatred.

But the butchery was short-lived. Sulla looked around in growing panic as a thundering shook the earth. It could only mean one thing—Kara's cavalry had come.

With a grim realisation, Sulla saw that his indulgence in hunting down Sir Amik had cost him the battle. Swiftly he led his bodyguard away, abandoning his men before the wall.

SEVENTY-THREE

To Sir Vyvin, the outcome of the battle was inevitable. The Kinshra were caught between the Imperial Guard and the remaining knights and militia that he commanded. All had witnessed Sir Amik's fall, and the apparent death of their leader made his men fight with a suicidal frenzy. Even young peons bested men twice their age, ignoring wounds that would have felled stronger warriors.

They hacked their way through the Kinshra ranks to where they believed Sir Amik to have fallen.

It was Sir Vyvin who first reached the prone figure. The fallen knight's head was cushioned on the flank of his horse, which lay dead beneath him. In his hands he held the two broken pieces of the banner.

Sir Vyvin knelt beside him. As he began to open the visor a pained grunt came from the man within.

Bhuler was alive.

"Do not open it," he said. "The boys are doing us proud. Let them fight until the end."

Sir Vyvin knew he did not have long to live.

"So it *is* you, Bhuler," he said. "I have suspected it since you spoke to me under the wall. Where is Sir Amik?"

Bhuler shook his head.

"He was too weak to join us. But I was not… and we needed our leader…"

A rider caught Sir Vyvin's attention. It was Theodore.

"Sir Amik!" he cried as he knelt by Sir Vyvin's side. "Tell me, sir, is there anything I can do?"

Bhuler stretched his hand out to Theodore, who took it reverently. "Bring Kara to me, Theodore," he said. "For I am Bhuler, and I wish to see her."

Theodore gaped in amazement. Sir Vyvin hushed him before he could speak.

"Go and bring Kara," he said quietly. "Tell no one of this, for only you and I know the truth."

The squire nodded and mounted his horse, while behind him the remaining knights formed a defensive circle around their fallen leader, fighting any Kinshra soldier that came within their reach.

The rune fizzed brightly in Ebenezer's open palm, lighting the chamber with a red glow. The small pebble gave off a plume of red-tinted smoke that gave the alchemist a sudden look of power. He had to concentrate on controlling the magic, however, rationing it so it would not burn too quickly—or even explode. The rune would last only a brief time, but he had a dozen more in his pocket.

"Marius?" he called as he stepped forward slowly. "Sir Tiffy?" He carried the magic fire with him and with each step illuminated more of the chamber's dark secrets.

"I am here," Marius said quietly, looking into the water at his feet.

There lay the traitor, opening his mouth silently in a muted plea, his hands clutched at a deadly wound in his right side.

"He is still alive," Marius said, his face contorted in barely-restrained rage. "This is for Bryant," he screamed suddenly, "and the countless others who have fallen because of your treachery."

The squire raised his right foot and placed it squarely on the traitor's chest, pushing him down under the surface of the shallow black water, ignoring the pleading look in his eyes.

"Shouldn't we take him back alive?" Ebenezer said. For a moment his concentration slipped and the rune flared dangerously.

"There may not be a city left to return to," the squire said flatly, staring down at the traitor, who splashed feebly in an attempt to get some air. "And you should help Sir Tiffy."

Ebenezer moved to where the old knight lay, and crouched to place his arm around Sir Tiffy's shoulders. The knight breathed steadily.

"I'll help you when I've finished here," Marius said. Ebenezer noted the tears on the young man's face. "We'll take Sir Tiffy back to the city and see what the situation is. If Falador still resists, then we shall join the fight, and if we win we shall return here to retrieve the bodies of Sir Pallas and Sir Erical."

"What about him?" Ebenezer asked as the splashing ceased at the squire's feet.

"I think this will be a suitable place for him to spend eternity," Marius said as he drove his sword into the traitor's body to be sure his betrayal was ended.

Together, the squire and the alchemist carried Sir Tiffy from the chamber, their way lit by Ebenezer's burning rune.

None could stand against Kara. The blades of her enemies broke against her own, while their armour was useless against the adamant weapon.

A young Kinshra warrior covered his eyes with his hands as he grasped at his wounded forehead. Kara ran him through with a single thrust, then stepped behind him, withdrawing her

BETRAYAL AT FALADOR 473

sword to deliver a killing blow on the back of his neck.

With every enemy that fell before her, her rage only increased. She had forgotten mercy and put aside forgiveness.

Gar'rth fought at her side, without a weapon. He used his speed and hideous strength, clawing and sometimes biting. For he no longer resembled a human. His skin had taken on the grey hue, its thickness turning away the thrusts of his desperate enemies. His eyes were black pools of infinite darkness, and his jaw was grotesquely extended. And while each blow hurt him, none had cut him.

On her other side was Doric. The dwarf drove the edge of his shield into the stomach of a Kinshra soldier. As the man doubled over he smashed his axe into the man's face, felling him instantly. The Kinshra will to fight was lost, and he watched with growing sadness as Kara slew men who were trying to flee.

Riding behind them, Castimir picked his targets sparingly. He, too, noted Kara's rage. The wizard looked to Doric and the dwarf shook his head bitterly.

"I'll seek Theodore," Castimir said. "There is no need for this to continue."

With a grim look as Kara ignored a plea for mercy, the wizard turned his horse and galloped west.

Sulla looked back at his army. Dozens were running now, stripping their armour and discarding their weapons as they fled. It was turning into a rout.

"It is lost to us, Sulla," one of his bodyguards said, using his name as if he were a common soldier. "Kara-Meir has defeated us!"

He held his anger. He knew no one could reverse the outcome of the battle now. It was better to live than to die.

"Give the order to retreat," he said. After a moment's hesitation, a messenger left to convey the instruction.

Sulla closed his eyes in anger. He knew the Kinshra ways—as the commander who had planned and executed what had resulted in their greatest defeat for decades, he would be vulnerable to those who sought to remove him. And he knew such an end would not be quick.

He needed a victory.

Theodore rode east toward Kara's banner. He knew she had deliberately led her soldiers into battle against the largest part of the Kinshra army, to personally slay as many of the enemy as she could.

The squire had ridden for only a minute when he heard the challenge. He pulled his mare up short and looked back to where a Kinshra horseman levelled a bloodied sword at him. Theodore raised his own sword and bowed his head in acknowledgement.

Both horses charged.

Both men yelled.

Theodore had practised for years in the lists of the knights, and he was regarded as one of the finest warriors of his group. But his enemy was a Kinshra officer with years of experience behind him.

As they closed, the squire leaned forward to extend his reach, intending to run his sword through his enemy's throat. Yet somehow the Kinshra officer parried his blade and delivered a stroke of his own, striking Theodore's breastplate and knocking him from the saddle. He landed painfully.

Swiftly the squire stood, his breathing tortuous. The blade hadn't penetrated his armour, but the fall had winded him.

The Kinshra warrior turned his horse slowly, taunting him. The man sheathed his blade and pulled from his belt a morning star. He swung the weapon in slow circles, which became faster as the iron ball pulled at the chain. With another cry, he charged.

Theodore ducked, raising his sword above him at the last

moment. He felt the chain grapple his blade and rip it from his hand as the horse rode by, leaving him unarmed.

The Kinshra warrior turned again, swinging his weapon in anticipation. He hurled Theodore's sword into the earth in contempt.

"Your life is mine to take," the black-armoured warrior said, goading his horse onward.

Theodore jumped to one side as the iron ball swung toward him, missing him by inches. But the Kinshra officer was uncannily calm. He did not bother to turn his horse for another charge.

Down the morning star came again, slamming into Theodore's back, and knocking him to the ground with a cry. He tasted blood in his mouth.

He knew he did not have the strength to continue. Too weak to move, he could only await the end as he heard his enemy swing the morning star again, leaning down to ensure he had enough reach to deliver a killing blow.

Theodore closed his eyes in prayer, grimly accepting his death.

SEVENTY-FOUR

Castimir saw Theodore collapse under the impact of the morning star. He saw the Kinshra officer lean down and prepare for the killing blow.

He advanced hurling one ball of fire after another to buy his friend a few more seconds.

The Kinshra officer cantered aside quickly, avoiding his magic. Then, faster than Castimir had expected, he galloped forward, swinging his morning star.

Castimir had one chance. If he missed again…

The Kinshra officer was fifteen yards away when he cast his fire strike. The flame exploded in front of the horse, causing it to tumble and sending its rider flying with a yell.

Castimir rode closer as the man struggled to stand.

"This is for my friend!" he called as the tip of his fire staff connected with the runes in his hand. The fireball struck the officer's breastplate and fire enveloped him. He screamed as his skin blistered underneath his armour. With one hand he tore at his helmet to prevent it from scalding him, whilst with the other he drew his sword.

Gods, the wizard thought, *he continues to fight on even though he is suffering terribly.*

Castimir cantered away, distancing himself from the screaming man. He had to finish it now, for his enemy would not stop. Coldly, the wizard once more ignited the runes in his hand with the tip of his staff. He gazed toward the flailing man calmly, making sure he could deliver a clean end. Then he hurled his second fire strike, straight into his enemy's exposed face.

The force of the blow bent metal already softened by heat, tearing flesh and cracking bone. The Kinshra officer fell backward without a cry.

Castimir gazed at the body, feeling neither triumph nor shame. Then he rode toward Theodore, who was slowly staggering to his feet.

"Kara! I must find Kara," the squire gasped.

"Then you must follow me, Theo," the wizard replied. "But Kara might not listen to anything you have to say, for she is enraged, cutting unarmed men down before her."

"What I must say to her will curb her anger," Theodore said through teeth gritted against the pain. "Come, lead me to her."

To Kara, it seemed as if this moment was everything she had lived for. Her life had been ruined by the Kinshra and she had vowed to destroy them. It was simple justice. As she exacted her terrible revenge, she imagined she could smell the burning smoke of her village and hear the cries of her neighbours.

She never hesitated, sundering their blades as if the Kinshra fought with mere toys. She tripped an enemy onto his back and dispatched him with a swift stab of her blade.

She had just beheaded a dying man, her eyes already looking to her next enemy, when a familiar voice carried through the red haze. Theodore.

"Kara! Enough of this," he said. "Our victory is complete. But a friend has fallen. Even now, in his last moments, he wishes to speak with you."

Kara noticed how pale Theodore looked, and she knew instinctively that he had been injured. The squire saw her concern and waved his hand dismissively.

"It is Bhuler," he explained. "I shall take you to him."

Commander Blenheim looked to her in concern. It was she who had commanded them so far, inspiring them in a way he could never have done.

"Continue the fight, commander," she instructed. "Push the Kinshra into the wall and crush them!" Then she climbed up behind Theodore, placing her arms loosely about his waist. Despite her delicacy, the squire grimaced from the pain of his injuries.

Gar'rth and Doric followed also, the dwarf leaping up onto Castimir's horse while the werewolf ran behind.

"They are coming, old friend," Sir Vyvin's words were faint and far away and Bhuler knew his end was imminent.

"Have I done ill, Sir Vyvin?" he asked with a painful sigh. "Have I condemned us all?"

"You commanded us as no other could have, my friend," the knight said earnestly. "This is your day, a triumphant day for our order and for all who would call themselves free. Your sacrifice will never be forgotten." Sir Vyvin held Bhuler's hand and wept, his tears falling on his stained breastplate.

"Tell Sir Amik that I am sorry for what I have done…" the valet whispered.

But Sir Vyvin calmed him.

"Do not speak, Bhuler, Knight of Falador. Save your strength, for Kara is here."

Kara dropped to the ground at a run, unclasping her helmet and discarding her sword and shield, the battle forgotten. She looked to Sir Vyvin first.

"It is Bhuler in Sir Amik's armour," he explained. "The men do not yet know, although we can tell them now. You can open his visor if you wish, Kara-Meir."

Kara did so, raising it as gently as possible. When she saw her friend's pale face she sobbed.

"Do not cry, Kara," Bhuler said, reaching up with one hand and wiping away her tears. "You have made us all so very proud, for you have saved us."

"I cannot lose you too, Bhuler!" she said through gasping sobs. "Master Phyllis is gone, and if you go also I will not have anyone left." Her face rested on his chest.

Bhuler breathed deeply.

"You are not alone, Kara. Falador owes everything to you. You have your friends—Theodore and Gar'rth, Doric and Castimir, and that crazy old alchemist…" Then his voice changed, and his eyes grew serious.

"You must promise me something, Kara."

Kara nodded.

"You must promise to let go of your anger. You cannot be angry all your life. It will destroy you in the end. Promise me that, Kara, so I can die in peace."

"It is not something I can promise!" She wept, for she did not want to disappoint the man who had offered her friendship when she had needed it most.

"Then you must learn to forgive. You must let go of your hate and accept your history. Promise me you will do it, Kara!"

Kara looked suddenly at the faces of her friends and she knew then what they had each seen in her on the battlefield— the hatred that had driven her to cut down any man who stood before her.

"Very well, Bhuler," she said, turning back to him. "I promise. I shall do it for your sake."

And with her oath given, Bhuler died.

Sir Vyvin raised the broken banner and rammed it into the
ground at Bhuler's side. All about him knights and peons
watched in reverence, for the fighting on the field was over and
the few remaining Kinshra were fleeing.

"Here fell Bhuler, Knight of Falador, hero of the city," he said
loudly enough that all could hear. "May his name be spoken
with honour by all men!"

From the circle of onlookers, men beat their swords against
their shields and shouted his name. But Kara hadn't moved. Her
head lay rested against the valet's chest as if she expected him
to wake.

Then from the city it came, rolling like a thunder clap.
Another cry, a second name that the men and women of the city
called out in celebration. It was the name of the one person who
had saved them all, the name of the girl who had inspired them
and who was touched by the gods.

"Kara-Meir! Kara-Meir!" the voices shouted, thousands
strong.

The cry was echoed by the dwarf warriors who had followed
her and by the Imperial Guard who had ridden into battle at
her side. It was her name they cried, for she was the saviour of
Asgarnia and they owed everything to her.

"Kara-Meir!" the cry continued, echoing across the plain.

As Kara heard it, she stood, not knowing what to do.

Theodore picked up her sword and presented it to her.

"They honour you, Kara."

But Kara-Meir said nothing.

She climbed onto the nearest horse and raised her sword in
salute, noting how the citizens from the wall responded to her
with another shout.

"What are you doing, Kara?" Theodore asked nervously.

"Pass me my helmet and my shield, Theodore. I am going to

find the one man who started all this bloodshed. I am going to make sure he doesn't do it again."

Theodore did as she asked and then clambered awkwardly atop his own mare. Castimir exchanged a worried look with the squire as Gar'rth and Doric mounted their horses behind the two friends.

"I am going after Sulla," Kara said, goading her horse to the northeast.

SEVENTY-FIVE

Despite the distance, Sulla heard the cries from the wall as the citizens of Falador taunted him with the name of the girl who had haunted his nightmares

Kara-Meir!

The shouting drew the attention of the fleeing army as it marched north. They turned their heads south with a nervousness that Sulla knew marked them as broken men.

But as he looked over his defeated army, he noticed thirty horsemen riding toward him, asking questions as they neared. Men answered with raised arms, pointing to his location.

"They are asking directions," one of his officers muttered. "What do they want, Sulla?" The man spoke without respect.

As they rode closer, Sulla saw Kara-Meir at their head. He knew exactly what they were searching for.

"They've come for me," he said.

The Kinshra soldiers had no will left to fight and none dared to prevent Kara from galloping past them. Their cowardice angered him, and yet he felt suddenly afraid of her.

Who are you Kara-Meir? he wondered to himself, noting how his men, his very bodyguard, had edged their horses away from him. *Why do you pursue me so?* No one would help him in this fight.

The woman finally halted before him, raising her visor as she pulled on the reins of her steed.

"Your men are free to go, Sulla, as long as they promise never to enter Asgarnia again. Also, they are to harm no person in their retreat." As she spoke, she drew her sword slowly.

Sulla didn't move. "That is very generous of you, Kara-Meir," he said, his voice sarcastic despite the fear that clawed at him. "And what is to become of me?"

"We have a history, Sulla, you and I. Today that history shall end." Kara dismounted, her sword levelled in his direction.

"You are challenging me? In front of my army?" He laughed incredulously, attempting to appear brave. But he knew from the worried looks of his men that his bravado had failed.

They doubt me! My own men doubt me!

"Your army is free to go provided they abide by the rules I have set them," she replied. "You, however, are not."

Sulla looked at his men and noted how none of them would return his gaze. Then he turned back to face his challenger.

"Very well, Kara-Meir. I shall fight you." With a sudden yell, he kicked his spurs into his horse's flank, attempting to run her down before she had time to dodge.

But she jumped aside, her sword flashing as she drew it across the animal's flank. She severed the leather straps that held Sulla's saddle in place, tipping him off the horse's back and onto the soft grass.

"You're pathetic," Kara spat, marching around him. "To think anyone ever feared you…"

Sulla laughed again as he stood.

"Sir Amik did," he replied defiantly. "When I killed him."

"I have news for you, Sulla—Sir Amik is not dead. The man you killed was not even a knight! He was Sir Amik's *valet*." As she spoke, she remembered what Bhuler had made her promise.

After Sulla, Bhuler, she thought. *That is my promise to you.* Before there could be forgiveness, she had to fulfil a pledge she had made to herself and her family years ago, on an island in a frozen lake.

Sulla shouted, his sword cutting down with a speed that caught Kara by surprise. Her shield parried the blade, but her arm was jarred painfully by the force of the blow. She backed away. He was a better fighter than she had imagined, moving quicker than she would have thought possible in his black armour. She could not afford to relax her guard even for a second.

"I will kill you. Here, today, this is where you die," he growled behind his visor, his sword swinging forward.

Instinctively, Kara swung her shield to intercept his blow, but as she did so she knew she had made a mistake. As she raised her shield her view was obscured and Sulla sidestepped, moving behind her and drawing a dagger from his belt.

He drew his arm toward her throat. But at the same time she kicked at him with her boot, using his body to push herself away, falling forward as she did so, losing her balance.

Sulla laughed. She had barely escaped him and her desperate attempt had made her look weak.

"Look at her run!" he shouted to his men, and some of the Kinshra started to smile. Slowly, they were getting their confidence back.

"Get up, Kara!" Castimir shouted. He had his hand on Gar'rth's shoulder to stop him interfering. If he did then the Kinshra would turn on them, and they were still outnumbered. This was a fight between their chosen champions, representatives of their gods on earth. No one dared interfere.

As Kara stood, a pain tore at her calf and her leg faltered. She staggered suddenly, hearing Gar'rth's cry of warning too late to avoid Sulla's thrown knife. In agony, her leg gave way and she fell to one knee.

She opened her visor to gasp for air as the Kinshra lord strode forward, swatting aside her sword with his own and stepping in close to her. With a vicious snarl he punched her once, twice, then a third time, each blow directed into her unprotected face.

Kara fell to the earth.

Sulla kicked her in the ribs as he stepped over her with total disdain.

"This is your captain?" he said loudly, stepping directly in front of Theodore. "This is the one who was supposed to defend you? She is just a girl! She is no warrior."

The Kinshra lord turned to look down at her.

"She is not without her charms, however. No wonder Sir Amik kept her at the castle." He turned to his men, raising his arms to encourage their laughter.

Kara wiped the blood from her face as she stood again, the knife still lodged in her leg.

Sulla spun and rushed toward her. His sword hissed through the air, aimed for her neck. But at the last moment came the sound of steel shattering on adamant as Kara parried his blow.

"I have killed many of your men today, Sulla," she said, her voice unnaturally calm. "You will be no different."

Sulla leapt back, out of Kara's reach, as she moved to the offensive. One of the Kinshra officers hurled his sword into the circle of men and Sulla seized it without ever taking his eye off her.

"I shall break any weapon you care to wield, Sulla." She lunged at him, eager to shatter his second weapon and to beat down his spirit.

Kara pressed him, hoping that his heavier armour would tire him out. She did not merely wish to kill Sulla—she wanted to destroy him in front of his men, to ensure that from that day forth, whenever his name was spoken it was spoken with contempt.

Then she saw her opening. Sulla's defence was repetitive,

predictable, his sword parrying hers at an eccentric angle to prevent it from breaking. He did it again and again, and instead of backing away he stood his ground.

It is his weakness!

Suddenly Kara directed her blade toward his. As his sword broke into two halves, the Kinshra lord stepped in, seizing her arm before she had a chance to reverse her swing. She had fallen for his ploy!

With his superior strength he forced Kara to the ground, his booted foot stamping down on her blade, pinning her weapon beneath his weight. He seized her helmet with his free hand, tearing it loose with an angry grunt.

Kara grimaced beneath him, her eyes brimming with hate-filled tears, her lips parted in defiance of everything he was.

Sulla seized his broken blade, its jagged edge sharp enough to cut human flesh with ease. With his free hand he dragged her face closer to the broken edge.

"I'll cut your pretty face first," he said to her in a low voice.

But the look in Kara's eyes made him hesitate. Even now, she wasn't afraid.

Kara hissed through gritted teeth as she pulled his dagger from her own calf and stabbed it into the top of Sulla's boot. He couldn't help but lift his foot from Kara's sword as he stumbled in sudden agony, clutching the hilt of his broken blade with both hands in preparation for delivering a death blow to the girl who had dared believe she could beat him.

Kara's sword swung upward, severing both Sulla's wrists as the adamant blade cut through his black armour. Both his hands fell to the earth along with the broken sword.

The Kinshra lord sagged to his knees as the blood emptied from his veins.

Kara stood. She placed the tip of her sword to Sulla's neck.

"Do it, if you have the courage!" Sulla spat, his voice fainter than before.

"It would be the easiest thing in the world," Kara replied. Her hands shook with excitement. "But I want to see your face first."

She took her sword away and tore open Sulla's visor, forcing him backward so she could look into his one good eye. Despite his appearance, she did not flinch.

"I made a vow years ago, Sulla, to avenge those you took from me."

Sulla shook his head.

"I don't even know who you are."

"You destroyed my family," she replied. "You killed my parents when my father begged for my mother's life. You denied him even that."

"I don't remember..." he gasped.

"That is the real tragedy, Sulla. You have done so much evil over so long a time that you do not even remember the faces of those you have slain."

She raised her sword, ready to destroy him forever. It was what she had dreamt of for as long as she could remember.

But she couldn't do it. She recalled Bhuler's words, begging her to forgive her enemy, making her promise to release her anger.

So Kara-Meir turned her sword at the last moment, ramming it into the earth at Sulla's side, her cries the only sound in the circle of men who looked on.

"I knew you couldn't do it!" Sulla taunted her. "I knew you lacked the courage. Your father lacked courage as well—he never begged for your mother's life. He offered her to me if I would spare him."

But she knew he lied.

"I will not kill you, Sulla. Not today. The words of a man a thousand times better than you prevent me from doing so. But

I shall take from you the only thing that has counted in your miserable life."

Kara bent down and picked up Sulla's severed right hand, examining it closely. Suddenly she held a glittering object up above her head.

"Men of the Kinshra, I have taken Sulla's hands. And from his hands I take this signet ring—the symbol of your leader. It is mine now! Take yourselves and be gone from here." She looked down at Sulla. "And take this man also. He is responsible for your defeat. Take him and do with him what you will."

Several Kinshra soldiers ran forward and dragged him away, slinging him over a horse and mounting their own steeds before heading north. Hundreds of others followed after them, none daring to meet Kara's gaze.

Swiftly her friends gathered about her, their hands on her shoulders in comfort. She wept as she knelt on the earth with her sword before her. Never had the weapon felt so alien in her grasp.

Kara-Meir wept. She wept because she was in pain, she wept because she was sad, she wept because she had had her vengeance. But mostly, Kara-Meir wept because she had kept her promise.

SEVENTY-SIX

Every day brought new heartache and sorrow, for the dead were many. The families of the missing prayed hourly that news would come of their safe return and rescue, but it rarely did. Before the end of the second day, when hearing that someone was still missing and unaccounted for, men and women would shake their heads in sorrow, knowing that only a corpse would be found.

Sir Amik took command of the clean-up efforts. The knights were deployed with the city guard to keep a watch over the dead, to ensure their bodies were not dishonoured by the carrion birds and animals or by human thieves.

On the third day it was decided to burn the dead. Burial parties were recruited from the men of the city, and slowly the corpses of both sides were lowered into the trench that the goblins had dug to guard Sulla's encampment. In their midst, dry straw packets were laid amongst the enemies who now slept side by side. When the trench was full, the pyre was lit. For three days and nights it burned, kept alight by the men of Falador who wished to purge their city of the dead and leave no trace for any beast to devour.

Only a few dozen bodies were retrieved from the field. Several of them were high-ranking knights who were interred in the chapel, stripped and washed before being laid to rest in the most hallowed chambers of the castle. Amongst these men were Sir Erical and Sir Pallas, retrieved by a dozen peons led by Sir Tiffy and Sir Vyvin.

A special place was reserved for the man who had sacrificed everything for the city he had cherished so much. Bhuler's funeral was attended by thousands, and his grave was not in the castle of the knights. Rather, in memory of his sacrifice, he was laid to rest at the foot of the newest part of the wall that was being rebuilt and strengthened through the skill of the dwarfs. His body a symbol to inspire future generations. He was wrapped in Kara-Meir's banner, and his horse was buried beneath him.

Kara was tempted to place her sword at his side, but her friends persuaded her to keep it, despite a change in her character since Sulla's defeat.

"Those touched by the gods aren't let off so easily, Kara," Theodore warned her. "And the sword was given to you by Master Phyllis. You should keep it as an heirloom of the family that adopted you."

Theodore was right, but she didn't want to fight again, not ever again. She recalled Bhuler's words to her as he had died. *You cannot be angry all your life.* And she wasn't angry any more. She was just tired.

The day after Bhuler's funeral, word reached Falador that Burthorpe had been liberated without a battle. Lord Radebaugh and the Imperial Guard had presented Lord Daquarius with Sulla's severed hands and his ring of office, which Kara had sent so that the Kinshra would realize it would be futile to fight. Within a day they had left the citadel.

Lord Radebaugh wrote to them of his discovery of the crown prince's secret shrine to Zamorak. He had destroyed it and the crown prince was confined for his own safety, raving like a madman. He finished his letter by informing Sir Amik that he would consult the druid Kaqemeex for help in curing the prince of his hallucinations.

It was a week of exhaustion for all, but by the end of it the traders could be seen at their stands again, the washerwomen at their laundry and the city guards—under their new chief, Colonel Ingrew—patrolling the streets.

Slowly, things returned to normal.

In the foothills of Ice Mountain a man drew a black dagger.

"I am tired of your whimpering! No one will miss you, Sulla. After the disaster you led us into, this dagger is going to be a swifter end than the one you deserve." The Kinshra soldier of the lowliest rank strode forward. None of his friends moved to stop him. None even spoke in protest.

The soldier placed the dagger to Sulla's throat.

Sulla pleaded weakly for his life.

"I wouldn't do that if I were you," a voice growled from the shadows of the fir trees. From under their low boughs a tall figure appeared, wearing a ragged red robe, his hand pressed against his wounded shoulder.

The Kinshra warrior stepped away.

"That is Sulla's demon," one of the men remarked, recognising Jerrod.

"I need one man," Jerrod said slowly, "for only a short service." His burning eyes fixed on the soldier who had planned to kill Sulla. "Will you aid me?"

The man glanced at his friends and shrugged. They all knew the werewolf had fought at their side in the battle. With a confident step, he approached. It was the last thing he ever did. Jerrod seized him by the throat and squeezed with such strength that the man didn't have time to scream.

"I told him it would be for a short service," Jerrod growled as he removed the man's fur cloak, wrapping it around Sulla.

The Kinshra soldiers fled into the woods, not daring to face him. He had expected nothing else of them.

"Why are you helping me?" Sulla muttered, his teeth chattering from the cold.

"I was going to kill you," the werewolf admitted. "But as I slept after the battle, an emissary of Zamorak himself spoke to me. He wants us working together, Sulla. Whatever game the gods are playing, it is not yet concluded. The first chapter only, but there is always a second."

Sulla lowered his head, cushioned by the warm cloak.

"I need food," he said.

Jerrod nodded.

"And you shall have it, my friend. I shall make a fire, for you would not like your meat raw. Sleep now, whilst I work."

The werewolf's eyes focused on the dead man. With a skill perfected by years of practice he began his dreadful work. In only a few minutes, under the boughs of the low trees, a fire crackled and a grim cut of meat cooked on a stick above the flames.

Jerrod smiled to himself, wondering what Sulla would say if he knew.

In the bowels of the Kinshra fortress an officer opened a wooden door without knocking.

"Who dares to enter my chamber?" the sybil cried.

"I have orders from Lord Daquarius, the new lord of the Kinshra. Your meddling led us into disaster. He has decided it would be best if you are no longer associated with our cause."

The officer nodded to the two men behind him. They strode forward and seized the old woman. The officer removed the lid of the huge cauldron that stood on an unlit fire at the centre of the room. A greenish liquid stirred inside and with a grimace the man nodded toward it. The two men heaved the sybil into the sickly potion. Before she could clamber out, the heavy lid was replaced, the men fastening it so that only a small gap remained.

A withered old hand, responsible for so much evil, forced its way through, trying in vain to lift the lid.

"Light the fire," the officer said flatly. "Call me when the water begins to boil."

The two soldiers grinned, kneeling to begin their grisly work. They ignored the sybil's threats of revenge as well as her pleas for mercy.

Soon the fire began to rage. The waters began to bubble. And the sybil began to scream.

SEVENTY-SEVEN

It was late. The fire burned in the hearth in the upstairs room of The Rising Sun. They sat around a large table, each deep in thought, no one willing to break the peaceful silence.

Finally the alchemist spoke, gazing into the wispy smoke of his pipe.

"So we are decided then. Each of us has made their choice. Each of us shall go their separate way over the next few months, and meet in Varrock in time for Midsummer's Eve."

Doric looked thoughtfully at his unfinished meal.

"I shall go and rebuild my house. The magistrate in Falador has looked favourably on my case. But first, I must act as a diplomat for the dwarf request to open the seams beneath the city. Sir Amik will give my people their mining guild in the northeast of Falador."

"And I shall go to the Wizards' Tower," Castimir said unhappily. "My wanderings are at their end and I must demonstrate what I have learned."

"But you have Master Segainus's spell books. Surely that is no small prize?" Ebenezer asked.

Castimir looked sly.

"Yes. That is a fortunate privilege. His years of experience are recorded in his books. It is knowledge I am fearful to learn, for

I know my superiors would not approve of someone of my age delving into such mysteries."

"Whenever has that stopped you before, Castimir?" Kara asked playfully.

The young wizard smiled, but still his eyes revealed concern. His friends knew immediately that he had already explored the pages of Master Segainus's books.

"Knowledge can be a dangerous thing," Ebenezer said. "The Kinshra used it to create their guns, and some men attempt to find the answer to eternal life. But it need not always be so— great and good things can be done by those strong enough to wield knowledge properly."

"As you have demonstrated time and again to our benefit," Castimir said with a nod to his old friend. "Maybe I am too young for such secrets. Maybe I should wait. I shall also write to Arisha."

Theodore glanced at Castimir with a smile.

The wizard looked bashfully away.

"She still has my belongings and my yak," he muttered.

It was Kara who spoke next.

"I shall go to the monastery and help rebuild it. I shall spend time with Abbot Langley and search among any of their records that may have survived. Hopefully, I shall find some information about my father and I would especially like to know my mother's name. I may also seek out my village, and place a marker where my parents died."

She knew what her friends were thinking.

"I am no longer looking for vengeance," she added. "The Kinshra will punish Sulla enough."

Ebenezer lowered his pipe and spoke next.

"I shall remain here. Lord Tremene and the city authorities have asked for my help in draining the moat around the castle. Falador's wealthier citizens want to retrieve the riches that they so hastily threw away in their madness. I shall need to send a message to some of my scientific friends in Varrock, for I need equipment that isn't available here."

The alchemist smiled cunningly.

"The work is going to make me a wealthy man. I have a handsome commission, so it is a job that is worth the labour."

The companions laughed at his acumen.

"I shall be going to Varrock," Theodore said. "And I will take your message, if it can wait for a few days. Sir Amik needs new recruits for the knights and he wants me to take advantage of my fame and act as a recruiting sergeant. Our losses were so great that we shall admit entrants who are older than usual, and Sir Amik has told me that they will cut a year off the training time in order to bolster our ranks quicker.

"And he has told me something else…" Theodore looked to his friends as if they were all part of a dark conspiracy. "I am to be made a knight on my return. In only a few more months, before the summer comes. So, too, is Marius."

Castimir stood and started clapping, and so did Kara, and then Ebenezer and Doric, followed by Gar'rth, who knew just enough words now to understand what was said.

"Congratulations, Theo!" Castimir said. "Everything you have worked so hard for is realised." The wizard's eyes filled with happy tears for his childhood friend.

But there was one amongst them who hadn't spoken. Gar'rth walked to the window after the friends had finished congratulating Theodore.

"And what shall you do, Gar'rth?" Theodore asked, looking at the sudden bitter expression on the youth's face as he stared out of the rain-battered pane and over the city.

"Jerrod lives," he said.

They had searched for the werewolf's body amongst the dead of the battlefield—the soldiers had been told to look out specifically for a man with black blood—but no corpse had been found.

Gar'rth had later caught his scent and had followed it for a day, first south and then east and north across the open countryside. It seemed likely that Jerrod had joined the Kinshra retreat.

He had told them of his wish to hunt his uncle down.

"He will not stop," he said. "So I must go to him." He had carefully rehearsed the words with Kara, and she knew that he was right, for Jerrod would one day return.

"Gar'rth will accompany me to the monastery," she added abruptly, her eyes resting on Theodore as he averted his gaze. Everyone was aware of the tension that still existed between them.

The alchemist raised his mug of ale briskly, diverting their attention as he stood.

"My youthful friends," he said. "And you also, Doric, if you so wish…" His voice was suddenly serious. "I will soon be a wealthy man, with more money than I can ever spend in my declining years. My children died of smallpox in their infancy and my wife died in childbirth many years ago. I have no family left. No one to care for me when my wits abandon me." He gave Castimir a sidelong glance, as if expecting the wizard to make a joke.

"Therefore, I wish to adopt each of you as my heirs, for we have braved so much together that it is only right."

Doric grumbled and got to his feet. "I am older than you, Ebenezer, and I am wealthy in my own right. I thank you for the consideration but this gift is best suited for the young."

The alchemist nodded and raised his ale again.

"So be it," he said. "To friends! And to family!"

And amongst them the woodcutter's daughter raised her drink, knowing suddenly that she had found what she had always truly sought, though she had masked it for years under the veil of anger and revenge.

Kara-Meir had found a family she could call her own.

THE END

ACKNOWLEDGEMENTS

There are many people who deserve my thanks for the completion of the novel. Firstly, there are the numerous test readers who criticise and offer valued feedback, and my thanks especially must go to the usual cohort: Rory, Marcus, Ben, Josh, John and Roddy.

Then there are those special people who are always there when things go wrong, like the Giraffe, who saw me through the many crises with her usual stoicism when the project seemed to be permanently under black clouds.

At RuneScape, two people at Jagex stand out in particular: Matt Ham, whose attention to detail saved me from many an amusing typo, and Mark Ogilvie, who threw his energy behind the project from the start. My gratitude must also be extended to the founders of RuneScape, Andrew and Paul, for giving the books the green light in the first place.

It would be remiss of me not to include Giuseppe Grassi also, for his excellent work over many hours on the covers and the map, which every good fantasy book needs. As an author, admitting that I would have trouble describing the feeling of elation when I held the final product for the first time is a testament to how good his instinct and artwork truly is.

And then there is the editor: Steve Saffel, who took the novel and polished it into the version that exists today. We have exchanged enough emails to write our own book on the intricacies of modern writing, I do believe, and I am the wiser for it. Thank you Steve.

My thanks must also go to Titan, and the enthusiasm that I found there for the project. Nick, Vivian, Tim, Katy and Cath. Thanks very much to each of you.

Finally, I must thank my business partner and brother, Josh, for the innumerable discussions we have had on the project, for his optimism, his ideas, and his input, and of course for taking care of the company whilst I was busy writing.

T.S. Church was born and educated in Worcestershire, England. He holds degrees in Information Systems and Business, as well as an MA in Marketing, all from the University of the West of England, Bristol. In his free time, he enjoys playing RuneScape. When not spending time in Gielinor, he likes to read and study history. He also participates (reluctantly) in adventure sports, from canoeing the length of the Thames to running half marathons. *Betrayal at Falador* is his first novel. To find out more, visit his website, www.tschurch.com.

RUNESCAPE: RETURN TO CANIFIS
T.S. CHURCH

Varrock is the greatest human city in the world, yet it is a city filled with dangerous secrets. People have been disappearing, taken by an inhuman abductor. Its victims murdered... or worse. For some are spirited away to Morytania, the land of the dead, where vampires rule.

As Kara-Meir and her friends—heroes of the Battle of Falador— gather for the Midsummer Festival, unrest grows against the crown. A conspiracy is unmasked, and the King is forced to send representatives across the holy river to Canifis, the capital of Morytania. For reasons of his own, he selects the now famous heroine Kara, as well as Gar'rth, unique in his knowledge of the land of the dead. They are accompanied by Theodore, Doric the dwarf, the wizard Castimir and the barbarian priestess Arisha, on a mission that will force Gar'rth to confront his violent heritage, and will reveal secrets that will test their loyalties to the limit.

For the price of failure in Morytania is far worse than death, and if their mission fails, then a new King will rule in Varrock. A King who is lord of both the living and the dead.

AVAILABLE IN FEBRUARY 2011